William John Fitzpatrick

The Life of Charles Lever

Vol. 1

William John Fitzpatrick

The Life of Charles Lever
Vol. 1

ISBN/EAN: 9783337427351

Printed in Europe, USA, Canada, Australia, Japan

Cover: Foto ©Raphael Reischuk / pixelio.de

More available books at **www.hansebooks.com**

THE LIFE

OF

CHARLES LEVER.

BY

W. J. FITZPATRICK, LL.D., M.R.I.A.

PROFESSOR OF HISTORY IN THE ROYAL HIBERNIAN ACADEMY; J.P.; BIOGRAPHER
OF BISHOP DOYLE, LADY MORGAN, LORD CLONCURRY, ETC.; AUTHOR OF
"THE SHAM SQUIRE, AND THE INFORMERS OF '98,"
"IRISH WITS AND WORTHIES," "IRELAND
BEFORE THE UNION," ETC.

IN TWO VOLUMES.—VOL. I.

LONDON:
CHAPMAN AND HALL, 193, PICCADILLY.
1879.

LONDON:
BRADBURY, AGNEW, & CO., PRINTERS, WHITEFRIARS.

TO

JOHN LEVER, ESQ.,

A.B., M.R.C.S.E.

SON AND REPRESENTATIVE OF

THE LATE REV. JOHN LEVER, RECTOR OF ARDNURCHUR.

THAT ONLY BROTHER WHOM

CHARLES LEVER

CALLED HIS "SECOND FATHER,"

The following Memoir

IS, BY PERMISSION, INSCRIBED.

PREFACE.

CRITICAL judgments on some recent biographies have convinced me that the free introduction of a man's private letters is often a mistake. The otherwise valuable " Life of the Rev. Charles Kingsley " may perhaps be taken as an example; in reviewing which the *Athenæum* * and other journals condemned as uninteresting, and calculated to create " disappointment," the letters with which his widow filled it. The most troublesome part of my labour was to digest the mass of Lever's correspondence, and to reject all that did not contain something characteristic of his life. I have read piles of his letters without being tempted to make many notes. Every point, however, marked by wit, or as furnishing fact for his life, I have carefully welded into the narrative. Many of his letters digress into discussion on the politics of the hour, which to quote in these memoirs would tend to re-open questions happily long closed. It is, moreover, as Lever himself writes,

* See No. 2564 for December 16, 1876.

"not always wise to invite spectators—already happy in theatrical illusion—to walk behind the scenes and view all the lath and plaster appliances and unsightly strings which make up stage effect."

I desire at the very outset to express my gratitude to Lever's life-long associate, Major D——, whom he designed to be his biographer, and who possessed his entire confidence. He placed all his treasures at my disposal, and his help has been prodigal all through. The Rev. Canon Hayman, Rector of Douglas, Cork, Lever's dear friend and correspondent, who would have discharged the present task so well had he been persuaded to undertake it, also deserves in a special degree my best thanks. I am under many obligations to the representatives of the late James McGlashan, Esq., Lever's publisher, who afforded me the perusal of nearly four hundred letters. For a similar aid I am indebted to the widow of the late Rev. Edward Johnson, to Miss Constance Anster, daughter of the late John Anster, Esq., LL.D., and to Mr. Bentley of New Burlington Street.

Mr. Pearce of Queen Anne Street, now a distinguished artist and formerly the amanuensis of Lever, rendered a double service to this book. Henry Innes, Esq., Lever's cousin and associate from boyhood, has supplied in writing very valuable information; while, for lesser aid

I am bound to thank John Adair, Esq. B.L.; Rev. A.
K. H. Boyd, D.D.; Rev. D. Babington; Dr. Banks;
M. J. Barry, Esq.; Dr. Bigger; Courtnay Boyle, Esq.,
Ex-Private Secretary to the Lord Lieutenant; Sir Bernard
Burke; the late Isaac Butt, Esq., M.P.; E. Clibborn,
Esq.; Rev. Geo. Craig, M.A.; Rev. Graham Craig, M.A.;
Sir John Crampton, Bart.; Dr. Cullinan; Sir Ralph
Cusack; Dr. Darby; Canon Dwyer; Baron Erlanger;
Canon Floyd, LL.D.; S. C. Hall, Esq.; Lord Houghton;
Dr. Hudson; Sir Henry James, Q.C.; Sir Kingston
James, Bart.; Dr. Benjamin Johnson; Jaspar Joly, Esq.,
LL.D.; F. A. Keane, Esq.; the late Judge Keogh;
his nephew, Dr. John Lever, A.B.; J. Lauder, Esq.;
W. Hartpole Lecky, Esq.; the late J. S. Lefanu; Dr.
Leet; the Bishop of Limerick; Mrs. Lever; Mrs.
Lodge; Judge Longfield; Mrs. Louche, relict of James
Lever's executor; Dr. Lytton MacIntyre; Dr. Nedley;
Major O'Beirne, M.P.; A. Palmer, Esq. F.T.C.D.;
Dr. Parkinson; Dr. Ridgeway; the late Dr. Seward;
General Seymour; Mrs. Sanger; Sir Hamilton Seymour,
formerly Minister at Brussels; Lord Spencer and his
cousin Miss Boyle; Colonel Steward; the late Dr.
Stokes; G. F. Shaw, Esq. F.T.C.D.; Anthony Trollope,
Esq.; Rev. Chancellor Tisdall; the late Dr. Tuohill; R.
Tyrrell, Esq., F.T.C.D.; Rev. C. A. Vignoles; Henry
West, Esq., Q.C.; the late Lord Chief Justice White-

side; the late Sir W. Wilde; B. Williamson, Esq., F.T.C.D.; Rev. H. Wilson White, M.A., &c. The courtesy I received from John George Adair, Esq., D.L., I must always remember gratefully.

It will be observed that this book largely embraces the earlier period of Lever's life—the period involved in most obscurity—and requiring more than ordinary labour to unfold and explore. In pursuing this course I have followed the subjoined prescription of Lever himself in a paper on " Grattan's Life by His Son," written when Lever was a practising physician at Brussels.

"Of the first period, during which biography is unconnected with history, the son can say nothing of his own knowledge: his memory cannot reach so far back. We may assume, as a very low average, that a man is forty-five years of age before his son is old enough to have any distinct perception and understanding of what passes before him; but the first period has passed long before he attains this age. Those early years are among the most interesting in a great man's biography: they are in general those of which we know least and desire to know most. We desire to know by what education his character was formed, and those abilities matured which afterwards led him to distinction; what were his early habits; what his natural disposition; what part of his conduct or character in youth gave promise of his future fame. For all this information we must look not to his son, but to his contemporaries, and we feel a wish that his biography had been undertaken by some of them. If the son possesses any peculiar advantages in obtaining traditionary information respecting his father, and in obtaining access to letters, and other private documents, it is, in our opinion, more than counterbalanced by that pious reverence for his parent's memory which causes him to attach importance to every trivial occurrence."

I undertook, not without diffidence, the task of writing the biography of the great novelist of my country; but observing some years ago that the men who intimately knew him were fast passing away—and that not one of the survivors was likely to take the labour in hand, I determined to go to work while their aid and counsel yet remained accessible. On looking over my book, I am sadly reminded that not a few of my informants have since followed him to whose memory they materially helped to build this monument.

Throughout its progress, I have received the prodigal help and counsel of highly-gifted friends, several of whom shared Lever's confidence from boyhood; but, some older men who knew him best had not the energy requisite to face the undertaking. One began it, but soon relinquished it, feeling that it required the ardour of a younger man and one better acquainted with the anatomy of biography, to grope for and grasp the various veins and arteries from which Lever's real life can alone be supplied.

In these volumes his eventful career will be found honestly traced; and if, in passing, many minor traits are noted, I have but followed the counsel of Johnson, who declares that "the incidents which give excellence to a biography are of a volatile and evanescent kind—such as soon escape the memory, and are rarely transmitted by tradition;" while his own biographer, Boswell, avers, "minute particulars are frequently characteristic, and always amusing, when they relate to a distinguished man."

HERBERT HOUSE, PEMBROKE ROAD,
    DUBLIN, *May 1st*, 1879.

CONTENTS.

CHAPTER I.

CHAPTER IV.

CHAPTER V.

CHAPTER VI.

CHAPTER VII.

CHAPTER VIII.

CHAPTER IX.

CHAPTER X.

CHAPTER XI.

ERRATUM.

Vol. I. p. 184, line 8 from top, *for* " Foot " *read* " Regt."

*** Whenever the note " D. U. M." appears it implies *Dublin University Magazine.*

LIFE OF CHARLES LEVER.

CHAPTER I.

Birth and Boyhood—James Lever's belongings—School-days and adventures—Theatrical Exploits—Military bias—Mr. Innes' Recollections—A Comical Portrait—The Battle of Mountjoy Fields, and what came of it—A Police Magistrate disgraced—Lever's first and only Love—Recollections of the boy Lever, by Henry West, Esq., an Irish County Judge.

CHARLES LEVER was not very accurately informed as regards his own age, and told Mr. McGlashan so in 1853. The memoir revised by himself in "Men of the Time," states his natal year as 1809. The obituary notices mechanically copied what they found; but a mortgage deed, preserved in the Registry Office, Dublin, establishes the truth :—" 1809. James Foxall to James Lever, carpenter and builder, premises, North Strand, dwelling-house, outhouses, yard, and garden held for lives of John Lever, eldest son of lessee, and Charles James Lever, his 2nd son : John then aged 13, Charles 3 years." Thus it appears that Charles Lever was born, not in 1809, but in 1806. The deed fixes the year; and, as regards the day of the month, he told the Rev. Samuel Hayman that his birthday was the 31st of August, adding a wish that the month had only thirty days, and he might have escaped the wear and tear of this work-a-day world.

Charles James Lever was born in the North Strand, Dublin, of which the name was changed to Amiens Street after the treaty of 1802.* His father's house faced some waste ground, on which the Northern Railway Terminus has since been built, and adjoined North Cope Street. now known as Talbot Street, famous for Beresford's Riding School, where in 1798 triangles were raised to aid in the administration of torture to suspected persons. But Dublin became at last used to this sort of thing; and a wag one day wrote over the door "Mangling done here by Beresford and Co."† "Triangles" had long been a familiar household word to young Lever, and when a phrenologist once criticised his head he said he had a decided predilection for the comic and not the slightest for conic sections—that

---

* The burial, baptismal, or other registers of St. Thomas's Church, Marlborough Street, throw no light upon the dates of James Lever's marriage, or even the births of his children ; and the old Dublin Directories ignore him altogether. This, perhaps, is due to the fact that Marlborough Green and a tract of waste ground intervened between Dublin proper and the suburban purlieus of Mabbot Street, North Strand, and Blenheim Street. The latter and Marlborough Green have since been swept away. To the Registry of Deeds Office we must look for information. The first record found of James Lever's existence is an assignment, dated May 26th, 1800, from "Samuel Taylor to James Lever, builder, Montgomery Street and North Strand." He afterwards extended his holding to Mabbot Street, of which a lease was given on June 1st, 1821, by Lord Blessington, husband of the rattling Irish girl, Margaret Power—afterwards famous for her pleasant receptions at Gore House—and for the warm reception she herself received as an authoress. James Lever's final move was to the small private house, 74. Talbot Street.

† The Right Hon. J. Claudius Beresford, see pp. 4, 5.

there never was a man with less mathematical head, and that he had as great a horror of triangles as though he had figured in the Irish Rebellion.

James Lever was an Englishman, and is said to have claimed kindred with no end of Levers, all more or less distinguished, including Ralph and Thomas Lever, both learned church writers in the 16th century; Christopher Lever, author of "Queen Elizabeth's Tears;" Sir Assheton Lever, of whom presently; and Darcy Lever, who wrote the " Sea Officer's Sheet Anchor." *

His family was an old Lancashire stock, part of the bone and sinew of that great nursery of self-reliant men. Near Bolton are three parishes—Darcy Lever, Great Lever, and Little Lever; and the name originally was derived from a locality, and written "De Lever." The senior line was seated at " Great Lever."

In the 16th century Adam Lever, Esquire, of Great Lever, had an only child and heiress, Margaret, who married in 1535 Sir Ralph Assheton, and brought with her the lordship of Lever. Thenceforth, the junior branches seem to have used Assheton as a baptismal name.† Charles Lever's great uncle, Sir Assheton Lever, was noted for his museum. The objects, chiefly in natural history, were dispersed by lottery in July,

---

* Particulars of these men may be found in Allibone. For fuller notices of prominent persons of the name, *vide* Index to the Publications of the Parker Society.

† They who care to know more of them would do well to see Baines' " History of Lancashire;" and "Assheton of Lever," &c., in Burke's " Extinct Baronetcies."

1806.* "Sir Assheton Lever," writes Charles, "was my father's uncle, an old hermit, who squandered a large fortune on stuffed birds and founded a museum—having beggared his family."

One of those stricken by vicissitude was James Lever, but, full of energy, he resolved to do for himself. The soil of Ireland was no *terra incognita* to him, one of his ancestors having been a soldier of fortune under the Commonwealth,† whose representatives are found in Ireland between the years 1753 and 1777.‡

Mr. Carolin, of Dublin, builder, an octogenarian, and for a long period the landlord and close neighbour of James Lever, describes him as an English carpenter and builder, who, emigrating to Ireland, obtained through Government favour the work of the Custom-house, and rose to wealth in the enjoyment of a monopoly much coveted by his brethren in the trade. A book called "Sketches of Irish Political Characters," published in 1799, describes the Custom-house, as then recently built by John Claudius Beresford, Commis-

---

* *Vide* an engraving of the Museum, and of the ticket of admission, in Hone's "Every-day Book," vol. ii. pp. 493 to 496.

† The list of adventurers printed in Mr. Prendergast's "Cromwellian Settlement of Ireland," includes the name of Robert Lever, jun., of Manchester, and in that city Lever Street may be found. Liverpool was anciently spelt Lever-pool.

‡ Searches in the registry office show in 1753, Richard Shaw, of Dublin, reciting his settlement with Ellen Lever, whose fortune is paid by her father to a trustee, Jas. Lever, of Wigan, Lancashire; and in 1777, Mrs. Lever, of Portobello, Dublin, executed a deed to Rev. John Lever, of Carlingford. There is not now in Dublin a person of the name. Later deeds describe the father of our novelist as James Lever, of Talbot Street, Esquire, showing the good position attained by him.

sioner of Revenue, nominally for the public service, but really as a palace for personal residence. He was the back-stairs Viceroy, who manipulated every department of the executive, and in comparison to whose power the Lord Lieutenant himself was a cypher. This potential race is still represented by persons wielding high influence. In a recent visit of the Lord Primate to the Solicitor's office in the Custom-house, he gazed so steadfastly around that a clerk ventured to say, "Your Grace seems to know this room!" "I ought," was the reply, "for I was born in that corner!" The patronage of Lever by the Beresfords proved no disadvantage to himself and family.

Until 1808, the Bank of Ireland stood in Mary's Abbey, when its business was transferred to the palatial walls once graced by the Irish Parliament. During the preliminary alterations, as Mr. Keane tells, James Lever acted as clerk of the works. Charles, fifty years ago, bemoans with something of personal feeling, that both the Senate and the Custom-house should find their occupation gone. He speaks of "walking the cold and comfortless corridors of the now deserted Custom-house, and refers to that splendid money-office, which was erst the house of Legislature of Old Ireland." *

The first important task which James Lever carried to completion was the ornate "Round Church," Dublin, built from designs by Johnston, and opened for service in March, 1807. He was also associated with Johnston

* "Dublin Literary Gazette," Feb. 6, 1830, p. 91.

in the erection of St. George's Church and the General Post Office. Johnston was a very influential man, and founded the Royal Hibernian Academy. Another architect, Mr. Louche, had a high opinion of James Lever, threw some work in his way, and was, at last, appointed executor under his will. It was jokingly said of Lever, that he became a great *contractor* in proportion as he enlarged the sphere of his labours.

Fifty years ago, the profession of architect was not very clearly defined. Many confounded it with that of builder—possibly influenced by the proverb, "a good architect buildeth on a sure foundation." James Lever was styled an architect quite as often as a "builder," and few were disposed to cavil at the honorary rank thus awarded.

He is described by his wife's family as a handsome, well-built man, famous for his prowess at athletic sports; with pleasant off-hand manners, and socially a great favourite. "He told a story better than any man I ever heard, his son not excepted." *

In 1795, James Lever married Julia, daughter of Mathew Candler, Esq., and niece of Archdeacon Helsham, both being Cromwellian families who had received grants of land, in virtue of their services as soldiers under the Protector. The precise date of the marriage cannot be ascertained, no deed of settlement having been executed.

* The reader is requested to see in the "Portfolio" appended to these volumes, the valuable recollections of H. Innes, Esq., which did not reach us until nearly the whole work was in type.

It was a love match; and both to the last comported themselves more like lovers than persons of advanced years; Mrs. Lever being described by her cousin as generally sitting on James Lever's knee at dinner, helping everybody and seldom eating anything herself.

By the will of James Lever, proved May 26th, 1833, all his property is devised between his sons John and Charles James. John, afterwards in orders, whose services as a preacher of charity sermons were often sought, had finally a quiet life of it in a rural parish, without a flock, and died long previous to his over-worked brother. "Better to wear out than rust out," were amongst his last words. No issue beyond the two sons marked the marriage of James Lever with Julia Candler. John was ten years the senior of Charles, who followed him on exactly the expiration of the decade. John Lever died in 1862, Charles in 1872; but John's birthday was in July, while that of his brother fell in August.

That Charles Lever attended three schools before he went to the Rev. George Wright's Academy, will be new even to his own descendants. Mr. Rosborough, of 33, Molesworth Street, Dublin, has been good enough to communicate some useful recollections of childhood, which will prove the more welcome when the words of Dr. Johnson are remembered: "Not to describe the schools or the masters of men illustrious in literature, is a kind of historical fraud by which honest fame is injuriously diminished":—

"My recollection of Charles Lever dates from his cradle, and it may be said that we were born under the same roof, a party-wall merely dividing my father's house from James Lever's. We were constantly together in infancy and through different stages of childhood, which it now gives me pleasure to retrace. In 1809 a schoolmaster named Ford came to lodge in my father's house, and opened an academy there. Charley Lever, then aged not more than three years, was one of the pupils. Ford's sister, a figure not unlike Mrs. Squeers, kept house for him. Among the boys, the wonder only was how 'one small head could carry all it knew;' but Ford was fearfully addicted to the brutal habits of his time and of his class. He daily flogged the boys with savage ferocity. Little Lever came in for his share; but it was not easy, even at that tender age, to beat out of his elastic nature its joyous buoyancy. Ford had forty pupils, of whom I am now the sole survivor; and he enjoyed in the locality some reputation as a teacher. One day a new boy having arrived, Ford flogged my elder brother out of his seat to make room for the new-comer—little Lever looking aghast at the outrage. My father was constantly out during the day, or his child's cries would have brought him to the rescue, but that evening he showed the welts on his arms and back; and my father, boiling with rage at the sight, rushed upstairs to where Ford was reposing in his easy chair, and seizing his birch rod, which he bore like a sceptre, thrashed him with such severity that he ran yelling out of the house, and was never seen more. I am bound to add, that it was the fashion of the day to flog boys savagely at school. Another of my masters—Mooney—would not be bothered flogging any isolated victim, but generally put twelve or fourteen in a row, and then rushed up and down their ranks cutting right and left with furious energy, and I afterwards had the satisfaction of seeing him flogged through the streets for a felonious assault on one of his female pupils.

"Mrs. Lever was very kind to me. There never was a pie or pudding in honour of Charley's birthday that I was not sent for to help in celebrating the event, or sharing the feast. She was a very orderly, tidy little woman, whose appearance is now vividly before me; very unostentatiously dressed, and such a perfect model of an English housewife, that I thought she must have come from the other side.

"My school connection with Lever did not stop here. We were both sent to 56, William Street, whither, satchel on backs, we made our daily journey. Our new preceptor bore the historic name of Florence Mac-Carthy. Like Ford, he also was a Roman Catholic; but no two men could differ more widely in characteristics. MacCarthy was a very accomplished and well-informed man, with a fine presence, whom it was impossible not to respect. He had entered Trinity College, and would have taken a scholarship with higher honours, but that his religion disqualified him. He was therefore driven to open a school next door to the City

Assembly House, which was attended by about eighty boys, of whom I do not know one now living but myself. Amongst them were two sons of Sir Charles Coote. William Coote was so wrong-headed, that Charles Lever loved to cram him with false data; and he certainly had a special knack in engrafting perverse principles upon his mind. Coote was quite proud of the progress which he was persuaded he had made; and every day for months he would shuffle along the form till he got to the head of the class, where he at once held forth with an air of mingled pomposity and importance indescribably amusing, and which threw the school into kinks of laughter, and in which our master himself was sometimes constrained to join. This system was going on for a long time before the absurd display was traced to the effects of practical joking, and still longer ere it leaked out that Lever, the handsome, fair-haired, innocent-looking boy, was the delinquent. I may add that Lever was very fat, but which did not prevent him taking an active part in the usual sports of boys. This play on Coote's credulity occurred in 1814, Lever being then eight years old. I can fix the date because of the heavy fall of snow which made that year memorable, and the streets impassable for several weeks. It gave rise to great distress among the poor; and to a collection of £10,000 in aid of them. While want and sorrow reigned, we boys pelted dull care away with snowballs.

"One day Charley and I mitched from school, and rambled off towards Crumlin, where, meeting a round car full of Quakers, with their broad beavers ' nid-nodding' at each other, Lever and I began to pelt them with small pellets, which led a 'Mawworm'-like man to smite the beast that drew the heavily-freighted car, and to lay on his flanks with cruel energy, hoping thereby to get away quickly from the jeers of two rude urchins. Lever's wit and vivacity were mainly fed in boyhood by association with a youth named Ottiwell, who often dropped into his father's house in the evening. Full of wit and humour, his visits were always welcome.

" I did not again meet Lever till after he returned from Göttingen, and when he was believed to be pursuing his medical studies at Stevens' Hospital.

" I say *believed*, for in passing Castle Street, as I daily did, about that time, his face repeatedly caught my eye, surrounded by officers in uniform, leaning out of the windows of the guard-room to the right of the Castle-gate. Again I lost sight of him for fourteen years, when he re-appeared in Dublin, and might be daily seen riding through the streets, attended by his auburn-haired children on ponies; while everybody paused to stare on the popular author of ' Charles O'Malley.' "

Leaving McCarthy's school, Lever attended as a day pupil that of William O'Callaghan, 113, Abbey Street, described as "a mathematician." "Here," writes his cousin, " dramas were acted by the boys previous to vacation. At Inistioge, in 1817, we young people from eight to twelve went nearly mad on being bitten by his Thespian taste. A loft was fitted up as a theatre, and

Lever did everything. He was scene-painter, prompter, played the fiddle, sang all the songs, acted all the chief parts, and dressed the performers. The favourite pieces were 'Bombastes Furioso' and the 'Warwickshire Wag,' but tragedies were not neglected, for I have a lively recollection of the sore bones I got dying on the hard boards."

A portrait of James Lever by Comerford is preserved in the family. It represents a sedate elderly gentleman in a white cravat, and with a high forehead, his hair brushed up at top into a sharp apex. The mouth indicates decision of character, and seems to reject the placidity of expression so frequently found in pictures before the discovery of the photograph. Charles Lever, some years ago, got Samuel Lover to execute a copy of this portrait.

Mr. Adair, who remembers him handing about the plate for the usual Sunday collection at St. Thomas's Church, Dublin, describes him as having "a rather peculiar appearance, reddish face, height about five feet eight inches, and a somewhat studied air and manner."

Mrs. Sophia Lodge, the daughter of James Lever's executor, Mr. John Louche, C.E., retains full and vivid recollections of Charles in boyhood. " Charley and I were born within a few weeks of each other, and we were play-mates together throughout a happy childhood. My father was an Englishman like Lever. They became much attached to each other, and Lever's counsel helped him more than once. James Lever's house on the North Strand presented the acme of comfort. The old couple without seeing company had always full and plenty for those who dropped in. Their house was called "the Sunny Bank," from the bright fires which shed rays of comfort in every room. My position every evening was on one knee of Mr. Lever while Charley occupied the other. After breakfast he would put on his father's spectacles, and affect to read aloud from the morning paper all sorts of stirring occurrences. The old people—more matter-of-fact—would listen attentively, and after Charley left the room, gravely discuss the matter, and sometimes vainly search the journal for these wondrous details. John Lever—then passing through college—had a study in the house. Many a time he gave us both money to keep out of it. He read so hard at the time that crushing headaches constantly affected him. Charley had a theatre at the rear of the house, with scenery which we patched and painted. He and I frequently figured in some impromptu scene, before an audience often restricted to the old cook, or the apprentice.*

* *A propos* of the apprentices one was named Windgrave, the other had lazy habits which did not coincide with James Lever's views, who was a man of thorough English energy. "Finding him one morning in bed at a late hour," observes Mrs. Lodge, "Mr. Lever took a stick and beat him from beneath the blankets. He ran from the house and enlisted. Twenty years after a gentleman sent up his card, on which 'Captain ———,' was written. 'You don't seem to remember me.' Mr. Lever said, 'No.' 'You made my fortune,' he said, 'and I have come to thank you. The chastisement you gave me for habits, which if unchecked could only end in my ruin, marked a new era in my life. It taught me energy, and discipline. I first got good conduct badges, promotion followed, and I now hold a commission in His Majesty's service.' Mrs. Lever was a most energetic housekeeper, and shortened her life by her exertions. As long as I remember her she was asthmatic. Charles did not care for meat; nothing but pies would satisfy him. So many of these were made that they sometimes got musty—which led him

Mrs. Lever encouraged this play, as it kept Charles out of John's way, and saved him from distraction at his studies. Charley was a capital singer of comic songs, and a wonderfully expert mimic, especially of O'Connell."

The boy was an apt scholar; his real preceptor deserves commemoration. "John Ottiwell," writes Lever's cousin, Mr. Innes, in his valued jottings, "was a hero; he could do everything, as we believed, better than anybody else. He rode, he swam, he ran, he jumped, he composed verses, he sang them, he ventriloquized; he had a voice as rough as that of a bear, also a sort of falsetto, as clear as a bell. He was a man six feet high, with features no way remarkable, except for the contortions he subjected them to. His eye-brows, his mouth, his ears, appeared under separate command. He was an ill-looking customer withal; unpleasant to meet at one minute, the next he was a jolly, beaming, bandy-legged

to call them 'pussy pies.' She had a brother who one day arrived from India bearing beautiful presents, but on returning to the East, just as he was about to step on board, he fell into the Liffey, and was lost. We kept the news from her for seven years, during which time she would often say, 'Is it not strange John never writes!' Mrs. Lever's hobby lay in a love of old china and buying up antique bargains in Liffey Street. When any new article of costume or furniture appeared in the house, or ware at meals, Charley would slily ask, 'Is this Liffey Street?' His own pocket-money was applied to buying old books and getting them bound. I never knew a more honourable fellow. He never made love to any girl whom he did not mean to make his wife. John was a thorough contrast to him—small and sedate, but of *chevaleresque* manners to ladies. He married his cousin, Miss Innes, a lady with a good fortune. His father bought for him the living of Tullamore; the Bishop promoted him. He preached so well that we called him 'St. Paul in the Pulpit.' On one of the last occasions that I met Charley at the old house he presented his mother with a handsome silk dress, slily observing, 'It's not from Liffey Street.'"

dwarf, begging for something to drink your honour's health. He was in Lever's eye an admirable Crichton, and many of his features are reproduced in Frank Webber. Ottiwell passed through Trinity with little credit, his talents notwithstanding; was called to the bar, joined O'Connell, and died early a disappointed man."

The "Dublin Directory" for the year 1819 records for the first time the name of the Rev. G. N. Wright, Principal of the Proprietary School in Great Denmark Street. To this academy, managed by a committee and regarded as a very select one, Charles Lever was now sent, and he is vividly remembered for his powers of story-telling by Mr. Adair and other school-fellows. He is described as a not very diligent student, fonder of turning over the leaves of romances than a new leaf in improvement, feeling no great love for grammars and lexicons, and rather disposed to interrupt the studies of the other boys by the narratives, "to be continued," concocted in his own brain wherewith he enchained them from day to day. Of Mr. Adair Lever was six years the senior, and his age naturally gave him an ascendancy and influence in the school.

The Rev. George Newenham Wright was a man with stern notions of discipline, who for a slight offence would expel a boy. He is described as combining the frown of Rhadamanthus with the muscular energy of Whackford Squeers. Lever received his share of strokes, but not to the extent of the other boys, for his school-fellows say he had a "silver end to his tongue" which pleased Mr. Wright, and some favouritism was certainly shown to him. As a classical scholar Wright would seem to have been over-rated, but he had a marked literary taste, wrote a life of the Duke of Wellington, and shortly before the visit of George the Fourth to Ireland he compiled a "Historical Guide to Dublin," in which Mr. Petrie was associated with him. This book, creditable to the candour and ability of the author, shows him to have been a man of liberal views and a sincere lover of his country. The King's visit in 1821 formed an epoch, and the boys of Wright's school trooped to see him off.

"Certainly that autumn eve when he went away," writes Lever, "it presented a glorious and most spirit-stirring sight, as the gorgeous western sun beamed down on the hundreds of thousands of loyal and lusty-voiced mortals, hallooing and shouting in grief as in gladness, now at his Majesty's departure, as erewhile when first he arrived. After all, there is an indescribable magic in the loud huzza of a million of reasoning bipeds, whether rushing to battle or hailing a king."*

Mr. Adair writes: "At school Lever used to amuse the other boys by telling stories, based on actual occurrences, that were carried on from day to day. He often held a book in his hand—not a school-book—during the school hours, and read stories from it, as if rehearsing his tasks with his companions."

Here we have the boy in his teens already at the

* "Irish National Magazine for June," 1830.

work of his future life, and moreover addressing the very same public for whom so many of his best works were written, namely, sons of Erin, some of whom at last became soldiers. No trace now remains of these juvenile tales, but it may be assumed from anecdotes which will be told of the martial practices of the boys, that the subject-matter was suited to the predilections of the audience.

In the days which followed Waterloo, Dublin was a great garrison-town, whose best streets, squares, and *salons* were thronged with gay uniforms. This is no longer the case: troops are still there; but the green island is now rarely dotted by red specks. Lever to the end addressed that "beloved public," which in his first sketches he styles it, and was perhaps fully understood by it only. The general public laughed with him; sometimes they laughed *at* what they regarded as his extravagancies, but the old Irish public of his first love warmed to him the more because the mirror he held out to them reflected their faults and frailties as well as their warm affections and social instincts. All this distraction of story-telling, however it may have affected the other boys, seems not to have interfered very seriously with Lever's own success in the school. In truth, it was rather a misfortune than otherwise that he should have been able to acquire with too great facility the amount of knowledge demanded from him. Greater things he would have mastered had narrow circumstances and severe discipline compelled him to work hard in his youth, and of this he was himself fully aware. John Lever, who was ten years his senior and most devotedly attached to him, assisted Charles in his studies; for " I well remember," writes Major D——, " the words with which the younger introduced me to the elder brother in 1842 : 'This is my brother John, whom you heard preach at the Mariners' Church this morning. But for him I should never have learned the little I know. He has been a second father to me.' "

Many of Lever's companions at Wright's school were of good family. Their fathers belonged to learned crafts, " and it was no doubt in this way," writes Major D——, " that he had whilst a mere schoolboy, and not more than twelve years old, already acquired in Dublin circles some fame as a story-teller. I myself remember hearing of him long before I knew him personally, which was not till 1825."

Not a little blue blood, indeed, coursed through the veins of the spirited youth of this school. His early association with them impregnated him with an aspiring aim, and the worthy builder showed his usual tact and progress in placing Charles in a higher social position than he himself enjoyed.

Corporal punishment was the order of the day, and in the proprietary school it was ungrudgingly dealt. But the only boy who, as Mr. Adair tells us, he saw stripped to nudity and flogged was Edward S. Dix, afterwards the well-known police magistrate in Dublin.

Some days later, when Knight Boswell, the late eminent solicitor, and at that time a strong muscular boy, was about to be subjected to a severe caning from his reverend preceptor, he—prompted by Lever—resisted the attempt at "assault and battery," and squaring at him defiantly, all but paralysed the arm which had been raised to smite.

The master, we are told, had authorities, like blows, on his fingers' ends, from the Scriptures to Locke, who notices with praise a mother who flogged her child eight times without subduing it; for, had she stopped at the seventh castigation, her infant would have been ruined. Mr. Wright's predilections were not lost on Lever, who, however, had measured his mental stamina. His searching eye discovered that Mr. Wright had failed to pass for full orders, having broken down on examination in the Greek Testament. The pupil took care to let him know, indirectly, that he was aware of this fact. The other boys chuckled over Lever's discovery, and the cane fell less heavily amongst them from that day. Mr. Wright felt small even among small boys, winced under their sneer, and by degrees ceased altogether to smite them. But he took strong courses in other ways, and even went the length of expelling Mr. C——, now the able officer of a great national institution. An inquiry having been held by the directorate, it appeared that Mr. C—— had been wrongly accused; Mr. Wright resigned, and was succeeded by the Rev. W. Jones. Wilkie's picture of the school in which more fun than work went on, often found its reflex here.* Relaxed discipline within led to wilder freaks without.

The north side of Dublin, then as now, was noted for the escapades of some young vagabonds who played malign tricks on unoffending citizens. Party feeling ran high in those days. The boys of Wright's school, who all represented families with unpopular sympathies, were more than once pelted as they passed. The roughs found allies in the pupils of another school, but of an inferior social caste, which stood in Grenville Street adjacent. These boys were under the able general-ship of a stripling not undistinguished in after life. Skirmishes took place, and at last it was agreed that a regular pitched battle should be fought in Mountjoy Fields, then a piece of waste ground on which Gardiner Street Church and Convent have since been built. Lever helped to organise the tiny troops. The little army had its companies, commander-in-chief, its out-lying pickets, reserves, and even its sappers and miners. Mr. Robert M——, an eminent engineer still living, an F.R.S. and a Ph. D., first showed his talents by mining

* George Downes, the Usher who taught Lever Latin, had been a draper's drudge, but Shekleton of Ballytore—the principal of Edmund Burke's Alma Mater—when visiting the shop, observing that he pored lovingly over a tattered Virgil, asked him some questions which elicited the fact that he had the classic completely by heart. On Shekleton's invitation he joined the Ballytore school, from which he was at length transferred to Mr. Wright's. Here a blow upon his head from a Virgil—as Lever used to tell—one day knocked him down. He was very fragile, and often threw up basins of blood in school. Downes eventually became a distinguished author, archæologist, and M. R. I. A., and was associated with Petrie in his work on the " Round Towers." He left no representative.

the ground on which the enemy were to be next day engaged. A small mine was worked, and several pounds of blasting powder laid. The opposite faction mustered at length in great force and opened the fight by a brisk discharge of sharp stones, which was returned by Mr. Wright's boys with shouts of defiance, and a fire of miniature cannon. A charge forward was then made by the roughs, some of whom were provided with black thorns which, if applied to the skulls of the juvenile army, would have inflicted "serious subsequent loss on letters, law, science, physic, and divinity." Dr. B——— of Dublin is now almost the only survivor who took part in this conflict. He held a high rank in the command, and just as the enemy was about to fall upon them like an avalanche, word was given to fire the mine, which a lighted cigar promptly accomplished. The explosion scattered dismay, and inflicted some slight bodily wounds. Lever's company suffered quite as much as the enemy; the faces on both sides were scorched and scratched. The army of the north retreated in disorder, leaving Mr. Wright's pupils in possession of the field——only to be scared, however, by the rapid approach of the police, who, with their glazed caps and side arms, the uniform of that day, entered Mountjoy Fields at every point.

Marlborough Street Police Office exhibited a scene of some excitement when the case came on next day. Hanging was still the penalty for incendiarism; and terrible forebodings of the gibbet or Botany Bay, smote the small prisoners brought up before Mr. Magrath, who, in his occasional ebullitions of temper, resembled Mr. Fang, Oliver Twist's stern judge, and Fang we know was a veritable portrait. Some fussy matrons were in attendance to testify that the north side had been all but blown into the southern division by the shock, while the weak police of that day, with "occupation well nigh gone," seem to have regarded the whole affair very much as a god-send. The boy-prisoners, including Edward Spencer Dix, afterwards police magistrate, are described by Dr. B—— as tongue-tied. Mr. Magrath said it was a bad case, and scowled. The police shook their heads, and a pin might be heard to drop.

At last a boy came forward as spokesman, and appealed to the bench. The magistrate declared that they were before him on a charge of riot and outrage, which it behoved him to suppress with a firm hand. Lever submitted that the provocation they received from a lawless gang justified them in inflicting condign punishment : that the vagabonds were the first aggressors ; that self-defence was the first law of nature, and that a war of juveniles was not worse in principle than war waged by wiser heads.

Mr. Magrath.—"But you are not to take the law into your own hands. Moreover, you use firearms and introduce gunpowder into a mine previously prepared and with malice prepense."

Master Lever.—"All sound and smoke, sir ; our cannon were only toy guns, and the mine a mimic mine. Most of us may take up arms yet in defence of our king and country; and might we not be worse employed than in learning the science at the most impressionable period of our lives?"

Mr. Magrath's attitude of hostility relaxed; without complimenting Lever on his eloquence, he certainly seemed struck by it; and he brought the case to a close by imposing sundry small fines, which would suffice, he said, to satisfy offended justice.*

This magistrate was himself soon after arraigned for much graver offences. He was proved guilty of embezzlement and banished. As to Master B——the juvenile commander-in-chief—he was flogged five successive days because of the determination with which he refused to divulge the spot where the subsequently famous engineer M—— had concealed his mining powder.

All this excitement soon found reaction in repose. Our next glimpse of the boy Lever is as an observer and thinker.

Old bookworms remember a fair-haired youth in ringlets passing from stall to stall—those old stores of accessible literature, now nearly all swept away,—and burying himself deep in the "Mysteries of Udolpho," or "The Adventures of Count Fathom." In this way he met some kindred spirits, whose contour struck his

* Since we gathered these details from the survivors of the little troop who fought shoulder to shoulder with Lever, and afterwards stood with him before an angry judge, we have found, in Chapter cv. of that semi-autobiography "O'Malley," an incident somewhat akin to it; but the University and College Green are made the site of the row, and Webber takes the place of Lever.

impressionable mind with photographic fidelity. As a boy, he possessed that keenness of observation, which in the old novelist of sixty was an admitted speciality.

"I remember when a boy"—he wrote in 'Blackwood'—"to have seen a man who passed his days wandering from one bookstall to another, stopping a while to read at each. His dress bespoke him as very poor, and there was a humility in his manner that still more indicated narrow fortune; he never would presume to occupy the place of a possible purchaser, but move respectfully away when such approached."

The child, Lever, was one of few who stepped forth from the busy world which swept past, to offer homage to those humble stores of wisdom.

"He was an object of much interest to me. I used to watch him as he read, and hasten to take up the book he had quitted, curious to see whether one class of reading had its principal attraction for him, and what that class might be. Often used I speculate as to how he came by this knowledge, and ask myself if it were a source of happiness to him. Again, would all this greedy pursuit of learning I saw in him survive if he were suddenly to become rich, the owner of a well-stocked library, abounding in every appliance of ease and comfort? Would he hang as enraptured over that volume in the deep recess of a cushioned-chair, as I have seen him when the rain beat against his face and the rude wind almost swept him and his treasure away?"

Good moralising follows, proving that there is a

something in those pleasures won by a sacrifice which have a sweetness all their own.

A military bias continued to assert itself in the boy. A paper describing a visit to Dublin in 1865, says that he verily believed the same carman drove him to his hotel, who used to take him, as a boy, to the Pigeonhouse. This is a famous fort situated in the Bay, and approached by a causeway raised above the water.

What if the military-struck youth should, in a burst of enthusiasm, enlist? An eye was kept to him by his elder brother, destined ere long to be a clergyman. John was now distinguished in college, having received his earlier education at a school in Mecklenburgh Street, presided over by John Fowler, grand Masonic secretary, who, in the estimation of his awe-stricken pupils, at least, wielded mysterious terrors by shouldering the poker and cane alternately.

" Lever, while yet a schoolboy," writes Dr. Waller, from information supplied by Mr. E. Clibborn, " was attracted by a pretty little girl who lived in the Marine School,* and thither he used to steal to get a sight of or a word with her almost daily. One of his acquaintances was in the habit of supplying him with flowers,

* It is not so certain that the house in which Miss Baker lived was at that time the Marine School. The directories fail to notice this academy until subsequent to Lever's scholastic course, when they thus describe it : " Hugh R. Baker, Hibernian Marine School." The earlier directories, contemporaneous with Lever's boyhood, record : " W. M. Baker, Deputy-Treasurer to the Navy and Greenwich Hospital, 89, Rogerson's Quay." Previously he is described as " Secretary to the European Insurance Company, 1, Eden Quay," and later of Dorset Street, " Esquire." Mr. Baker's position was in-

which were sometimes given by the boy-lover to the girl, sometimes thrown to her through the iron gate of the courtyard, which was guarded by an old sailor. It was a matter of arrangement among his companions to attract the attention of the old janitor while Lever pursued his love-making."

It may be interesting to add, as it is certainly creditable to Lever, that the little girl thus described was his future wife, Katharine Baker. It has been said that this is one of the few cases in which a man is found marrying his first love, but from the Recollections of his cousin, it appears that Lever had one attachment previously. The friend from whom the flowers came was Mr. Clibborn, who had a nice garden at Leeson Park, and was a classfellow of Lever's at Wright's school.

Thackeray sang to the maid of Newtownlimavady, and Lysaght to Kate of Garnavilla. Kate Baker's home— on Sir John Rogerson's Quay—was of equally interminable orthography. Here the love scenes were of frequent occurrence. Flowers fell in bright profusion before the girl's path; "Charley is my Darling" became a favoured song in her répertoire. Hurried interviews—sweet and stolen—continuously passed. The young folk pledged their troth and proved loyal to their

deed very respectable, and he had seen some military service, which made his home the more attractive to Lever. A few of his stories are re-told in "Lorrequer," as our seventh chapter will reveal. His son, Thomas Harrison Baker, afterwards medical doctor, opened a school at Parsonstown. A younger brother, who died young, succeeded for a short time his father as Master of the Royal Marine School. Both brothers were able, intellectual men.

fervidly whispered vows, though the long-looked-for union was far distant yet.

As well it might be. Lever was still a mere boy, and had not even entered college. Mr. Wright petted him. Years after, when the boy had become famous, and his old master had offered congratulations, he is said to have paraphrased a reply of Curran's, to the effect that the work was his—" What you see is but the stucco upon the building of which you laid the foundation."

He had little taste for the sort of building in which his father was engaged, and seemed more desirous of "building the lofty rhyme "—as Milton has it—and a literary reputation as well. He learned enough of the craft, however, to be able, in after life, to draw useful illustrations from what he saw, while hitting, at the same time, some critics by whom he had been reviled. " By the universal law," he writes, " everything has its place somewhere. The gnarled and bent sapling that would be rejected by the builder is exactly the piece adapted for the knee-timber of a frigate; and perhaps on the same principle dull lawyers make excellent judges, and the people who cannot speak within the limits of Lindley Murray are admirable public writers and excellent critics."

Lever, as a boy, was not without ambition; but his views the matter-of-fact builder stigmatised as building castles in the air. These so-called châteaux en Espagne afterwards developed into such successful Spanish pictures as we find in " O'Malley," and showed that the road to Fame was not necessarily paved with bricks.

How he told stories at school—danced—fenced—laughed—and then rode off on a pony, the letter of Henry West, Esq., an Irish county judge, records :—

"You ask me to communicate to you my impressions and recollections of Charles Lever at school.

"For this purpose I must go back more than fifty years; I have a most vivid recollection of him, and you will readily understand that his subsequent career has kept him green in my memory.

"The school, though nominally Mr. Wright's, was a proprietary academy under the direction of a committee, the Rev. George N. Wright being the salaried head-master. The house—No. 2, Great Denmark Street—had belonged to Lord Ashtown, and was finished in the best style.

"I never saw Lever in the drawing-rooms, where the classics, etc., were taught; he came, after lesson hours were over, to a sort of theatre built in the rear of the garden, to take lessons in fencing and dancing only. He was a prime favourite with Sattell, the French fencing master, and the pride of Montague, the professor of dancing. At this time he resided at Coolock with his father; he was always gaily dressed, and had a pony to take him from the school.

"Mr. Wright, not being satisfied with his position, opened an establishment of his own in Rutland Square, and carried off many of the pupils, and among them I should think Lever, for I cannot remember to have seen him in the time of the new head-master, Mr. Jones.

" He was even then a vigilant observer, and a brisk *raconteur*. I remember a story he told us with great zest of Lord Chief Justice Norbury, who lived next door to the school, and whom the boys used to watch alighting from his horse, with top boots and cheeks puffing, like Æolus, as depicted in the caricatures of the day. The story was that, being in the habit of calling on a brother judge (Vandeleur) in Rutland Square, on his way to Court, and being one day challenged for being too late at the door, he searched for his watch in his fob, and not finding it, called out with an oath that he had left it in the pocket of the bed. On his return he desired his butler to fetch it; the astonished servant informed him that he had handed it to a man who had asked for it for his lordship, giving as a token the place where it was to be found.

" Of all our schoolfellows, an average of one hundred and twenty, I remember but two living.

" The recollection of the other survivor agrees entirely with mine. We were both wonderfully surprised with his literary success.

" I have met him since in Brussels, Munich, Spezzia, and more than once in this house, and he never was without some lively story energetically told; I never could hear him or read his books without being reminded of the vigour and agility of his dancing, he being the only boy in the school who could cut five, a favourite *pas* of the professor's."

The dancing referred to by Mr. West as having been

carried on in a sort of theatre at the rear of Wright's school, was much stimulated by the occasional presence of veritable girls from a ladies' seminary in Mountjoy Square. Dr. Stoker remembers Lever, all grace and agility, leading off with a Miss Briscoe, while he, with a Miss Adair, figured as his *vis-à-vis*. He describes Lever as one of the handsomest boys he had ever seen. His long hair fell in glossy ringlets, and his smile was sweetness itself. These grand Terpsichorean fêtes generally followed the examinations; and the parents of the children sat round the room, while Mr. Montague, fiddle in hand, put the tiny dancers through their evolutions. Lever, in "Jack Hinton," utilised some of the recollections of these days :—

"When the dancing-master is excited by passion, he never loses sight of the unities. If he flies down the floor to chide, he contrives to do it with a step, a spring, and a hop, to the time of one, two, three. Is there a confusion in the figure—he advances to rectify it with a chassé rigadoon? Does Mr. Somebody turn his toes too much out, or is Miss So-and-so holding her petticoats too high—he fugles the correction in his own person, first imitating the deformity he would expose, and then displaying the perfection he would point to?"

This was a habit with Montague, and Lever manifestly alludes to him, though in the novel he is called Mr. Harkin. A paper of Lever's in the "Dublin Literary Gazette" of January 18, 1830, refers to Montague by name.

CHAPTER II.

LEVER's boyhood was a little luxury very unlike that of Dickens, who was engaged at this very time in tying and labelling blacking-jars at a window, before which a small crowd would stop to watch his marvellous rapidity at work. Lever had his pony to ride to school, where his studies seem to have been confined mostly to the fun of fencing, the pleasant whirl of the waltz, or the romance of love-making. The iron had not entered his soul like that of his great contemporary—the ill-fed, ill-clad, uneducated, and uncared-for boy as he complains to have been; and doubtless we may trace to the joy of Lever's youth that wonderful flow of animal spirits, which in manhood bubbled over with pleasant sparkles, and made him the incarnation of fun. This luxurious little life in which nobody contradicted him, helped to produce that endearing equanimity and domestic devotion which Dickens, with all his philosophy, was never able to attain.

Mr. Cuthbert—one of the survivors of the Monks of the Screw—took a fancy to Lever, and contributed to the happiness of his life by telling him stories of Old Dublin. An historic Preface to the "Knight of Gwynne" —penned shortly before his death—tells us, *à propos* of the corrupt means by which the Union was carried :—

"As a boy it was my fortune to listen to the narratives of the men who had been actors in the events of that exciting era, and who could even show me in modern Dublin the scenes where memorable events occurred, and not unfrequently the very houses where celebrated convivialities occurred. And thus from Drogheda Street, the modern Sackville Street, where the beaux of the day lounged in all their bravery, to the Circular Road, where a long file of carriages, six in hand, evidenced the luxury and tone of display of the capital, I was deeply imbued with the features of the time, and ransacked the old newspapers and magazines with a zest which only great familiarity with the names of the leading characters could have inspired."

Among other houses thus pointed out to the child were Wright's school, and the adjoining mansion of Lord Norbury. The former, as Mr. West reminds us, had been the residence of Lord Ashtown—who, like Lord Norbury, was a leading actor in the struggle which cost Ireland her Parliament. The deserted palace of the Powerscourts stood within a door or two of MacCarthy's school.

Important recollections of Lever's rural life, contributed by his cousin, Mr. Innes, will be found in "the

Portfolio" appended to these memoirs—how he became acquainted with Hewitson Nixon, of Brownsbarn, a man who, although blind from childhood, had passed through most extraordinary adventures, and quite charmed Lever by his marvellous power in describing them; also how the boy, having attended the meets and hunts in Kilkenny, and cut a splash "just as the hare was taken," found his exploits commemorated in a ballad sold at fairs and races for one half-penny.

The Rector of Portumna, fifty years ago, was a somewhat peculiar shepherd, who wielded flageolet as well as pastoral staff. Octogenarian survivors of his flock say that "the only part of the church service he could be induced to read was the first morning lesson for the 19th Sunday after Trinity—the constant reiteration of the words ' cornet, flute, harp, sackbut, psaltery, dulcimer, and all kinds of music,' seeming to afford him intense pleasure." To this musical minister who, in days when discordant party-cries ran high, lived in harmony with all, John Lever, on receiving Orders, was sent as curate. Years after, when officiating near Tullamore, John followed his example by accepting the hospitalities of the local " P.P."

" John Lever came to Portumna as curate in the year 1821—and remained till 1825 "—writes Mr. Palmer, "and during those years his brother Charles spent generally from two to three months every summer with him. They had a pleasure boat on the Shannon, and went out every other day, sailing about and calling in at the several harbours along the shore; and Charlie seemed to derive great pleasure in taking a round of the different houses, and hearing stories from all who could tell them; and on our return in the evening would make sketches of all the country people, and concoct some amusing story connected with our day's rambling. I once had lots of those sketches and stories; but was very young then, and have lost them all."

The careful memoranda of his cousin informs us that in these boating excursions he was often joined by officers of a Highland regiment, who taught him to sing Scotch songs and to make Irish stew; an accomplishment, it is added, of which he was not a little proud, almost as much so, indeed, as of the attentions of the Countess Clanricarde and her daughter, Lady Emily de Burgh, afterwards wife of Earl Howth; "the first persons of rank," adds Mr. Innes, "whom he knew."

The Waverley novels awakened in Lever's mind a strong spirit of story telling, and a generous desire to emulate their heroes of romance. A paper contributed, long after, to "Blackwood," tells us, "I can remember the time when, as freshmen in our first year, we went about talking to each other of 'Ivanhoe' and 'Kenilworth,' and when the glorious spirit of those novels had so possessed us, that our romance elevated and warmed us to an unconscious imitation of the noble thoughts and deeds we had been reading."

It was from these days too, that Lever's love for Galway dates. Portumna stands at the point where the

Shannon begins to dilate into the beautiful expanse of Lough Derg, which, after forming sundry bays and receiving a number of smaller streams, once more narrows itself at episcopal Killaloe. The country bordering this lake is most interesting, not only from its picturesque beauty, which Americans pronounce equal to any lake scenery in Europe, but also on account of the fine specimens of ancient architecture which dot it. These were the sites of some stirring episodes in Irish history; and at the time of Lever's story, traditions which proudly called on Erin to remember its "Days of Old" lingered amongst the then numerous but now mostly expatriated peasantry. In the three Counties of Galway, Clare, and Tipperary, bordering Lough Derg, may, even now, be found the remnants of, at least, three distinct Celtic races, intermixed with representatives of the successive conquerors of Ireland. Charles Lever was not the man to enter deeply into ethnological or historical questions affecting the country, but it was impossible for a youth, constituted as he was, to live close to the Norman Castle of the De Burghs at Portumna, the ruined Abbey of Lorrha—to sail past Ireton's Castle, on Derry Island; and perhaps, on the same forenoon, to see the mysterious round tower rise from Inniscealtha, or Brian Boroihme's home near Killaloe,—without recognizing in these and other monuments, a sad epitome of the history of Ireland. The youth of English descent seems to have been deeply impressed by these Irish sermons in stones;

and his own warm nature with its tender susceptibility
and kindliness readily awoke kindred responses in the
sociable hearts of the Irish peasantry. There is a
peculiar charm in all lake scenery, but Lough Derg
combines beauties seldom found elsewhere; the colouring is so rich, the light so subdued, the tone of the
whole scenery so wild, so lone, interrupted only by
the plaintive cry of the curlew, that one feels whilst
gliding on its waters a dreamy pleasure not unmixed
with pain, chastened indeed, but yet the lingering echo
of a lament for men and things irrevocably gone. But
its charms are so pure, that no trace of bitterness can
possibly intrude. It was here perhaps, more than
anywhere else, that the young *romancier's* genius was
nursed, and acquired some of its most vivid and lasting impressions; his name too, has become associated
with the district to this day; O'Malley refers to it;
and a duel similar to that described was actually fought
at Derry Island on the Tipperary side of the lake.

On October the 14th, 1822, Lever entered Trinity
College, Dublin, as a pensioner, being then $16\frac{1}{2}$ years of
age. Men " go up " for the University, as it is called,
earlier in Dublin than at Oxford or Cambridge—a
practice in some respects objectionable, but it is the
consequence of the want in Ireland of schools like Eton
and Harrow; and may also be traced to the system which
permits the students to keep their terms and attend
lectures whilst living with their parents in town.

In all the obituary notices of Lever as well as in

dictionaries of contemporaneous biography, it was stated that he received his education at Cambridge. This is an error, and must have arisen from the fact that Cambridge has a "Trinity College" as well as Dublin—the former founded by Henry VIII.

Equally at fault was Dr. Maginn who, in reviewing "O'Malley," denied that Lever had ever been "a Trinity College man" in Dublin. Maginn himself had entered that University at the age of ten years, was warmly attached to his Alma Mater, and strongly resented any imputation upon its discipline. It is, nevertheless, true, that at Trinity College, Dublin, Lever went through his course without incurring any disgrace, and without earning much distinction, more creditably, perhaps, than Goldsmith, and with less diligence than Sheridan. He seems chiefly remembered for his rollicking fun and unflagging industry in the manufacture of pleasant tales. He liked to read character rather than books.

"His naturally joyous temperament," writes a fellow student, "his robust health and physical completeness led him to dash into the midst of the fray, in which he was everybody's customer in his own light-hearted kindly way. It was very difficult to take offence at anything Charles Lever said, the weapons he used were often as keen as they were brilliant; but it was so evident to his friends and associates that he never willingly inflicted real pain, that if a slight scar remained it was regarded rather as a thing to be proud of, than as a blemish."

"Give me but the making of the ballads and I care not who should make the laws of a nation" is an apophthegm attributed to Chatham and Voltaire, but in reality the words of Fletcher of Saltoun. From the days of "Lilliburlero," a war of ballads was waged between the rival races and parties of Ireland. "The wearing of the green" was answered by "Croppies, Lie Down," and the "Shan Van Voght" by "Protestant Boys." Both sexes followed the craft of street ballad-singing. Dublin had been, until the last twenty years, famous for its vocal powers in this line; and it is recorded of Goldsmith that, when a sizar, he wrote some of these ballads, and, "creeping within dark shadows of the ill-lighted streets," would watch the effect produced on the motley audience. Lever has also been known to glide from Trinity College at night, on a kindred but more sensational mission. Many of the old Dublin ballads were coarse and scurrilous, which tried to make up in bitterness of innuendo for their deficiency in humour; but occasionally were found real gems of passionate feeling sparkling with native wit, and possessing the true ring, which were at once caught up and carolled from end to end of the city. In the composition of many of these ballads Lever, no doubt, was directly concerned. He saturated his mind in such portions of the ballad literature of Ireland as deserved attention; "and on one occasion," observes the fellow student to whom we are indebted for so much that is valuable in these details, "having hired the uniform and accoutrements of the prototype of Rhoudlum—an historical personage still remembered in Dublin, and introduced in the ' Knight of Gwynne '—he went the length of singing, in one of the most frequented parts of Dublin, a political ballad of his own composition, judged to be too strong by the regular professionals. A great row ensued, but a party of fellow students were at hand to rescue the amateur singer and bear him off in triumph."

His confederate on this occasion was Keane, who will be found hereafter associated in a practical joke played on Surgeon Cusack's class. If they received rough usage as ballad-singers, they also received something more consoling. Dr. Tweedy says that Lever and Keane returned that night with thirty shillings in half-pence. He was greatly attached to Keane, and seemed in a paroxysm of tears when, sometime later, he announced his death to Dr. Tweedy. Readers of Lever's works will not fail to have remarked the frequent and effective use he makes of ballads and ballad-singers ; and all those acquainted with Dublin thirty years ago, will also recognise how perfectly in his own acknowledged compositions he caught not only the form but the tone and spirit of the best Dublin ballad. In his last work, " Kilgobbin," Joe Allic is made to do this very same task of writing ballads for the streets —a souvenir of times never more to return. The glorious days of Dublin ballad-singing were before the new policeman came to say " Move on ! " Major D——, to whom we are indebted for the above anecdote, tells us that he perfectly recollects the grotesque figure of Rhoudlum singing ballads. Lever, in the "Knight of Gwynne," describes the choral crone as "a fiend-like old woman, with one eye, and a voice like a cracked bassoon. She was dressed in a cast-off soldier's coat, and a man's hat, and either from face or costume had few feminine traits. She was followed by a mob of admiring amateurs, who seemed to form her body-guard and her chorus." Lever ran some risk of popular chastisement from the freedom with which he used favourite names.

> "Och, Dublin city, there is no doubtin',
>   Bates every city upon the say ;
> 'Tis there you'd hear O'Connell spoutin',
>   An' Lady Morgan makin' tay.
> For 'tis the capital o' the finest nation,
>   Wid charmin' pisintry upon a fruitful sod,
> Fightin' like divils for conciliation,
>   An' hatin' each other for the love of God."

His careful studies of the Irish ballad-singer stood him in good stead ever after. The important *rôle* played by Darby—disguised as a hag of this character —will be remembered by readers of "Tom Burke."* "It will be easily understood," resumes our esteemed informant, the Major, "why a character like Lever should, even in his earliest years, have acquired a cer-

---

* "Don't be crowdin' an me that away. There it is now—ye're tearin' the cloak aff' the back o' me ! Divil receave the note I'll sing, if ye don't behave ! And look at his honour up there, with a tenpenny bit in the heel of his fist for me. The Lord reward your purty face—'tis yourself has the darlin' blue eyes. Bad scran to yez, ye blaggards—look at my ilegant bonnet the way you've made it !"—*Vide* "Tom Burke," chaps. xviii., *et seq.*

tain ascendancy, and no small degree of popularity amongst his fellow students. What ensured his social position very much, was the fact that, although Lever's name was constantly heard of in connection with all manner of wild and daring exploits, it was well known that he was never mixed up with aught in the slightest degree objectionable, and this, no doubt, partly because he never was a drinking man, although Dublin, forty years ago, was as much given to inebriety as any city that can be found either north or south of the Tweed. An audacious bit of fun, but pure fun unmixed with coarseness, was Lever's delight—something at which all parties were sure in the end to laugh, after it had produced a momentary sensation."

His life in Trinity was of an enjoyable character. It is not necessary, as college men know, to read hard in order to obtain a degree. He drove and rode much; and the "curricle" rather than the curriculum attracted his thoughts. According to Charles Knight, who, however, does not employ the antithesis, some of Lever's time was devoted to breaking horses as well as to breaking hearts. His rooms in college were at No. 2 on the ground floor—not No. 2 to the left of the gate on entering, but No. 2 "Botany Bay,"—and from their situation the orgies, in which he and his chum Boyle indulged, were readily heard. This person figures under the name of Frank Webber in "O'Malley." Lever used to say of him that if now living he would certainly be a Fenian head-centre, and prove himself a far more for-

midable foe to England than any of the tried leaders of
that movement:—"He was one of my earliest friends,
my chum in college, and in the very chambers where I
have located Charles O'Malley in old Trinity. He was
a man of the highest order of abilities, and with a
memory that never forgot, but ruined and run to seed
by the idleness that came of a discursive, uncertain
temperament. Capable of anything, he spent his youth
in follies and eccentricities, every one of which, however, gave indications of a mind inexhaustible in
resources, and abounding in devices and contrivances
that none other but himself would have thought of.
Poor fellow, he died young, and perhaps it is better it
should have been so."

Lever does not seem to know that Robert Torrens
Boyle finally became a clergyman. In 1850 he was
curate at Stradbally, and afterwards rector of Timogue,
Leighlin. Here Mr. Burrowes Kelly specially remarked
him for his prim and staid demeanour. Boyle at this
period married a co-heiress, by whom he had no
children, sank into a state of mental imbecility, and
retired to Donegal, where he died about the same time
as Lever himself. Boyle's family tell us that at college
he stopped at no daring feat, from a conspiracy to
capture Major Sirr, the Fouché of Dublin, and a
notorious Terrorist, to practical jokes on the dean
of his University. Associated with Lever in some
pleasant pranks were Babington and Norcott—the
latter supplying the name of one of his last novels.

In " O'Malley " is introduced the Vice-Provost, Dr. Barrett, a figure so grotesque that even Lever could hardly caricature the reality.* Barrett died in 1821, and as Lever entered college in 1822, he could not have known him there ; but Barrett had been the guest of Lever's father, and furnished the observant boy with large material for future pencilling. Barrett's eccentricities were welded into the work at the special desire of McGlashan, the publisher. The collegiate progress of our student, as detailed there, though probably embellished, is, we are assured, autobiographic. The chief freaks ascribed to Webber, however, were performed by Lever himself—a fact known to his fellow students, some of whom now occupy distinguished status.

Except reading, there was nothing our collegians did not do. Among their avocations, we are told, were " training hacks for a race in the Phœnix, arranging a rowing match, getting up a mock duel between two white-feather friends, or organising ' the Association for discountenancing Watchmen.' "

Chapters xiv., xvi., and xx., of " O'Malley " may be fairly consulted by those who desire to enjoy a good laugh while gathering an insight into Lever's college life. *There* will be seen the endless practical jokes which pursued the Dons. How, on one occasion, dragoons in full uniform, on our student's invitation,

* In the " D. U. M." will be found (Vol. xviii., pages 350—358) a characteristic portrait and amusing memoir from his pen of this eccentric though gifted person. "But Lever's first piece appeared,' writes Mr. Innes, "in ' Bolster's Quarterly Magazine,' published at Cork in 1826." *Vide* " Portfolio."

excited dismay by unbuckling their belts and sabres, and seating themselves at the Fellows' table at dinner; how the loud orgies at night in the rooms jointly occupied by Webber and his chum, necessitated a nocturnal visit from the Burser;* how a hot skirmish ensued between the collegians and porters, whose wrath relaxed on being sprinkled with ambrosial punch; and how the Board threatened penalties next day, but on hearing an ingenious defence, relented. We suspect, however, that the real secret of Webber's (Robert Boyle's) escape was that he claimed kindred to the provost, Dr. Kyle, afterwards Bishop of Cork. The incident at the Fellows' table is remembered in Dublin University to this day as a veritable occurrence. Lever, perhaps, used it as a tradition rather than a personal reminiscence, but that it took place there can be no doubt. Dr. Maginn questioned the accuracy of the description, and declared that Lever could not have been an alumnus, adding :—

"A Trinity College man would have known that had any persons intruded themselves into a society where no guests are received, where none, excepting those members of the University actually resident within the walls, can enter, they would infallibly have been kicked first out of the hall by the gentlemen and then out of the gates by the porter."

---

* Dr. Maginn declared that this designation " of the inoffensive Treasurer of the College" was as absurd as "to send him to do the duty of the Dean in suppressing a disturbance." (" Fraser," No. CLIV.) No adverse criticism, however, ever made Lever alter a line that he had once written.

The Irish gentleman of the old school, however, especially if a highly educated one, is proverbial for his courtesy, and it is quite possible that the Fellows, rather than sanction so gross an outrage as that suggested, connived for once at the presence round their table, of military visitors—clearly strangers in Dublin,—on whose breasts hung the medals of Talavera and Waterloo, and who found themselves, possibly by some mistake, guests at the Fellows' table.

But this incident pales beside others duly described, including a proposal to blow up the great bell, which had so often intruded on their morning convivialities. This was overruled, and O'Malley satisfied his wild spirit in igniting some squibs and crackers which had been previously disposed in the gown of a certain worthy doctor. "The terrors of the 'Board' were never fulminated against me. The threat of giving publicity to the entire proceedings by the papers, and the dread of figuring in a sixpenny caricature, were too much for the worthy doctor, and he took the wiser course, and held his peace."

All this, besides furnishing a glimpse of Lever's life in Alma Mater, affords a good specimen of the fun—free from frailty—which was a specialty with him. The convivial indulgence described is overdrawn, so far as Lever's own case is concerned, it being positively asserted by Major D—— and others who knew him in college, that he was not addicted to hard drinking : and we know on the same authority that he never smoked.

The confession reveals no worse than ungovernable animal spirits, rollicking fun, and the exuberant buoyancy of boys—and Lever was, to the last, "a child of larger growth." The scene is a rich harlequinade, at which we laugh without feeling the worse for it.

"His writings," observes a critic, "are absolutely without anything which is base in itself or lowering in its tendencies. The animalism in which he revels is the animalism of which we need not be ashamed. No youthful mind was ever impregnated with a single seed of unwholesome appetite or desire by the novels of Charles Lever. They are infected by no moral taint. Their atmosphere is free indeed and uncontrolled. Their hilarity runs high, and is sometimes boisterous. Their heroes are often enough impossible and extravagant. We are introduced to *noctes cœnæque deorum* not a few, but there is nothing that an English parent need hesitate to entrust to the leisure-hour reading of an inquiring English boy." *

Who knows but that his hard hits at the academic asceticism of that day, and his exaggerated pictures of the collegiate laxity, of which it was almost necessarily the fruit, may have helped to soften the rigour of its rules? Trinity College, now-a-days, is widely different from the old Trinity of fifty years ago, and how few would credit the prediction, if then made, that balls, attended by the belles of Dublin, would now be openly allowed in that ancient seat of learning.

* The *Standard*, No. 14,928, June 4, 1872.

Lever was attacked by Dr. Maginn for presenting, in "O'Malley," pictures of relaxed discipline in Alma Mater—adding that he could not have been a Trinity College man to defile the Temple; but the heads of the University far from viewed his sketchwork in this peevish spirit, of which we have proof in the fact that, not very long after, they solicited him to become their representative in Parliament, and, although holding a Doctor's degree from a continental college, presented him, at last, with a diploma of LL.D. *Honoris Causâ.*

Lever having entered College in 1822, should have been in a position to graduate as B.A. early in 1826. He must, therefore, have lost an entire year in some way, for the College books show that he did not take that degree until autumn, 1827. Whatever time he lost was mostly spent in

> "Wit, eloquence, and poesy—
> Arts which I loved, for they, my friend! were thine."

How his time passed his friend Major D—— helps to tell in those wonderful notes he has so fully placed in our hands. "About the year 1826 a scion of a good family in Connaught, who resided in Trinity College, made himself conspicuous amongst the students by his very exaggerated self-importance and pretension, wholly unwarranted by the possession of talents or attainments. Lever, having undertaken to admonish his inordinate vanity, accomplished the task first, by inserting paragraphs in one of the Dublin newspapers, proclaiming in the most pompous style, all this gentleman's movements real or pretended, as for instance, " We are glad to be able to announce the arrival—from his family seat, county ——, of that distinguished young gentleman, Mr. A. B., who purposes residing, for the time being, at No. 340, Trinity College," or, " We hear that Mr. A. B. has taken up his residence for a week at Gresham's Hotel, Kingstown, where his presence cannot fail to attract all the leaders of fashion in our metropolis, &c., &c., &c." The poor young man swallowed the bait most eagerly, and really began to imagine himself a person of great importance, whilst his appearance in society afforded general amusement. The climax was reached when Lever appeared at A. B.'s rooms in college at the head of a deputation, dressed in their caps and gowns, to present a mock heroic address from a pretended meeting of students, expressing, in very inflated terms, their high sentiments of respect for A. B.—the whole of which was taken literally, and swallowed with infinite complacency. This precious address appeared in one of the Dublin newspapers next morning, with a number of names annexed to it, and a reply from A. B., showing how completely he fell into the trap so adroitly laid to catch his self-conceit. There is no saying how far this farce might have gone, but that a copy of the newspaper falling into the hands of some friends of A. B.'s highly respectable family, that young gentleman was removed to other spheres, and, for aught I know, may be still adorning society in his native region. I may add, in reference to the address, that amongst other names unauthorisedly appended was my own, to the great disgust of an uncle, a staid old gentleman, who had an equal claim to it. The whole thing left a particular impression on me, for I remember getting well blown-up on the circulation of the news by officious friends."

A tedious search for this address has terminated in its discovery at a date subsequent to that which Lever's friend assigns to it. The address and reply appear in *Saunders' News Letter* of April the 4th, 1831, but the successful formality of the Presentation took place very appropriately on the 1st of April. The document, with other amusing adjuncts, will be found in the portfolio appended to this memoir. It may be added, on the authority of Dr. H——, one of the signatories, that this spark of Lever's wit ignited a train of practical jokes which completely blew B—— out of Dublin—culminating in the arrival, one morning, at his door of a hearse, which, on a hoaxing order, came to remove his remains.

It will hardly have failed to strike the reader ere our narrative ends, that Lever's characteristics, whether by accident or design, bore a marked resemblance to those of Theodore Hook, the Stanislaus Hoax of Disraeli's "Vivian Grey." We are told by Hook's biographer that his "joking proclivities had nearly cost him his matriculation." He is believed to have been the prime mover of the Berners Street Hoax, in 1809—but, it is added, "a record of his practical jokes, boisterous buffooneries, adventures, and fits of frolic would fill a volume." Both Hook and Lever shone to infinitely better advantage at the table than in their writings. The parallel must, however, stop here. Hook revelled in _double-entendre_,—Lever was never known throughout the forty years of Major D.'s association with him to make one joke to which the most fastidious could object.

Now-a-days when folk are constantly on the wing, travelling over not only every European land, but all parts of the world, it will be hard to understand the stay-at-home life that fifty years ago our fathers led. The long series of wars lasting from 1792 to 1815 had well nigh weaned British subjects from Continental travel; and it was not till ten or twelve years after Waterloo that the younger generation, especially of Irishmen, began to yearn for further acquaintance with the outward world. Lever felt this impulse very early, and with him it was an irresistible one. His previous trips had sharpened his appetite for further travel. If living was cheap in those days, transit was slow, and Lever's time being limited by his medical studies, he adopted an ingenious mode of inexpensively gratifying his love for roaming, while discharging, at the same time, a professional _rôle_. It was precisely at the period when Dr. Lardner, T.C.D., sought to demonstrate, by rigid mathematical calculation, the impossibility of steam-ship communication being ever established between Ireland and America, that the Irish exodus which attained such vast dimensions of late years had its birth, and sailing ships were fitted out in Irish ports for transatlantic emigration. Frightful occurrences had taken place on board some of these vessels in consequence of the outbreak of fever and other diseases, and the Government issued an order to compel each ship carrying emigrants, to carry also a duly qualified medical officer. The ship-owners interpreted "duly qualified" to mean a medical student of perhaps two years' standing who could procure a certificate of proficiency in the treatment of accidents and common fevers, the remuneration being a small sum, a free place at the skipper's table, and a gratuitous passage home.

Provided with credentials of higher mark than seems to have been necessary to secure the appointment, Lever obtained charge of an emigrant ship bound for Quebec, in the spring of 1829. With a case of instruments, and a small valise, he got on board, probably whistling as he went "The girl I left behind me." In those days no Board of Emigration existed, and no records of such matters were kept by the Custom House, Dublin, so that it has been found impossible to ascertain the name of the vessel, or any particulars of the voyage. But some reminiscences of it may be gathered from his subsequent writings. A Review by him of "Marryat's America,"* after noticing the great sea-serpent, of which there has recently been a revival, says:

"We ourselves can vouch for having made the voyage across the Atlantic under the guidance of a Yankee

* D. U. M., vol. xiv. p. 516.

'skipper,' who assured us that he sailed for two days on a wind alongside of one, and only 'got to the end of him when the breeze freshened to eight knots an hour.'"

In the thirtieth chapter of "O'Malley," giving a graphic description of a ship becalmed, will be found reminiscences of this voyage; and there are also traces of the visit to Canada in "Lorrequer;" whilst Bagenal Daly and his man Sandy, together with the wild Indian character described in the "Knight of Gwynne," are evidently derived from the impressions of his trip to North America. In "Con Cregan," too, he utilizes some experiences of this time. We have a chapter headed "The Voyage out;" another, "Quebec;" a third, "An emigrant's first step on shore;" a fourth, "A night in the Lower Town;" a fifth, "A scene, and my lucubrations on the St. Lawrence;" a sixth, "On board the Cristobel;" a seventh, "A log hut at Brazos;" an eighth, "A night in a forest of Texas"— and so on. Going out, he speaks of "passing at sunset the great headlands of the south of Ireland—at first seemingly clear, and at last like hazy fog banks, while our light vessel scudded along to North America." He tells us that he sometimes dropped into the steerage to listen to some seaman's yarn of storm and shipwreck, but far oftener into the cuisine. "I resolved," he writes, "upon making a tour of Canada and the States, in order to pick up a few notions, and increase my store of experiences, ere I adopted any fixed career."

Very graphic is his sketch of Quebec, which he at

last reluctantly left; but more interesting evidence of the reproduction of adventures actually experienced at this time lies before us.

A letter, addressed to us by the clergyman who shared so largely Lever's confidence, states, "He wrote to me in June, 1843, saying that in return for a secret I confided to him he would tell me one in return respecting the story of 'O'Leary,' then appearing. The shipmate, the tale, and the adventures, *à gaspé* were facts, and happened to himself. He spent the summer of 1829 in Canada and the States, visited some of the Indian settlements and Lake Erie, and went as far as Inscarara. The Indian 'Post' was a true man, and the journey was made, he added, exactly as described.

"Lever narrated to me his landing in America and his rapidly passing from civilised districts to the prairie —with the determination to seek the experiences of forest life with an Indian tribe. He easily found the red man's haunts, and was admitted into fellowship. For a time, a life free from the restraints imposed by civilization upon us was to him of the highest enjoyable character. The nights under the open air, the days in the pine forest or by some majestic river, were transcendentally happy. He got so thoroughly in accord with them, that the Indian sachem formally admitted him into tribal privileges, and initiated him into membership." *

* Letter of Rev. Samuel Hayman, Feb. 21, 1876.

Lever became the more reconciled to native companions from the savage boorishness he had met on the route from white ones. His review of "Marryat's America," after referring to the combination of vulgar egotism with impertinent curiosity, which marked the emigrant population of Canada, goes on to say:

" 'Two Turks are not so bad as one renegade,' so, in fact, two 'genuine Yankees' are less insufferable than one adopted son of this land of independence. A few years ago, when making a short tour in America, we made one of a coach party going from Utica to the 'Springs.' A swarthy, well-dressed personage opposite interrupted a remark, by saying 'You are an Irishman I guess, friend?' Having replied in the affirmative, he added, with a chuckle, 'Well, I thought so, your countrymen are such damned ugly men.' " Such barbarous rebuffs fanned his adventurous spirit — Lever flung himself into the ranks of the less repulsive red men.

Mr. Hayman resumes :—

"For a time, Lever said, this was pleasurable; but only for a time. He grew weary of barbarism, and sighed for civilisation. He endeavoured to hide his emotions, and he succeeded with the men ; but one of the squaws, looking at him fixedly, read his thoughts. 'Your heart, stranger,' said she, 'is not with us now. You wish for your own people. But you will never see them again. Our chief will kill you, if you leave us. It is the law of our tribe, that none joining us can go away. No ! no ! You will never see the pale faces again, nor go back to your country. How could *you* find the forest tracks for yourself, if you fled? You would be instantly followed, and found; and when found you would be slain. O stay!' He feigned to be convinced by her arguments; but all his thoughts were fixed on the one object—flight. How could he effect it?"*

"Every day and every hour he studied to find opportunity; but it was all in vain. He found the customs of the tribe to be as the woman described. There was to be no separation from them; or death the penalty. The same squaw noticed the change in his spirits, and ere long in his health; and her 'woman's' heart was touched with compassion. She even devised the means of his getting away.

"A red Indian, named Tahata, came to the tribe once a year, bringing tobacco and brandy from some British settlement, and exchanging them for the peltry the hunters had collected from his previous visit. The squaw told Lever that she would sound this man ('the Post' he was called), and see whether for a sum of money he would appoint some place of *rendezvous* for him in the forest, and be his guide through its mazes until some outpost or town would be reached. Lever had no money, but 'the Post' was to be remunerated by his countrymen on his reaching them. The offer was accepted. Lever, at the squaw's suggestion, feigned sickness, and was left behind in the wigwams with the

---

* Letter of the Rev. Samuel Hayman, Grange Erin, Douglas, Cork, March 6th, 1876.

women, while the tribe were out hunting. In the men's absence he made his escape. Tahata was faithful."

The following is from " O'Leary," a book which Lever admitted to Mr. Hayman, correctly described his own progress at this time.

" Then began a series of adventures, to which all I have hitherto told you are as nothing. It was the wild life of the prairies in companionship with one who felt as much at home in the dark recesses of a pine forest, as ever I did in the snug corner of mine inn. Now it was a night spent under the starry sky, beside some clear river's bank, where the fish lay motionless beneath the red glare of our watch-fire; now we bivouacked in a gloomy forest, planting stockades around to keep off the wild beasts; then we would chance upon some small Indian settlement, where we were regaled with hospitality, and spent half the night listening to the low chant of a red man's song, as he deplored the downfall of his nation, and the loss of their hunting grounds. Through all, my guide preserved the steady equability of one who was travelling a well-worn path—some notched tree, some small stone heap, some fissured rock, being his guide through wastes, where it seemed to me no human foot had ever trod. He lightened the road with many a song, and many a story, the latter always displaying some curious trait of his people, whose high sense of truth and unswerving fidelity to their word, once pledged, appeared to be an invariable feature in every narrative; and though he could well account for

the feeling that makes a man more attached to his own
nation, he more than once half expressed his surprise
how, having lived among the simple minded children of
the forest, I could ever return to the haunts of the
plotting and designing white men." *

"The fugitives were pursued," continued Mr. Hayman, "but not overtaken; Lever reached Quebec in
safety. 'I walked through the streets,' he said to me,
'in the moccasins and with head-feathers. I found a
merchant who knew my father, and gave me the reward
for the guide, and who crowned his kindness by lodging
and boarding me until he paid my passage back to
Europe.' I give you," adds Mr. Hayman, "Lever's
narrative as nearly as I can in his own words."

His arrival in Quebec was, as he says, on a bright,
clear, frosty day in December, when all the world was
astir; sledges flying here and there, men slipping
along in rackets, women wrapped up in furs, sitting
snugly in chairs, and pushed along the ice some ten or
twelve miles the hour; all gay, all lively, and all
merry looking.

In his books he constantly recurs for material supplied
in these early adventures. Thus, Roland Cashel details
to Olivia his history when a prisoner with the Caman-
ches, a savage American tribe. About this time he
also visited the States; and in reviewing "Marryat's
America," after praising Upper Canada as the finest

* D. U. M., July, 1843, p. 6.

portion of North America, adds: "The Americans themselves we part with here, as we did some years since from their shores, *sans regret.*"[*] His allusions, however, to their "whittling and spitting propensities," with other habits, show that Lever had no opportunity of meeting well-educated Americans.

On the whole, however, these early travels proved of use in forming his mind and character. A magazine paper on "Foreign Travel" dilates on the benefits derived from "intercourse with strangers, and the opportunities of correcting, by personal observation, the impressions already received by study. "No one sets a higher price on this than I do; no one estimates more fully the advantages of tempering one's nationality by the candid comparison of our own institutions with those of other countries; no one values more highly the unbiassed frame of mind produced by extending the field of our observation, and, instead of limiting our experience by the details of a book, reading from the wide-spread page of human nature itself."[†]

He recognised the importance of travel, but yet often throughout this period of expatriation, felt inclined to lilt from a song of his own—

> "I would dance like a fairy,
> To see old Dunleary!"

He was glad, therefore, to set foot once more on its beach, and to find that Ireland had been in the interim

---

[*] D. U. M., vol. xix. p. 323.

[†] *Ibid.*, vol. xiv. p. 521.

emancipated. In his last preface to "The Martins," he speaks of this "as one of the most memorable eras in its history, and when an act of the Legislature assumed to redress irregularities, compose differences, and allay jealousies of centuries' growth, and make of two widely different races one contented people!"

Lever's luggage home was swelled by an unusual adjunct. An old friend of his, Dr. Maunsell, remembers him bringing home a canoe from Canada, and being taken, in company with another youth, to try it on the Grand Canal near Dublin.

Lever pursued his medical studies, but Dr. D—— tells us that he was more remarkable for acuteness in prognosis than diagnosis. His general diligence of observation, however, was great. Its keenness is proved by the fidelity with which he always sketches German manners prevalent in those old German towns at a time when the small Courts were in the full enjoyment of their superficial honours—scenes quite as graphically pourtrayed as his picturesque glimpses of "Dear Dublin" and the West.

To this city, endeared to him by birth and the associations of a happy boyhood, he is now found speeding once more.

CHAPTER III.

"Jacky Barrett"—Cologne and Coblentz—Life at Göttingen — Blumenbach—A duel—Louis Napoleon—At Heidelberg—Vienna and Weimar
—Goethe—Return to Dublin—Studies medicine—A startling resur-
rection—Personates Mr. Cusack to the class—Pursuit at the hands of
the hoaxed—Recollections by Drs. Ridgeway and Cullinan, "the
wrestling doctor."

JAMES LEVER rented from Sir Compton Domville
some land near Clontarf, on which he built a handsome
villa, known as Moatfield,* where Charles passed many
early days. It afterwards became the residence of Mr.
Staunton, a well-known Irish journalist, noticed by
Moore in his diary, and later an important public officer,
who took it direct from James Lever. To Clontarf,
Lever devotes a Chapter of "O'Donoghue," and describes it as "the then fashionable watering-place of the
citizens of Dublin;" while its "Green Lanes," receive
honourable mention in that "Boy of Norcotts."

Men of mark were occasionally entertained by James
Lever; but he was a calculating man of business, and
rarely dispensed festivity without an object. We catch

---

* Charles Lever was the last life in the lease, and in 1872 Moatfield
became the subject of the first case for litigation under the new Land Act—
known to lawyers as *Holland* v. *Domville*—when compensation for permanent improvements was claimed, and came on appeal before Baron
Deasy from a decree made by the county chairman.

a glimpse of these pleasant evenings in a memoir by
Lever of Dr. Barrett, a don of Dublin University.

"A gentleman at Clontarf who wished to become
tenant of some college lands, invited him, when bursar,
with other Fellows to dinner. He had not been so far
from college since his childhood. It was then, that
passing by Lord Charlemont's beautiful demesne, and
seeing the sheep grazing, he asked what extraordinary
animals they were, and when told expressed the greatest delight at seeing for the first time live mutton.
As he passed along the shore, the sea attracted his
particular admiration. He described it as "a broad flat
superficies, like Euclid's definition of a line expanding
itself into a surface and blue, like Xenophon's plain
covered with wormwood."

"The college bell," adds Lever, "hung at that time
to a high steeple in the front square, and when it tolled
at night the roll was distinctly heard across the bay at
Clontarf, like Milton's curfew :—

> ' Over some wide watered shore,
>   Swinging slow with sullen roar.'

"After dinner, when the guests, as was then usual,
began to drink to the health of favourite ladies, the
Doctor was asked for his belle: 'I'll give you,' said he,
'the college bell; for I'm told she's finer than Big Tom
of Lincoln.' This was not meant as a play upon words,
which he could not comprehend and never attempted.
The bell he always called ' she ' from the same vul-
garism that makes a gun or a ship of the feminine

gender. This was perhaps the only occasion on which he dined out of the Commons hall for nearly forty years."[*]

Moatfield, situated on a spot traditionally the scene of fairy gambols, had nice gardens round it, from which Charlie could now cull roses to his heart's content, eloquent of full-blown love. He had no longer need to look to Edward Clibborn for bouquets to lay at Kate Baker's feet. James Lever had, at first, some idea of putting Charles to the Bar, and would have much preferred to see him cultivating the flowers of rhetoric or even camomile flowers and poppy-heads, rather than those which engaged his attention. At length, the youth tamed down somewhat under parental remonstrance, took out his degree as Bachelor in a staid sense; and decided on proceeding to Göttingen to study Physic rather than Psyche. Increased sobriety of thought gradually grew up. "Whether," he writes, "we regard the physician as a man of science, cultivating, as the daily business of his life, the highest order of mental pursuits—or look upon him more nearly in his immediate relation to society, he has ever appeared to us a most interesting character."[†] "He became a traveller in his 'teens," writes Mr. Hayman. "His father gave him sufficient means. 'I shall know always, Charlie,' said the father to him, 'from your letters how you are conducting yourself. An altered

* D. U. M., vol. xviii. p. 354.
† "Physic and Physicians," D. U. M., Dec. 1839, p. 653.

life will bring an altered tone, that you will not be able to hide, and I shall judge for myself.' " *

The date of his journey to Göttingen can be but inferentially known. We were at first disposed to place it before the Canadian trip; but in his account of Cologne he alludes to the emotions he had previously felt on viewing Niagara. The first part of his " Log-Book of a Rambler," appeared in the " Dublin Literary Gazette " for January 16, 1830, and was probably written towards the end of 1829. " In the early part of last year," he writes, " I was waiting at Rotterdam " —which fixes the date, namely, 1828. At Göttingen he passed the winter of that year and the ensuing spring. His " Log-Book," published in the " Dublin Literary Gazette," which serial, by the way, was stamped out after an existence of six months, by the Stamp Office insisting on each number being furnished with a twopenny stamp—narrates his experiences *en route* to the Great German University. The notes begin with some account of Rotterdam, where, awaiting the arrival of a friend, he sojourned for some time. Snatches of impromptu song, and pleasant gossip are agreeably blended, and favourably contrast with the Dryasdust school of writing travels previously in vogue. The public are grasped warmly by the hand, and asked—

> " Know ye the land of dull dykes and dank ditches ;
> Whose waters are waveless and stagnantly green ;
> Where Mynheer, in Batavian expansion of breeches,
> And cigar-invoked stupor, sits still and serene ?'

---

* Letter of the Rev. Samuel Hayman, March 6, 1876.

The coming man at last makes his appearance, and the two friends start for Cologne, in order to be present at the great Musical Festival held in the then ruinous cathedral. The scenery along the Lower Rhine is pooh-poohed, and regret expressed that the French spoken by some Dutch fellow-travellers was unintelligible to him; and it subsequently appears that the German at Cologne was equally so. From which it may be inferred that, although he had acquired a tolerably good acquaintance with both languages, so far as books and masters enabled him, his ear had not as yet been made. "Lever," writes that old friend so retentive in recollection, "was never very accurate in foreign tongues; all his sympathies were at first in favour of Germany and its language, and I can remember perfectly his saying to me in 1830, that although an Englishman may reasonably hope to become a tolerably perfect German scholar, he can never become a really good French one. There is much truth in this remark, but it is curious enough that Lever's sympathies took, later on, quite the contrary direction, and became at one time as decidedly French as they had previously been German. Those who have studied his works or who were personally intimate with him, must have remarked that his genius was much more French in its character than either English or German." This peculiarity will become more apparent when we come to notice "Tom Burke."

Some details of his progress and a spice of his powers

of observation are found in the journal of 1830. He stands at the door of the Cathedral, wedged in a human mass whose decorum contradicted Swift's adage that a crowd is a mob even if composed of bishops.

"The swell of the music, as borne upon the wind, mingled with the din of the multitude, forcibly reminded me of the far-off roar of Niagara, when first I heard it booming in the distance.

"Never shall I forget the effect of that moment. The vast building lay before me, crowded with human beings to the roof; while the loud bray of the organ, mingling its artillery of sound with the deafening peal of several hundred instruments, was tremendous.

"The Cologne belles, with their tight-laced bodices of velvet, their black eyes, and still blacker hair, rarely covered by anything but a silk handkerchief lightly thrown over it, formed a strong contrast to the fair complexioned, blue-eyed daughters of Holland, whose demure and almost *minaudière* demeanour, was curiously contrasted with the air of coquetry which the others have borrowed from their French neighbours."

He adds that he wrote a very full description of "this Festival and the music, and made mems of some pleasant fellows with whom he dined, and of the pretty partners with whom he had waltzed," and asks—

> " Know ye the land where professors are tripping
>   In the light airy waltz and the swift galopade ;
>   Or retired within dark groves their negus are sipping,
>   And mixing soft speeches with stout kalte-shale :"

He attended a *fête* at Drachenfels—graphically described—where he got something better than kalte-shale, which is simply warm beer grated with nutmeg and sugar. Coblentz he reaches late in the evening, and had to go supperless to bed, the Duke of Clarence, who had just arrived, having ordered everything eatable in the town for himself and suite! He praises Wilhelmshöh and its water-works, but is shocked at seeing "the splendid carriage of the Elector, who sat in all the glory of a rich uniform and moustaches *à la Prusse*, smoking beside a young lady, not his Duchess. After stopping here for three days, which passed most agreeably, he again took flight, and at the end of a forty miles' excursion,

> "In our stage-coach waggon trotting in,
> We made our entrance to the U-
> Niversity of Göttingen."

The third part of the " Rambler's Log " appeared on April 17th, 1830, and is heralded, as usual, with metrical queries happily improvised, and sketching so vividly the life by which he was surrounded:

> " Know ye the land where the students pugnacious
> Strut the streets in long frocks, and loose trowsers and caps ;
> Who, proud in the glory of pipe and moustaches,
> Drink the downfall of nations in flat beer or schnaps ?"

"In three days," he writes, "I was enrolled a student of Göttingen, which, besides conferring on me the undoubted advantages of one of the finest libraries in Europe, with admission to various lectures, collections, botanical gardens, etc., also bestowed on me the more equivocal honour of being eligible to fight a duel, and drink '*bruderschaft*,' in the beer cellar of the university."

At length he sallies forth accoutred in a suit of sables, one hand holding a large canister of Dublin snuff, which he had brought as a propitiatory offering to the "greatest nose in Europe," and the other bearing some letters of introduction.

He describes himself as conducted by his guide to the house of a great Professor. Ascending the stairs, he knocked at a particular door specially labelled. "'Herein !' in a voice of thunder, was the answer from within to my still small knock. I entered, and beheld a small, venerable-looking old man, with white hair flowing in careless profusion upon his neck and shoulders; his head, almost preternaturally large, was surmounted by a green velvet cap placed a little on one side. He was grotesquely enveloped in fur cloak with large sleeves, and altogether presented the most extraordinary figure I had ever seen. I was again roused by the sound of his voice interrogating me in no less than six successive languages (ere I found my tongue) as to my name, country, &c., &c. I immediately presented my letters and present, with which he seemed highly pleased, and informed me that his 'guter freund,' Lord Talbot, always brought him Irish snuff; and then welcoming me to Göttingen, he seized my hands, pressed me down upon a seat, and began talking concerning my travels, plans, probable stay at the University, &c. I now felt myself relieved from the awe with which I had at first awaited the interview, and looked around with a mingled feeling of admiration and surprise at the odd *mélange* of curiosities in natural history, skulls, drawings, models, and even toys, which filled the cabinet. But, indeed, the worthy professor was by far the greatest lion of the collection." Lever remarked that the newest English publications reposed on his table, and even some from Dublin. "On standing up to take my leave, I asked him whether the Gall and Spurzheim theories were to compose part of my university-creed course of study; to which he answered, 'No! but if you will wait to October, we are to have a new system broached;' and then, chuckling at this hit at the fondness of his countrymen for speculating, he pressed me soon to revisit him and see his collection; and thus ended my interview with the great Blumenbach.'

Lever did not misname the eminent man. A letter once addressed "Blumenbach, Europe," found him.

"I was lolling one evening upon my sofa, enjoying a volume of 'Kotzebue' over my coffee," Lever goes on to say, "when my door opened, and a tall young man entered. His light blue frock, and long sabre, bespoke him a Prussian, no less than the white stripe upon his cloth cap, which, placed upon one side of his head, with true Burschen familiarity, he made no motion to remove. He immediately addressed me as follows—

'You are an Englishman studying here?' 'Yes.' 'You deal for coffee, &c., with Vaust, in the Weender Strasse?' 'Yes.' 'Well, then, do so no longer.' This was said without any menacing air, but with a most business-like composure. He seemed to think he had said enough; but, judging from my look of surprise that I had not clearly comprehended the full force of the *sorites* which led to this conclusion, he added, by way of explanation, 'I have lived two years in his house, and on my asking this morning he refused to lend me fourteen Louis d'ors.' Immediately perceiving the drift of his visit, I recovered presence of mind enough to ask, what the consequence would be if I neglected this injunction? 'You will then fight us; we are forty-eight in number, and Prussians—Adieu!' Having said this with the most provoking nonchalance, he withdrew, and the door closed after him, leaving me with an unfinished abjuration of groceries upon my lips. Ere the following day elapsed, he again visited me, to say that Vaust was no longer under ban, having complied with his demand. I could give many such instances but—*ex uno disce omnes.*

"And now," adds Lever, "that I have shown you the dark side of the picture, let me assure you there is a better one. For firm adherence to each other, for true brotherhood, the German student is above any other I ever met with; and although the principle of honour be overstrained, yet, in many respects, the consequences are good, and the chivalrous feeling thus inculcated renders him incapable of a mean or unworthy action."*

Pictures of student life in Göttingen follow, including a sensation glimpse of a duel in which Lever bore a part, but humanely: for at one time, when he saw the breast of Eisendaller covered, and his opponent was about to draw the trigger, he "felt an impulse to rush forward and arrest his arm." This duel, however, had no fatal termination. Hansel fired straight over his head. Eisendaller had been his playfellow in happier days. Throwing his arms around his neck, he exclaimed, "Mein bruder!" and wept like a child.

At last comes the fourth and last chip of the "Log."

"I was not long a resident in Göttingen ere I became enamoured of many of the Burschen institutions. I had already begun to think that students were a very superior order of people; that duelling was an agreeable after-dinner amusement; and that nothing could be more becoming or appropriate than a black frock, braided, and fur collar thereto, even in the month of July."

The pleasant "Irlander" became a favourite. He danced delightfully; sang with spirit and expression; and won golden opinions by translating into German verse, "The king, God bless him!" for a banquet commemorative of Waterloo.

* Dublin Literary Gazette, April 17, 1830. To this serial he is also found contributing some papers headed "Horæ Germanicæ,"—criticism on German music and poetry, chiefly "Der Freischütz."

This piece of autobiography, so little, if at all known, goes on to tell—

"My life now, although somewhat monotonous, was by no means an uninteresting one. The mornings were occupied at lectures, and then I dined, as did all the students, at one, after which we generally adjourned in parties to one another's lodgings, where we drank coffee and smoked till about three; after which we again heard lectures, till we met together at Blumenbach's in the Botanical Gardens in the evening, when we listened to the venerable professor explaining the mysteries of calyx and corolla to some half dozen young ladies, by far the most attentive of his pupils. The evening was then usually concluded by a drive to Geismar, or some other little village five or six miles from Göttingen, when having supped on sour milk thickened with brown bread and brown sugar, (a beverage which, notwithstanding my Burschen prejudices, I must confess neither ' cheers nor inebriates,') we returned home about eleven; and although I wished much that University restrictions had not forbade our having a Theatre in the town, and also that professors' minds were relieved from their dread of the students misbehaving, and would have permitted them to associate with their daughters, (for I was as completely secluded from the society of ladies as ever St. Kevin was,) yet was I happy and content withal." *

* Dublin Literary Gazette, Saturday June 26, 1830, No. 26.

There was a Kathleen with blue eyes and flowing hair praying far away for Charlie's safe return, and who, we may be assured, entirely approved the professors' disinclination to allow their daughters to associate with the students.

This life at Göttingen bore good fruit to Lever, independent of what he may have professionally gathered. Major D——, who was with him in College, and afterwards acquired an intimate knowledge of German life by long residence, observes, in the MS. notes placed at our disposal :—

"It was no small gain for a Dublin student of those days to discover that a great deal of social intercourse and agreeable society may be enjoyed by young men without having recourse to beverages which inebriate without cheering; and Lever, who was himself passionately fond of music, and had a very good voice, soon became aware that the chorus-singing of the German students, and the cultivation of good music (not the tantalising so-called comic song of the music-hall), had no small share in diminishing the consumption of exciseable commodities, discovered something equally valuable in himself and his friends, namely, a power of becoming a leader and social chief amongst his contemporaries; and, moreover, he must have even then determined on effecting a reformation of student life at his own University, for he very carefully collected materials for carrying such a project into effect; but of this hereafter."

In a review of Dr. Graves' "Clinical Medicine," Lever shows the difference between medical education in Germany and at home. There "the State provides the means and dictates the ordeal of study—while with us, the Colleges of Physicians and Surgeons possess chartered powers, under which they legislate for the two professions." *

Lever had a decided prejudice in favour of the continental physician; and in a similar paper, written three years earlier, he bitterly notices the want of encouragement which the progressive physiologist too often finds at home.

" Look at the professorships nobly endowed in France; look at the rewards conferred upon Blumenbach, Meckel, Tiedemann, Graefe, Langanbeck, and others in Germany. The man who abroad devotes his time and talents to the laborious pursuit of science in his cabinet, in preference to the more healthful and inspiriting duties of a practising physician, is not, by adopting the severer career, neglecting the more profitable. His government is able and willing to reward his services, and they never go unrequited. Not so with us, for all the benefits to accrue to one's children, and all the worldly advantages and consideration to one's self, better far to be the humblest apothecary that ever bestrode a ten pound hackney, 'arising for his half-crown fee,' than the enlightened discoverer of a subtle analysis or the in-

* D. U. M., vol. xxi. p. 308 (June, 1843).

ventor of a remedy which may confer lasting blessings upon mankind."*

In "Arthur O'Leary" we find some of Lever's Göttingen experiences reproduced. One chapter thus concludes: "But I must leave Göttingen and its memories. They recall happy days it is true; but they who made them so—where are they?"

Lever told Mr. J. G. Adair, his executor, that when in Germany at this time, a group of students, of whom he was the central figure, were often joined by one known as Morony; whose habitual taciturnity unfitted him from contributing to their social circle unless as a listener. Thirty years after Lever met in Italy one of the survivors, of whom he asked many questions regarding early friends, including Morony. "You don't seem to know that Morony was no other than the present Emperor Napoleon," was the reply. Napoleon was at this time in the zenith of his power; the guns of Solferino boomed their note of triumph almost simultaneously with this answer; and Lever declared that never had he been taken more completely by surprise.

From Göttingen Lever proceeded to Heidelberg; where he fell in with two friends, both, like himself, medical students; and one of whom, Dr. Maunsell, is still living, and not undistinguished as a journalist.

A very full account of the revolt of the Heidelberg

* D. U. M., vol. xiii. p. 662 (Dec. 1839).

students is supplied by Lever in the *Dublin Literary
Gazette* of 1830, in the last part of his " Rambler's
Log."

Another stirring narrative—well worth attention—
called a " A peep at the mysteries of the Heidelberg
students," appears in the *University Magazine*, Vol. 27,
pp. 173-183. In that paper will be found ample details
of the duels to which they are prone; and of a certain
upward stroke well known among experienced duellists,
and which, if successful, puts an end to the combat by
dividing the sinew of the sword-arm. *There* also is
recorded, besides the lyrics sung, an account of a supper
at which Lever was entertained—where at the head
and foot of every table two schlagers with basket
hilts, adorned with green and white ribbands, lay
crossed.*

Lever and his two companions at length went on to

* D. U. M., pp. 440-452, April 1846. Turn over some 300 pages further,
and more autobiographic detail may be gleaned. A long paper, headed
" Recollections of the Burschenschaft of Germany," describes the funeral by
torchlight of one who fell—two schlagers laid across the coffin with his
chore band and cap, two lines of students following—each carrying his
drawn sword with its point turned to the ground. As silent and slow the
procession passed on—the wail of music—the blue steel glancing in the
torchlight—all formed a solemn spectacle.

Records of what he saw at Heidelberg, possibly at a later date—the
Harmonie Ball—the duels—the interior of the students' chamber—may be
found in his sketches of Burschen life (pp. 54-67, vol. 28). The causes of
quarrels, he tells us, are frequently quite as trivial as that sought for by
the Irishman at Donnybrook fair, who trailed his coat and challenged any
man to stand on it. A more pleasing view of the Heidelberg youths is
afforded by Lever's account of the departure from College of one who had
been popular with his companions, when a procession, marked by pomp,
escorted him for miles.

Vienna. "I wished to contrast," he writes, "that well-policed and aristocratic capital with the almost licentious freedom of a university in another part of the confederation." *

Of Vienna he retained ever after pleasant memories —how he danced at the Landstrasse and the Elysium —was worried by the police about his passport, and mulcted by the janitor who guards every residence, and admits no one after ten at night unless on payment of a fee.

One of the two friends who accompanied him to the Austrian capital writes: "W—— and I used often to laugh at a mistake made by Lever when explaining to some ladies at Vienna, who were desirous of information about Ireland, how the victims of agrarian law were done to death in that country. The mistake consisted in Lever's having forgotten to change the vowel in conjugating the verb 'todschiessen,' so that instead of the participle 'todtgesckossen,' he used, to the great horror and confusion of the ladies, a word of totally different signification."

A paper contributed to "Blackwood" in 1864, mentions that he also made some stay at Weimar, and knew Goethe there who soon after died. It has been stated that the present Duke of Wellington studied with Lever at Weimar; but his Grace informs us that, although he was at Weimar in 1829, and knew Lever

<hr>

* Dublin Literary Gazette, June 26, 1830.

well afterwards, they had not then met. If Lever knew
Lord Douro by appearance at this time, it does not
follow that his Lordship knew the obscure Irish student.
Lever describes " Weimar as a small village-like capital,
with a miniature palace, a miniature theatre, a quaint
old park, and a quaint old Platz," and that in the
evening "society" assembled in a sombre old house
occupied by a large white-haired man, specially fond of
talking to a number of young Englishmen then at
Weimar for military education, "amongst them one who
is now a duke,* with one of the greatest historic names
in Europe." Goethe's talk was marked by touches of
picturesque description and humour, with, "now and
then a deep feeling which held his little auditory in rapt
astonishment that he could hold them there entranced,
while they could not, when he had done, recall any of
the magic by which he worked his spell. I myself
remember to have tried to repeat a story he told, and
once, more hazardous still, to convey some impression of
how he talked; and with what lamentable failure let my
present confession atone."

If it were only to have seen Goethe, Lever was well
repaid by this trip to Germany. He now wended his
way homeward, most probably through Bavaria and *viâ*
Strasbourg, and Paris, to England. The theatre-scene

* The " Duke with the historic name" writes (London, 28th May, 1877) :
" I was in Weimar in the winter of 1828-9, and Charles Lever was not, I
believe, then there ; I knew him afterwards very well in several places in
Germany, and if he did me the honour to allude to our acquaintance it was
probably to Goethe."

at Strasbourg, and many of the other incidents described in "Lorrequer," and subsequently in "Arthur O'Leary," demonstrate that he must have passed through Bavaria and been in France and at Paris previously to the Revolution of 1830. This explains, too, how Lever came to offer to his friend the opinion and advice already alluded to with regard to the study of German in preference to French. He must himself have experienced a difficulty in accommodating his ear to French after having accustomed it to German for some time. "Subsequently, indeed, the contrary was the case," writes his fellow-student, "for he understood the French language and literature much better than the German. In his works this becomes very apparent, for his French quotations are, if not all at least with few exceptions incorrect; whilst in quoting German or introducing German expressions into his dialogue, he follows the example given by Sir Walter Scott, in whose works not one single correct German quotation is to be found." *

The nice subtleties of German idiom, Lever, Grand Lama of the Burschenschaft as he was, never mastered.

---

* It is due to Lever to insert here some directions to his printer when "Lorrequer" was passing through the press, from which it is clear that many of the mistakes in foreign orthography imputed to him were typographical. "Look very closely to the proof this time, and above all to the French and German words, which are usually rendered Coptic and Norwegian by the devils." "It's a mercy I'm not near the printer who set up Number 18. I'm sorely afraid I should appear at Kilmainham the next quarter sessions." The spelling of the proper names was, he said, in many cases most improper. Lever was living at Brussels during the progress of "Lorrequer" and "O'Malley," and difficulties attended the transmission of the proofs.

Having lain fallow for a time, he now produced somewhat fuller fruit on resuming the culture of his craft. From some of his notes now before us, made in 1843, the secret thoughts and experiences of the young doctor to the period of their date may be learned, as well as the reflections that led him to select the medical profession in preference to others; and they not unpleasingly foreshadow the career that is coming. The elder Lever had become a clergyman, and though his knowledge of character was restricted, he possessed a judgment calm and clear, which rendered him, as mingled Censor and Mentor, of vast advantage in pruning the redundant sallies of his brother.

"No other class," he writes, "whose minds are trained by a course of labour, have so many opportunities of mixing with their fellow-men of every grade as the physician. The clergyman is limited by the very nature of his sacred calling to one species of intercourse with his flock. Worldly subjects and daily interests he is almost forbidden to touch upon or mingle with; his efforts, more directed to withdraw the minds of his hearers from passing events and fix them upon things of deeper and higher importance, he has less sympathy with sorrows and cares which spring from sources he undervalues, and therefore his knowledge of character, his insight into the human heart, will, by the very practice of his profession, be restricted.

"The lawyer, whose life is a continued mental struggle either in the detection and assertion, or in the concealment of truth, looks on the world but as one wide arena of litigation. Habits of distrust and suspicion tinge and colour to him every relation of life, and he arranges mankind into the two classes of Plaintiff and Defendant, with an intuitive readiness which enables him to take bold and striking views of society; but with the finer traits of human feeling—with the more minute springs that stir his heart—his occupation brings him into no contact. The very ingenuity to which he has trained his mind, the very sophistry which it is his daily habit to exercise, are so many causes of perversion to his judgment. Less eager in the pursuit of truth than desirous to fashion and mould it when found to his own peculiar purposes, he rejects the good that is not adapted to his views, and only unveils falsehood when it may be serviceable to his case. His discrimination of right and wrong will always be made more with refer- ence to legal than moral guilt or innocence; and he whose occupation it is by every trick of ingenuity, and every subtlety, to induce his hearers to adopt his views, will often find himself a special pleader to his own heart."

The craft of M.D. Lever preferred; though not be- cause he was necessarily in love with medicine. "He is alternately the encourager, the dissuader, and the comforter of his patients; and his character, moulded by the very exigency of his position, will put him in relation with feelings and sympathies of every varying condition in life. That any man so placed should obtain a deep insight into the world and its ways is not surprising; but when we add to these advantages the fruit of a study whose object it is to detect the secret working of the mind in every derangement of the body—to behold intellect 'cribbed, cabined, and confined' by every little morbid action of the system—his opportunities are great indeed. If, then, he possess such a widespread view of mankind by the nature of his profession, his requisites for its study are no less difficult and important,"—and he goes on to say, that the few in any great city who rise to eminence is a sufficient proof that the race is an arduous one.

A sample of the cynical talk which went on in his father's house and elsewhere, respecting the choice of a profession, peeps forth in the following:—

"I am old enough to remember the anxious discussion there used to be about overstocked professions. I can recall a time when people spoke of thatching their barns with unemployed barristers, and making corduroy roads with idle curates. Grumbles there are about under-pay occasionally; but it is rare to hear a man say there are too many doctors or attorneys. Novel-reading indeed is perhaps the only career overstocked; but the fiction writers have their uses too: they have banished from society colloquial novelists, the most intense bore —so we should be grateful to them as to the dogs in Constantinople: there are no other scavengers—and but for them the streets would be impassable."

When Lever joined the profession it was gradually

emancipating itself, under the guidance of Graves in Ireland and Todd in England, from much of that charlatanry of which a sample is found in the prescription, signed by fourteen doctors, for Charles the Second when almost in his last agony—comprising a volatile liquid distilled from human skulls, and the application of red-hot irons to the head that had borne a crown !

The physician of the nineteenth century, unlike the quack of the seventeenth, was a man of progress, on whose arm Lever leant.   Though he himself never attained a high rank in the profession, his views in respect to it were sound.   And the experience of old age but served to confirm his appreciation of the craft. Just before his death, in a paper "about doctors," he referred, among other matters, to their importance as an agent in checking "Spiritualism,"—thereby anticipating the recent detections of Dr. Lankaster.

One of Lever's visits on returning to Ireland was to Mr. and Mrs. Louche.   " 'I not only walked all the Hospitals of Germany,' he said, 'but I literally walked Germany, exploring everything.'   Long after my husband met him one day coming out of a musical publisher's in great glee.   'Only think,' he said, 'that a German Lied I brought home with me and translated has sold prodigiously.   I had forgot all about it—until Logier surprised me by saying that there is £300 to my credit.' "   Logier's shop in Sackville Street became eventually occupied by James McGlashan.

From the time of the premature death of the *Dublin*

Literary Gazette until the establishment of the *University Magazine*, Lever's pen seems to have been laid aside in favour of the lancet and scalpel. At Stevens' hospital, and the medical schools of Dublin, both were brought into play under Cusack, Hart, and MacCartney. The latter, a strange but able man, set up in the yard of the dissecting-room a marble tablet (afterwards plastered over, but now once more exposed), stating that it was consecrated to the remains of those whose bodies had been used for the purposes of science.

Lever's chief instruction, however, in the arcana of anatomy was received in a since extinct school in Park Street, called the "Medico-Chirurgical"—and now replaced by St. Mark's Ophthalmic Hospital. Here Dr. Tuohill and Lever met daily for dissections; and a friendship sprung up between them which continued uninterrupted to the end. We can imagine Lever at this time with the *Dublin Dissector* in one hand, and *Bell's Life in London* in the other: the solemn student of medicine one hour: the sporting squire the next.

The lecturer at Park Street was Mr. Hart, referred to by Lever in his "Log Book," and of whom he says Blumenbach asked him at Göttingen some questions. It is impossible to conceive two men more unlike than Hart and his pupil. The *Irish National Magazine* for November, 1830, contains a paper entitled "Schools of Surgery," which, describing a lecture at Park Street, speaks of Mr. Hart as "a most metaphysical-looking man; his countenance appeared scathed by the rays of the midnight lamp. He was a member of the Temperance Society, after the straitest manner of that sect. He read his own lecture with painful difficulty—such readings as we have heard from our devil when he came across some of that MS. which often puzzles ourselves— English written in Chinese characters." To Hart, Graves presented quite a contrast. The local gazette for which Lever wrote, mentions, in December, 1830, Graves "delivering, with great effect, a lecture from a written document, but occasionally throwing it aside, and explaining, familiarly, those parts which he seemed to think required elucidation."

Dr. B——, who had held a command with Lever in the miniature army which Wright's school sent forth, met him again at this time attending the Lectures of Graves in Sir Patrick Dunn's hospital. He describes Lever as arriving always half an hour before the lecture begun, and exercising the privilege of *entrée* to Graves' private room. This Lever appreciated and enjoyed, much in the same spirit as when in later days he was allowed "to go behind" and lounge in the Greenroom. Graves showed paternal kindness to the handsome student who, when a great magazine editor later on, returned the courtesy by eulogising his "Clinical Medicine."

Conjointly with Tuohill and others, he attended a medical debating club, whose meetings were held at Mr. Fannin's, 41, Grafton Street. "Lever spoke with such overpowering volubility, and energy,—he dis-

played such extraordinary fertility and felicity of illustration, that it was whispered in the club he must have taken
opium previous to these efforts." So said Dr. Tuohill.

Lever, though a resident student at Stevens', walked
the wards of Sir Patrick Dunn's Hospital with another
youth, Mr. now Sir Robert Kane. But he had time for
scribbling, and contributed the "Story of a Surgeon"
to the "National Magazine" for February, 1831. The
writer says that "his chief reason for residing in
Stevens' was to avail himself of the facility with
which immediate post-mortem examinations could be
obtained." One night a fever patient died; the
student took up his candle and proceeded to the dissecting-room. "To an uninitiated stranger it would have
appeared a horrible and ghastly sight; yet so much
are we the slaves of habit, that the young surgeon sat
down to his revolting task as indifferently as opening
a chess-board. The room was lofty and badly lighted,
his flickering taper scarcely revealing the ancient
writings that he was about to peruse. On the table
before him lay the subject wrapped in a long sheet,
his case of instruments resting on it; he read on for
some time unheeding the storm which raged without,
and threatened to blow in the casements, against which
the rain beat in large drops; 'and this,' said he, looking on the body and pursuing the train of his thoughts,
'this mass of lifelessness, coldness, and inaction, is all
we know of that alteration of our being, that mysterious
modification of our existence by which our vital intel-

ligence is launched into the worlds beyond—a breath, and we are here—a breath, and we are gone.' He raised his knife and opened a vein in the foot, a faint shriek, and a start, which overset the table, and extinguished the light, were the effects of his temerity.

"Turning to relight his taper he heard through the darkness a long-drawn sigh, and in weak accents, 'O doctor, I am better now!' He covered up the man thus wonderfully re-awakened from almost a fatal trance, carried him back, and laid him in his bed. In a week after, the patient was discharged from the hospital cured."

He is now found giving much attention to the collection of Ana, and proving himself a close observer of life and death around him. Nothing likely to aid the conversationalist or storyteller seems to have escaped his notice; all was stored up in his retentive memory to be drawn on when required.[*]

From grave to gay was the order of the day at Stevens'. A pleasant dance was given there by the matron, Miss Thompson, a lady of great intelligence, who, in her will afterwards, bequeathed £7,000 to the

---

[*] Dr. Ridgeway, the highest authority on any point connected with Stevens' Hospital from 1828 to 1833, tells us that he has heard the incident above described. To Dr. Cullinan it is new, but he can tell other things not quite so sensational. "I went down to the dead-room one night at Stevens' to fetch a 'preparation' I was 'macerating,' and which was low down in a barrel used for such purposes. My taper fell out of the candlestick while I was stooping over and holding the candle so as to show light into the barrel. Of course I was a little scared, and had to grope my way through a very unpleasant region."—Letter, August 5, 1876.

hospital. Dr. Tweedy describes Lever as in great form at her ball, and as he held forth to an admiring circle of listeners, it was clear that all other attractions in the room would soon be deserted in his favour. To Mrs. Cusack and Miss Thompson—the former the wife of his chief—and both elderly ladies, he mainly addressed his sallies. It struck Dr. Tweedy that when he danced or told stories, his attentions were not directed to handsome girls, but to people of mature age, likely to appreciate real wit. At supper he kept the table in a roar, improvising the while no end of witty stanzas in which the name of every guest present was pleasantly put.

The late eminent Mr. Cusack, afterwards surgeon to the Queen, was the resident surgeon at Stevens' Hospital. On this personage many a characteristic trick was played by Lever. Like his co-novelist, Dickens, he was full of dramatic talent, and one morning absolutely succeeded in personating Cusack to the class. This freak will be found recorded with due dramatic effect in "O'Malley;" but the scene is laid at Trinity College, instead of the hospital, while in lieu of Lever, Frank Webber plays the prank; and Doctor Mooney takes the place of Surgeon Cusack.

Two of the students present on this occasion, and who have since attained high rank in the profession, have kindly committed to writing their recollections of the incident. We allude to Mr. Cullinan, F.R.C.S.I., J.P., Ennis; and Mr. Ridgeway, F.R.C.S.I., Oldcastle.

"The circumstances attending Lever's personation of

Mr. Cusack were as follows," writes Dr. Cullinan: "Mr. Cusack used to sleep at the hospital when there were important cases under treatment, and particularly after the performance of capital operations. When he entered the hospital at night the porter would ring a bell to announce his arrival, and the resident pupils used to muster to see such cases as Mr. Cusack thought it necessary to visit. After making the usual round, Mr. Cusack directed his pupils to attend in his bedroom in the morning to be examined on a subject which he then specified. On the morning referred to I was going round the hospital at an early hour, and learned that Cusack had unexpectedly left during the night and had not returned. I met Lever on his way to Cusack's rooms, and told him he was not there, that he had left during the night, and we conspired together to have 'a lark.' Mr. Cusack's bedroom had a double door, the inner (a baize door) was acted on by a 'dumb porter,' which creaked when the door was opened or closed. Lever went into Cusack's bed, wrapped himself up in the blankets, and put on the red silk nightcap of his chief. I remained in the room. 'The bell boomed' —to quote Lever's words—'the sounds of feet were heard on the stairs, the door creaked, and gradually the room was filled with shivering students, some half asleep and trying to rouse themselves into some approach to attention.'" Dr. Cullinan continues:

"K., one of the apprentices, came in; Lever, in an admirably disguised voice, asked, 'Who is that?'

'K., sir,' was the answer. The next to arrive was O'R. (who was always called by his christian name, Gerald), and the usual question was asked, 'Who is that?' The answer was 'Gerald, sir.'

"Others came in succession, and Lever, selecting the subjects for his mock examination, began. After a few queries, he asked, 'What is the next subject, Gerald?'

"*O'R.*—Cancer, sir.

"Here a normal snore resounded from the bed.

"*Lever.*—Cancer, O'R? (interrogatively).

"*O'R.*—What about it, sir?

"*Lever.*—What about it yourself?—(giving a yawn as though he would dislocate his jaw).

"*O'R.*—Cancer, sir, is a malignant disease.

"*Lever* (after a few snores).—Well?

"*O'R.*—Well, sir?

"*Lever.*—You are a stupid ass, O'R. What do *you* know about it, K.? (K. was not very brilliant, and spoke with a lisp).

"*K.*—Cancew, sir, affects the lower lip of males.

"*Lever.*—What more? What colour is it?

"*K.*—Wed, sir.

"*Lever.*—Red? (doubtingly).

"*K.* (prompted by me).—It is yellow, sir.

"*Lever* (still more doubtingly).—Yellow?

"*K.* (after another prompt).—Bloo, sir.

"K. would probably have been led through all the colours of the spectrum before satisfying his preceptor as to the colour of cancer, but Lever could preserve his gravity no longer, and starting up to the amazement of Gerald and K. and the glee of the others, flung his night-cap into K.'s face, and jumped out of bed."

It is said that among the questions the sham Cusack asked was, "Where's Lever?" and the party answered "Absent, sir." "Sorry for it. Lever is a man of first-rate capacity, and were he only to apply, I am not certain to what eminence his abilities might raise him."

The late Sir W. Wilde told us that he often heard Lever describe this laughable adventure in presence of the great surgeon,* whom he had ventured to personate. Sundry small details, not given in the book, were added, such as Lever placing on the bed, ere the class arrived, Cusack's boot-jack and slippers, wherewith he wreaked summary chastisement on the heads of those who had failed to answer to his satisfaction.

Dr. Ridgeway has also given us his recollections of the scene, viewed through surgical spectacles; but, as some of the details would involve a repetition, we venture to make an amputation. "Lever," writes Dr. Ridgeway, "knew not his profession deeply, and it was a slip he made in the examination of a senior student which led to his detection, and it was only with some difficulty he was saved from the enraged class, whom for half-an-hour he had so successfully hoaxed." The

* Lever's intimacy with the Cusack family continued to the last. In July, 1871, two grandsons of Cusack, when travelling with the Rev. C. Baker, spent several weeks with Lever at Trieste.

remainder of the elaborate document drawn up by Dr. Ridgeway will be found in our Portfolio.

"No one when at Stevens' knew Lever better than Dr. Ridgeway," writes Mr. Cullinan; the written memoranda of the latter, however, are more illustrative of the man.

"I knew Lever from the year 1825 to 1831," resumes Mr. Cullinan. "He and I were fellow-apprentices and very intimate friends; we may be considered respectively the idle and industrious apprentices in a limited and literal sense. When his apprenticeship was about completed Mr. Cusack, who felt a great interest in Lever, sent him to live with me in my rooms in Stevens' Hospital, with the object and hope that he might read diligently for his approaching examination at the College of Surgeons. We read together steadily for some time, and examined each other daily in about sixty papers of the most important professional classbooks; but Lever's social habits and genial disposition prevailed, and after a few weeks he quitted my rooms, and we ceased to work together. Some time afterwards Lever 'went in' for his examination at the college, and having answered unsatisfactorily on the first day's examination,* he did not go in on the second, and he never got the licence of the college." ["The dismay of his father,"

* We are bound to say that, according to the Records of Trinity College, Dublin, he got from it, in 1831 (Æst.), the degree of Bachelor of Medicine, a high distinction, capable of enlargement to that of M.D. for a few pounds. He graduated as B.A. "Vern. 1827."—Ed. The "Diary of a late Physician," appeared in "Blackwood" in 1830—1. "When many eminent M.D.'s were mystified about it," writes Canon Hayman to us; "Lever saw through the disguise. He told me there were mistakes in it such as a tyro in

observes Mrs. Louche, "on learning that Charley had failed to pass was strongly manifested. But no remonstrance from him or from my husband could persuade Charles to go up again, as many others had done. He told us that so 'shot' was he on recognizing among the Examiners a man who had previously made himself disagreeable to him—that in his nervousness every thing he had learned at once flew from his mind." It may be interesting to add that the Examiners (then called Censors) were, in 1831, Wm. Aukenleck, Maurice Collis, Arthur Jacob, W. H. Porter, S. Wilmot, and Francis White. The man whom Lever feared will be found pointedly referred to at p. 118, *infra.*] "He left the hospital soon after," resumes Dr. Cullinan; "nor did I see him again until the 18th June, 1843, when Mrs. Lever and he were making a tour in the south-west of Ireland, and they passed through Ennis and named a day to dine with me.

"When I became an apprentice, I was invited to breakfast at Stevens' by one of the pupils whom I had previously known. The meal was very homely indeed, but the breakfast-table was elaborately ornamented with choice 'preparations,' consisting of dried skulls, thigh-bones, an ossified larynx, etc. etc. To do me honour, probably, Lever and two or three other fellows were invited to the breakfast, and I was introduced to him.

medicine would readily fall into, but which no well-educated doctor could make. This betokens more medical lore than our author might have been credited with, but the truth is, Lever was capable of grander and greater things than he ever accomplished."

He astonished me by his volubility and playful wit, and the extent of his knowledge of things in general. He talked of everything except 'shop.' Lever brought a tea-spoon to breakfast, to supplement our host's limited stock, and his teaspoon fell to my lot; after I had sweetened my tea, 'the first stirring event of the day,' as he said, I proceeded to sip it in the usual way, but there was nothing to sip, there being a hole in the bottom of the spoon. I was laughed at pretty generally, and I have no doubt I looked rather foolish, while Lever expressed the gravest sympathy with me for the unworthy trick practised upon me.

" Lever was very genial and festive; we used sometimes to pass a jolly evening together in some fellow's room; we played cards, sang songs, had tea with bread and butter, and generally finished off with a *glass* of punch out of a tea-cup. Lever enlivened these reunions by the introduction of a kind of doggerel, made extemporaneously, and containing playful allusions to some local and personal matters. There was a chorus which I never understood,* namely,

> ' Once so merrily hopped she,' &c. (*repeated thrice.*)
> ' Heigh-ho, Heigh-ho, Heigh-ho.'

He was wonderfully clever and witty in improvising such verses. Everyone was obliged to compose a verse in turn, which was always good or bad enough to afford an excuse for fun, and often much immoderate laughter.

* This is the old glee, " A pie sat on a pear-tree."

"While we lived together, he and I used to walk from the hospital to the lecture-room, about a mile distant, and, in order to utilise the time, would write down on scraps of paper some professional matters desirable to commit to memory, such as chemical formula, etc., which we learned by heart as we walked along, and then examined one another. Our shortest route was by the quays of the Liffey, but there was a glue factory on the quays, the odour from which was very strong. I remember that one day we both agreed it was probably like the smell of the skins of the sea-calves, which Ulysses found so intolerable when he had been covered with them by a friendly nymph to conceal him from her father, and which Homer called ὀλοώτατος ὀδμή. Lever used to go by the streets to avoid passing this factory, thereby increasing the distance to the lecture-rooms considerably. I objected to the loss of time so incurred, observing that I rather *liked* the smell from the glue works, which from habit I had really learned not to loath. He expressed his disgust very emphatically, and suggested that I should test the opinions of other persons by putting some of the glue stuff in my hair at the next crowded dance to which I might be invited, and where I might desire more room than people generally had in such places.

"Another subject of contention between him and me was that when crossing from one side of the street to the other he always went straight across and at right angles and at a 'crossing,' while I passed obliquely.

He objected to my practice as unusual and inconvenient, to which I replied that my object was to save time and distance, for that any two sides of a triangle were greater than the third; to which he rejoined, 'You may take the hypothenuse, if you wish to be ridiculous; but I shall not be guilty of vulgarity in order to make such a display of my knowledge of practical geometry.'

"I remember some of his facetiæ. Mr. Cusack was remarkable for paying scant attention to his apparel, and most of it had seen better days; on one occasion he got a new suit of a showy brown colour. Lever surveyed the garments with a scrutinising and critical stare, which Cusack mistook for admiration, and asked what he thought of his new clothes. Lever answered, 'Oh, Cullinan had told me that you had fallen into a keg of brown paint, but I am happy to see he was mistaken.' Cusack went off a good deal mystified, and not pleased.

"One day Professor Porter was about to deliver a lecture, to be illustrated with 'preparations.' One of Mr. Porter's pupils, who had been charged with providing and arranging the 'preparations,' had not arrived, and Mr. Porter was angry and impatient. He accosted some of the students who were waiting about, and Lever, looking into his eyes fixedly, said, 'I fear Mr. Porter you are getting *iritis* (inflammation of iris). Porter was a good deal startled, and exclaimed, 'Why do you think so?' Lever said gravely, 'your *pupils* are quite irregular, sir,' irregularity of the pupils being one of the prominent symptoms of iritis.

"On another occasion Mr. Cusack was passing behind the back of T., one of his apprentices, an idle fellow and a fop. This person was sitting on a stool at a table with a 'subject' before him, and wore a fashionable cloak, with a mitred cape. The cloak and cape were very fantastical, and quite an unsuitable dress for a man occupied as T. was. Cusack looked at him contemptuously, and said, 'How can that fellow ever hope to get on?' Lever said, 'I don't agree with you; I call that the "Cape of Good Hope,"' pointing to T.'s cape.

"Knott and Tighe were two of Cusack's apprentices. Lever and I were sitting at lecture one day, Knott and Tighe being also present. I had a note-book in my hand, making mems. occasionally, while Lever was not paying much attention to the lecture. He surprised me by asking me to lend him my note-book, and on his returning it I found the following epigram:

> " Knott said to Tighe, ' Can you tell why
> Two different names we've got ? '
> Tighe said to Knott, ' You have forgot,
> I'm Tighe and you are Not.' "

Other stories might be told to show his light-hearted nature. While at Stevens', he would ramble in the Phœnix Park, and return circuitously by Kilmainham and Mount Browne. One evening, when accompanied by his brother John, and their genial little friend Alexander Spencer, their attention was drawn to a large cradle hewn out of stone and neatly chiselled, which hung in front of the Foundling Hospital. Whenever a deserted child found itself flung into this receptacle, a wire communicating with a bell immediately raised an alarm and brought assistance to the spot. On this particular occasion Mr. Spencer was suddenly seized by Lever and raised into the yawning crib; and it was not without roars of laughter—very characteristic of the man—that his tiny friend was at last extricated from his comical position by the janitors, who rushed forth upon hearing the tinkle of the bell. It may be added that the stone cradle disappeared about forty years ago, during the alterations attendant on the conversion of the Foundling Hospital into a Poor House.*

To Mr. Spencer—small in size but large in heart—Lever inscribed the first edition of his " Knight of Gwynne " —styling him " the oldest friend he had in the world ;" and expressing a hope that the public would prove only half as indulgent to the faults and demerits of the book, as Mr. Spencer had been to those of its author.

* This institution, founded A.D. 1704, mainly with a view to educate children in the State religion, ceased to exist in 1831. The enormous cost to the country, the fearful mortality among the children, the difficulty of disposing of the survivors, and its baneful effect on the public morals, left the Government no alternative but to extinguish it. The bloodiest battles in history would not show a death-roll like theirs. In six years, out of 12,786 admissions, death had overtaken 7,807 ; and in the twelve years ending 1796, of 25,352 children adopted by the Foundling Hospital more than 17,000 died. On inquiry it appeared that a potent bottle had long been held in high favour with the head nurse, the ingredients of which she knew nothing beyond that they had the effect of making the children lie quiet after drinking it. A History of the Foundling Hospital has lately been published by W. D. Wodsworth, S.L.C.B.L., in whose department its ancient muniments repose.

A physician of rare humour was brought into association with Lever at this time—Dr. Brennan, the well-known "wrestling doctor." His early acquaintance with Brennan transpires in a review of Croker's "Songs of Ireland." This review was written by Lever, who regretted that none of Brennan's pieces had been included in the volume.

"The last thing we heard from the Doctor, he writes, was one day we met him in Sackville Street, a short time before his death.* A well-known Dublin shopkeeper, with his tawdry spouse were passing at the moment, neither looking very remarkable for neatness or propriety. ' Look at K—— and his wife,' he said, ' with the Liffey before their door, and their shop full of soap, and they're the dirtiest pair in Dublin.'

" Brennan was a hard-tongued fellow," adds Lever, " but always witty. He called the well-known Mr. Ireland—from a certain laudatory tendency he indulged towards his own acts—" Erin-go-Brag." Observing of another practitioner not famed for free hospitality he said, " The cat would get the rheumatism any day in his kitchen-grate." †

That " doctors differ," was illustrated in every phase of Brennan's career—

> Choose the grave you'd wish to be buried in
> Before you send for Dr. Sheriden—

was his significant estimate of a brother M.D.; and

---

* Dr. Brennan died in July, 1830.
† D. U. M. vol. xiv. p. 96.

not less than fifty other doctors received hits as hard.

These things we give not for their point, but because they reveal, on Lever's showing, that when a student he received comic grind from the witty Doctor whose sayings, pruned of thorns and slang, had effect upon the mind and character of the subsequently brilliant Humorist.

Lever got on very pleasantly in Dublin, and liked it the more from being able to compare it with continental cities. It struck Dickens with being " nearly as big as Paris, of which the quays along the river specially reminded him ; and but for the dress of the common people he could have thought himself on the Toledo."*
Lever was just the man to strive and make it still more continental ; he therefore planned the Burschenschaft, and helped to get up some successful Carnivals of which due mention will, bye and bye, be made.

* Life, vol. ii. pp. 198-9.

CHAPTER IV.

"I REMEMBER," writes the same graphic pen to which
we owe the communication of so much important detail
in Lever's life, "I remember seeing about this time, in
the courts of Trinity College, Dublin, some eight or ten
young men gathering round a figure that out-topped
them; every now and then a peal of hearty laughter
burst forth from the group, which scattered for a
moment as if recoiling from the explosion of a shell, and
then once more swarmed like bees round the central
figure. This naturally attracted my attention, and I
asked a bystander what it was all about. "Oh! its
only Charlie Lever, all the fellows are running after him
like mad." I had frequently heard the name before,
but it was the first time I had ever seen the man, who
was the kindest and most true-hearted friend anyone
could rely on. I approached nearer, and must confess
that the first superficial glance was not quite satisfactory.
I saw indeed a tall, athletic, erect and manly figure, that
never rested for a moment, but kept veering and tacking

about, the head being fixed for an instant to deliver a shot at some of the skirmishers who came to close quarters, or thrown backwards in hearty enjoyment of some happy repartee : but this figure was clad literally from head to foot, with the sole exception of his boots and as much of his shirt as was visible, in one uniform suit of Lincoln green, cut after a German fashion totally new to me. I perfectly remember that I muttered to myself—'This is the green man become restless;' but I went nearer, hoping to catch a glimpse of his head. In this I only partially succeeded, for Lever then wore a profusion of long hair hanging in wavy curls over his neck. After a time, indeed, I caught a good view of his wonderfully expressive face, his kindly smile, his brilliant though somewhat deeply set eye, that sometimes flashed fire and then again twinkled with mirth, but I am no portrait painter, and the impression made by that same face when I saw it for the last time one afternoon in June, 1871, is still so vividly and regretfully impressed on my memory, that I cannot even attempt to describe what it was in all the glow and fervency of youth, strength and hope; all I can say is, that the old face was to me equally attractive as the young one had been, and its expression was, although chastened and overcast even then by the shadow of death, more affectionate and tender than ever. That last loving look can never be forgotten."

The society which received Lever on his return to

Ireland chilled him. At some tables the jargon of technicality and shop held sway. In one set " stuck-up-ism " tied their tongues : in a sphere somewhat lower *mauvais honte* produced the same effect—eliciting at table the remark " awful *pause*," whereupon a lady, thinking the allusion was to her hands, at once buried them in her lap.

He liked the less formal and more accessible circles of the continent. He longed for conversational society in which he already began to feel his own superiority. He was too young and too little known to make his way at the dinner-tables where he sometimes appeared as guest, and he left them disappointed rather than exhilarated. Writing in a local gazette, (June 19th, 1830,) he speaks of the " ennui and display which attend soirées in Dublin. We have stupid dinner-parties, where men of law and physic talk a chaos of detainers, alibis, and ex-officios, or the still more unintelligible jargon of atrophy, hypertrophy, and syncope of the tribe of Esculapius. We are too social to go to the theatre. We are too social to form clubs as in London. In a word, we are too social to go much into society."

To correct this slow life, he applied his muscular shoulder to the wheel ; and the present joyous tone of society in Dublin has not been uninfluenced by his efforts.

Among the first of his social achievements was the Burschenschaft. Weary of feeling pulses, plying stethoscopes, and viewing tongues, he organised in 1830 the Burschen Club, which he resolved should present in its features an improvement on all previous gatherings of a social character, and be widely different from

> " The jolly members of that toping club,
>   Whose members were like staves hoop'd into a tub ;
>   And in a close confederacy link
>   For nothing else but only to hold drink."

Lever's club, on the contrary, was one, as Samuel Lover said, where " society in its brightest form quaffed the cup rather to lubricate the throat hoarse with uttering wit than to gratify the sensual gust of palate."

The Burschen—all song and sparkle—elected Lever Grand Lama. Thoroughly German in its proclivities, this social reunion evidenced a love of all things German, unless, perhaps, German silver, if the title of one of its high officers "Hereditary Bearer of the Wooden Spoon" may be taken as evidence. German songs were sung and translated by Lever, who afterwards gave them a place in "Lorrequer." So thoroughly Teutonic did Lever seem at this time, that nothing can divest his most intimate friend Francis Keene of the impression, that Lever's father had been himself a German.

The doctors and lawyers avoided "shop," true to Lever's inculcation. " Among the members," observes Dr. Parkinson, "was my brother William, who afterwards succeeded Lever as physician to the British Legation in Brussels, Cuthbert Eccles and Moore—both lawyers. Often my brother told me that Lever as president was the life and soul of the club, owing to his inimitable humour, conversational powers, and general good-nature."*

Another of the members was Mr.—afterwards Sir Francis—Smyth, between whom and Dr. Cullinan—who, however, never joined the Burschen—there was an affair of honour in which Lever bore a part. Jet Fitzgerald, brother of the present Baron of the Exchequer, was likewise a member. "'Poor Jet is dead,' writes Major D——. 'Many years ago he went out to Spain with De Lacy Evans's forces as assistant-surgeon, and was standing under a tree, looking on at some engagement, when a Carlist lancer charged him and pinned him to the tree.'

"The same pointed pen goes on to say :—'As to the statutes of the Burschenschaft of which I was an unworthy member, I can only recollect that it was required of us to abjure the use of white hats and shepherd's plaid pants, to abstain from evil words, including oaths or adjurations, to contribute to the amusement and good-fellowship of the club to the best of our abilities, without exceeding in liquor, and to address all the office-bearers by their proper titles.'

"Lever was naturally our president; and the title by which he was addressed was 'most noble grand!' There was a Turko-ecclesiastical official or expounder, a man of Friar Tuck circumference, the mufti (Mr. Maunsell), also a doomster (O'Leary); further a clerk of the punch-bowl, whose place at table was *vis-à-vis* the

* Letter of J. R. Parkinson, Esq., M.D., Wexford, December 27th, 1875.

mufti, the punch-bowl intervening. There were several other high officials whose proper designations I prefer not attempting to recall, lest I should be led into flights of imagination.* One, however, must be mentioned—the minstrel, *i. e.*, Samuel Lover, painter, poet, musician, novelist, dramatist. The Burschen all wore scarlet vests with gilt buttons, which were intended to bear a German student's duelling-sabre and porcelain 'pipe proper on a field gules;' but the Dublin artist who was employed, having never seen either one or the other, substituted, in his ignorance, the Dublin Lord Mayor's great sword of state and a common clay. I have not been able to recover one of these buttons, nor one of the red skull-caps with white tassels which completed our official uniform. The paraphernalia appertaining to the Bur-schenschaft consisted of, first, a huge misshapen meer-schaum, furnished with a multiplicity of tassels, and smelling vilely of every variety of tobacco that the old or new world ever produced."

All this was German enough, but it has been well observed by Bayle Bernard that instead of the hacking sword-play in which the German soul delights, the worthier contests of the brain were essayed wherein the only cut and thrust were those of repartee.

" Then there was a mighty book with antique binding and brazen clasps," resumes the Major, " containing a legend of the supposed origin of the society in the reign

* A writer in " Macmillan," who claimed to be a survivor, had spoken of the State Squeezer of the Lemons, the Steward of the Salt-box, &c.

of King O'Toole, and illuminated very handsomely after the fashion of a missal. The legend, I need scarcely say, was the production of the 'most noble grand' himself, whilst the illuminations were executed by the minstrel.

" In order to impart the requisite air of antiquity to this quasi-venerable book, it had been first thrown into the fire for a moment, then plunged into a pail of water, and finally buried in a coal-cellar. Thirdly, there was also some kind of sword that had probably belonged to a drummer of volunteers in 1798. Some years ago Lever told me that he still had in his possession the regalia.*

" There was a nice, plain, cold supper, a very small allowance of wine, and a strictly limited punch-bowl, for the double purpose of rendering the evening inexpensive and preventing excess. At first, such of the members as were used to more copious libations growled; but they soon found they could enjoy themselves to their heart's content.

" Lever proved himself a most courteous and brilliant host, and set everyone completely at his ease. After a few moments' chat, or when new members were to be admitted, the formula of instalment had been gone through, the whole party sat down to supper. This ceremony, when developed, became a very amusing parody on that used in Dublin University for conferring the higher degrees. The 'most noble grand' and his high officers of state, notables, the mufti, and one or two

---

* The German meerschaum, as Bayle Bernard reminds us, was eventually laid aside for the *dudeen*, or short clay-pipe of the Irish peasant, "supposed to have belonged to St. Patrick."

others had each their several parts assigned, and the whole dialogue used, being in rhyme, was sung with solo parts and chorus adapted to music, and all from the chorus 'Ein freies Leben' in Schiller's 'Robbers.' The admonition of the 'most noble grand' to the candidate, after his election, commenced—

> " ' You'll truly swear
>   Our Vest to wear,
>   And be a loyal Bursche,' &c. &c.

There was a pianoforte in the room, at which the minstrel presided; and the get-up of the whole ceremony was very creditable to the candidates, however difficult they frequently found it to preserve their gravity.

"Both before and after supper the regular charter songs of the Burschenschaft were duly sung. One of them was 'The Pope he leads a happy life,' of which Thackeray said, in my presence, to Lever in 1842, ' that he would be prouder to have written that translation than anything he had himself ever done.' But Thackeray at that period had not written 'Vanity Fair.' Many of Lever's and Lover's lyrical pieces were, in fact, written for and sung at the Burschen meetings.

"Our reunions were occasionally honoured by visits from staid old gentlemen; amongst others Mr. Cuthbert, who well remembered Curran's 'Monks of the Screw,' and said to Lever that the evening Burschen had been quite as brilliant and pleasant as any of the ante-union ones. There were, indeed, some highly talented men and gifted conversationalists amongst the Burschen, some of whom subsequently attained high positions at the bar and on the bench, and Lever was just the man to make the best of any good materials that came under his hands. The wind-up of the evening, after the treasurer had collected some trifling dues, was a pretty chorus introduced in ‘O’Malley,’

> “ The morning breezes chill,
> And yet we linger still,
> Where we’ve so happy been.”

“Lever’s Burschenschaft was most agreeable and useful, it gave many of us a relish for more intellectual enjoyments and society; and the few remaining Burschen still living can testify that the ‘ most noble grand ’ conducted our concerns with infinite tact and delicacy, never permitting for a moment the slightest impropriety, and thereby gaining in an equal degree our esteem and affection; indeed, I feel certain that much of his popularity and the very kindly feelings entertained towards him so generally was due to the admirable way in which he presided over his Burschen. That he himself was also a gainer is equally true; he learned how to lead, and he also acquired a juster estimate of and greater confidence in his own powers. No one, indeed, seems to have suspected, even at that time, what was really in the man. Some, perhaps, even shook their heads in doubt as to what good could ever come out of the sort of pre-eminence he had attained, being, as it was, the reverse of professional.”

Thus far Major D——. Lever’s own recollections of

the same time will be found in a paper contributed to *Blackwood* in 1865 (p. 211):—

"We were altogether, as I then thought—and now, with thirty more years of life, still think—the wittiest, pleasantest, jolliest, and most *spirituel* fellows that ever sat round a punch-bowl. Oh dear, when I think of writing the charter song of our order and bringing it down to the club, and teaching my comrades the grand old German Lied, I am half ready to believe it was but yesterday we met; and I think I see the great meerschaum on the red cushion, the symbol of our union; and as my eyes grow dimmer, visions of the gay company in their scarlet waistcoats come thronging around me; and what fine, generous hearts beat under those bright vests, and what good fellowship linked us!

"It was very fine fooling, let me tell you; and for a witty doggerel on the topic of the hour, a smart epigram, or a clever bit of drollery, all I have ever since met of *beaux esprits* in my own or in other countries could not approach comparison with the Burschen."

It continued its gay bright course, and, like the ballet-dancer's leg, daily increased in strength and thickness. Thirty-five years after, Lover was greatly affected on meeting some of the survivors. "In the emotion with which they recalled those glorious nights, I could mark how bright these spots shone through all the dreary savannahs of life, how they clung to them and treasured them, firmly persuaded that no accident, no hazard, no fortuitous concurrence of events could ever bring to-

gether again such spirits as made the Burschenschaft.
Let no one tell me that there is not a soul in a hearty,
racy conviviality, and that in those gatherings where
men who like each other blend emotions as they mingle
in song, rising with the exaltation of the hour to inter-
change of friendly pledges, that in such there is not a
spirit of affectionate attachment that survives time and
distance, so that he on the Himalaya shall toast him on
the Baltic coast, and the ice-bound sailor in Behrings
Strait remembers him who is roasting away under the
sun of India." *

Unlike Moore, Lever kept no diary; but we are able
to say in whose company he dined on August the 2nd,
1830. His memoir of Maxwell—in a magazine for 1841
—mentions incidentally:—"We remember well when
the news of the last revolution in France reached us:
we were dining in company with that most accomplished
man, Charles Kemble. The fall of the exiled monarch,
elicited from all around the table some testimony of
opinion in accordance with the political leanings of the
speaker; but when it came to his turn, he paused for a
second or two, as if meditating, and then finishing off

---

* Queries as to the site of these Burschen meetings have elicited the reply
that they were held in the first storey of a confectioner's shop, No. 16,
Dame Street, afterwards known as "the Civet Cat." The Club subsequently met in a large back room in the Commercial Buildings—we believe
that since used as the Stock Exchange—"and here might be seen," adds
Major D——, "for a long time after, a *daïs* covered with cloth or baize
with a representation of a sword and tobacco-pipe crossed, in brass-headed
nails, on which the 'most noble grand,' *i.e.*, Lever, had his chair placed on
all occasions."

his glass, gravely remarked, 'Charles X. has lost a d—d good engagement.' "

Lever at no time showed any very marked preference for theatrical society; but he loved an artiste, no matter in what walk he found him. One of the unacknowledged papers of veritable history contributed by him to the magazine of his selection, tells us :—

" It has been my fortune, good or ill as you like to call it, to have mixed much in the society of poet, painter, musician, sculptor, song-writer, playwright, actor, author. Now I by no means would insist, that a man cannot keep better, but he certainly cannot keep pleasanter company. The very dark sides of their character are so relieved by the flashes of genius which illustrate their works, their foibles, their vanities, their egotisms, their fits of sulkiness, and ill-humour, are all so tinged with the ' couleur de rose ' light that plays over their happier moments, that what in less gifted temperaments had degenerated into coarse selfishness, or morose isolation, with them is but the black cloud shadowing the landscape as it passes, deepening every dell and ravine, where the instant after the bright sun will be sparkling and glittering." *

This affords a glimpse of the sort of men with whom Lever loved to mix previous to the year 1841. Shiel had been contributing to *Colburn's New Monthly* about this time semi-political papers " On the state of parties

---

* Memoir of W. H. Maxwell, D. U. M., vol. xviii., p. 220 (August 1841).

in Dublin;" and the same heading, descriptive of parties in a more festive sense, was employed by Lever in his first attempt at humorous writing—"The Log Book of a Rambler," being chiefly didactic. His remarks " On the state of parties," however, is full of humour, though of a grade inferior to that marking his more matured sketches, and bearing much the same relation to them as Thackeray's story of "Dando the oyster-eater" does to "Vanity Fair." The paper, however, merits attention as throwing light on Lever's life and thoughts at this period.

He condemns the dances then fashionable in Dublin, especially on the north side. He hates Payne's quadrilles, and the pianoforte performances of some young lady all compliance and diffidence: he looks forward to supper for recompense; but there is none. In place of it "you have two odd-looking men, in air, manner and occupation wonderfully like vendors of Bath buns, parading the room with the concentrated essence of ague and indigestion in the insidious garb of lemon-ice and sponge-cake."

This paper, written possibly in dyspeptic disgust after some freezing festive failure, goes on to propose the establishment of a society for the suppression of tray suppers and Payne's quadrilles, and to promote the knowledge and practice of waltzing and wild fowl, mazurka and merriment, conversation and cutlets.

Lever then proceeds to describe himself leaving at midnight this chilly clime, and, after gliding over a line of streets, at last reaching Carlisle Bridge, which he jokingly calls the verge of the kingdom. "You there experience that peculiar mental excitement which a traveller feels when, after crossing some vast American forest, and bivouacked among the red men for weeks sharing their raw flesh, he at last approaches a civilised Yankee town." * The latter experience, it will be remembered, was a veritable adventure.

There is much amusing exaggeration in the contrast he draws between the north and the south side of Dublin, which the Liffey divides. He was himself a native of the former, and he seems to have retained a chilling impression of the friends with whom he had mostly mixed. By degrees he got into a wider social sphere, and his account of a ball in Merrion Square is most genial and flattering.

He entreats the really well meaning but misled people of the north, not to forget, in their intemperate quadrilling, the words of the Irishman who, when the people were trotting at the funeral of his wife, reproved them by calling out, "Asy! asy! ye thieves of the world! can't yez for to not be making a toil of a pleasure!" †

Mrs. Louche has retained a most amusing recollection of a ball to which Lever was invited by an opulent

* *Dublin Literary Gazette,* June 19, 1830.

† His prejudice against the north side is partly due to the fact, sufficiently well known in his family, that the house property which had been left him as his patrimony was situated in that region and rarely brought him anything but trouble.

ironmonger, whose brother afterwards became a baronet. A ware-room off the shop was allotted to dancing and to a fine *orchestre*. Green baise neatly concealed piles of fenders and fire-irons, which covered the walls from the floor to the ceiling. Military officers in full uniform spun round in the waltz : but one having leant his back in a *dégagé* manner against, as he supposed, the wall, a pile of ironmongery became dislocated, and fell to the ground with a fearful crash. Mrs. Louche was greatly amused on recognising in " Lorrequer" this incident— one illustrated by Phiz in his best vein.

His ambition at first seems to have been to make a name for himself as a conversational *Raconteur*. This attained, his society was eagerly sought. His Jottings (1830–31) give a glimpse of the pleasant social expectations which his advent never failed to awaken.

The *Dublin Literary Gazette*, full of promise at its birth, and of power while it lived, died, after a career of six months, as a weekly publication; though a bold effort was made to merge it into a monthly serial, known as the *National Magazine*.

Lever's literary passion, which had first begun to assert vitality beneath its ægis, was well-nigh extinguished in the *débris* of the *Gazette*, and his pen for years after lay inactive. The first impress of his hand, traceable in the *National Magazine*, is a sketch of " The Aquatic Sports in Dublin Bay," published in July, 1830. It describes a recent regatta at Kingstown, and is signed " Pepperpot"—the same name which supplies some allusions to Göttingen in the "Plantagonals" of the same serial. His account of the Rock Road thronged with the washed and unwashed of Dublin, hurrying to the *fête*—we had no railway then—is amusing; to say nothing of the sudden downpour of rain which at last placed all comers on a perfect footing of equality—and spread panic around, especially to "woe-begotten dandies with inconceivables that once were white and which now, mud-draggled, clung to their shapely thighs." Watching the progress of the viceroy, the people, and the race, he noted everything calculated to raise a smile. From the too often rain-charged sky of his native land he drew drops of crystal consolation, maintaining that "Irish clouds are by far the most beautiful in the world. I have never witnessed the same variety of form and tint elsewhere, and I have seen as much of the world as most men. I attribute the circumstance chiefly to the combined dampness and warmth of our climate." The welcome he found at a hotel, the good dinner, and the wine, "so refreshing after the fatigues of the day," are described with characteristic gusto.*

Some of the best members of the Burschen Club were gradually compelled to relinquish their connection with

---

* "An Evening in College," (*Nat. Mag.*) January, 1831, is most likely also Lever's. Opening in a style suggestive of the earlier chapters of "O'Malley," we are introduced to an "unlucky junior sophister, who had been cautioned that day by the inexorable Doctor, and who now, with the aid of a few friends, a spatch-cock, and some three-year-old October, was endeavouring to banish care, in the drawing-room floor of Botany-bay Square."

it by imperative calls to other lands. In 1832 it was still existing, but with vitality on the wane.

A favourite boarding-house known as "Lisle House," 33, Molesworth Street, presented some attraction to him. "Here," observes Dr. Darby, "Lever, with John Blake, brother of the eminent K.C. of that name, and one or two others, formed a most agreeable coterie. As a teller of stories Lever was altogether unmatched. Most of these,—at least, when I knew him in early days, —were impromptu 'flams' circumstantially related. He was so genial, and told such amusing stories, that he was much sought after. In this way he gained the lasting friendship of the Rev. W. Fausset,"—of whom we may add more anon.

Another old *habitué* of Lisle House was Surgeon Cusack Rooney, whom Lever introduces in "Lorrequer" as Surgeon MacCulloch. This gentleman, like Blake, who died in Australia, is no longer living. Both could have furnished many amusing details of Lever at Lisle House.

His first introduction to it is described in Chapter XIII. of "Lorrequer." Entering the drawing-room before dinner, and on his name being yelled forth he is congratulated on its escape from the hash of which all names were usually made by a careless lackey—Mr. Blennerhasset having just been announced as "Misther Blather-hashit."

No time was lost by O'Flaherty—the name given to the veritable Blake—in presenting him to sundry persons, to be cut hereafter—as he whispered—including Miss Riley, in a bird of paradise plume and corked eyebrows, Mrs. Clanfrizzle, some old ladies in turbans, Mr. Garret Cudmore, a doctor in blue "winkers," several ancient vestals, and a host of others.

At last Lever was booked as a resident of the House, "a lover to at least five elderly and three young ladies, a patient, a client, and a second in a duel. O'Flaherty told me all this was requisite to my being well received, though no one thought much of my breach of compact subsequently."

During dinner O'Flaherty, seizing an idle moment from his operation of carving, asks the new-comer to take wine with him, and to name what wine he drank, intending thereby, as afterwards appeared, to send from his end of the table what wine his guest selected. Not conceiving the object of the inquiry, and having hitherto helped himself from a neighbouring decanter, he immediately turned for correct information to the bottle itself, upon whose neck reposed a slip of paper. His endeavour to decipher the writing occupied time sufficient again to make his host ask, "Well, will you have port?" "No, thanks, I'll stick to my old friend here, Bob McGrotty "—" for thus," writes Lever, " I rendered familiarly the name of Robert McGrotty on the decanter, and which I believed to be the boarding-house *sobriquet* for bad sherry. That Mr. McGrotty himself little relished my familiarity with either his name or property, I had a very decisive proof; for, turning round upon his chair and surveying my person from head to foot with a look of fiery wrath, he thundered out in very broad Scotch : "And, by my saul, ye may just as weel finish it noo, for de'il a glass o' his ain wine did Bob McGrotty, as ye ca' him, swallow this day."

Lever in his fictions, instead of coining names as Dickens did, loved to introduce those which had once been familiar to him. A Mr. McGrotty will be found further on at Coleraine, where Lever was brought into constant contact with him.

Physic bottles, quite as much as decanters, were now in Lever's hands. In Midsummer, 1831, he received his degree as a Bachelor of Medicine in Trinity College, Dublin; and henceforth we find him consulted by patients. But as this nice distinction failed to carry weight with the ignorant, he seems to have remitted at a later date to Louvain* the amount requisite for obtaining the diploma of M.D. *in absentia.* With many it gave him prestige; it injured him with a few. "Abernethy would have shaken his head at it."†

A Louvain degree also gave the title of Doctor to his

---

* About thirty sketches of Lever, published in biographic dictionaries and elsewhere, describe him, but incorrectly, as an M.D. of Göttingen.

† Lever could shake his head at Abernethy when he liked. A magazine paper of his, besides supplying a bit of autobiographic detail, states :—

"Abernethy's character as a wit was for the most part acquired in the Lecture-room ; and very little experience of such an arena enables us to predict that the smallest offering of the jocose is ever most gratefully acknowledged there. Our very heart sinks at the remembrance of the scholastic jests in anatomy and surgery, to which we were doomed to listen each winter for five years of our student's existence. Of one little professor of ophthalmic surgery, we have a mournful memory to this day.

co-novelist and countryman, Goldsmith, who, having one day said, "I prescribe only for my friends," was playfully answered by Beauclerc, "Reserve your prescriptions for your enemies." But, unlike Goldy, Lever was really successful in medical treatment. Had he contented himself, however, with the B.M. of Dublin University, it would have proved a prouder possession.

Some old account-books of James Lever, replete with domestic interest, are preserved, and seem to have been most carefully kept. The portion for 1830 devotes many entries to Master Charles, including the payment of various fees to his master in anatomy, Doctor McCartney, and no end of disbursements for gloves, which never exceed two shillings a pair, while his boots sometimes cost as high as two pounds. He seems to have been a great patron of the Drama,* his theatrical outlay on one night sometimes amounting to twenty-four shillings,

Though happily removed from ear-shot of his piercing voice, and far from the scenes of his trite witticisms, yet so clear is our recollection of his pointless jests and stingless severity, that we shudder at it even to this hour."—" Physic and Physicians," D. U. M., December, 1839, p. 635. Lever, notwithstanding his character for indomitable fun, was alive to the duty of maintaining, in the schools of anatomy, the decorum befitting the gravity of his studies.

* The following are extracts from the day-book of James Lever :—

	£	s.	d.
1830—March 17. Cash to Charles .	0	10	0
„ 23. Cash to Charles . .	0	4	6
„ 26. Pd. Thompson for Charles' Boots . . .	2	0	0
April 2. Pd. for Boots for Charles .	1	4	0
„ 10. Pd. for Charles' breakfasts at Steevens' Hospital .	1	0	0

though as a dramatic critic he might well claim the
right of free admission. His general tone, however,
was so much the reverse of laudatory that perhaps he
thought himself hardly entitled to ask a compliment
from the lessee. A specimen of this bold tone, and
how his evenings passed, are found in a sketch published
forty-seven years ago in the *Dublin Gazette*, and which
thus wound up :—

"We placed ourselves in a box near the stage, the
reason of our selection being that it was the only one
inhabited. Two grave-looking men occupied the seat
before us, whom by their conversation we discovered to

		£	s.	d.
April 14. Cash to Charles for his Surgical Examination	.	31	10	0
July 7. To Charles for his breakfasts at Steevens' Hospital .	.	2	0	0
November 26. Pd. for hat and two waistcoats for Charles		1	16	0
To Charles for College porter . .	.	0	2	6
December 6. Pd. Charles cash for his breakfasts at Steevens'		5	0	0
Cash for his medical tickets . .	. .	19	4	0
1831—February 23. Pd. for a silk handkerchief Charles got	.	0	4	0
Pd. for two pairs of gloves Charles got also	. .	0	2	0
May 18. Cash to Charles for the porters		0	7	0
August 9. Cash to Charles for his degree . . .	.	24	0	0
November 29. Pd. Charles, borrowed money . .	. .	1	10	0
December 17. Cash to Charles (theatre money) .	. .	1	4	0

be bond-holders mourning over the melancholy prospects of the house. Lulled by the drowsy orchestra, in which our old friend the bass-viol seemed to have taken an opiate, we soon fell asleep, and did not wake till it was time to dress for Lady L——'s* *soirée.*"

The day ended thus, but how did it open? A visitor presented himself to Lever, "enveloped in a box-coat and Belcher muffler." There was something in his appearance which awed him, "and I instinctively hurried my widespread MSS. into an open drawer, dreading lest the great unknown might be an angry author coming to take signal vengeance upon his reviewer."

Thus it would appear that he wrote more largely as a critic than has hitherto transpired. The following shows that no booksellers' drudge had a worse time of it!

"If, according to the Northern proverb, 'he has need o' a lang shankit speene that sups kail wi' the deil,' so he requires a sharp-pointed pen who corrects proofs for him; and the deuce of it is, that after you have revised your proof as clear as a whistle, and got to bed with eyes and fingers wearied and aching at four in the morning, you find next day, as I know from sad experience, that the paper is published with half your corrections blundered anew."

The visitor, when denuded of dreadnoughts, proves

<hr>

* Probably Sophia, Lady Lees, wife of the Rev. Sir Harcourt Lees, a prolific pamphleteer in aid of Church and State. He is introduced, *en passant,* in "Charles O'Malley."

to be an old College chum, who claims Lever as guide in viewing the local lions and in comparing the changes which time had wrought. Lever mentally hears the "muttered maledictions of an enraged editor" as he accompanies his friend. He takes a fling at some local blots not yet erased, especially the dirt of the streets, by suggesting a placard announcing the sale of "a great variety of mudspoons, scrapers, shovels, spades, scoops, and scavengers, all which, being very little used, are nearly as good as new."

They visit the Law Courts, and finally a well-known divan * to get their mulls replenished ; and then follow sketches of some once familiar figures, but who for forty years have been quietly inurned. "An invitation to sup on devilled kidneys comes," accompanied by a request that "I should prepare myself to be particularly brilliant and facetious in conversation.

"After this I rode out, visited various public places, heard all the *on dits* of the day, and then returned to my lodgings, ordering my servant to deny me to all comers, being determined to bottle up my conversation for the evening, and not even trust myself to an interview with a member of the Deaf and Dumb Institution!"

There was then no " United Service Club " in Dublin —or indeed hardly a club of any sort. It now boasts

* Mr. Fairholt, in his " History of Tobacco," remarks that men of large mind have been almost all snuff-takers. It will be remembered that he brought to Blumenbach a canister of Dublin snuff, "an offering to the finest nose in Europe." Lever must have early broke himself of snuff-taking ; for the last twenty years of his life he never carried a box.

nine.   Military officers never laid aside their uniforms,
bed-time alone excepted ; they dined in them,—danced in
them.   The tables at Hayes' Hotel were to be found
daily thronged with red-coats ; and here it was that
Lever first acquired his intimate acquaintance with *ex
officio* " mess " life.   Charley and his friend are now
drawing over their chairs at Hayes'.*

" Shades of Kitchener, how odoriferous is Calipash—
how restorative Mullagatawny !   Hayes is in possession
of the receipt for that valuable sauce, described as one
with which, ' on peut manger son père ; ' we commend
ourselves to the tender mercies of the he-cook—and
elbowing our way through some dozen of booted, spurred,
moustached, and spruce-looking heroes, reach a table in
safety."

These and other passages show that Lever, during
his medical course, gave his study quite as much to
culinary as to higher lore ; and that, as he said, while
reading Dr. Wells on shrivelled kidneys (Bright had
not written till 1837), he was not unmindful of Dr.
Kitchener on devilled kidneys as well.   Edgar A. Poe,
in a review of Lever, noticed his frequent allusions to
this savoury viand.

* Dublin Literary Gazette, February 6, 1830, p. 91.

CHAPTER V.

IT was about this time that an incident which greatly
excited Dublin occurred. By a feat of ventriloquism,
people were led to tear up the pavement, for the purpose
of rescuing from a sewer a man who announced himself
as just escaped from prison, but who, in making for the
Liffey, had taken the wrong turn, and was well nigh
suffocated for his pains. One of the shrewdest professors
of the College of Surgeons, Mr. Benson, was so deceived,
that he reprimanded a young doctor present for his heart-
lessness in laughing at the sufferings of a fellow-creature.

Lever, with a free brush, paints the picture in
"O'Malley," and describes the police as beaten back with
stones by the mob, on attempting to disperse it; until, at
last, dragoons with drawn sabres were obliged to charge
the excited people, who, after digging a hole into which
a coach might be driven, had come to the painful conclusion that the poor prisoner for debt had been smothered
in his bold attempt to regain the sweets of liberty.

Shortly before the death, in 1877, of the amateur

ventriloquist, Dr. Seward, he was good enough to commit to paper the particulars of the affair in which he whilom figured. They occur in a letter to Dr. Benson, specially prepared for the purposes of this memoir.

"On a wet December evening, in the year 1832, I was returning from the College of Surgeons, accompanied by Samuel Bennet and George Burke. Passing the corner of Bridgefoot Street, opposite St. Catherine's Church, Bennet said, 'Come, Seward, give us a touch of your ventriloquism in that sewer there.' I complied, but did not intend that anyone but the two should hear me. I called from the sewer as if there was a person anxious to be let out, saying he was a prisoner who had made his way there from the Four Courts Marshalsea, adjacent, that he was very weak, and would shortly die if not released. It so happened that at the corner was an apple-woman's stall, the owner of which heard the dialogue from the sewer. We left at once, and heard her calling lustily for help. This happened about 5 o'clock P.M. The postman called at my place in James Street to deliver a letter about 6 o'clock. 'Oh, sir,' said he, 'there's desperate work in Thomas Street: the prisoners have escaped from the Marshalsea, and they are digging them out of the sewer in the street.' It was raining very hard, and I ran down to the place. There was a large crowd, some with umbrellas, holding lighted lanterns, and men working for the very life with spades and picks, ripping up the sewer down Dirty Lane. I ran across Thomas Street to a grating near St. Catherine's

Church, and threw my voice into that opening. A person passing was attracted by the voice, and at once called out that he heard the man there. The scene of operations continued with undiminished activity. That grating was at once torn up, and the street ripped open from one side to the other, stopping all traffic for the time being, then a great inconvenience, as Thomas Street was the leading thoroughfare to the south of Ireland for the mail coaches, and all of which were obliged to go by Usher's Island instead. Of course the news was all over Dublin in the morning, and I was received at the College as a hero—students flocking round me, and begging of me to speak in all quarters. Dr. West was a demonstrator at the College at that time, and he asked me to speak down a small sewer in the College court. I did so, and at that moment Dr. Benson, who was then also a demonstrator, happened to pass by, and inquired what was the matter. Dr. West replied that it was a prisoner who had escaped from Richmond Bridewell, and had made his way there.

"Dr. Benson, a kind-hearted man, instantly directed that a porter named Graham should be sent for, and to bring a crowbar and pick. The man came, and with the crowbar struck between a joint on the flagging. West burst out laughing, and implored of the man *to desist*, not wishing to have the court injured. Dr. Benson desired the man to *go on*, and said that West was a most ill-natured person to laugh so at a fellow-creature in distress. West was laughing so heartily, he could scarcely articulate 'It's Seward.' Dr. Benson turned away, saying, 'Never was so sold in my life; and *I* after demonstrating on the larynx this morning.' "

A sketch of this adventure appears in *Saunders* of the day, contributed, we suspect, by Lever, who, in "O'Malley," frequently speaks of having furnished squibs to it.

There also will be found his account of a grand Fancy Ball at the Mansion House, on April 30, 1831, including "a new Pittay-atee woman," with a babe in her arms (Samuel Lover), and "Mrs. O'Flaherty, who ogled and simpered, ate ices, and drank negus with every one, nothing loth." "Ogle" was a favourite word with Lever, and Thackeray twitted him for the use of it.* The sketch of Sir George Dashwood's ball in "O'Malley," where Frank Webber so successfully personates Judy Macan, was probably suggested by this incident. A long detail in the morning paper concludes, singing :—

> " Oh, a fancy ball's a strange affair,
> Made up of silks and leathers,
> Light heads, light heels, false hearts, false hair,
> Pins, paint, and ostrich feathers."

But this was nothing to the Grand Carnival held in the Rotundo two months later, and which the same pen alliteratively word-paints. " Kings and Queens, Punches and Judys, Terryalts and Turks, Terry Regans and Tumblers, Pipers and Pastry-cooks, Draymen and Doctors, Harlequins and Hop Merchants, Quakers and Coiffeurs— all mingled in *mélange*, or, as Terry said, like peas in a sieve. In one set we saw Dr. O'Toole dance with Miss

* *Vide,* p. 339, *infra.*

Belinda Blue Stockings, Jeremy Diddler with Judy Kearney—a fishwoman, from Pill Lane—and so on to the end of the chapter. 'But, true it is, in our heart's recesses we dress in fancies quite as strange as these our fancy dresses.'" Conversations, at both balls, between the Viceroy, Lord Anglesey, and the various characters, are pleasantly reported.*

Those with whom Lever mixed describe him as very temperate. Among his German tendencies was a love of tea as thorough as ever Uhland breathed in his "Lied": "O Thee! Du sieber eine Mythe."

Almost the last entry penned by old James Lever in his "Day Book," is:—"1832. November: Tea-pot, Charles having taken mine, 8s. 6d."

While Lever was playing practical jokes in Dublin,—his naturally high spirits primed by strong tea,—John Lever, a man of sedate mien, was discharging curate's duties, first at Kilbride and later at Durrow Abbey, Tullamore, amongst which was the sad one of attending, in his last moments, the murdered Earl of Norbury. Meanwhile Mrs. Lever, senior, died in Dublin in January, 1833, and her remains were consigned to the

---

* "Cons" and epigrams on topics of the hour are freely found. These are clearly Lever's. He was fond of talking of the Caliph of Bagdad (*vide* p. 328, *infra*). *Saunders*, of March 9, 1831, invokes the same personage in "a Con" of purely ephemeral intelligibility. Old Lever's emoluments were eventually much diminished by the rivalry of cheap competitors. *Saunders* sings :—

> " Ye architects and builders pray beware,
>   Be not too hasty—let your work be sound ;
> What takes such little time to raise in air,
>   Takes still less time to tumble to the ground."

vaults of St. Thomas's Church. A few days previously she had called upon Mrs. Louche to ask if she could take into her keeping a chest to which she attached much value. Mrs. Louche consented, and, two days later, hearing some noise at the hall door, she concluded that the chest had come; but was greatly shocked to learn that Mrs. Lever was dead, and that Mr. Lever, stunned by the blow, required the immediate presence of Mr. Louche. On his return, it appeared that Mrs. Lever had been found dead in her bed—the body leaning over the side. She is described by her daughter-in-law as having been a bright, black-eyed little woman several years younger than her husband. He took her death so much to heart that he left the house in Talbot Street; and, on the invitation of the Rev. John Lever and his amiable wife, went down to Tullamore, where he resided with them until his own dissolution.*

Charles Lever, who held in 1833 a medical appointment in Ulster, was present at his father's funeral, but not at his death. The obsequies over, the will was read— a simple document drawn up by the Rev. John Lever, and tremulously signed by the dying man. Mrs. Louche, the widow of his executor, states that he left between his sons near £500 a-year. After some minor bequests, including a debenture on the Theatre, the will goes on to say:—

* The following has been furnished through the courtesy of the Rector of Kilbride. " James Lever, late of Talbot Street, Dublin, died at St. Catherine's, Tullamore, and was buried April 1st, 1833, aged 69 years and 10 months. Ceremony performed by Nathaniel Slater, Curate of the parish.—Graham Craig, Rector, 31 July, 1876."

"The drawing-room furniture to be the portion of Charles, with the exception of the pier cabinet, fender and fire irons, which I give to John. I give the furniture of the parlour also to my son Charles James, save the chairs, &c. My gold watch I leave to Charles and his mother's large ring."

John Lever finally became Rector of Ardnurcher, Horseleap, near Moate, in the diocese of Meath, and is described as a powerful and popular preacher. He also officiated as chaplain to the Earl of Charleville. "In 1845 he left Tullamore," the Rector writes, "and was appointed by the Bishop to Ardnurchur, a country parish in this neighbourhood. It brought him a higher income, but I believe in every other respect he much regretted the change. Here he was considered a very eloquent preacher, but I hear never could reconcile himself to the meagre audience of Ardnurchur."

The congregation seems, indeed, to have been of the character indicated by Swift, who described a preacher interlarding his sermon with "dearly beloved Roger." Lever often visited Tullamore from the time he assisted to bury his father there; but it was not love of the locality which brought him. Canon Floyd tells us that the following impromptu in doggrel has been attributed to Lever by the humorists of that region :

"Open ye bogs and swallow down
That horrid place called Philipstown ;
And if you've room for any more,
Then swallow dirty Tullamore."

In Ardnurchur, more picturesque though less populous, John Lever found his occupation gone. The small living Charles once playfully Anglicised "Hard-Nurture." John was disabled, for some years before his death by painful illness, when the Rev. F. Marsh did duty for him. He died in 1862, ten years previous to his brother. An attachment the most warm and tender always subsisted between them : but no two brothers could be more unlike than the tiny form of the one presented to the burly physique of the other, and while John to the last evinced a retiring disposition, Charles for thirty years was the reverse. John Lever did not for some time know who Harry Lorrequer was. Charles hesitated to avow the authorship even to him, fearing that the more severe judgment of the Churchman would deprecate as a bar to professional progress, the light and ludicrous tone of "Harry." There can be no impropriety in now disclosing that the later novels *did* receive the benefit of the elder Lever's revision.*

For a short time Charles continued to occupy his father's house in Talbot Street as a medical man ; but without being engaged in any pharmaceutical employ-

* On the 15th November, 1850, he writes to the publisher : "I trust you will find the proofs all right, that is, when we understand the author's meaning, I shall be always ready to give you a hand in this way, whenever you think it convenient to call upon me. 'Maurice Tiernay' [the Soldier of Fortune] is manifestly improving, since he reached Ireland."

The introduction by Charles of an anecdote pointing to Dr. Singer, F.T.C.D., afterwards Bishop of Meath, is believed in the family to have operated injuriously against John's preferment.

ment. "Hobbling gout and wheezing age" came to his door with many symptoms, but few fees.

On the table of the little back parlour, by courtesy called the "waiting room," reposed a well-thumbed copy of the "Dublin Literary Gazette," containing the then proudly owned, but since unacknowledged "Sketches of a Rambler." On rare occasions, the dismal tinkle of his night-bell blended its tones with the moanings of the night wind, and disturbed the doctor in his sleep, to administer a sedative probably to some restless sufferer. This life was slow enough for a man of his temperament, and he was not sorry to resign it for a more exciting round of duty.

Since 1650, fifteen years prior to the Plague which swept London, Ireland had been free from epidemic visitation; but in 1832 it became the theatre of a series of sad scenes. On the outburst of cholera, Lever was appointed to minister professionally to the suffering people of Clare. It is impossible to conceive a greater contrast than was presented by the horrors of this time to the fun, frolic, and festivity of the previous year. The Grand Láma of the Burschen Club, clad in sombre raiment, proceeded on his gloomy mission—appointed not by the Government as has been alleged, but by the Board of Health in connection with the Irish Privy Council. A number of young men were told off, to use the technical phrase—at the same time, and on the same duty; not a few declined to act, including Lever's fellow-student, Dr. Tuohill. Lever girded for battle, and furnished with all the artillery of medicine, resolutely advanced to meet the dark visitor now grown into a giant from its cradle in the East.

The poverty of the people of Kilrush and Kilkee had predisposed them to a ready reception of the malady, and amongst the poor fishermen it had made sad havoc. Sheds were erected for those suddenly stricken. Dr. Lever with intrepidity, if not always with success, did his best so far as the scanty knowledge, then possessed by the college of physicians, of their ghastly visitant enabled him. He went to work with his wonted stock of pleasant philosophy—resolved to distil honey from every cup of bitters. In concert with higher members of the Tory party, he pronounced the cholera a retributive scourge for the Radical Reform Bill of 1832. One of his prescriptions ran :—

> " Fear not, but be serenely gay,
>   Prudence in living shew,
>   Ye who would have the mens *say nay*
>   In corpore, *say no !* "—*Saunders,* Nov. 18, 1831.*

---

* A physician who has since filled high office, and who received with Lever his appointment as cholera doctor, has given us a curious account of the treatment prescribed for the plague-stricken at that time. The patients were bled by lancet, leech, and cup ; often blood refused to pour, being thick as treacle, and scarcely moving in the veins. Sometimes salts were injected to liquify it and restore the circulation, which gave rise to the remark that, however it might be with swine, salting a patient was not synonymous with curing him.

To the back of the neck blisters were applied, calomel was administered, which our informant on afterwards dissecting the dead found unabsorbed in the stomach. For calomel, corrosive sublimate was sometimes employed. Alcoholic stimuli too, were used to such an extent, that sufferers who recovered from cholera, fell often into low fever and died. In the stage of collapse powerful drastics, chiefly elaterium and croton oil were plied, in

On reading the cholera statistics of 1832, and the treatment there revealed, the wonder is, not that so many should have died, but that any survived the nostrums of the Medical Board. Probably not the least useful part of the arrangements made by the Board of Health in 1832, was that Dr. Lever and his colleague should receive ten shillings a day, to be raised eventually to a guinea.

It must be admitted that some of the doctors were in advance of the teaching of their day, and refused to be led. One of Lever's fellow-labourers in this duty was Dr. Hogan of Clare, through whose hands five thousand cases of cholera passed. He tells us as the fruit of his ripe experience, that the grand secret of successful treatment was to avoid mercurial or other medicines; to admit a free current of fresh air; to inspire the patients with confidence in their own recovery, and to seem cheerful in ministering to them. This, there can be no doubt, explains much of Lever's luck in dealing with the plague. Decanters of brandy, says Dr. Hogan, lay on a table at the cholera hospital in Limerick, which the more timid of the doctors imbibed, before entering on their work—but though it nerved them for a moment, it was succeeded by a fatal reaction, and predisposed to the disease instead of foiling it. Morning after morning

the hope of expelling the foe ; but this was like trying to quench a fire by pouring oil upon it. Death often took place in the course of two hours ; the hapless sufferer was often made to inhale oxide or laughing gas. Lever lived to see and say, *Nous avons changé tout cela*, and that opium is their sheet anchor.

Dr. Hogan saw biers borne to the graveyard, with the remains of physicians who had resorted to stimulants. Among the few, who used brandy and escaped, was Lever. He imbibed it, not to nerve a heart which knew not fear, though he had modesty enough, but in deference to a medical theory since exploded. His indomitable courage and cheerful mind saved him. Dr. Hogan adds, that wherever Lever went he won all hearts by his kindliness and generally cheerful mood.*

If fine air could check cholera Kilkee would not have suffered. But all previous theories were negatived by the eccentric ravages of this novel scourge. The fine strand of Kilkee, sheltered by a ledge of noble rocks stretching along the bay, has long been esteemed as a favourite convalescent nursery.

Lever, in " St. Patrick's Eve," and more fully in " The Martins," draws upon his memory for much of the painful experience gathered at that time. And

* A curiosity of medical treatment, since obsolete, was practised at this exciting time. Dr. Hogan tells us that when wives were in the last stage of the disease, he has transfused into their veins blood drawn from the husbands', and that the women rose miraculously from their prostration, seemed quite happy, but after living a few days invariably died. The haste with which bodies received sepulchre was startling. Dr. Hogan on visiting the Cholera Hospital at Limerick, saw a huge pile of remains waiting for the shells which could not be supplied fast enough, and detecting some peculiarity of hue in one, was induced to get it pulled forth from the heap and examined with care. The body, though apparently dead, was placed in bed, and at length restored to consciousness. The difficulty of recognizing the existence of lingering life, was increased by a phenomenon in the dead, noticed by Dr. Watson. " Half an hour and more after the breathing had ceased," and other signs of animation had departed, spasmodic quiverings, and motions of the muscles would take place, and even distinct movements of the limbs in consequence of the spasms."

twelve years later we find him thus recurring to the theme. "Of its fearful ravages in the west, in the wilds of Clare, and that lonely promontory that stretches at the mouth of the Shannon into the Atlantic, I had been the daily witness; and even to recall some of the incidents passingly was an effort of great pain. Of one feature of the people at this disastrous time I could not say enough, nor could any words of mine do justice to the splendid heroism with which they bore up, and the noble generosity they showed each other in misfortune. It is but too often remarked how selfish men are made by misery, and how fatal is a common affliction to that charity that cares for others. There was none of this here; I never, in any condition or class, recognised more traits of thoughtful kindness, and self-denial, than I did amongst these poor, famished, and forgotten people. I never witnessed, in the same perfection, how a wide-spread affliction could call up a humanity great as itself, and make very commonplace natures something actually heroic and glorious.

"Nothing short of the fatal tendency I have to digression, and the watchful care I am bound to bestow against this fault, prevented me from narrating several incidents within my own experience. It was only by an effort I overcame the temptation to recall them.

"If a nation," he adds, "is to be judged by her bearing under calamity, Ireland—and she has had some experiences—comes well through the ordeal. That we may yet see how she will sustain her part in happier circumstances, and that the time be not too far off, is my hope and my prayer."

Tyrone Power described an incident of the cholera in Clare, at the time that Lever and his colleagues officially stemmed it. The disease attacked a remote police barrack, killed three, and left the rest prostrate. The doctor on arrival found corpses decomposing, and the air pestilential. " With his own hands he had to put the bodies into shells, and nail down the lids." There was no hut or house of any sort for miles around— except two. He applied for admission where he had a legitimate claim, and was refused. He arrived at, the priest's house faint, sick, and despairing. He got off his horse, and leaned his head against the gable. He prayed God to look down upon him, thinking that if he who had been so lately succouring others was now himself seized with the disease, he must die like an unowned dog. The priest heard his story, received him as a son; gave him to eat and to drink, and shared with him the only bed which his poor dwelling owned.

Ludlow, referring to a vast tract in Clare, said that it had not a tree to hang a man on, water to drown him, or soil to bury him in. But Lever was not the man to go from coast to coast—even though ravaged by plague —and say "'tis all barren." Hence his mind is found deriving at this time, a series of impressions full of photographic accuracy, which in future books are all vividly reproduced.

The ill wind which swept the pestilence southward

blew good fruit to Lever. Had not the cholera brought our young doctor to Clare, we should never have heard of Harry Lorrequer. It was there he learned how to know character, to read motives, to analyse idiosyncracies, to seize and hold up to laughter the weaknesses and inconsistencies of men. A paper in his own magazine, pointing out a specially high idiosyncrasy, said:

"He should be a Clare man—none other have the same shrewd insight into character, the same intuitive knowledge of life: none others detect like them the flaws and fractures in human nature. There may be more mathematical genius in Cork, and more classic lore in Kerry; there may be, I know there is, a more astute and painstaking spirit of calculation in the northern counties; but for the man who is only to have one rapid glance at the game, and say how it fares to throw a quick *coup d'œil* on the board and declare the winner, Clare for ever! Were I a lawgiver, I would admit any attorney to practice, who should produce sufficient evidence of his having served half the usual time of apprenticeship in Ennis. The Pontine marshes are not so prolific of fever as the air of that country of ready-witted intelligence and smartness." *

Besides meeting men who taught him to read character, just as Graves and Cusack had taught him to diagnose disease, Lever found in Clare rich materials "cut and dry" before him. His lot was cast among men who filled his fertile brain with the rudiment of fruit

* D. U. M. for Jan., 1843, p. 110.

yet in embryo. Further, they taught him to shake off *mauvaise-honte* which had tended to tie his progress. In his " Widow Malone " he sings of Clare :

> " 'Tis little they care
> For blushing down there ! "

As he mingled with its people, he gathered confidence which, by degrees, grew into self-reliance. It becomes our duty to trace these moulders of his real destiny—all of whom, with one exception, have long been dead. Queries instituted in Clare led to a whisper that to Francis A. Keane, Esq., of Ennis, we owe not a few of the stories so happily worked up by Lever in " Lorrequer "; but different attempts to elicit by letter Mr. Keane's recollections of his friend failed. In reply to one application he says, " I am too old to write a history of matters which occurred near half a century ago."

Later, however, we got access to some notes which he had made after Lever's death, and here they are :—

" In May, 1832, Doctor Charles Lever came to Kilrush, one of a score of young medical men sent to remote districts by the Dublin Board of Health, on the outbreak of cholera. On his arrival he found the town sunk in gloom and despondency, owing to the ravages of the fearful disease. There was not a little jealousy on the part of the old doctor and the old apothecary,* at the idea of sending a stripling of his kind to

* Fitzgerald, the local apothecary, was a native of Kerry, and claimed kindred with him who derives his title from that ancient " kingdom." He lived freely. Perpetual processes pursued him. At a dinner in Ennis, which the legal profession attended in numbers, his health was proposed

teach them their business. He was not more than six and twenty, and even for that was young looking. After a few days Lever's good-natured and cheerful manner gained on every one, and on none more than the two above named. In Lever I recognised my brother's friend, whom he had known at Stevens' Hospital and Trinity College, where both had been associated in some escapades, including the impersonation of ballad-singers, and of their own master, Surgeon Cusack; and I at once introduced myself.

"There was, at this time, in Kilrush, a very social well-informed set, consisting of Bobby Unthank, whose wit and humour Clare men well remember; Tomkins Brew, John Jackson (who wrote as Terry Driscol), Maurice Fitzgerald, and John Lucas, a descendant of Grattan's great contemporary; they met every evening at their respective houses, or at the Cholera Hospital. Lever was then rather nervous and retiring, but with good manners. These men had seen a great deal of life, and each had plenty of anecdote which he recounted freely—one was well versed in current literature; another a first-rate story-teller, well acquainted with the habits of the middle and lower classes.

"Lever's cheerfulness kept up the spirits of the in-

by a local attorney, who praised his skill in the name of many present who had often been his patients. "In return," it was added, "we ought all come to an agreement to act for him gratuitously ; and not only that, but when we are opposed to him, to take out Decrees without costs !" "The latter part is the most important boon offered," replied Fitzgerald, "for it will add a considerable amount to my annual income."

habitants generally; as no matter how dismal the news of the day was, you parted from the young doctor in a roar of laughter. He was a great practical joker, but so playful that no one could take offence even though they themselves might have been the subject of the joke. He was suspected at the time to take notes of amusing occurrences, and to write squibs for the papers.

"Lever remained for four months amongst us, and as far as Kilrush was concerned he was lost sight of until the first number of "Harry Lorrequer" appeared in April, 1837, the second chapter of which revealed to his old companions there *who* the writer was, though unknown to the world.

" It seems to me, however, that what he says of Father Malachy Brennan, by whom he is well known to have meant Father Malachy Duggan, was drawn from his own imagination; as a more unobtrusive, simple-minded, hospitable and moral clergyman of his class there was not in Ireland; he was by no means the rollicking Father Malachy that Lever portrays. He had often seen this priest in the streets of Kilrush, and as he said himself, took his measure and was taken with his name. Lever had a good deal of private practice in Kilrush during his short stay there, and was a general favourite. One lady doing a thriving business, and of a robust appearance, complained of nervousness and low spirits; she was suspected of imbibing; but be this as it may she thought fit to consult the young doctor. Lever was called in, and being aware of her propensity, prescribed, in addition to a tonic, that on rising in the morning she should take a tablespoonful of burned spirits, 'just to take the smell of the feathers off her.' Need I say that the lady rose early, improved in health, and Lever in reputation."

Two recent interviews with Mr. Keane elicited a few more waifs. For notes of these we are indebted first to Canon Dwyer, Rector of Dromcliffe, Ennis, and secondly, to M. Kenny, Esq., solicitor, who had the kindness to wait personally on Mr. Keane in Clare.*

"The gloom of the sad visitation," writes Canon Dwyer, "was alleviated by Lever's joyousness. His associates were driven to account for his wondrous exuberance even after he had been sitting up night after night, by supposing that he was excited in some unknown but unnatural manner. They formed a social Board of Health, and Lever was president of it.

"Kilrush was then a jolly little place. Railroads had not yet carried away men of small means to Dublin, and the terrible potato famine had not smashed the middlemen. The little town had a circle of six or

---

* That Mr. Keane should be living near half a century after to describe these early days is remarkable, when the mortality of Kilrush is remembered. In 1844 Lever made a pilgrimage to Kilrush and revisited, not without emotion, the scenes of happier days. Writing at this time he enumerates as missing nearly all the men he had known, so that, he added, the old feature of mortality still clung to it. "The Burton Arms which Harry Lorrequer remembers is a sad ruin—the once buxom hostess dead." It is pleasant to find thirty-two years after, a gossiping survivor in Mr. Keane. His glimpses of Lever's early life show how much that is real has been recorded in "Lorrequer." In a cancelled preface, Lever remarks that some persons have doubted the veracity of the adventures. He hesitates to appeal to credible witnesses ; but pledges himself that every tittle advanced was as true as that his name was Lorrequer !

eight educated companionable men, who had read, and could observe—among these was John Jackson, better known by his weekly letter of the most quaint and purely Celtic peculiarities. He reported, too, for the London *Herald*, the curious outcomes of life and strife as appearing in the weekly court at Kilrush. Unthank, a converted Quaker, and a capital singer, was another pillar in this social group.*

"The coterie played their cards at a nominal risk of money. They laid open their stores of quaint local lore to Lever. He fell on a mine of Irish diamonds, and he worked it well. "When 'Lorrequer' came out, our Kilrushites were in consternation. The question was: 'Who turned traitor? Who let the cat out of the bag?'" And yet whoever published to the world their local cut and dry stories and rifled their stores of wit, was not charged guilty of personality or of offence, so kind and considerate was the heart of him who became the author.

"The Callonbys' sumptuous residence in that lovely glen was the beautiful house and place of Colonel Macnamara, which Lever's genius took the liberty of wafting towards Kilrush. The grand coast scenery in those happy equestrian excursions of the lucky Harry are along the stupendous cliffs of Moher. Mrs. Healy, of the Kilrush Inn, that scold of incurable volubility, com-

---

* Unthank was, moreover, a good classical scholar. Mr. Kenny writes, "He attended some social gatherings in Ennis held at the rooms of a fair restaurateur, to whom Mr. A—, it was whispered, had been paying court. The latter having handed round a plate to defray the hire of the rooms, Unthank, quoting from Virgil, exclaimed, 'Domus et placens uxor!'"

plained that her maternal and moral proportions were photographed by the cruel eye and pen of the doctor.

"The collection after the supper at Father Malachy's was a story of what had occurred at a wedding at Kilmaly near Ennis. Mr. Keane was present and told it to Lever; and Lever took poetic license to introduce it in all its richness and reality, although at the wrong time and place. Posterity may rejoice to be informed that, at the original wedding feast of Pat Magaurin's blooming daughter, the sum of £17 was collected.

"Lever was rebuked at Kilrush by Mr. Bevan, a rigid fanatic, for not writing upon a religious subject for edification. His reply was pointed, but not unkind. 'I will bring Moses and Aaron into my next novel, but you must assure me that they will pay as well as Harry and Lord Kilkee.'"

"Mr. Keane gave me the impression," observes Mr. Kenny, "that Lever, at Kilrush, was retiring and evidently nervous,—perhaps at the responsibility of his position there."*

To Mr. Keane we owe the introduction of this shy

---

* He continues : "the story of Miss Biddy, *alanna*, the thing you know is at the door"—the announcement which paralysed Miss O'Dowd when playing whist at Lord Callonby's—originated in an incident which Mr. Keane mentioned to Lever. This gentleman's sister and all the family were invited to a party at Mr. Moroney's, but on proposing to the coachman to drive them there, he assured them that no spring carriage could travel on the road, and it was determined that they should all go in a car with a bed as described by Lever. Larry, the coachman, came to the drawing-room door, and in a stage whisper, announced to one of the young ladies, 'that the thing, you know, was at the door.' The incident was at once mentioned to the party, and they left early, having a long journey before them, loudly cheered by all the remaining guests."

débutant to a circle of genial well-informed men. Had not means been taken to draw him out, the genius within might have flickered and sunk.*

After the publication of "Lorrequer" Lever spent some time with Mr. Keane at Kilkee, and in order to avert the suspicion of having pilloried old friends, told him that the only real character in the "Confessions" was "Pether," a cob which belonged to Mr. Keane, with an untiring canter such as Lever describes. "Lord Callonby and Lord Kilkee were fictitious characters, and the Marquis of Conyngham is not likely to have sat for either, as has been whispered. Lever expressed great regret that Father Malachy's feelings were hurt; in fact, he would not willingly give offence to any-one!"

The name of one man with whom Lever was most intimate in Clare does not occur in the notes contributed by our correspondents. From the recollections of this period the scenes as well as the names in "Lorrequer" were mainly drawn—even to the incident of "Dr. Finu-cane and the Grey Mare." The Doctor was a veritable character who had served in the Royal Navy and fought under Nelson at the Nile. He lived at Ennistimon, was the soul of hospitality, enjoyed a high reputation

---

* Mr. Keane's impression is confirmed by Lever's conduct before his examiners (p. 92, *ante*). The feeling finally merged into an involuntary motion of the muscles of the mouth, which those who knew Lever in later life must have observed, especially when he had been excited by oral descrip-tion. A closing chapter will find him dining at the Fellows' Table in Trinity College, where Bishops and Dons thronged to hear him. He was in "great form," but the twitch did not escape attention.

for patching up heads battered in faction fights, had a weakness for punch, and possessed the podgy "physique" portrayed in the novel. His son succeeded him in his practice and appointments, and we learn from his widow that the scene in which Phiz depicts him actually occurred. Clare men recognised old friends in "Lorrequer" with mingled emotions of surprise and pleasure.

Another man not unknown to Lever during these early days was one who subsequently obtained fame as "Head Pacificator of Ireland." Honest Tom Steele, a pleasant Clare man and graduate of Cambridge, given to grog, Greek, *Gosther*,* "galavanting," and scribbling, is alluded to by Lever as having once remarked of a stranger who for some months inhabited Ennis and was suspected to be a lord in disguise—"If so," quoth Tom, "he is the best disguised lord I ever met with."†

Father Comyns of Kilkee—the son of a gentleman and the brother of a Crown official—was a man completely after Lever's heart. Mr. Inspector Macmahon, a friend of Lever's, once undertook to prefer a request to this priest, which his own parishioners shrank from making. It was to lend his school house for a ball, and the favour was granted. Not the least amusing incident of the night was the recognition of his face about 2 A.M. peeping through a blind to see that the orderly arrangements promised were duly carried out.

* *Anglice* "talk."

† Lever applied this in December, 1839, to a clumsy chapter of a book under review, which seemed very unlike what it professed to be—satire.

The talk, habits, and belongings of these men all formed valuable material in that literary crucible which the fire of his fancy was destined, ere long, to heat. They had their charms for Lever; but the beauties of picturesque scenery and an intimate intercourse with the peasantry shared his attentions, and left, a deep impression upon him. A critique on Lady Chatterton's "Rambles in the South of Ireland" told us how well he remembered "a sunset on the Shannon below Kilrush, where the dim mistiness of the Kerry shore, the long golden light upon the sea, the clear reflection of the green island of Scattery, all brought to our mind the great Claude of the Dresden Gallery.

"Where, then," he proceeds, "to the shrewd observer of human nature is there such a field? Where is the book of the human heart laid so open before him as in Ireland? Where do passion, feelings, prejudices lie so much on the surface? And where is the mystery which wraps her anomalous condition more worthy of study? Where, amid poverty and hardship, are such happiness and contentment to be met with? Where the natural and ever ready courtesy, the kind and polite attention, the freely offered hospitality, as in the Irish peasant? In a word, where is self most forgotten in all this wide and weary world? We answer fearlessly, in the cabin of the poor Irishman. We have travelled in most countries of the old Continent and much of the new, and—we say it advisedly—we know of nothing, either for qualities of heart or head, to call their equal."*

* D. U. M. Vol. xiv. p. 98.

CHAPTER VI.

Docror Lever having spilt blood freely in the discharge of his duty, sheathed his sword, or rather his lancet, and persuaded himself that he had conquered the cholera. Wisely judging that some relaxation was due to him, he mixed in all sorts of society, sacerdotal and otherwise. The famous P.P. of Kilkee, Father Comyns, saw much of him.

The character of Father Tom Loftus in " Jack Hinton " is said to have been drawn from this great original. He was a man of mind and mark, of masculine beauty, of worth and wit. Father Malachy Duggan, P.P. of Carrigaholt, exhibited a contrast to the imposing presence of Father Comyns. The strange scene in " Lorrequer," descriptive of " a supper at Father Malachy's," and the etching by Phiz of the same incident, will not be forgotten. This Patriot Pastor presented a fair sample of the muscular priest by whose aid O'Connell mainly won the Clare election, the turning-point of the Catholic question: bright black silk stockings encased a pair of well-developed calves, which Lever likened to the balustrades of Carlisle Bridge. The sketch was striking if not strictly accurate. Mr. M. Kenny was the first to show Father Malachy the picture and the chapter devoted to him. The priest recognising both, described the circumstances of some early intercourse with Lever which enabled the novelist long after to recur for material to the recollections awakened by it. Carrigaholt was so remote and so little known—the priest's house being then almost its only structure—that some readers supposed it was a name of Lever's coinage. Not only, however, is Father Malachy's cognomen given without alteration — the surname "Brennan" being merely substituted for "Duggan" —but the title of his parish remains unchanged.* Father Malachy was a worthy man, though not a polished pastor, and presented vulnerable points to Lever's scalpel. He says in the last edition of "Lorrequer" that he contributed "nothing of exaggeration to the character of Father Malachy." In the same breath, however, he adds that "when the Padre saw himself in print and in picture, he evinced some mock indignation, for he was too racy a humourist and too genuine a lover of fun to be really angry at this caricature of him."

Father Malachy's friends, however, were not so good-humoured; and Lever handsomely expressed regret that a passage should have escaped him which gave

* Brennan was the Priest's man—a study in himself.

offence. Even the ministers of another Church recognised him as a pastor of great worth. Canon Dwyer, Ennis, author of the "History of the Diocese of Killaloe," observes, in part of the MS. which has been obligingly communicated to us, "Censure has been expressed by those who knew not the man nor his manner of writing. People assumed that allusion had been made to a most respectable Catholic priest, Father Malachy Duggan; and a distinguished Irish hierarch, in an angry diatribe, directed against an unpopular Judge, referred to the Judge's companionship with Lever, who had painted the Irish priesthood as an undignified set. Lever repudiated at the time anything more reflecting on this one section of Irish life than on any other. He was a painter of social life, and, like Fielding and all the rest, who were cunning hands, he took materials from real life, and coloured them to suit his purpose, took also material from ideal life, and put all together into his brilliant tissue of joyous fancy. But as touching the real and original 'Father Malachy,' he was a most eloquent and able man, very quiet and stay-at-home, highly respectable, not exactly scholarly after the Anglican pattern, but yet able on an occasion to come forth as with thunder and lightning. His was the most telling speech—a speech in the Irish tongue at the Clare election of 1829. But Lever had no sting in his wit,—no malice or hatred in his heart. The object of the convulsed laughter of the little group himself laughed the heartiest of them all at the grotesque descriptions given of himself."

A priest who officiated with Father Malachy writes:—"Lever was stationed, during the cholera, near Carrigaholt—a place full of interest to a man like him, especially its old castle where the people to this day believe that Clare's dragoons may be seen by moonlight ploughing the lake with glittering sabres. Here he made the acquaintance of Father Malachy, a man racy of the school now passed away. Hospitality personified, his roof was the only shelter within miles; he kept open-house for all; he *made* Carrigaholt; he was a man of republican simplicity, and though not versed in black letter lore—having read men more than books—he always formed an accurate estimate of character. He was anxious for the diffusion of newspaper literature amongst his flock—a primitive race of people—"to bring," according to his own quaint phraseology, "the focus of uncultivated minds to a proper intonation."

Honest Father Malachy is now a quarter of a century dead; but the burly physique of his quondam curate, whose figure author and artist also sketched, might till recently be seen hurrying on a sick call through the mountains of Clare; or reading his Breviary by the banks of the Shannon. His real name was Dollard, and he is described by his friends as of primitive habits, easily roused to irascible feeling whenever the name of "Lorrequer" happened to be broached. Some years before his death "the coadjutor of Father Malachy," was appointed by Bishop Vaughan parish priest of Kilmichael.

On his reputation the breath of censure never fell. This it is due to him to say, for Lorrequer in an unlucky passage, impugned the red-haired Coadjutor's morals. Father Dollard's weakness lay in his strength of tongue. Language had rather the command of *him* than he of language. He never cut with a razor, but dealt double-handed blows with a blackthorn.

As Lever fails to avow the originals of those sacerdotal studies, it perhaps becomes our duty to supply authentic details regarding them.

Long after " Lorrequer's Confessions" came to an end, Father Malachy continued to hold a favoured niche in Lever's fancy. In Feb. 1841 he made the following proposal to McGlashan. " What do you think of ' the Wild Songs of the West, edited by Father Malachy Duggan, P.P.' A mock collection of pseudo-original Irish ballads written by myself; like the Limburg Jaco-bite relics, with notes historical, antiquarian, political, polemical, and nonsensical; one volume with plates, woodcuts, music, &c., &c. It would be a great hit if well done—'Martin Hanigan's Aunt' on the title and a portrait of Father Malachy. It would offer a great field for Irish anecdote, ' à la Barrington,' and in every respect open a road to fun of all kinds."

This idea was never practically worked out. Arch-bishop Whately once said " that the Parsonage House is the nucleus of civilization in remote parts of Ireland ; "

but the remark hardly applied to Kilkee, where in Lever's time, service had to be performed in a cabin. Roman Catholicism was in the ascendant here, which may serve to show why Lever found himself thrown so much among priests. "Different from Father Malachy," writes a brother cleric, " the P.P. of Kilkee (said to have sat for Father Loftus), was more of the modern school, a manly, bold, and somewhat desultory character. He enjoyed large revenue from his parish, and kept a Baronial Hall where everyone was welcome, particularly the impoverished and unemployed members of his own profession."

Lever made so good a name for himself in treating the epidemic which ravaged Ireland, that he was offered the post of Chief Physician to a cholera hospital in the West; but he preferred a permanent medical appointment if such a thing would turn up. His recent experiences in Clare riveted his attachment to Ireland. The conviviality of friends, and the magnanimity of the people equally evoked his praise.

He once more repaired to Dublin, full of buoyancy as usual, without any very clear ideas as to his future career, and, in truth, not giving himself much uneasiness about it. His chief trouble seems to have been how to while away the hours till dinner, and he remarks, Dublin was the only city of its size in the world where there is no lounge, no promenade; "Heaven help the gentlemen so left in Dublin, say I."

One morning he saw, in glancing over a Dublin print,

that the dispensary at Portstewart, not far from the Giant's Causeway, had lost its medical attendant. He thought of the grand scenery which his old master, Mr. Wright, had graphically painted in "a guide" to that region; he liked the change, and exclaimed 'twas just the thing for him. Furnished with credentials from Cusack and Crampton, he made a low bow before the committee in whose gift the appointment lay. He had few competitors, and the office without difficulty was won. The date of this event can be approximated only. There are not at present any records in the Portstewart Dispensary belonging to the time that Lever was its medical officer. The earliest date of any register preserved there is the 1st January 1836; a letter, however, dated the 26th Sept. 1832, refers to his recent appointment at Portstewart. Lever's first sight of it was obtained under favourable circumstances. It was summer; and legions of gaily dressed visitors issued from the whitewashed cottages which, in winter became the abode of poor fishermen. In the "Knight of Gwynne" (Chapters XXVI.–LX.) he praises the picturesque beauty of its situation. Two jutting promontories sheltered the bay both eastward and westward; in front, the distant island of Islay and the Scottish coast could be seen. Dr. Knox in his "Irish Watering Places" describes it as now one of the most frequented, and Sir H. Inglis compares it to Biarritz in Bayonne. But as winter approached the pleasant scene changed. "The transformation of a little summer watering-place into the dismal village of some poor fishermen in winter," writes Lever, " is a sad spectacle; nor was the picture relieved by the presence of the fragments of a large vessel, which, lately lost with all its crew, hung on the rocks, thumping and clattering with every motion of the waves."

During such exciting scenes and struggles Lever was not inactive; but ordinarily the work proved light enough. His general duty involved no severe efforts at diagnosis, and was mainly confined to administering to rural sufferers castor oil and Epsom salts, and, if summoned again,—"The mixture as before." No obscure forms of disease with delightfully novel symptoms, came before him to justify a paper for the *Medical Press* or *Lancet*. Part of Lever's dispensary experience will be found reproduced in "The Martins of Cro' Martin."* Certain doctors, with whom Lever found himself often in consultation at this critical time, have found a type in Billy Trenor of the " Fortunes of Glencore."

" I am the nearest thing to a doctor going," says Billy; " I can breathe a vein against any man in the barony. I can't say that for any articular congestion of the aortis valve, or for a seropulmonic diathesis, d'ye mind, that there isn't as good as me; but for the ould School of Physic, the humoral diagnostic touch, who can beat me ? "

An appointment to some small medical practice at

* With a little bitterness fostered by past wrong—he notices how the peasantry glory in an exaggerated description of their own sufferings. A remarkable scene illustrative of this tendency is quoted in the new edition of Chambers' " Cyclopædia of English Literature."

Portrush, in the same locality, came not unacceptably, if only for its fine fish and grand outline of coast. Its hills, formed solely of sand, swept up by northern winds, are in themselves an object of interest.*

While doing dispensary duty at Portstewart, Lever was invited by the Coleraine Board of Health to take charge of their hospital. This is not more than three miles from the dispensary, and the appointment seemed opportune. At Coleraine, however, he had not much to do. Medical tradition tells that, owing to the salubrity of its air, few fatal cases occurred in the visitation of typhus in 1817, and later of the cholera. But, notwithstanding its sanitary reputation, the local physicians have not been long-lived, Doctors Gordon and Babington, who succeeded Lever, being both dead.

The change from Clare to Derry was fresh, bracing, and marked. Sterling Coyne in his book on Irish scenery, when describing the country between Coleraine and Londonderry says that it wore more the look of England than any other place he had seen.

Lever had been but a short time in work at his dispensary, when he obtained leave of absence to visit Dublin, in order to complete some arrangements which he had been planning; and while here he was nominated by the Derry Board of Health to their cholera hospital. Meanwhile pains of cholic at Portstewart cried for relief:

---

* A few years before, during a great storm which drifted away the land, an ancient town peeped forth, gradually disclosing elk horns, domestic implements, spear heads, kelts, and other instruments of warfare.

and Lever was denounced as a heartless hygiest. To Mr. Cromie—the lord of the soil and Chairman of the Dispensary Board—he appealed in September, 1832, to the effect, that the suddenness of his departure from Coleraine, and the unceasing attention he had been obliged to devote in Derry to his professional duties, must plead his excuse for not explaining his situation sooner. When he obtained leave of absence from the dispensary until October, it was to make arrangements in Dublin to settle in the country; for which reason he declined the post of Chief Physician to a cholera hospital in Connaught. But, when nominated by the Coleraine Board to their hospital, he quite thought that this application had been made with the concurrence of the Portstewart committee, and complied with it, his sole reason being to establish his professional character with those among whom his lot would be cast. In Dublin he received the invitation of the Derry Board, which he accepted on condition, that if the cholera returned to Coleraine he should resume his duties there. At Derry he induced many to avail themselves of hospital aid who would not otherwise do so, thereby greatly checking mortality. The people whose confidence he had secured, finding he was leaving Derry, memorialized the Board to prevent it, and expressed their conviction that trust in him personally had induced the poor to go to hospital. Lever added, that although well aware of that peculiar feeling of the people which made them rely more upon the stranger than those they had been accustomed to, yet he had been led to remain for the present in Derry at the request of the Board. In conclusion, he assured Mr. Cromie that his avocations there should not interfere with the discharge of his duties in Portstewart whenever it might be requisite to resume them. He reminded him that, as it was under his auspices he had first visited the county, he felt bound to obey him implicitly, and if he could obtain leave of absence even for one day, would certainly wait upon him.

The appointment which Lever held at Derry terminated with the cessation of the epidemic which he had helped to stamp out. While engaged as cholera doctor a large and populous district lay under his supervision, including the city of Derry, and the towns of Limavady and Coleraine. The splendid scenery of the district, and the bright historic memories spangling it, made his peregrinatory life in Ulster very enjoyable. The impressions and experiences of this time are reproduced in " The Knight of Gwynne "—the very title being in itself suggested by a family of that name, with whom Lever was brought into peculiar contact at Portstewart. A boarding house* at Coleraine is also described, where the fictitious Lady Eleanor of the novel, when straitened in means, takes temporary refuge. To this house—described as Mrs. Fumbally's— Lever was no stranger professionally or socially. Everything about it left an impression on him, even to the fur-

---

* This boarding house stood on an area known as " the Diamond," every part of which has since been swept away.

tive efforts made to plant two square plots of yellow grass
in front. "The dead shrubs in default of leaves displaying a large crop of stockings, night-caps, and other wear-
ables, which flaunted as gaily in the breeze as the owners
were doing on the beach." The gentlemen figured in
costumes "ingeniously a cross between the sporting
world and the naval service;" while the ladies displayed
"a pleasing *negligée*, half sea-nymph half shepherdess."

Lever had some hard work in Derry. But the
maiden city holds a less prominent place in his books
than other localities to which early ties had bound him.
Mr. McGlashan having urged him to be more respectful
in his references to the Black North, Lever replied that
he had every right to be civil to it, especially as he had
just been appointed Surgeon to the Derry Militia, by
Colonel Sir R. Ferguson. There are few Derry people
now living who remember Lever. Mrs. Watt says that
he was frequently at the house of her late husband, who
saw a good deal of company, and that "Dr. Lever was
at all times hailed as a most delightful acquisition."
The Rev. George Craig, A.M., writing from Aghanlo
Glebe, Derry, says "that he often heard Lever very
favourably spoken of, especially by Mrs. Smith, who
resided at Bann, near Coleraine, of which I was then
curate. Mrs. Smith, a daughter of Archbishop Magee,
was very competent to form a sound judgment of
character, and often predicted that the doctor was sure
to rise." Lever liked the North, which is in many
respects so wholly different from the South and West of

Ireland, that it seemed a perfectly new country peopled by another race. Derry liked him and he liked Derry. As cholera doctor, he was popular with the poor from his cheerful efforts to mitigate their sufferings, while from higher classes of society, he received the homage due to eminent social gifts.

"When I came to this parish in 1836," writes the Rev. J. Gwynne, Rector of Portstewart, "I found Doctor Lever dwelling in the village. We were near neighbours, and became very intimate friends—all the more as he was physician not only to myself and my family, but to my then existing school department, including upwards of thirty boys. His appointment to the dispensary he had, I think, resigned before my arrival here, Doctor Lever confining himself to private practice."

Lever rendered an important service to Mr. Gwynne, which has been always remembered gratefully. Mrs. Gwynne, when bathing, was drowned, and during a long and anxious interval no trace could be got of her body. At length it was washed ashore at Islay, on the western part of Argyllshire, and in due time was identified by a ring borne on her wasted finger. To get the remains removed to Ireland under the auspices of an undertaker would have involved painful delay and great cost; but Lever adroitly negotiated with the owner of a herring boat, who, after offering sundry objections to the proposed freight, finally agreed to oblige the popular doctor. Accompanied by a few hands he went to sea, and, not without risk, accomplished his gloomy mission.

Lever's attachment to Ulster, and to Letters, was greatly strengthened by his companionship with William Hamilton Maxwell. How he first came to know the pleasant prebendary and successful novelist, transpires in a sketch of Maxwell, contributed by Lever in 1841, to a local magazine.

"We well remember the first occasion of our meeting with him. It was at some remote village on the coast, where the preparations for an humble regatta were going forward. The little authorities of the place, ourselves amongst the number, were busily engaged in the legislation of our destined *fête*, with all the ceremony and parade of such a proceeding; the course, the prizes, the *déjeuner*, the band, the invitations—the very order of precedence of certain county beauties, were all being discussed; when suddenly there appeared in the midst of us a tall distinguished-looking person, whose dress, without anything one could particularize exactly, bespoke the man whose lounge was as often down Piccadilly, as over the blue flower of the heath mountain. With a certain air of easy *convenance*, he took his place; entered into all our plans, suggested, devised, corrected, and arranged everything; with a consummate tact overcame difficulties we had stood stupidly still at; conciliated rival interests, and in half an hour, drew up a flash paragraph for the local paper and astonished our weak notions, and left us wondering who the deuce our clever and accomplished friend could be; who knew everything from the cut of a jib to the flounce of a petticoat, and seemed equally conversant with belles, buoys, bands and boatmen, punch, prizes, and precedence. [Speculations as to his identity are expressed.]

" In fact, we were all in fault. We could only agree upon one point,—that we had never met his equal before, and that he was the best-mannered, best-looking, and apparently the best-tempered fellow we had ever the good fortune to foregather with. Some pronounced him a dragoon, others hinted they had seen him in a grenadier company, one ventured to drop a suspicion that he was the new Irish secretary, Lord Leveson Gower, just then come over, but none suspected that in our easy unaffected acquaintance we had met the talented author of the most popular book of the day."

In Lever's " One of Them," we learn that £280 was annually voted for the local regatta—just noticed—while the poor dispensary doctor was thought not ill paid with £80 a year. This regatta was usually held upon the Ban.

The cholera, wrapt in its black shroud, having stalked through the length and breadth of Ireland, vanished one night as suddenly as it came; and Lever, with satisfaction, found his " occupation gone." He returned to Portstewart and resumed dispensary duty. The usual number of aged females suffering from colic and cramps presented themselves; but students of his life would no doubt like to learn more of those Derry days.

Robert Kyle Knox, Esq., LL.D., writing from Coleraine in reply to some of our earlier queries, " feared that the people who knew Lever there were all dead."

But though Derry folk who knew him no longer
live among the scenes endeared by early association,
survivors are to be found scattered in other places,
discharging various *rôles* of duty. Mr. Boyle, now a
public officer in Dublin, has preserved some interesting
recollections of Lever's life at this time.

To Portstewart all the Derry gentry flocked in
summer time; but, as at Kilrush, there were half-a-
dozen companionable men—some of more than average
acumen, and others rich in humour, accessible to Lever
all the year round. These are described as Colonel
Cairns, well stocked with anecdotes of his military
experience in India; Colonel Babington, John Barré
Beresford, the scion of a highly influential family, Mr.
Orr, Dr. Boyd, afterwards M.P. for Coleraine, Mr.
Fletcher, agent to the Irish Society, and Captain Drew.

With these men Lever maintained frequent and
intimate intercourse; and most of them became warmly
attached to him. Dr. Boyd long after, addressing Major
Leech, said, "Round that mahogany the best of the
stories to be found in Lever's tales were originally
told." Each as a narrator, vied with his neighbour,
and plaudits fell fast around.

As an oral story teller he is described as exceeding
in charm anything ever produced by his pen. At every
party his presence was joyously hailed. Hours sped
apace when he appeared; the evening passed delightfully, and at the sitting suppers with which they wound
up, he would improvise a song, bringing in the names

of all the company to comic rhymes, but untinged by the slightest ill nature. This usually went to the air of "Vive la Compagnie"—sometimes he would "drink to the graces, law, physic, divinity," and playfully hit the representatives of all three.

He had much of the vivacity of Sheridan; sang "Let the Toast pass" to perfection; and all the more effectively from the improvised lines with which it glowed.

> "Here's to the maiden of blushing fifteen,
>   Here's to the damsel that's merry,
>   Here's to the flaunting extravagant queen,
>   And here's to the widow of Derry."

The guests never separated until Lever had organised two or three picnic excursions to the Lonely Rock and Ruin of Dunluce; to Dunmull Hill and its Druidical circle; Beardiville and its Pagan altar; to the far-famed Causeway, or the Fairy Bridge of Carrig-a-Rede, as he styles it in "Tony Butler," making those less likely to be fatigued promise that next day they would all join in a bracing walk along the strand to mature the arrangements outlined overnight. Sometimes an expedition to the Corvey was planned, *i.e.*, the hulk of an old frigate, wrecked many years before, and which lay on the opposite side of the bay on Innishowan strand. The Corvey, sometimes called the Ark, was let in lodgings during the summer season, and became more than once the scene of great fun and festivity. Lever's thoughts recurred to the Corvey when writing his "Knight of Gwynne," an entire chapter of which is devoted to this strange specimen of architecture, placed keel uppermost, as most consistent with terrestrial notions of building. From this spot westward glowed rich sunsets in all their golden glory, tipping the rolling waves with freckled lustre, and throwing a haze of violet-coloured light over the white swells. That walk along the strand, with Lever as guide, must have been eminently delightful.

"Perhaps, in all the sea-board of the empire," he writes, "nothing of the same extent can vie in awful sublimity with this iron-bound coast. Gigantic cliffs of four and five hundred feet, straight as a wall, are seen perforated beneath by lofty tunnels, through which the wild waters plunge madly. Fragments of basalt, large enough to be called islands, are studded along the shore, the outlines fanciful and strange as beating waves and winds can make them."

The brightness and vivacity of the *cicerone* capitally relieved the solemnity with which pilgrimages to the Causeway were invested by those who, studying God's wondrous works, mingled awe with their admiration. "The country as you approach the Causeway," he writes, "has as aspect of dreary desolation that only needs the leaden sky and the drifting storm of winter to make it the most melancholy of all landscapes." Waves beat against giant cliffs like the booming of distant artillery—the whole presenting picturesque beauties which attracted tourists to that lonely region.

Bright girls came, and proved a welcome accession to the picnics organised by Lever, to say nothing of some pleasant but very select local balls which, through the same instrumentality, were held during the season in the Portstewart Hotel.

Lever, while dancing at balls, was dancing attendance with bright vigilance by the bedside of suffering humanity : and this his worst Evangelical enemies were constrained to confess. Now whirling in the Waltz—a few minutes later by the bedside of danger. Back to the ball again!—engaging Miss Dashwood for the "Lancers"—hurrying away to see the cataplasm removed, and with his own hand administering relief, or spreading the balm. He arrives just in time to take his place with the Belle of the Ball; but the intermittent pulse of the little sufferer still throbs at his own heart; the glance of its glassy eye is before him ; and he is less impressionable than usual to that " hazel and blue " which evoked his best lyric. He is back with the sick girl again — gives a stimulant — she rallies; within ten minutes he is doing the same for himself at the supper-table. Happier now, he is in a state of supreme felicity when dancing that "Morning-Bell Galop," with which the rout winds up. He goes home, revolving in his mind some tonic wherewith to "set up" the convalescent, and probably whistling :

"You may talk if you please,
Of the brown Portuguese,
But wherever you roam, wherever you roam,
You nothing will meet,
Half so lovely or sweet,
As the girls at home, the girls at home !"

CHAPTER VII.

CAPTAIN DREW may be said to have been the least
conversible man in the coterie of which Lever, at Portstewart, was the central figure. Often he would say of
a wet day, looking forth from the windows of the local
inn in which a few men had sauntered and shivered, " I
see nothing to be done but to go out and draw Drew."
No one better knew how to utilise material of this sort
than Lever.

Portstewart without Maxwell was like Twickenham
without Pope, Ferney without Voltaire, or Tinnehinch
without Grattan. No place would be dull where Lever
lived. But monotony at times threatened Portstewart,
and we find him seeking more exhilarating society and
pursuits. To the latter we shall presently come. As
regards society, he formed the bold resolve of forthwith marrying, with small means, the pretty girl of his
choice, especially as the difficulties which beset his path
to Hymen's altar now seemed dissolving.

The scene now changes from the wild desolation of

the Derry coast, with its leaden sky and cutting blast, to Cromwell's pet plantation of Meath, teeming with fertility and clad in luxuriant verdure. At Navan— where Lever's future father-in-law, Mr. Baker, was now master of the Endowed School—he is frequently found about this time. The local Surgeon no longer lives to tell of his doings, as he often did, but the reminiscence of a lady claims mention here. "It interested me much to observe Lever constantly boating on the Boyne with the *petite* and pleasing girl to whom he was *fiancé*. Her dress could not fail, in itself, to arrest attention, being black, white, and pink, cut in diamond pattern. The fine romantic scenery of the historic Boyne heightened the interest and attracted me to the same fairy spot. Often our little boat went abreast with Lever's, and we sang the 'Canadian Boat Song' in concert, as both glided on. 'The Jolly Young Waterman,' Lever, was a capital rower, but when our boats could not hold all the picnic parties which he got up, we hired lighters and went to Beau Parc or Slane, and dined on the sod. On those picnics they had generally lovers' quarrels which the undisguised amusement of spectators did not tend to smooth—but in their sails on the Boyne all was happiness—he throwing his bait, she casting her net of fascination, 'all earth forgot, all heaven around them.'" On their return one evening another informant met him at Mrs. Charlton's of Navan, when he sung a pleasantly improvised song and accompanied himself on the piano.

Mr. Baker is remembered in Navan for his gossip

and his gout—for his social habits and his scholarly
attainments. He is said to have previously held a
commission in the North Cork Militia; and as we are
informed by Dr. Hudson, formerly of Navan and a
fellow-student with Lever in college, some of the
"Lorrequer" stories were at once recognized in Meath
as Baker's.

Lever had loved Kate Baker from childhood. This
attachment lasted undiminished through life, and had no
small share in moulding his destiny. There is a Kate in
nearly all his books, and in the later ones a Julia, the name
of his eldest daughter. An old friend of Lever's notices
"the peculiarly chaste and tender tone pervading his
works. It was perfectly spontaneous. He delighted in
writing for women; his constant wish was to please and
interest them; and much of this must be traced to that
early romantic love which was the ruling power and the
blessing of his entire life."

Old Mr. Lever had had strong hopes of a great future
for his son. He had wished him to marry the daughter
of a wealthy trader, but Charlie recoiled from the proposal like a true hero of romance. To marry for love
seemed lunacy in the elder Lever's eyes; he continued
to his death "dead against his son's love project." His
dissolution on March 29th, 1833, left Charles at last free
to follow his own wishes, or to avow a marriage whispered
to have already taken place. That he had been pri-
vately married, Mr. Louche, James Lever's executor,
always said. This throws light on the strangely vague

way in which the parson—perhaps on Charley's prompting—executed the entry in the Registry.* One can picture Lever nervously going through the ceremony, and imagining that his father, with his wonted energy of character, was on his track, and might at any moment in full chase arrive! Mrs. Lever, shortly before her death, had called on Mrs. Louche, to say that Charley had just been importuning her, in a very excited state,

---

* The registries of St. Mark's and St. Thomas's were vainly searched for some record of Lever's marriage before inquiry traced him to Navan. Luckily the data usually furnished by Registries are not in this case needed as legal evidence. The clergyman in charge of Navan Parish writes :—

"I am extremely sorry that my Registry Book has been most carelessly kept in times past; for whole years no entries were made of any kind; it seems to have been often in the custody of some ignorant clerk. I have searched every record in my possession, bearing in any way on your subject. I give you an extract copy of the Marriage Register of 1833.

"No. (none entered)

"Doctor Lever of the Parish
—Baker of this Parish, were married in this church by licence this
day of   in the year one thousand eight hundred and   by
me,   JAMES MORTON.

"This marriage was solemnized between us

"In presence of

"No date is given; the name of Miss Baker is not given; nor did the parties named as the witnesses sign the register. One can hardly credit such monstrous carelessness."

The Rector adds, that the entry of marriage preceding Lever's is dated August, 1832; and the succeeding one August, 1833. Lever's, therefore, lay between. It has been said, that the ceremony was performed by Lever's brother, who was a clergyman in the diocese to which Navan belonged; but he did not even assist Mr. Morton. The latter was a cousin of the Marchioness of Headfort.

Two members of the Baker family are mentioned in some more accurately kept records preserved at Navan. Henry Baker died there in September 1835; and John Scott Baker attended and signed the minutes of the Easter Vestries held in 1831 and 1833, and retired from Navan College in 1836.

to use her influence with his father to induce him to relent ; but she had declined to interfere, and Charles left the house in anger. In point of fact the selection of Kate Baker as " his lawfully wedded wife " was a wise one; and it is well known to the profession that marriage often proves a good stroke of business, by giving to the young physician an *entrée* to the rooms of fair invalids, which, as a bachelor, he could not at all times command.

There is something of personal feeling in a passage dated 1872,—a few months before his death—and occurring in the final preface to " O'Donoghue."

" I am not of those who think that the married life of a man is but the second volume of his bachelor existence. I rather incline to believe that he starts afresh in life under circumstances very favourable to the development of whatever is best, and to the extinguishment of what is worst in him. That is, of course, where he marries well, and where he allies himself to qualities of temper and tastes which will serve as the complement or at times the correctives of his own." *

---

* To Lever's wife is due the merit of having broken him of snuff-taking and other habits, all the better of being lopped off. A writer has powerfully put the advantage a man derives from conjugal grind. "A wife is the grand wielder of the moral pruning-knife. Had Johnson's wife lived, there would have been no hoarding of bits of orange peel, no touching all the posts in walking along the streets, no eating and drinking with a disgusting voracity. If Goldsmith had been married he would never have worn that memorable and ridiculous coat. Wives generally have much more sense than their husbands, especially when their husbands are clever men. The wife's advices are like the ballast that keeps the ship steady, or the wholesome, though painful, shears snipping off little growths of self-conceit and folly."

Lever read all his novels to his wife; and pruned as she pleased. From the day she died, he felt that his right hand had lost its cunning; and in dedicating "Lord Kilgobbin" to her memory he declares that it must be his last.

To judge from the exploits of "Lorrequer" and "O'Malley" in the field of flirtation, Lever might well be supposed to have had considerable experience and aptitude as a Lothario; but his companion from youth, Major D——, assures us that this was in reality not the case, for "although delighting in female society, he seems to have never had but one real love affair—the one which began in his boyhood and ended only with his life; and indeed he very soon ceased to represent his heroes as being quite so desultory and his heroines so off-hand in their attachments as he had at first depicted them."

The brightness of the honeymoon was heightened about this time by an invitation which came from Lady Garvagh to attend a grand fancy ball at the picturesque seat from which her title is derived. The dignity of D. L. had for the first time been extended to Ireland; several donned the red uniform of the office, and the ball, spangled by its presence, originated partly in celebration of this event. Excitement pervaded the county at the festive news, and matrons finessed for cards. The journey through a mountainous district was long and tortuous; but what of that? There were people so anxious to go that, like Lough Derg Pilgrims, they would have walked every inch of the way if necessary, even to wearing peas in their shoes. Worst of all there was a great dearth of conveyances. "Every available vehicle in Limavady and Coleraine was hired, even to Turbot's furniture van, a hearse, and a mourning coach from the undertaker."

Lever organised the Coleraine contingent, and took the command of it dressed as Jeremy Diddler. Coming back that night heavily freighted, the van broke down at Castle Coe, some miles from Coleraine, and just at the gate of a gentleman who enjoyed in the county a reputation for hospitality. Lever thought that he had only to use what, it will be remembered, one of his schoolfellows described as "the silver end of his tongue" and explain the accident to receive prompt shelter for his party; but the people of the house, roused from their sleep and with temper also roused, peremptorily declined the request. Lever as spokesman, and still dressed as the Bohemian, expostulated. The family assumed a still more firm attitude, and, glancing at the furniture van, which quite resembled an itinerant theatre, vowed they would not admit to their house a party of showmen, gipsies, and play actors! Lever's powers of persuasion failed. Followed by his party, whose gay motley garb seemed to ill assort with their haggard mien and sleepladen lids, they returned to the van, and slept there anyhow till day. The accident would have been amusing enough were it not that Lever evinced great anxiety for his wife, whose condition was certainly interesting. Luckily, however, her slumber proved quite as sound as though enjoyed on a spring mattress, and not the smashed springs of a van.*

Next morning a messenger for additional horses was despatched to Mr. B——, who obligingly complied, and the furniture van, with its fantastic crew, made its "triumphal entry" into Coleraine on a market-day within lines of gaping spectators who, when their surprise abated, lustily cheered the cavalcade. In the latter was Mr. S——, brother of an eminent physician. He had personated the Man in the Moon, one half of his person being black and the other half white. Lever cannot be said to have enjoyed this adventure on the whole, and contrary to his usual system it has never been reproduced in his books.

Mr. C——, who swayed the councils of the Dispensary Committee, wielded large territorial influence. His only child Helen married the brother of a duke,† and his sister became the wife of a peer and Privy Councillor. Both noblemen conformed to the Roman Catholic Church, but Mr. C—— continued a strong evangelical, solemnly

---

* The accuracy of our informant's recollection is confirmed by the following letter from the Hon. A. D. G. Canning, written at the request of the Dowager Lady Garvagh, and which supplies the date of the Fancy Ball.

"My mother wishes me to answer your letter respecting the late Mr. Charles Lever. He came with his wife to a Fancy Ball given here in March, 1833. Mrs. Lever came as a gipsy, and Mr. Lever was also in character; but we cannot at present ascertain what it was. The Levers came with a party of friends from Coleraine.—Garvagh, Co. Derry, November 22nd, 1876."

A friend tells us that he has still preserved a card of Lever's, presented by himself, "Mr. Jeremy Diddler."

† The Duke of Manchester.

opposed to fun and to the convivial board. Lever was summoned, admonished, and warned by Mr. C—— that such pranks were unseemly and wholly unbefitting the gravity and dignity of a medical officer. He replied " that all work and no play make Jack a dull boy ; that man was sent into the world for something else besides work and worry ; that the enjoyment of harmless pleasures occupied an honoured place in the code of human economy ; and that the duties of his office were not neglected, of which the affection of the people for him was in itself a proof." This logic, however, failed to convince Mr. C—— ; but he decided upon giving Lever one more chance. He soon found that he continued the life and soul of a coterie, the reverse of strait-laced, and came to the conclusion at last that it would be a meritorious act to get rid of the jolly doctor. But everybody else seemed to like him so well that this was easier said than done. A periodic election took place at the dispensary which presented a promising opportunity. Every one who paid a guinea had a vote, and it was whispered that the local magnate had been paying subscriptions for voters, and bringing them up with the object of ejecting Lever.

" This must not be," said Colonel Cairns. " Sharp's the word," said Colonel Babington. And immediately a counter-subscription was organised to " outflank," as the Colonel said, the strategic movement of the enemy. Voters poured in from every side next day. Lever's friends, by doubling their subscriptions, doubled their votes. Much excitement prevailed, and on a scrutiny it appeared that the Leverites had won.

The ladies seemed quite on Lever's side. Mrs. Maxwell, of Coleraine, admiring him as a friend and valuing him as a physician, presented him with a gift of substantial worth; Mrs. R——, a widow,—of whom hereafter—was quite a partisan in his favour.

A very remarkable man participated not less in the excitement of the contest than the jubilee of the victory, William Hamilton Maxwell, author of " The Wild Sports of the West," deserted them at times for the bracing breezes of the North. He joined the coterie which grasped Cairns, Babington, Boyd, Beresford, and Lever, and a marvellously pleasant accession he proved. Some reference here to the practical jokes in which Lever and Maxwell acted as co-conspirators will throw light on the causes of Mr. C——'s pious horror of both. An Introduction to the last edition of " Lorrequer " notices his first acquaintance with Maxwell " at a little watering place," but does not say it was Portstewart.

" We often exchanged our experiences of Irish character and life, and in our gossiping stories were told, added to, and amplified in such a way between us that I believe neither of us could have pronounced at last who gave the initiative of an incident, or on which side lay the authorship of any particular event.

" It would have been well had our intercourse stopped with these confidences, but unfortunately it did not.

We often indulged in little practical jokes on our more well-conducted neighbours; and I remember that the old soldier from whom I drew some of the features I have given to Colonel Kamworth was especially the mark of these harmless pleasantries.

"Our Colonel was an excellent fellow, kind-hearted and hospitable, but so infatuated with a propensity to meddle with every one, and to be a partner to the joys, the afflictions, the failures, or the successes of all around him, that with the best possible intentions, and the most sincere desire to be useful to his neighbours, he became the cause of daily misconceptions and mistakes, sowed discord where he meant unity, and, in fact, originated more trouble and more distrust than the most malevolent mischief-maker of the whole country side.

"I am forced to own that the small persecutions with which my friend Maxwell and myself followed the worthy Colonel, the wrong intelligence with which we supplied him, particularly as regarded the rank and station of the various visitors who came down during the bathing season, the false scents on which we sent him, and the absurd enterprises on which we embarked him, even to the extent of a mock address which induced him to stand for the 'Borough'—the address to the constituency being our joint production—all these follies, I say, more or less disposed me, to that incessant flow of absurd incident which runs through this book, and which, after all, has really little other than the reflex of our daily plottings and contrivings."*

The "mock address" was of course aimed at the adjacent borough of Coleraine, and however innocuous a document of that sort may have been, it was represented by Mr. C—— that practical jokes which had the effect of "sowing discord" can hardly be regarded as "harmless pleasantries." Another blemish on the bright buoyancy of Lorrequer's life at this time was his seeming unconsciousness of the breach of good manners shown in accepting the hospitality of men, and afterwards laughing at their foibles. Fathers Duggan and Comyns had complained of this treatment, and to the "Colonel" at least an apology was tardily, and we may add gracefully offered.

"I believe my old friend the Colonel is still living; if he be, and if he should read these lines, let him also read that I have other memories of him than those of mere jest and pleasantry—memories of his cordial hospitality and genial good nature—and that there are few things I would like better than to meet and talk with him over bygones, knowing no one more likely to relish a pleasant reminiscence than himself, or to forgive a long-passed liberty taken with him."†

* Dickens, like Lever, was much given to the fun of playing on the credulity of unsuspecting folk. His biographer describes him even during the wretched thraldom of his early struggles, as deriving pleasure from such freaks. At page 40, vol. 1, he is found telling "astonishing fictions."

† This preface is dated 1872. Our correspondence in trying to trace him would fill a chapter. Lever was not aware that Colonel Cairns had died many years previously.

Other practical jokes—possibly prompted by Maxwell —may be traced to Lever at this time. The effects of the Rev. Mr. Blacker—brother to the famous Colonel of that name—were advertised to be sold by auction at the Rectory near Coleraine. Lever impressed upon Captain D——, a man of wealth and in his own conception, of importance, that he owed it to his position to buy Blacker's coach. D —— nodded away until the auctioneer's hammer fell at £95. "When you want horses to draw it home, I hope you won't send to me," said Mr. McGrotty, the innkeeper of Coleraine: "two elephants could hardly move it." Mr. D—— was not a social man, and failed to cultivate habits of hospitality. But Lever by his tact and fun wrought a wondrous change in him. He gave D——- to understand that at the last meeting of the fellows some injurious reports as to his solvency had, with deep regret, been referred to. "The best way to convince them of its falsity," said Lever, "is to ask them all to dinner." D—— swallowed the bait, and a dozen jovial souls swallowed his good cheer. That night Lever, in glowing terms, proposed the health of the usually taciturn host, who to save himself the trouble of a speech replied that the best way of expressing his appreciation of those who so cordially drank his health was to invite them again for that day week.

Dickens played practical jokes from love of fun. Lever, when jaded by work, resorted to it as a relaxation. The small persecution to which he was subjected

by those who condemned his general *abandon* and
enjoyment of passing pleasures was clearly in his mind
when reviewing " Physic and Physicians " (" D. U. M.,"
Dec., 1839). " Nothing is too severe : nothing too
illiberal to be said of the doctor when, the hours of a
painful and laborious day passed, should he either
unbend in the lighter amusements of the world, or
avail himself of the recreations which to over-worked
minds are almost a necessity of existence.   No, no—
we never can forgive the man who has listened to our
narrative of gouty suffering or dyspeptic ill-temper, if
he be seen the same evening enjoying himself at the
opera, or the next morning breathing the free air of
the hunting field."

It has been said that the life of a country doctor is
one either of stagnation or overwork : but Lever took
care to avoid both Scylla and Charybdis.   One of his
successors in office told Major D——, from whose
manuscript we quote, that " when he went to Derry
some years later, he found the whole country still full
of stories and anecdotes of ' the wild young Doctor,'
who himself performed in Coleraine the feat of jumping
over a cart and horse, which Lever attributes to O'Malley
at Lisbon.   He is also described as riding backward
and forward through the entire night between the bed
of some child that was dangerously ill, and a ball given
by the officers of a regiment then at Coleraine, and that
too in his evening dress."

If Lever had studied appearances, and looked solemn

while his heart was glad, his purse would have become
more fat from fees. He rejected the white cravat and
gold-headed stick—preferred Byronic ties and riding-
whips—inculcated active exercise in fresh air as ardently
as ever Hawthorn did in "My Dog and my Gun," and,
instead of dosing patients and pocketing their gold,
prescribed Dryden's specific :

> " Better to hunt in fields for health unbought,
> Than fee the doctor for a nauseous draught :
> The wise for cure on exercise depend ;
> God never made his work for man to mend."

Some persons have pooh-poohed Lever's skill as a
physician, but unfairly. Dr. Lytton McIntyre, who
succeeded him in dispensary duty at Portstewart,
writes : "Doctor Barr, the oldest medical practitioner
now in Coleraine, tells me he knew him well, and he
speaks in the highest terms of his medical skill. There
is scarcely a resident in Portstewart now who existed in
Lever's time. Many years ago I knew several of his
friends there, and my impression, from their description,
was that he is universally esteemed, and that for his attainments and disposition his society was greatly sought."

In that chapter of "The Barringtons" headed "The
Country Doctor," we obtain an insight into the feelings
of the lowly practitioner, under circumstances of which
Lever had manifestly the experience. For instance, the
sensitive suffering of the doctor is described when his
services are relinquished for those of some more pompous
physician—the change from a good to a bad doctor being

often merely from a pound to one-pound-five. He was fond of recurring to the scenes endeared to him at this time. Thirty-five years after, he is found in "Tony Butler," sketching the cot once occupied by himself.

The bathing season over, Portstewart became the "Deserted Village;" and the houses which had previously been the scenes of joyous coteries, were once more held by poor fishermen clad in the oilskin panoply of their craft. Although Lever's position was far enough removed from that "stagnation" to which it is said the life of a country doctor is prone, he took good care to guard against it by cultivating the society of Maxwell. He was Rector of Balla, in Mayo; but those who remember his dashing disposition will not be surprised to learn that difficulties overtook him, and led to his rustication "on the basaltic peninsula—Portrush," in the hope, it is said, of evading duns. A congeniality of tastes brought Lever and Maxwell closely together. The latter, as the author of "Captain Blake of the Rifles," may be said to have been the founder of the military novel; and Lever's plans, which had been long simmering in his brain, gradually attained boiling heat in the fervid companionship of the brilliant parson, who enjoyed wine and punch at night, and was given more to soda-water than "sermons" the next morning.

Mr. Maxwell had never been in the army—the statements in published sketches of him to the contrary notwithstanding. But little would persuade him to put on the uniform, and show how easy it was to boil a black lobster red. He had, indeed, a sympathetic knowledge of military life and manners; and while Rector of Balla enjoyed the privilege of having apartments in the barracks of Castlebar, so genial a companion did he prove to the officers quartered there. At the time Lever met him at Portstewart, he had just entered the lists with O'Connell on the Tithe Question, for which he got a Roland for his Oliver. The great Agitator in a public letter, which playfully pilloried him, began: "Prebendary of Balla, thou art a wag!" To which the reply was made, "Ay, by the mass! and the verier wag of the two." And by his own side the parson was declared to have had the best in the shindy.

About the same time, he was reminded that duties which he received pay for discharging remained neglected in Mayo, and he thought it right to put in an appearance there. Promising to introduce Lever "to the Wild Sports of the West," he returned to his living, while Lever went on a visit to him, and was brought into close association with the military, and met Jackson, the author of some pleasant papers, "The Kilrush Petty Sessions,"* contributed to the *Morning Herald.*

* Mr. O'Gorman of Kilrush, High Sheriff of Clare, 1878, tells us, that these sketches were written in his back parlour, and embodied many points made by the late Mr. Merritt and by himself.

Jackson, "a man whose genial satire left no sting behind," had been a reporter on the *Herald*, but having given up to the Government his short-hand notes of a speech made by Mr. O'Connell, he was very properly dismissed by the proprietary. To compensate him for this loss, Jackson received from the Crown an appointment in Dublin Castle worth £150 a year; which he enjoyed until his death in 1857.

These sketches are said to have had some effect in stimulating Lever's pen. His real model, though, was Maxwell. For several years Maxwell and Lever pursued the same road, but the pupil soon distanced the master: when two men get upon the same hobby horse, one must go behind.

How Maxwell first acquired that military taste which he afterwards engrafted upon Lever, claims a word in passing; and if it savours of digression, it is allowable in a memoir of Lever, who himself continually indulged in it.

The 10th Foot, quartered many years ago in Dublin, is remembered chiefly for its impudence. At a pleasant ball, they uniformly replied to a polite proffer from the hostess to provide them with partners, "the Tenth don't dance!" Losing all patience, at last, she exclaimed. pointing to the door, "Perhaps the Tenth can march!" The lady had influence enough to get this supercilious corps removed from Dublin, and transferred

> "To Castlebar and Ballinrobe,
> The dullest dens upon the globe."

In such quarters they were often driven to their wit's ends in devising recreation. A pleasant trio turned up in the Prebendary of Balla, Dr. Hamilton, a local surgeon, and Mr. sub-Sheriff Burke. Their companionship was secured by the regiments successively stationed in Mayo. Maxwell introduced them to capital shooting, dined at their mess daily; and while draining their decanters drained their memories of those stirring recollections which he turned to account in his "Stories of Waterloo," and of "The Peninsular War." "As a *bon raconteur*, he was second only to Sheridan," writes Sir W. Wilde; "and when he had no story precisely suited to his hearers, or to the circumstances around him, he invented one. In gratitude for delightful hours spent in his company, and as a souvenir of bright convivial moments not likely to be renewed, the officers, when under orders to march, presented to Maxwell the residue of what wine the barrack cellars contained. On some of this "Waterloo" port Lever was himself regaled; and it strengthened that martial bias which at last carried him away, and left his "leader" far behind. Here it was that Lever wrote :

> " We talked of pipe-clay, regulation caps,
> Long twenty fours—short culverins and mortars—
> Denounced the Horse Guards for a set of Raps,
> And cursed our fate at being in such quarters.
> Some smoked, some sighed, and some were heard to snore,
> Some wished themselves five fathoms 'neath the Solway ;
> And some did pray—who never prayed before,
> That they might get the ' Route ' for Cork or Galway."*

The scenery about Castlebar and Westport, to which Maxwell introduced him at this time, is described in the " Knight of Gwynne." One picturesque spot, known as

---

* Many anecdotes furnished by the late Sir William Wilde might here be told, exhibiting a view of the men with whom Lever mixed, and of the scenes which left their impress on his mind ; but our limits warn us that they must be reserved. As regards Mr. Maxwell, English readers must not regard him as a type of the Irish parson.

"Maxwell's Leap," and pointed out to tourists, shows the active life our prebendary led.[*]

"The Wild Sports of the West" over for a time, Lever resumed, in more senses than one, the "Recreations of Christopher *North*."[†] He retraced his steps to Ulster, which he had come to love so much during his five years' connection, that he rather claimed to be a northern for a long time after. For example, a review of Otway's "Connaught," written during Lever's earlier career, and when the sly introduction of an advertisement may be regarded as venial, observes,—after reminding us that if it had not been for an Ulsterman, the "Wild Sports of the West" would still be unwritten—

"Ulster sent Harry Lorrequer to do for Galway what its thirteen tribes, and six-and-twenty half-tribes, would never have done for themselves. But for the black north, these positive Blakes; passionate Bodkins; Fighting Frenches; stout D'Arcys; and all the rest of that dashing, duelling, foxhunting race of squires, whose

---

[*] Mr. Maxwell survived to December 29th, 1850, when he died at Musselburgh, North Britain, in indigence. He was kindly succoured in his last illness, and professionally served, by Dr. Moir, the "Delta" of *Blackwood*. Through the kindness of the Rev. Mr. Dobbin, his papers have been searched, but no letters from Lever can be found. In explanation, it is said, that for several years they met daily, which rendered written correspondence unnecessary.

[†] He contributed to the "National Magazine"—the "Pantagonals," written in imitation of the "Noctes Ambrosianæ" of C. North. Lever, to the last worshipped "North." "As a boy," he wrote, "the greatest happiness of my life was in your writings ; and among all my faults and failures, I can trace not one to your influence ; while if I have ever been momentarily successful in upholding the right and denouncing the wrong, I owe more of the spirit that suggested the effort to yourself, than to any other man breathing."

whims and oddities are now, by Harry's labours, as well known in Baden-Baden and St. Petersburg, as they are in Ballinasloe or the Claddagh, should have gone down to posterity with no other record of their virtues than that which is furnished by O'Kelly's 'Western Endosologist,' or the files of her Majesty's Courts of Common Law and Equity." *

This paper, written in 1839, said:—

" In spite of the sharp accent, and high cheek bones of its population, our hearts, we confess, ever warms to the dear black north,"—and his subsequent novels from the " Knight " to " Tony Butler," prove the steady consistency of this " dévouement."

Dr. Quicksilver, as some of the dames called him, had not been much tamed by his recent apprenticeship as parlour boarder to Maxwell. His attentions were divided equally between the maiden city and Coleraine; but judging by subsequent allusions, the latter presented a pleasanter retrospect than Derry. " Ah," he writes,

> " Were you wiser, 'tis plain
> You'd be now at Coleraine ! "

" Once," writes Major D——, " when galloping to visit some patient, he came full tilt against a turf cart as it suddenly emerged from a side street, and not having room to pull up his horse, he ' put in ' the spurs and ' lifted ' him over the load of turf, which feat, by the way, gained him the name of the ' Mad Doctor.' "

* In the " D. U. M." for 1829.

The pleasant physician is found prosecuting dispensary duty at Portstewart until 1836, and embracing such chance practice among the local gentry and middle classes as came in his way. He was as busy as possible, plying the pestle and mortar one minute, stirring the literary crucible the next. A nice little *ménage* was that at Portstewart—our doctor a mixture of Garth and Galen, while two blue eyes shedding purest rays shone lovingly.

Brightly the honeymoon beamed on—though not without a passing cloud. He received his share of what, in the jargon of the dispensary, are called "red runners," tickets printed in red type which make the ill-paid recipient fly forthwith to some bedside, often miles away. But then the road, running along a great basaltic range, was grandly picturesque; especially at those points near the estuary of the Bann, or the mouth of Lough Foyle, where the peninsula of Innishowan towered before the muffled Doctor as, braced by the sea breeze, he sped to the relief of suffering humanity. In the "Knight" he speaks of "those giant cliffs which, straight as a wall, formed the barriers against the ocean," and we are told of a certain "little footpath across the fields"—doubtless often trod by himself—"which, from time to time, approached the seaside, and wound again through the gently undulating surface of that ever changing tract."

The clouds besetting his honeymoon were not without a silver lining. The plague of the "red runners," had

the advantage of giving our plethorically threatened
doctor ample exercise, which neutralised the ill effects
of sedentary pursuits with " Lorrequer," or boon companionship with Maxwell. It will readily be believed
that the man who "topped a mule cart with his cob,"
and who never was without a kind word and sweet
smile for the lowliest of his patients, or townsfolk,
enjoyed, for the most part, a popularity amongst them,
amounting in a few instances to idolatry.

In a magazine sketch we find crowding to his mind
thoughts of those bright old summer days. " Denied
those high rewards so lavishly bestowed on all other
professions, the doctor's comparatively humble career
would have little to compensate the arduous hours of
his toil, were it not that, in the estimation of the world
he lives in, he finds a rich harvest of grateful acknowledgment for kindness, and that hold upon the affections and sympathies of his fellow men, which he alone
can have, whose duties have so often exhibited him as
the confidant, the friend, the benefactor. In that little
space, bounded upon one side by health, and by death
upon the other, his narrow walk is placed. Forgotten
in the exciting struggle of political ascendancy—
neglected in the gayer hours of pleasure—lost amid
the thousand distractions of the world—we rarely think
of him upon whose sympathies we may suddenly have
to lean for support, and upon whose skill we may have
to trust, under God, for our lives. And yet to him—
the stranger of an hour previous—we hesitate not to

lay bare the cherished secret of our lives—the pain, the suffering—the shame itself, that we dared not reveal to a brother—to him, without a blush, we confess the fear of death, the longing for life, to acknowledge which is to make the hearer your master." *

Undaunted meanwhile by evangelical scowls, Lever, on principle, moved in the best society he could find, and cultivated a wide field of relaxation. But, like the cultivation of other fields which amateur farmers know to their cost, this sort of thing failed to pay, and perhaps had he been less generous he would have been a richer man. Whatever his income may have been he probably lived beyond it. Dr. Benjamin Johnston writes from Middleton, Co. Cork:—" In the year 1835 my father's family occupied the Low Castle near Portstewart for the summer months, and I remember Lever attending daily my eldest brother. He seemed to live in good style, drove a pair of grey bloods, and was then writing, we heard, for the magazines."

Meanwhile his intimacy with the Prebendary of Balla became closer. The parson inoculated his young friend with his views; and Lever flung himself into the same manner of life. Like Maxwell, he also was threatened with service of writs, and one day he is said to have asked his mentor to recommend him some refugium, without being obliged to start for Douglas or Boulogne. Maxwell counselled him by no means to leave the land of bright eyes and potatoes, and that Ireland contained

* "D. U. M.," Vol. XIII., p. 653.

many spots of picturesque beauty hitherto unexplored
by bailiffs, and eminently suited for literary men requiring retirement or inspiration.

In those days no railway existed in Ireland unless
that between Dublin and Kingstown. Kilkee and
Ennistimon were instanced as places hardly known to
the people of Ulster. To Clare, therefore, Lever decided
upon retiring—more especially as he wielded some
influence there from his previous official connection
with the county. Leaving Dr. Gordon as *locum tenens*
at Portstewart, Lever bent his course to Ennistimon
where Dr. Finucane lived, and finally to Kilkee, the
parish priest of which had already expressed himself
" willing to extend the shelter of his hermitage." *

We give the story as told by friends of Lever; but
it is quite possible that his health may have required
the relaxation of a change of air.

Father Comyns possessed great social gifts. " I was
once walking along the road near Kilkee," observes
Dr. Cullinan, " and my attention was attracted by a
jovial song lilted by a gentleman mounted on a handsome, ambling cob, and swaying a silver-mounted whip
in time to the melody." This was Father Comyns.

Lever is said to have continued for some days the
guest of this genial man, famous for his " solid priestly
Port." And when, long after, the character of Father

* We have been at some pains to test by inquiry the truth of Lever's
alleged intimacy with Father Comyns. Dr. Griffin of Kilkee writes, " Lever
was a little before my time, but I often heard Mr. Comyns speak of him as
one whom he knew well."

Tom Loftus was introduced to the public, no one more promptly recognised the portrait than Mr. Comyns himself.

It should be remembered that Lever did not enter his house with the object of depicting him; he simply recurred to some material supplied by early acquaintance when many years after he wrote "Jack Hinton." In that book we find a pleasant sketch of the priest's kitchen, his parlour, his stables, and his servant, and finally of his library.*

The chapter must not be taken as a literal history. Jack Hinton is made a denizen of the priest's cottage rather from illness induced by the effort to rescue a drowning heroine; while Major Mahon is the party represented as in debt, but at last most comically caught by bailiffs in female garb—Mahon having indiscreetly left his retreat to pay court to a "widow Moriarty."

When we come to the events of the year 1842, and to examine "Jack Hinton," we shall have more to say of Father Comyns of Kilkee.

---

* "The good father's shelves, I found, for the most part, were filled with portly tomes of divinity and polemics, huge folio copies of St. Augustine, Origen, Eusebius, and others; innumerable volumes of learned tractates on disputed points in theology, none of which possessed any interest for me. In one corner, however, beside the fire, whose convenience to the habitual seat of Father Tom argued that they were not least in favour with his reverence, was an admirable collection of the French dramatists, Molière, Beaumarchais, Racine, and several more; these were a real treat, and, seating myself beside the window, I prepared to read 'La Folle Journée.'"

CHAPTER VIII.

ALL this while Dr. Gordon had charge of the Portstewart Dispensary, Lever nominally continuing its medical officer. Previous to returning thither he passed some time in Dublin, and, of this stage in his life, Jaspar Joly, Esq., LL.D., has preserved an interesting reminiscence. A club of old Peninsular officers, numbering eight, dined daily at the London Tavern, D'Olier Street, and talked over the pleasant adventures and stirring events of the great campaign. The president of the club was Captain Plunkett, an infirm man, who "shouldered his crutch to show how fields were won."

Mr. Joly was at that time going through his College course, but dined daily at this tavern, with ears open to catch the marvellous oral flow which, fed by generous draughts, continued uninterrupted till a late hour. One fair young man occupied a seat at the club, as unlike the weather-beaten faces around him as May to December. He is described by Dr. Joly as mild and gentle, in the flower of early manhood, with a voice soft and balmy, not often heard, and then merely to express some comment in a deferential and winning way. Dr. Joly was delighted with the conversation, and always made it a point to sit at the table nearest to the genial group. Day after day he was at his post, and day after day Lever was there too.

Had Mr. Joly been a literary detective placed by Clio to watch the future Lorrequer and the sources from which he drew his stories, the *surveillance* of our informant could not have been more untiring. "Lorrequer's Confessions" were given to the world three years later, and Dr. Joly tells us that he at once recognised not in this book only but also in "O'Malley" and "Tom Burke," a number of the anecdotes and even expressions to which he had been an attentive listener.

Meanwhile Lever returned to Portstewart, and once more got into harness. He was glad to grasp again by the hand men whose friendship he had won, and to see in the enjoyment of renewed health some of the lowliest in his list of patients. These were mostly poor fishermen and their families, who marked their gratitude to the Doctor by glittering gifts from their nets. The "Irish National Magazine" died on April the 1st, 1831, and in January, 1833, the "Dublin University" began. Of "Blackwood" and "Fraser" it aimed to be the political ally and the literary rival.

This serial, enjoying at one time a world-wide fame owing to Lever's contributions, was inaugurated by a few college students who, for literary improvement, had formed a reunion, styled after the manner of the ancients, "The Stoa," or "Porch." Mr. Butt, M.P., in a letter addressed to us, while kindly eulogising our efforts "to preserve incidents of Irish history which ought not to be forgotten," details the circumstances under which the serial originated.

"The 'Dublin University Magazine' was started on the first of January, 1833, by six Collegians, each of us subscribing ten pounds, four of us undergraduates. At the end of the first six months we sold it to Curry and McGlashan; Charles Stanford was its editor for the first eighteen months. I succeeded him.* As well as I recollect Lever only contributed one article before 'Harry Lorrequer.' I was editor when the first chapter of Lorrequer appeared."

The paper of Lever thus referred to was "The Black Mask," published in May, 1836. Mr. Butt adds that

* The Rev. Samuel Hayman, referring to these literary Collegians observes, December 10, 1878 :—"They cordially loved the Muses, but differed in political sentiment. The majority, who were Tories, started the 'D. U. M.' under Charles Stuart Stanford; while the Whig minority originated the D. U. Review, under Cæsar George Otway. In the Memoir of the premier editor, the Rev. C. S. Stanford ('D. U. M.,' Sept., 1840), this divergence of opinions and actions was described Politics in this, as in every other Irish undertaking, became the stumbling-block ; but his strong Tory bias did not prevent him marrying the grand-daughter of Lord Edward Fitzgerald." Further details of the origin of the elder serial— planned over a roaring fire, in the winter of 1832—may be found in vol. xiv., pp. 266-7.

it was not very successful. It was, in fact, discovered that the paper had previously appeared in another publication ; and Mr. Carleton, the Irish novelist, and then sole purveyor of Tales to the magazine, was the first to cry in half fun, half earnest, " Stop Thief," adding that his acumen had penetrated " The Black Mask."

The awkward discovery was conveyed to Lever as delicately as possible. Carleton, it appears, had told the editor that *another translation* of " The Black Mask " had already appeared in a work called "The Storyteller." Lever explained that it was not a translation; but was written originally at his own fireside, and he sent the Irish novelist word that the only " storyteller " in question was that very successful one Mr. Carleton himself.

This explanation did not mend matters much ; but, luckily for Lever's fame, we have discovered an important document which frees him from the stigma of base disingenuousness sought to be cast. He states that the circumstances attending " The Black Mask " were at last unravelled to him by the memory of Mrs. Lever, who remembers a transaction that had long escaped his mind. In 1833, being desirous of publishing two volumes of stories, he entered into correspondence on the subject and transmitted as a specimen " The Black Mask " to London through L——, a bookseller in Grafton Street, who was then going over; from that day he never saw his MS., and after repeated efforts to find out its destiny, L——

having always evaded his enquiries, in despair Lever
gave up the matter and re-wrote the story from memory.
The whole affair had long been forgotten, and he could
not believe, till he read in "The Storyteller" his own
words, that the thing had previously appeared in print.
It was inserted without his knowledge or permission,
L—— having thus surreptitiously obtained what was
entrusted only to his care, and who by a direct fraud
appropriated to his own purposes the property of
another.

Lever during his three years of married life at
Portstewart continued to practise : but all this time he
was writing something more than prescriptions. He
was indeed constantly relapsing into his old habit ; and
different magazine papers fell from his hand. His
medical practice was not sufficiently large to occupy
his whole time, or to afford him an adequate income ;
and he felt irresistibly attracted towards a literary
career. At this time he is found making frequent
allusion to the enormous difficulties which the then
exorbitant rate of postage opposed to literary correspondence, and the strange shifts to which authors
were compelled to resort. No other class of working
men have probably benefited so much by Rowland
Hill's innovation.

Among his first lucubrations were the "MSS. of King
O'Toole," part of the regalia of the Burschen Club ; but
this paper does not seem to have been inserted.
"Lever's second paper," observes the Rev. Samuel

Hayman, " 'The Post-mortem Recollections of a Medical Student,' appeared in the June number, 1836. It is powerfully written. I admired it so much, that (at my request) he introduced it into 'O'Leary,' one of his very best books *me judice*."

"Nights in Kildare Street," was his next performance; but these papers—somewhat in the style of "Noctes Ambrosianæ,"—never appeared: then came "The Emigrant's Tale," * which was inserted.

On the staff of the magazine, at this time, were Dr., afterwards Judge Longfield, Professor of Political Economy, T.C.D., William Carleton, Samuel (now Sir) Ferguson, Doctor Anster, Mortimer and Samuel O'Sullivan, both clergymen, Rev. W. Archer Butler, Rev. Samuel (now Canon) Hayman, Rev. Mr. Maturin, Rev. Charles Stanford, Rev. Cæsar Otway, Digby P. Storkey, and others distinguished in the Church and in letters. It will be perceived that the ecclesiastical element predominated, and the enlistment of Lever's buoyancy was a wise stroke. All put their shoulders energetically to the wheel; but, notwithstanding such able aid, "Dea" had very uphill work until the muscle of

---

* This tale (" D. U. M.," July, 1836), descriptive of Canadian forest life and Irish character happily blended, is, no doubt, Lever's. It seems a sequel to the "Planter's Tale," which follows the "Post-mortem Recollections" in the July number. These tales belong to the class of which "O'Leary" was afterwards made up, and into which the first of them was welded at the suggestion of Mr. Hayman. This gentleman knows nothing of "The Planter's Tale" and "The Emigrant's Tale," but they are obviously, as we have said, of the "O'Leary" family, which includes "Mine Host's Tale," "The Smuggler's Story," "The Abbé's Tale," and "The Baron's Story."

"Lorrequer" and the unflagging life of "O'Malley"
pushed the vehicle at last to the top; when, amid
joyous shouts and ringing horn, it rattled along at a
pace for which the driver, Mr. McGlashan, was himself
unprepared. Just as "Blackwood" was known as
"Maga," and "Fraser" as "Regina," the "University,"
from August 1834, claimed the name of "Dea."

About this time Lever is found contributing occasionally to Colburn's "New Monthly," and there is a
tradition that "Lorrequer" was declined somewhat in
the words of the Twopenny Post-Bag Missive :—

> "Per post, Sir, we send your MS.—look'd it thro'—
> Very sorry—but can't undertake—'twouldn't do.
> Clever work, Sir !—would *get up* prodigiously well—
> Its only defect is—it never would sell !
> And though *statesmen* may glory in being *unbought*,
> In an *author*, we think, Sir, that's *rather* a fault."

To compensate for this rejection, Mr. Colburn asked
him to furnish a three-volume novel; but Lever replied
that he was not in the vein just then for anything more
elaborate than magazine work.

Samuel Lover was invited by Lever to read the
earlier chapters and recommend the subject to his publishers, who, however, were unwilling to touch it, though
they are said to have at last so far relented as to agree
to print on condition that "o" was substituted for "e,"
and that the book came out as Mr. Lover's, but we have
little faith in this story. Certain it is that the first gush
of the "Confessions" appeared in the "University Magazine" for February, 1837, but it may be found announced

in the number for December, 1836. Either the hero's name was slightly altered, or the printer made a blunder in the title, which is spelt by him "LOVESQUE."

It was some time ere McGlashan, a Scot of great literary discernment, decided upon admitting these "Confessions," and we find him taking into an hour's partnership an old schoolfellow, Mr. George Mason, to help him in making up his mind.

Lever's previous sketches were mostly confined to German and Canadian soil. He liked to describe the "Cologne belles with their tight-laced boddice, their black eyes, and thin black hair;" * "the ceaseless roar of the Danube which poured along its thundering course amid masses of frozen snow," "the joyóus call of the Jäger's horn," or "the blazing fires of the bivouac round which huntsmen caroused and told the adventures of the day."† But from the hour that Maxwell impregnated his mind with the more legitimate love of Erin, he entirely transferred his affections, and saw beauties in her brogue as well as honey in her blarney.

The free air of Ulster blew into flame the light of Lever's genius. Writing in the Magazine (August, 1839), he says that "it is a fine, healthy, breezy, ballad-loving, romantic land." Here his mind and heart opened freely. "Confession" after "confession" rapidly dropped, in which many gay recollections of·

* "Dublin Literary Gazette," January 16, 1830.
† "D. U. M.," May, 1836.

Clare lurked. One week they did not come; but it was explained that the apparent break-down was due to the influenza that spares not dogs nor doctors. He modestly besought the editor not to compare him to Carleton—so very far beyond the standard by which he could wish anything of his measured. The seal of these " Confessions " was for months inviolably kept; and not even to Lever's brother, the clergyman, was "Confiteor" said. " Dea " was, as yet, the sole depository of his secret. " John Lever told me," writes Mr. Innes, " that he became aware that his brother was the author of 'Harry Lorrequer' from the story of Father Darrè and the Pope. But, ah !" he added, " how inferior to my father's mode of telling it." For more on this point see Chapter the First of our second volume, and " The Portfolio."

Mr. McGlashan—the managing partner of Curry & Co.—had not been long in discovering that he had drawn a prize. Grumblers there were who poohpoohed Lorrequer's adventures as an attempt to poach upon Maxwell's manor; but the Prebendary cried " Bravo !" and the grumblers bowed. Meanwhile Mr. Colburn entered the field and aspired to bag the game. The shrewd Scot advised his more stolid partner to look sharp. A confidential officer in their employ was therefore deputed to go personally to Portstewart and fetch back as much MS. as could conveniently be secured. Mr. George Herbert—afterwards the well-known Dublin publisher—went and received from Lever a large sheaf of the " Confessions," with the remark that if Mc-

Glashan had been Archbishop Murray or Dr. MacHale, he could not have made a "cleaner breast." "Mr. Lever having asked me to breakfast, I travelled ten miles from Coleraine on a very wet morning, and after breakfast got the MS. which I brought back to Dublin to Curry & Co. He struck me as a man of most winning manners, which indeed were shared by his wife, to whom, in the course of my visit, he asked me to give my arm. The broad Atlantic came up almost to the steps of his door."

The obscure country doctor in a remote Irish village was now not unknown in Paternoster Row. This was a period of great anxiety, perhaps more to his wife than to himself. The prospect of spending his whole life as a country doctor was not very encouraging, and on the other hand it seemed a very hazardous step to abandon his profession and embrace the precarious life of a drudging scribe. His sojourn on the Continent had left a most pleasant impression, and a trip he made to France in 1836 renewed it strongly. He told McGlashan that he was about to steer for the land of dykes and broad breeches, from which, however, he meant to return ere long. His mind was, in fact, most unsettled as to what he should do. Meanwhile he continued to relieve his breast of Lorrequer's confessions. The glow of their success made incandescent a mass of material lying latent. His mind had been from boyhood most observant, and a large storehouse was the result. The popularity of "Lorrequer" grew, and

Mr. Curry found the sale of his serial spreading. He wrote to Lever, telling him to send more sprigs from the the same shillelagh.

"Though I have been," writes Lever, "what the sarcastic French moralist called 'blessed with a bad memory' all my life, I can still recall the delight with which I heard my attempt at authorship was successful. I did not awake, indeed, 'to find myself famous,' but I well remember the thrill of triumphant joy with which I read the letter that said 'Go on,' and the entrancing ecstasy I felt at the bare possibility of my one day becoming known as a writer. I have had, since then, some moments in which a partial success has made me very happy and very grateful, but I do not believe that all these put together, or indeed any possible favour the world might mete to me, would impart a tithe of the enjoyment I felt on hearing that 'Harry Lorrequer' had been liked, and that they had asked for more of him." *

Just as those who wish to trace Fielding's career, must needs consult Captain Booth and Amelia, the student of Lever's life will find in " One of Them " a remarkable series of chapters descriptive of his own life at this time. Encouraged by the example of Mr. Forster, the biographer of Dickens, who quotes episodes

* The London press, almost without exception, remained silent, but the " Observer " thirty years after confessed that " amidst all the reckless extravagance, the uproarious humour and brilliant slap-dash, they read between the lines of 'Lorrequer' a power of description, an insight into character, a mine of thought which one might look for in vain in works of far higher pretensions." No. 4,230, June, 1872.

from " Copperfield " to help to tell the story of Dickens' life, we shall make an excerpt or two here. Lever had many friends in Derry : but like all men of mark, he had also foes. The irregularity of his attendance at the dispensary had of late placed a fatal weapon of assault in their hands. The tenth chapter of " One of Them " describes Layton the dispensary doctor near Coleraine, while Phiz has ably sketched the various specimens of suffering humanity who were wont to throng the door. Lever was at this time much vexed by the adverse plots and reports ; and he thus recalls his annoyances :—

" Another low tap at the door aroused him from his musings, and the low voice he knew so well gently told him it was his morning to attend the dispensary, three miles off. More than one complaint had been already made of his irregularity and neglect, and intending to pay more attention in future, he had charged his wife to keep him mindful of his duties.

" ' You will scarcely reach Ballintray * before one o'clock,' she said, in her habitually timid tone.

" ' What if I should not try ? What if I throw up the beggarly office at once ? What if I burst through this slavery of patrons, and chairmen, and boards ? Do you fancy we should starve ? '

" ' O, no,' cried she ; ' I have no fears for our future.' "

He tells her that her courage is greater than his, and taking his hat he set off for the dispensary.

" ' Yer unco' late, docther, this morning,' said one,

* Ballintray is situated near Portstewart.

in that rebukeful tone the northern Irishman never scruples to employ when he thinks he has just cause of complaint.

"'It's na the way to heal folk to keep them waitin' twa hours at a closed door,' said another."

In reply he merely muttered that he could not cure them as kings used to cure the evil, by royal touch; but that he would do his best. On inquiry, however, it appeared that a local magnate had been to the dispensary and carried off the key, declaring that a doctor with such habits should not be entrusted with such a charge. One sturdy farmer said he had not come there to ask for charity. The doctor beckoned him to follow him into an adjacent ale-house, and offered refreshment while he described his case. A long interview is told, after which the doctor threw off a letter "with the ease of one to whom composition was familiar," and set out homewards "turning away from the coast." *

"It was the early evening, one of those brief seasons when the wind lulls and a sort of brief calm supervenes in the boisterous climate of northern Ireland. Along the narrow lane he trod, tall foxgloves and variegated ferns grew luxuriantly, imparting a half-shade to a scene usually desolate and bare; and Layton lingered along it as though its calm seclusion soothed him.

"The last flickerings of twilight guided him down the steep path of the cliff, and tired he reached home.

* The letter referred to tendered his resignation, and he personally delivered it at the chairman's door.

"'What a wearisome day you must have had,' said his wife, as she stooped for the hat and cane he had thrown beside him.

"'I mustn't complain, [Kate],' said he, with a sad sort of smile. 'It is the last of such fatigues.'

"'How, or what do you mean?' asked she, eagerly.

"'I have given it up. I have resigned my charge of the dispensary. Don't ask my reasons, girl,' broke he in, hastily; 'for I scarcely know them myself. All I can tell you is, it is done!'"

Two incidents had paved the way to this resolve which there is no need to leave untold. Lever's wife, as the book tells, was full of grace, softness, and love. The doctor, now all buoyancy and *abandon*—anon philosophically ruminative—was one day chewing the cud of sweet and bitter fancy, when an invitation arrived from a local swell asking Dr. and Mrs. Lever to a grand ball. This episode we give as nearly as possible in the words of his early friend Dr. D——. "The usual difficulty about a new dress to wear was represented. Lever wrote to his friend the Rev. William Faussett, Chaplain to the Royal Marine School, saying that they had been asked to the dance to which of all others Kate was most anxious to go. He could not think of disappointing her; and, although the £20 note which he enclosed constituted all his 'ready rhino,' he asked Mr. Faussett to invest it in a dress that would at once do credit to his wife and confer pleasure on the wearer."

The old clergyman * took an opportunity of showing
this communication to the Surgeon-General, Sir Philip
Crampton, a person of most kindly impulses, and who
wielded much influence in diplomatic and general
society. "Lorrequer" had won for Lever many
admirers including Sir Philip himself, who in early life
—as Moore's diary reveals—was given to the same
rollicking fun. He entered cordially into the matter,
urged that Lever ought to proceed to Brussels, where
he was more likely to advance himself, and wrote some
letters of introduction on his behalf, including one to
his son, then Secretary to the British Legation in
Belgium. Lever, who when his struggles were hardest
could, with great facility, construct " Châteaux en
Espagne," at once considered his fortune made, and that
he was, virtually, Physician to the British Embassy
from that hour. His young wife shared this sanguine
feeling. Visions of Brussels lace and Brussels carpets
enriched the pleasant prospect, while the doctor, gathering up his papers and "traps," proceeded to bid adieu
to Ulster, whistling, possibly, as he did so " Down,
Derry, Down." This has been pronounced the turning
point in Lever's destiny; but one of his last confidences
to a gifted friend sadly remarks, that both had failed
in life, and expresses regret that he should have ever
ceased to be the humble Dispensary Doctor of Derry.

* The son of this old friend is the Rev. A. R. Faussett, Rector of St.
Cuthbert's, York, himself an author of distinction, who tells us that he well
remembers Charles Lever at the Hibernian Marine School in 1830, "full
of sparkling wit and cheery pleasantry."

Another incident which hastened his departure must be told. Lever's great patron at Portstewart was an obese widow, whom he loved to mimic, especially the grunt with which she rose from her chair. To this lady he introduced his college grinder, Mr. C——l, and when, months later, he begun to touch her sore points with caustic scorch, C——l cut him short by saying that Mrs. R—— had been much hurt by his levity, and requesting he would not repeat it, as the lady and he were engaged. Within a month the grinder and the widow joined hands in wedlock; and Lever left Portstewart never more to return.

An intelligent grocer named Williams lived at Portstewart, and long after Lever became famous he maintained friendly relations with this early acquaintance by occasionally writing to him. A letter dated Thornhill, Stillorgan, in March, 1842, addressed by Lever to him, has been preserved, but contains no special points of interest. Mr. Williams still lives, and his sister writes: —"We both have many pleasing recollections of Dr. Lever. He was a kind friend, and lived next door to us at Portstewart. We have in our possession a table we got from Dr. Lever, when he was removing from this place. It was part of the furniture of King William's camp at the Boyne: and was given to an ancestor of Dr. Lever's after the battle : and he set great value upon it."

Although the literary attitude of Lorrequer indicates "confidence," Lever was in fact distrustful of his own powers. On removing to Brussels, his first determina-

tion was to relinquish all continuation of Lorrequer, and
with it every pretension to the profession of letters ;
and it was not without the exercise of some persuasion
on the publisher's part that he at last relented.

No incompatibility of disposition, as in the case of
some of Lever's most illustrious contemporaries, marred
his wedded life. "In 1839," observes Mr. Inspector
McMahon, "I was introduced to Lever and his wife
at a ball given by General St. John Clarke, and both
seemed to live for each other, and to be laughing the
entire night." Those who met them twenty years later
at the balls in Florence, describe Lever, unshackled by
strict etiquette, dancing unceasingly with his wife.
Finally, it will be seen how he at once sank when death
claimed her who, as he said, had made the happiness of
a long life ; and "whose loss had left him helpless."

Behind the mask of O'Dowd, having Kate's image
present with him, he exclaims in extravagant apo-
strophe :— "You are not alone more beautiful, and more
graceful, more charmingly feminine, and more fascinating
in every way than all the other women in Europe ; but
you are more sweet-voiced and more gentle, and ten
thousand times more loveable than them all ! "

Of Dr. Robert Gordon, who assisted Lever in his
dispensary, and finally succeeded him there, it needs
that we should give a passing word. He was no
common man. He largely contributed, under the pseu-
donym of Coul Goppagh, to the serial for which Lever
wrote. Rich in sonnets, he displayed, in other

verses, the wild sweetness of Coleridge. That he was
an opium eater is inferrible from his " Laudanum and
Rum—A vision of Negrohead and Havannah "—one of
the finest, quaintest pieces of prose we have read.*
Like De Quincey, Lever did a little as an opium eater
himself; and in more ways than one his example
influenced Gordon.

"Men of the Time," Allibone—all the leading journals,
in fact, every biographical memoir which has appeared of
Lever, state that in 1837 he received the appointment
of Physician to the British Embassy at Brussels. It
has been inferred that this appointment was a lucrative
one, and that he must have had high interest to get it.
In different prefaces to his works, he speaks of having
filled this office. We were therefore surprised to receive,
in the course of our inquiries, the following letter,
dated Foreign Office, December 18, 1875 :—

" I am directed by the Earl of Derby to inform you
that there does not appear to be any record in the
correspondence in the library of the Foreign Office, of
Mr. Charles Lever ever having been appointed as
Physician to the British Mission in Brussels."

In reply to further inquiries, Dr. Darby writes :—

---

* " D. U. M." vol. xii., pp. 632-659. Dr. Gordon died Sept. 16, 1857.
One who knew him well, writes :—" He was rich in the possessions of the
heart and intellect ; but as to material wealth, his was the scant reward
which awaits the hard-worked, toil-worn, but greatly useful country practitioner. His days were spent in the exercise of his noble profession, in
acts of charity that never tired, and were limited only by his means." He
left, indeed, little behind him, unless his orphans ; who will be glad, we
trust, to see this tribute to their father.

" I always understood that Lever was Physician to the British Embassy at Brussels. He told me so himself, and I have seen letters from an Irish gentleman, stating that when he was ill at Brussels he was attended by a fellow countryman, Dr. Lever, Physician to the Embassy. Dr. William Parkinson succeeded him in the office, whatever it was."

Dr. J. B. Parkinson, writing from Wexford, December the 27th, 1875, observes :—" I think my brother William was appointed to the post of Physician to the British Legation at Brussels by Sir Hamilton Seymour."

It has been said that Lever was indebted for this alleged appointment to Sir Philip Crampton, who exercised vast influence with every Viceroy, from Lord Whitworth down. Hoping to settle the question, we addressed Sir John Crampton, Minister successively at Washington, Hanover, St. Petersburg and Madrid, who thus replied :—" Charles Lever was certainly not indebted to my father, or anybody else, for an appiontment at Brussels. No such appointment as Physician to that Legation ever existed. I was myself one of the secretaries to that Legation during the whole time of Lever's residence at Brussels, and was intimate with him. He had brought me an introduction from my father and from my cousin John G. Smyly, Q.C., to whom he was well-known in the north of Ireland. He practised as a physician at Brussels for some years with considerable success." *

* Letter of Sir John Crampton, Bart., dated Bushy Park, Enniskerry, January 4th, 1876.

This would probably be regarded by most persons as quite settling the question : but one high source yet remained to be consulted, and not without diffidence we sought it. Sir Hamilton Seymour, originally private secretary to Lord Castlereagh, and who was Minister at Brussels when Lever, forty years ago, arrived there, happily still lives. This eminent and venerable man, addressing the present writer in a letter from 10, Grosvenor Crescent, London, 25th of February, 1876, goes on to say, in terms which we shall be excused for not mutilating :—

" Some few years ago, I should have been able to give effect in a certain degree to your wishes which now I can no longer do ; as the infirmities of advanced age have come upon me—and naturally enough among them, is a hand so shaking that it is with some difficulty that I write at all.

" I regret this the more, as it would have been very agreeable to talk about my valued friend Charles Lever, and to descant upon his numerous and *very* agreeable qualities. Our acquaintance was made in this way. I was Minister at Brussels when a gentleman, quite a stranger, called upon me and signified his intention of practising as a medical man in Belgium. His object was that I should appoint him Physician to H. M. Mission at Brussels.

" This I explained was impossible, that we were much too humble people to have a physician, etc. etc. ; in fact, that no such appointment ever existed.*

* There is some confusion of ideas regarding the " importance " of this appointment. Chambers's " Cyclopædia of English Literature " states that

"I went on to say how he had been highly recommended by Sir Philip Crampton, and that it would be agreeable to me, if he would reckon my wife and children as his patients, in case any of us should require his assistance.

"The proposal was readily acceded to, and this it was which led in the first instance to acquaintance, and later on to intimacy.

"But my writing powers are nearly exhausted.

"I am, however, eager to state how, knowing Lever for years abroad, and in various countries, I consider Charles Lever as one of the most agreeable men of the four or five agreeable men I ever fell in with.

"I often, indeed, ask myself whether, when quite at his ease, he did not shine even more in conversation than in writing; what is certain is, that he was very pre-eminent in both faculties.

"I will only add that you are quite right in stating that some of his stories were taken from the records of my own life and experience, in fairness I ought to state that the most of those stories owe their merit very principally to his way of narrating them." *

he received the post of Physician to the Embassy as a recognition of his successful labours in connection with the cholera in Ireland.

* Sir Hamilton Seymour after leaving Brussels became Envoy at Lisbon, and subsequently at St. Petersburg, where he exercised a check on the aggressive designs of the Czar, from whose Court he was recalled in 1854, on the proclamation of war between England and Russia. In 1855, on account of his great experience, he was appointed to represent England at Vienna. Since the year 1858 Sir Hamilton has lived in retirement. In April, 1878, we had the honour of an interview with him in London—

One recognises in this letter traces of that " grace "
which Lever, when inscribing " Lorrequer " to Sir
Hamilton Seymour, describes as a specialty with that
bon raconteur.

" Could I have stolen, for my story, any portion of
the grace and humour with which I have heard you
adorn many of your own, while deeming it more worthy
of your acceptance, I should also feel more confident
of its reception by the public."

A joyous intercourse began from the day of Lever's
introduction to the Minister, which continued uninterrupted to the end.   But all was not, at first, *couleur de
rose.*   To his father's executor he explained, in April,
1837, that owing to the great difficulty of obtaining
" le permis " to practise in Belgium, every English
physician had been deterred from trying Brussels as
a residence.   It was necessary to pass an examination before a jury *d'examen des Médecins,* all interested
in the rejection of the candidates, and only anxious to
make Brussels a close borough for themselves and their
friends.   He added, although he was appointed physician to the Embassy, and was so at that moment—he had
no right, strictly speaking, to practise, nor was he likely
to get it, yet through the protection of the Ambassador
he hoped to continue to exercise " les droits d'un
Médecin "—if not *sans peur* at least *sans reproche ;* and

touching Charles Lever, when it was easy to see how sensibly he felt that
men who had rendered less services to their Sovereign should have received
high honours, while his own have been comparatively forgotten.

if they were to proceed legally against him, the King would interfere and remit his fine; at least, so Lever had been assured, and at last if the prosecution should continue, he had only to study for a month and obtain a Louvain degree, which settles all difficulties by one stroke. At least four hundred a year might be made, and as everything was cheap except rent and taxes, a man could do very comfortably. He meant to start on an early day to bring over his wife and "wees," and settle at once. His patients were all the first people, Lord Stafford, Lady Faulkener among the number, and all expressed a desire to keep him and serve his interest. A fair prospect for success had offered, but he must needs raise a little money to furnish a house and bring over a family; and if Mr. Spencer would put him in the way of obtaining £250, he would not sell Moatfield, as otherwise he should be obliged to do. The opening was such that some one must fill it at once and for ever. His step did not admit of delay, and when he reached Ireland he should leave for Brussels almost immediately.

Meanwhile, a very flattering report of "Harry Lorrequer's" reception was conveyed to him by the editor of the Magazine, Mr. Butt. Lever replied, that Molière's Bourgeois Gentleman was not more surprised to hear that he had been speaking prose for forty years, than he was on learning that he was a successful author.

It has more than once been asserted, that with difficulty he was persuaded to continue the early instalments of "Lorrequer;" and, with equal diffidence, he first pooh-poohed the suggestion that it deserved reprint in a separate volume. He, in vain, urged as one of the miseries of human life, "the being obliged to listen to the repetition of a badly sung song, because some well wishing, rather than discreet, friend had called for an encore." He argued that it would be far wiser on his part to retire from the boards "in the pleasing delusion of success," content with the still small voice of a few partial friends. Again, "he had some little character at stake; his credit was only a five pound note; but he was dreadfully alarmed for the safety of the bank"—these were the pleasant figures with which he bantered good-natured friends. His modest attitude belied that character for overweening confidence and dauntless cheek which those who only half knew Lever gave him.

In a similar moment of weakness he would seem to have been about to decamp from Brussels. A Magazine paper (Jan. 1841) says:—"On the eighth day after my arrival at Brussels, I told my wife to pack up; for, as the lawyer who promised to write had not done so, we had nothing to wait for. We had seen Waterloo, visited the Musée, skated about in list slippers, through the Palais d'Orange, dined at Dubois, ate ice at Velloni's, bought half the old lace in the Rue de la Madeleine, and almost caught an ague in the Allée Verte. This was certainly pleasure enough for one week; so I ordered my bill, and prepared to evacuate Flanders."

He thought better of it, however, and stayed the tiny

hand about to repack his box. In Brussels the best society was opened to Lever, and a rich field for the study and seizure of character as well. A magazine paper in 1839, gives us an insight into the experience which he gradually gained. He was not unknown, personally or professionally, to King Leopold.

"He who to-day is the confidant of his king, and to-morrow leans over the sick bed of the starving tenant of a garret, must needs see life in various aspects; and it would be to deny him powers that his very position demands, not to confess, that to him more of the romance of life is presented than to any other man. So truly is this the case, that we would fearlessly ask any great practising physician if the scenes so powerfully recorded in a late work of fiction do not fall far short in pathos and tragic result of many of those he has witnessed in the course of his professional career." *

"Thus," writes one who knew him, "he bounded from the dreary drudgery of a dispensary, to the glittering gaiety of an embassy—from the repulsive squalor of the fever-reeking cabin, to the coquettish gravity of the palatial sick room."

"When Lever resided at Brussels," the Rev. Samuel Hayman writes, "his house was near the ambassador's, Sir Hamilton Seymour. Receptions at the Embassy closed for the public at 8 p.m., and none remained later, save on special invitations which constituted them private guests. Lever always opened *his* house on the

* "D. U. M.," vol. xiii., p. 653.

reception evenings at 8 p.m., when all who could not
remain at the envoy's poured in on him. Strangest
meetings were the consequence. Doctor Whately, Archbishop of Dublin, when his guest, would have no one
near him for the evening but the Papal Nuncio."

Stranger still—this Nuncio was no other than the
present Pontiff, Pope Leo XIII.—better known, perhaps,
as the genial Cardinal Pecci, whose relations with a
protestant King were so cordial and conciliatory.* He
sat beside Queen Victoria one day at dinner; and afterwards attended her Drawing-Room, presented by Lord Pal-
merston—the only Pope of whom such things can be told.

Midsummer, 1839, found Lever in good practice,
doctoring Peel, Polignac, Bishop Philpotts, Brougham
and Lyndhurst—not to speak of a mob of valetudina-
rians, sent by Dr. Granville to drink of German Spas;
and Lever bitterly complained that all expected him to
supply an analysis of every spring or fetid puddle from
Pyrmont to the Pyrenees, and that his mornings were
passed discussing chalybeates and sulphurets with all
the scarlet and pimpled faces that Harrogate and Buxton

---

* Some of these conversations have been recorded, from which it is clear
that Cardinal Pecci added the grace of the courtier to the culture of the
ecclesiastic. Leopold said, "I often forget Pecci is an Italian, and his
French is so fluent that, if I were not a German, I should certainly find
myself some day converted by the charm of his diction as well as the logic
of his reasoning." Leopold one day said to him at Laeken, "I am sorry
I cannot suffer myself to be converted by you, but you are so winning a
theologian that I shall ask the Pope to give you a cardinal's hat." "Ah,"
replied the Nuncio, "a hundred times more grateful than the hat would it
be to me to make some impression on your heart." " Oh, I have no heart,"
exclaimed the King, laughing. " Then, better still, on your majesty's mind."

had turned off incurable! Many of them were only hippish; but by the time they reached Brussels on their way back, their constitutions were so impaired by the fat, grease and acidity of German cookery, that we learn they all stood in need of Lever before they could get their passports for Antwerp. The English, who travelled for pleasure, seldom failed to bring with them some family ailment, which French wines and high living combined to make troublesome, and Lever's rooms were constantly visited by pleasant people of this sort. But some "unlicked cubs," as he called them, greatly disgusted him by the false impressions they conveyed to foreigners of what Englishmen really are. What they came for puzzled him—they could not be escaping from debt, for nobody would trust them—and they could not be swindlers who now-a-days were men of captivating address. He rejoiced to think that they would be cheated by the money changers, bullied by the police, and poisoned by the diet. But Lever's heart never nurtured a prejudice; and within six weeks he complained to McGlashan that he had been swindled out of £145 by a patient to whom, in a moment of weakness, he had lent it.

Lever was greatly amused by these curiosities of medical experience, and he plied his patients with stinging stanzas quite as much as French flies.

"Run, boys, run, for all the world is sipping it;
   Surely such a time as this was never known,
From Naples now to Norway poor John Bull is dripping wet,
   With sulphur and chalybeate, he is frantic grown.

> There's not a stream, how small it seems,
>   But if it only have a taint
> Of horses' legs, and rotten eggs
>   Is sure to cure a heart complaint.
> The very swells cut Bath and Wells,
>   And even all the knowing men
> Eschew the vine, and change their wine
>   For sulphuretted hydrogen."

A series of papers, called "Continental Gossipings," were contributed by Lever to the Magazine in April, May, and July, 1839; and next year were resumed. These, which do not seem to have ever been reprinted, are mainly devoted to notices of Louis Philippe, politics, Maisons de jeu, the Café Tortoni, the Bourse, the Legion of Honour, Criminal Law in France, the Procureur du Roi, English Ministers abroad, Tourists, &c.

Again Lever got what he called "the fidgets," and was half tempted to cut Brussels. He informed a friend in May, 1839, that he was not quite well, and was trying to get some one to order him to travel— adding that as old Lady B—l—e always found a doctor who knew her constitution, and told her to take Curaçoa frequently, he hoped to find an intelligent physician too. He might perhaps turn up in Dublin; but his trip was so very contingent upon the people who would not be sick just then, but were "keeping it all" for July or August, that he hardly knew what to say or do. He had some idea of visiting the German Spas, and trying if he could not beat "that arch humbug and bore, old Granville." Mortimer O'Sullivan, moreover, had suggested that he should write sketches of the German universities, give every city with most of the travelled routes, and some untravelled ones, taking in literature, politics and manners—mingled with incident, song and story—praising and abusing to " the top of his bent," and making up a slap-dash ramble abroad, that would astonish better behaved and more sedate travellers—the whole illustrated by Phiz! Counselled by his wife, Lever relinquished these projects and became, at last, more reconciled to his own " shop," as he called it. He resumed his practice and receptions in Brussels; and more than once sang for the present Pope his grand old Burschen ballad song, " The Pope he leads a happy life : " and no doubt the success of " Lorrequer" was promoted by the introduction of that fine lyric. Just as the drinking song "Jolly Nose," which made Ainsworth's " Blueskin " famous, is a translation from the Norman Anacreon Basselin, so Lever's well-known song comes from the German Studenten-lied, " Der Papst lebt herrlich in der Welt."

Canon Hayman continues:—

" Lever was then writing ' Harry Lorrequer,' and his copy was sent to Curry in the ambassador's private letter-bag. The two or three concluding chapters somehow went astray; and McGlashan wrote in dismay to the author about them. No enquiry at the time could unearth them; and poor Lever was constrained to write them over again. Time passed on, and in some accidental way the missing MSS. turned up, which I now place in your hands. They differ in many respects from the printed copies, as you will find by comparison." *

Lever bore this trying loss good-humouredly, exclaiming to Mr. Bentley: "They have made a series of blunders at the Foreign Office—Heaven grant they may make no more serious ones." He was at this time a very strong Tory, and liked to hit at the Opposition. When asking liberal terms from his publishers he said: "My Budget is in a more deplorable state of deficiency than the Whigs'!" and touching another of the many miscarriages of MS. which constantly tried his temper, he expressed (October, 1839) surprise to find himself not in print as usual in the Magazine, "like Bloomsbury in the St. Leger, not placed nowhere." Was he led astray in the Foreign Office, and had the lucubrations of the unfortunate "Lorrequer" been mistaken for a protocol and forwarded to Lord Ponsonby at Constantinople? One comfort there was in such case, they were nearly as *apropos* as most of the documents issuing from that quarter.

The last Introduction to "Lorrequer" notices autobiographically these incidents.

"If this sort of thing amuses them, thought I, I can go on for ever; and believing this to be true, I launched forth with all that prodigal waste of material, which, if it forms one of the reasons of the success, is, strictly speaking, one among the many demerits of this story. That I neither husbanded my resources, nor

* Letter to the author, March 6, 1876.

imagined that they ever could fail me, were not my only mistakes; and I am tempted to show how little I understood of the responsibilities of authorship by repeating"—and here he describes the blunder at the Foreign Office, where the last chapters of "Lorrequer" had been possibly mistaken for a dispatch.

"In this strait my publisher wrote to me in a strain that the trade alone knows how to employ towards an unknown author. Stung by his reproaches, and they were not mild, I wrote back enclosing another conclusion, and telling him to print either or both, as he pleased.

"Years after I saw the first MSS., which came to hand at last, bound in my publisher's library and lettered, Another Ending to 'Harry Lorrequer.' " *

From these and other passages, written for the public eye, it might be inferred that a marvellous facility blessed his progress; but the letters penned behind the scenes show that all this boastful tone should be taken with some qualification. On the stage Grimaldi's laugh reached from ear to ear; behind the proscenium he often writhed while medical treatment chafed his swollen

---

* This unused finale of "Lorrequer" was sent through McGlashan's London agent, but no acknowledgment came. The Foreign Office, he said, was bad enough, but "he seemed the stupidest bookseller—G— mend him !—that ever the Row beheld." The MSS., as bound, form a volume, nine inches by seven, which lies before us as we write. "Lorrequer" in the "D. U. M." contained fifty-three chapters ; this interesting folio has an additional chapter, and is lettered in gold, "Conclusion of Harry Lorrequer MS.," so that our author's recollection of its designation was not quite exact.

limbs. So it was with Lever. Twinges of torture perpetually pervade his private correspondence. Bodily pain, and at times utter mental prostration, receive due record. This was the penalty of pleasure—the reaction of that excitement in which "Lorrequer" and "O'Malley" loved to revel. To his publisher he often alluded to the festive life he led, adding as an additional reason for receiving a remittance, that dinner-giving and going out were very expensive pastimes.

In August, 1839, he is found adding more to his family than to "Harry"—and expressing great joy at the birth of a daughter. In October, 1839, he implored McGlashan to send him any critiques which appeared, and to be prompt with his proofs, as the season would soon commence in Brussels, when blue pill and rhubarb would not fail to eject all that appertained to "Harry Lorrequer." He said it was only the occasional prod of the spur that ever made him move. It appeared, however, that McGlashan's inactivity had been due to serious illness; but Dr. Graves at last wrote to say that he had restored him to the rank of a biped. Lever declared it would have been dreadful had McGlashan died with such a sin on his soul as the frightfully blundered proofs he had sent. They were as Shakspeare said, "most damning proofs," and it appeared that nearly every proof cost him seven shillings postage!

The illustrations by Phiz, however, greatly pleased him. When he did find fault, it was of no graver character than to express regret that Lorrequer at

"The Supper Scene" in Number 2, should be made so like his contemporary Nicholas Nickleby. It was unfortunate; and could not fail to strike every reader. Any plagiarisms in the book, he begged to say, were the author's prerogative.

Distracted by mingled gaieties and duties he was not always up to time with his monthly instalments. Some numbers of "Dea"* appeared minus the "Confessions," which solely led many persons to invest their half-crowns in it, and one or two lame excuses came, but, practice makes perfect. Ere long he acquired the same sort of facility in bounding over literary difficulties, as his dashing heroes evinced when clearing five-barred gates and laughably impregnable ha-has.

"Lorrequer" professed to be little better than an amplified note-book of the men he had met, the good stories he had heard, and the amusing scenes he saw. The incident which describes the pompous baronet, Sir Stewart Moore, mistaken for the steward of the ship, when the suffering widow, prompted by Harry, screams, "Steward!—Steward!—Steward-Moore, I say!" is said to have occurred to Sir Stewart Bruce, gentleman usher at the Irish Court. His flight from the cabin, night-cap on head, and with suspenders hanging, is very comically sketched by Phiz. At Lisle Boarding House, Dublin, during Lever's stay there, the amusing scene described

* "Lorrequer" appeared in the Magazine previous to its issue in shilling numbers. The part for August, 1834, claims the name of "Dea," though less felicitously than "Blackwood" did that of "Maga," or Enchantress.

by Lorrequer and sketched by Phiz, "Mr. Cudmore and the Teapot," occurred. This awkward collegian from Kerry, who, when handing and finally spilling the kettle, declared he would no longer act as "Skip" to the landlady, was a Mr. B——, brother of a subsequent Q.C.

It was a great pleasure to Lever to revisit in "Lorrequer" scenes endeared to him in the old land. What can be more picturesque than his sketch of the road to Callonby from Kilrush, where, for two miles, "it led along the margin of the lofty cliffs of Moher, now jutting out into bold promontories, and again retreating and forming mimic harbours into which the heavy swell of the broad Atlantic was rolling its deep blue tide." But Lever confuses his impressions of the scenes he had formerly seen, for the cliffs of Moher are at least twenty miles from Kilrush.

A line to McGlashan, at this time, urged him to conciliate the Press by every means, and that if *he* were in Dublin he should give a *soirée* of Devils to stand well with the men of Ink.

"Lorrequer," though written in defiance of the canons of criticism, proved a palpable hit. The public clapped; the critics coughed; the cynics hissed. It was not till long after that the censer swung. Its success, and that of the books which followed it, was partly due to their disregard of the small niceties and intricacies of book-making. Full of *abandon* they seemed a labour of love rather than laboured works of art. Hence the sporting world, from the first, liked them. N. P. Willis said that the highest honour and compliment which could be paid to a man would be to have the winner of the Derby named after him. Among items of news in July, 1840, we read:—"'Harry Lorrequer,' a horse belonging to the Prince de Chenez, has just won the gold cup at Ghent."

A German translation of "Lorrequer" having been announced at Leipsic, Lever remarked that it must have been rather thorny work for the translator. He was very much of Voltaire's opinion—"Woe to him who says all he can on any subject"—and urged McGlashan to close in ten numbers. The publisher suggested a prolonged and rather sentimental conclusion, of which Lever did not fully approve. He said that as the thing had done well it was not right that the badness of the cheese should obliterate the remembrance of the soup, fish, and *entrées*. If the public laughed at first it ought not to be sent home disposed to cry. A handsomely bound copy of "Lorrequer" having been sent to Lever by his publisher, the modest author exclaimed, "I feel, at seeing myself in such gay attire, very like the little old woman in the tale, and ready to say, 'Sure this is none o' me.'" He had all the sensibility and some of the weaknesses of a woman. Later on, finding McGlashan slow in communicating the laudatory notices of the Press, and without which, he said, he would never have check to continue, Lever told of a handsome Frenchwoman, to whom Chateaubriand complained that though ever so clever, flattery of her was too difficult; to which she replied, "*N'importe! Savonnez-moi toujours!*" "So I," he added, "without any of the same reason for the practice, would beg of you, Give me sugar-plums."

Gradually he gained more confidence, his later letters this year displaying in the left corner beneath the address the autograph "C. O'Malley," puzzling no doubt the postal officials, whose duty it was to pass free twelve letters a-day for every M.P.

The London journals ignored "Lorrequer," as "the opinions of the Press" gathered by McGlashan and prefixed to the magazine show. The praise is all cited from provincial papers, with the exception of one from a military journal, where the reviewer declared that he would rather be the author of "Lorrequer" than of all the "Pickwicks" or "Nicklebys" in the world.* Ere long, however, Lever took his stand among the most popular of European novelists.

The first good review he got was from "Fraser," in September, 1840, then edited by his countryman, Maginn, and proved more useful than if thick-spread praise. Hisses as well as kisses were mouthed. The two etchings prefixed to each monthly part of "Lorrequer," and which, in the subsequent serials of Dickens, Thackeray and

---

* This passage, with others of a similar drift, continued, long after, to arrest in advertisement the reader's eye,—giving much annoyance to Dickens, who, at last, responded angrily to a civil letter of Lever's, and it was not for years that friendly relations were resumed. With the comparison or the advertisement Lever had nothing to do, and far from trying to imitate Dickens, he had previously prayed Phiz not to make Harry Lorrequer so like Nicholas Nickleby.

Lever, formed no small element of attraction, were condemned, though not on artistic grounds. "The presence of these illustrations is a positive nuisance; they are anticipating you at every turn, and marring, whenever you have the misfortune to cast your eyes upon them, the laugh that was in store for you."

Behind the scenes, all was the reverse of laughter. In July, 1840, he described himself as having been bled, blistered, doctored, night-capped, and chicken-brothed, nearly out of this wicked world, gout promenading at discretion from his ankles to his eye-balls—the large cavities, as the faculty call them, included; but at last, with an elephant leg and a gaunt cheek, propped up in a window, resuming work.

A Preface published in 1863, and afterwards cancelled, repudiated the idea that the details in "Lorrequer" had application to himself personally. As he got older he became more open. The last preface, dated Trieste, 1872, adds to "The Confessions of Harry Lorrequer" one which for thirty years had been withheld: "In sketching Harry Lorrequer, I was in a great measure depicting myself, and becoming allegorically an autobiographist."

The suppressed preface, in alluding to the blended fact and fancy which made up the volume, declared that "in almost every case the improbable incident was the real one, and the commonplace event had only fiction for its foundation."

It was stated in the "Cyclopædia of English Literature," after his first and freshest books appeared, that his "chief fault was mistaking farce for comedy—mere animal spirits for wit and humour." But Lever in the earlier freaks of his pen had no higher aim than farce, and he no more mistook farce for comedy than Madison Morton did, whose broad farces, like "Ici on parle Français," pay better than the most ambitious comedy. Lever, while letting animal spirits loose, made no attempt to cut with diamond wit, and it might as well be said that in his racy smacks of Irish life he mistook Poteen for Curaçoa.

Tyrone Power, reviewing "Lorrequer," said that "it contained a superabundance of incident, and a constant succession of the most ludicrous surprises, so that it would furnish materials for at least half-a-hundred farces." "Lorrequer" was quite after the heart of him who, in a piece of his own, sang—

> "The first of all boys for love, fighting, and noise,
> Are the boys of the Irish Brigade!"

"Lorrequer," as a book, is very much the same as it appeared in the Magazine, with this exception, that several of the chapters in their primitive form are surmounted by citations which disappear in the reprint. A chapter entitled "The Chase" is thus garnished—

> "Then on we went, all galloping, galloping,
> All our legs went walloping, walloping.
> 'De'il take the last,' said Neil O'Bralaghan,
>   Whoever the same may be."

And to Chapter VI. is prefixed—

> " Land of Potatoe, Tithe, and Priest,
> Punch, Peeler, Proclamation,
> Bog, Bull, and Blarney, famine, feast,
> And fearful agitation."

Lever felt that this tone towards his Fatherland was unworthy of a national novelist; and on revision eschewed it. Some of the original headings never appeared in print at all, thanks to McGlashan's pruning knife. For example, we find in the first draft of Chapter II.—

> " Smoking, sleeping, poteen drinking,
> And ogling the Curate's daughters,
> Doing everything but thinking,—
> Such is life, in Country Quarters!"

The following, from " Percy's Reliques," also fell—

> " And theye lookede aboate for a rudelie manne,
> That was valiante at knife and forke,
> And who never desertede flagon nor canne,
> And him made they Mayor of Corke."

The above was meant to grace—and not inapplicably—that memorable first chapter where Alderman Beamish, under alcoholic influence, is found recumbent in his scarlet cloak.

CHAPTER IX.

WITH the exception of the short-lived triumphs of "Eclipse" in 1789, no Irish horse—till Harkaway's *début* in 1840—could win upon the English turf. There seemed to be a conspiracy to taboo all Hibernian horseflesh, in which men of the ring, trainers, stable-keepers, and jockeys, all it is said, joined. Harkaway at last burst bounds, took the lead, and cleared all before him. What was whispered of horses was also said of authors. John Dalton once told us, that when he went to London to dispose of his "History of Ireland," Mr. L—, an eminent publisher, said, "alter one letter and make it *Iceland*, and we may take the matter up; but as long as it remains Ireland, we cannot touch it."

Lorrequer, who had known few folk outside the chimes of the Post-office clock in Dublin, or the bells of Shandon, now made his bow before the fastidious folk who live within the sound of Bow Bells. He entered the lists unaided by puffing, and made his way well through the fogs of London. From the hour he let loose his dashing bursts of fun and frolic, one could see that he had conquered public prejudice, and was destined to take the lead, to keep it, and to win. The professional critics treated "Lorrequer" and "O'Malley" with stolid silence, and Lever's victory was therefore the more signal. These were the days of turnpikes and other obstacles, but, like Turpin, he cleared them all. Maginn compared him to "a race-horse, and urged England to make the best use of him before he slipped his shoulder or was worse doctored than when he was dubbed an M.D."

"Ireland for the Irish" had long been the cry; but at last the attractiveness of "Ireland for the English" became plain enough. A newspaper leader casually recorded : "Many Rugbeans who in 1838 were drinking in wisdom and learning at the feet of great Dr. Arnold will remember, that one of the most terrible fights ever decided in the school-close, was between two boys who quarrelled about the ownership of a magazine which contained an instalment of 'Lorrequer.'"*

A critic echoing the tone of some publisher who had refused a paraphrase of the book of Job, unless the author would throw a little more humour into it, complained that "Lorrequer" was wanting in scenes of pathetic interest. Seemingly to correct this want, "a sequel," "Lorrequer Married," was jestingly announced. The idea, however, wanted originality—assuming that Lever

* "Daily Telegraph," No. 5,298.

seriously held it—Hook's "Gurney" having just been followed by "Gurney Married." Alluding to "Lorrequer Married," Lever said to McGlashan, when the expenses of a house and family seemed yearly multiplying, that unfortunately for that state, it took the fun out of better men than poor Harry, and left them very little they'd like to confess to. "Lorrequer" had been written in the first person, and described a number of amusing scenes in which Lever himself had played a part. When urged to write a second book, he replied gloomily and with diffidence, "If the plank swam with one, it might sink with two." There was more fun in another answer to the same request, "Like the lucky Cockney, who having shot a swallow on the wing in his first effort, I am reluctant to reload my piece for a second trial. Small as the success is I have no fancy to peril it. My silence might foster many a speculation of what I might have been, were I only prudent enough not to destroy the illusion. Single-speech Hamilton is a celebrity to this hour, and there is great wisdom in the example."

McGlashan urged him to have confidence and to go on. "These publishers are wonderful fellows," said Lever long after. "They hold the curtain which hangs between the author and the public, and even at the chance glimpses they permit you to catch of 'the house,' they suggest most ambitious longings for the applause of the crowded benches before you. My first impulse on receiving his letter was to say 'No'; the thing has made a hit, let me live on it so long as it lasts, and be forgotten when it ceases to be remembered. Good spirits, which mainly prompted all I have said, are not to be summoned at will. Who knows what temperament might prevail during another and a longer effort."

Applause, however, was wafted across the German Ocean so freely, that he gathered courage; refreshed by this incense, he proceeded to draw on a vein which he soon found inexhaustible.

A shrewd caterer for the public taste, the late Mr. Richard Bentley, was struck by the promise displayed in the writings of the young and nameless author; and, while making overtures to him, suggested that the adventurous career of an Irish military officer would be a good subject for a new book. Lever replied that he had already meditated such a work; but Mr. Bentley's suggestion impregnated, we think, the fecund brain of Lever, who always distrusted his own fancies, and loved to follow the dictates of other judgments. Lever, his fancies strengthened by Bentley's counsel, began seriously to weave them into golden thread. He thought of calling the new book " Charles O'Hara " : * but the authors of the O'Hara Tales were then writing : and the name "O'Malley" received the final preference. In some of

* Here again he narrowly escaped the awkwardness of employing the name of a veritable Irish gentleman whose career was not uneventful. Charles O'Hara, a magistrate of Limerick, and at one time enjoying an income of £2500 a year, went through such strange vicissitudes that at his death in London he left money insufficient to bury him. His son, Charles O'Hara, still alive, enlisted as a private soldier.

his letters to Mr. Bentley, he speaks of lying fallow for a time and reading nonsense rather than writing it. He finally wished that his dragoon should fight under Bentley's banner—provided he gave him the uniform he wished—namely, monthly numbers, in a red cover, rather than three plethoric volumes. But the negotiation fell into abeyance; and the dragoon ere long was cutting his way through Dublin, rather than shrieking " Faugh-a-Ballagh " * in New Burlington Street.

Second ventures are often ticklish experiments. "When," said one of Lever's critics, with inimitable truth and humour, " we see a boy in the street standing on his head, if we are in a good humour we fling him a penny, but the next time we see him turning a somersault, we only say, ' There's that boy again ! ' and button up our pockets." We do not know that the exhibitor, even if a woman, is treated with more gallantry. " Uncle Tom's Cabin " created on its publication a noise almost unprecedented, and was absurdly called the book of the age; but the sequel and all subsequent stories from the same hand failed to attract attention. Many similar instances might be cited. But the case of "O'Malley" was exceptional. For fun intense and irresistible, it is really unmatched. To Sir Walter Scott has been attributed the apothegm—" If it be the highest praise of pathetic composition that it draws forth tears, why should it not be esteemed the greatest excellence of the ludicrous that it compels laughter? The one tribute

---

* Anglicè, "Clear the Way ! " the motto of the Connaught Rangers.

is at least as genuine an expression of natural feeling as
the other."

We certainly owe more to the man who makes us
laugh, than to him who is successful in making us cry.
Lever says, " I wrote as I felt ; sometimes in good
spirits, sometimes in bad—always carelessly, for, God
help me ! I can do no better."

It must be confessed that the clever illustrations by
Phiz contributed not a little to the success of the book.
Lever besought him to make O'Malley the same person
throughout, and not as Lorrequer was depicted,—old,
young, good-looking and ill-looking in every alternate
number. Phiz at this time knew little or nothing of
Irish physiognomy, a knowledge of which was so
essential to the effectiveness of the stories—and Lever
begged him to go down to the House and study the Tail
—as the most accessible way of obtaining an insight
into the Irish. " The Tail " was a familiar epithet for
the Irish members who followed O'Connell.

From Trieste, a few months before his death, he
writes :—

" When I set to write ' O'Malley ' I was, as I have
ever been, very low with fortune, and the success of a new
venture was pretty much as eventful to me as the turn
of the right colour at *rouge et noir*. At the same time
I had then an amount of spring in my temperament,
and a power of enjoying life, which I can honestly say
I never found surpassed. The world had for me all
the interest of an admirable comedy, in which the part

allotted myself, if not a high or a foreground one, was eminently suited to my taste, and brought me, besides, sufficiently often on the stage to enable me to follow all the fortunes of the piece. Brussels was adorned at the period by a most agreeable English society. Some leaders of the fashionable world of London had come there to refit and recruit, both in body and estate. There were several pleasant and a great number of pretty people among them; and the fashionable dramas of Belgrave Square and its vicinity were being performed in the Rue Royale and the Boulevard de Waterloo with considerable success. There were dinners, balls, *déjeûners*, and picnics in the Bois de Cambre, excursions to Waterloo, and select little parties to Boisfort, a charming little resort in the forest, whose intense cockneyism became perfectly inoffensive as being in a foreign land, and remote from the invasion of home-bred vulgarity. I mention all these things to show the adjuncts by which I was aided, and the rattle of gaiety by which I was, as it were, 'accompanied' when I next tried my voice. The soldier element tinctured our society most agreeably. Several old Peninsulars, with Lord Combermere, were of this number, and another of our set was an officer who accompanied, if indeed he did not command, the first boat party who crossed the Douro. It is needless to say how I cultivated a society so full of all the storied details I was eager to obtain. On topography especially were they valuable to me, and with such good result that I have been more than

once complimented on the accuracy of my descriptions
of places which I have never seen, and whose features
I have derived entirely from the narratives of my
friends."

As Lever omits the name of the Marquis of L——,
it is not for us to supply it. He told McGlashan that
the Douro chapter had been written from this Peer's
description ; and thus we trace Lever's object in giving
him that costly entertainment which Thackeray—mistaking his motive—called *Lordolatry.*

"Lever," writes the Rev. Samuel Hayman, "mentioned to me this fêting of the Peninsular hero, and he
seemed quite sore with the treatment he received at the
hand of Lord L——, who in a weak Book of Travels
makes slighting reference to the very bill of fare Lever
set before him."

One of the best chapters in Thackeray's "Book of
Snobs" has been hitherto imperfectly understood ; but
we find in the above remark a key to it.*

* "Here is an instance, out of Lord L——'s Travels," writes Thackeray,
"of that calm, goodnatured, undoubting way in which a great man accepts
the homage of his inferiors. After making some profound and ingenious
remarks about the town of Brussels, his lordship says :—'Staying some
days at the Hôtel de Belle Vue, I made acquaintance with Dr. L——, the
physician of the Mission. He was desirous of doing the honours of the place
to us, and he ordered for us a *dîner en gourmand* at the chief restaurateur's,
maintaining it surpassed the Rocher at Paris. Six or eight partook of the
entertainment, and we all agreed it was infinitely inferior to the Paris
display, and much more extravagant. So much for the copy !'

"And so much for the gentleman who gave the dinner," proceeds
Thackeray. "Dr. L——, desirous to do his lordship the 'honours of the
place,' feasts him with the best victuals the place could procure—and my
lord finds the entertainment extravagant and inferior. Extravagant ! it was

Niemeyer, the great German physician, opines that a doctor ought to give nearly as much study to diet and cooking as to physic, and said that it did a physician no harm to bear the reputation of a gourmand. This counsel Lever faithfully followed; but practical proof of his adhesion made inroads on time which might have been more profitably employed, and led to still heavier penalties.

In March, 1840, he describes himself as horribly afflicted with gout, and obliged to consult the doctors, who—confound them !—had stopped his grog and limited him to a pint of claret. This regimen he found, as he said, such "a floorer" that he was actually afraid to write, lest "O'Malley" should smack of low diet, &c., as well as its author. Droll reasons for again dining out to a more than ordinary extent are assigned, of which the chief was that he had bought a new coat.

Some chapters of "O'Malley" had appeared in the "University Magazine," and the separate publication of his new story had been advertised with illustrations by

not extravagant to *him.* Inferior ! Mr. L—— did his best to satisfy those noble jaws, and my lord receives the entertainment, and dismisses the giver with a rebuke.

"But how could it be otherwise in a country where lordolatry is part of our creed, and when our children are brought up to respect the 'Peerage' as the Englishman's second Bible ?"

Lever, in his letters home, stated that he was invited on a visit to Lord Boyle, and that the Marquis of Worcester conveyed to Ireland the MS. of "O'Malley:" but a weakness for lord worship should not be inferred from Thackeray's remark. His heart overflowed with kindness to all, and a disposition to oblige even strangers was often conspicuous. Thackeray's *Irish Sketch Book* came out long before the "Snobs ;" and Lever, when reviewing it, awards hearty praise for its condemnation of "lord worship."

Phiz, when Lever was much worried, first by remonstrances, and finally by threats, from a gentleman named O'Malley, who conceived that the author had specially pointed to him.

Lever was so fond of giving real names to his characters—unlike Dickens, who evinced felicity in concocting his Verisophts and Micawbers—that one cannot indeed wonder if certain Charles O'Malleys and Tom Burkes of Ours felt themselves somewhat awkwardly placed.

"I remember well," observes Dr. Waller, "the amusement created amongst the Bar of Ireland after a few numbers of 'O'Malley' had appeared. Amongst its members was one who came from the Far West, whose name was Charles O'Malley; and, stranger still, he had been first in a cavalry regiment ere he subscribed to the sentiment 'Cedant arma togae,' and, dolling shako and sabretashe, took to the wig and gown. He was a fine dashing pleasant fellow, good-natured, yet irascible, and retained to the last much of his military air, brandishing his brief much as he would have done his sabre. It was a standing joke to tell O'Malley that Lever had taken him for his model, and as each number came out with some new escapade of the hero,—some quarrel over his cups, or some misadventure in his gallantries,—there was some good-natured friend ready to bring it under the notice of the lawyer, and expatiate upon the injury such travesties must cause to his professional prospects. This was sure to fire his Celtic blood, and send it up into a face naturally one of the reddest, and so he was kept in a state of monthly exacerbation. It was indeed said that he was driven to challenge the author, but for the truth of this I will not vouch. Had he done so, I feel no doubt that Lever would have made the most ample and cordial *amende*, and declared, as was the truth, that the coincidence was totally fortuitous."

Charles O'Malley, Esq., of Temple Street, Dublin, "called in 1823," is the gentleman alluded to by his barrister brother. The monthly exacerbation sending the blood up to a face naturally indicating a strong sanguineous determination may at last have culminated in apoplexy—for we find his death recorded soon after the final development of plot in "O'Malley."

A letter of Lever's, written at the time, refers very fully to the coincidence just described, and shows that even before the final number of "O'Malley" appeared, a strong effort was made, through influential intervention, to make Lever alter his hero's name. John Adair, Esq., in a letter dated June the 17th, 1872, writes:—

"I was in our library at Court when Lever came there, as I was told at the time, to be introduced to O'Malley, and explain that he had not the least intention to allude to *him*. I remember at that occasion speaking to Lever, and hearing it said by barrister friends that O'Malley had consulted Edward Litton, afterwards Master in Chancery, a great friend of his, as to bringing an action against Lever for what he wrote."

This episode is quite as amusing and as sensational as anything in "O'Malley." Lever informed McGlashan in January, 1840, that the gentleman in question had written to demand a change of title. The author declared it preposterous that Mr. O'Malley should be exempt from mention any more than Messrs. Burke, Blake, French, Trench, Considine, Bodkin, and Co., and he could not comprehend why, because he advertises a work of pure fiction with that title, he is to be supposed as inditing the personal adventures of any Mr. Charles O'Malley in particular. He submitted that, if the common and proper names of the island were not open to Irish novelists, where are we to look for them? and that he trembled to think that some fine morning a Mr. Harry Lorrequer would present himself in Brussels and threaten fire and sword for Lever's eleven numbers of defamation. The absurd principle would lead them into endless difficulty. If Mr. O'Malley were changed, what was he to say to Messrs. Burke, Blake, O'Flaherty, & Co. Was he to change for them also, and adopt French names? or was he to yield foolishly to Mr. O'Malley, that he might engage recklessly the whole West? "The request was absurd, conceived in gross ignorance of the world, and not deserving temperate consideration—*Non sunt sola mea verba.*" Lever consulted Lord Sussex Lennox and Lord Ranelagh, and both laughed at the idea of attending to such a demand.

McGlashan was frightened, and seemed willing to

yield. Lever besought him to stand firm, for the sake of the book in which both were so intimately interested, for the sake of themselves, for the sake of his own bones (for, if it be a shindy, 'twere better it should be with Mr. O'Malley than all Galway, which must be the alternative if they yield). Mr. O'Malley obtained the intervention of Mr. Haire, and matters seemed looking serious, when Lever allayed hostility by declaring that he was ready to put on his title page that the gentleman described was not Mr. O'Malley, barrister-at-law, residing in Temple Street, but Charles O'Malley, campaigning with Wellington and fighting at Waterloo. Mr. O'Malley he had never known or heard of. His name suggested itself merely as being one of an old and respected house, and not unbefitting one whom, as his hero, he neither held up to ridicule or sarcasm, but delineated as far as in him lay as a gentleman and a soldier. McGlashan still seemed uneasy; but Lever reassured him by declaring it was impossible to overrate the importance it would prove to the success of their new book if the title remained unchanged. The Scot was slow as a correspondent, and Lever often wrote him five letters for one he replied to. He constantly addressed remonstrances to the publishers on this point, and complained they did not send him the friendly notices which had appeared—that he would prefer four lines of praise to a haunch of venison—that criticisms were in fact the spurs which nerved him to best exertion—that the non-arrival of proofs dreadfully worried him—and that sometimes the MS. miscarried altogether, necessitating the re-writing of several chapters.

McGlashan's slowness he bore nearly always with good humour; but one day he lost temper, and declared that he was ready to burst a blood-vessel with pure passion. When the prudent Scot did write, it was *multum in parvo.* If Dr. Lever's characters had vitality, depend on it they would do something, and if they have not, the sooner they die the better. With assurances such as these he set to work, fashioning his creatures, hoping that some at least among them might have the life-like element he described. If Lever once or twice boiled over with impatience, he generally contrived to let this feeling escape in such harmless and pleasant explosives, as the following hit at McGlashan's Magazine. "The Curse of McGlashan," suggested by "The Curse of Kehama," and reverently preserved among McGlashan's papers—runs—

> May your steamer be sunk,
> May Carleton get drunk,
> May [——] overwhelm you with lumber,
> May your merriest articles,
> Tell of Greek particles,
> A critique stolen fresh from the *Warder*, *
> With no light paragraph,
> Give your readers a laugh,
> But tell how Butt beat the Recorder.
>
> With your politics Chartist,
> May Sharp be your artist, †

* The Magazine had just been assailed by the *Warder*.

† The R. H. A.'s used to say that all Mr. Sharp's pictures looked as if the colours had been flung on the canvas, just as a mason "dashes."

> And your favourite subject Repeal.
>   Publish " Bunyan " critique,
>   Or " Tennant " * next week,
> And wind up with a sketch of Tom Steele. †
>
>   May Addison's letters
>   Hang round you like fetters ;
> May ‡ Remmy pitch into the number ;
>   And when death comes to take you,
>   May § long Sam forsake you,
> And hand you to him with a hoof,
>   Who'll shamefully use you,
>   With nought to amuse you,
> But correcting some " damnable proof."

The anathema, " may Sharp be your artist," was stimulated by a portrait of Lever, from the brush of that gentleman, which hung in the Exhibition of the Royal Hibernian Academy in 1841. Lever pronounced it an insane caricature, though there was one consolation : it was so unlike as not to lead to recognition ; but as no one cares to be prejudiced in the eyes of his neighbour, he asked the hanging committee to put in the Catalogue : " Portrait of Micky Free." " Remmy " is described pitching into the number. Lever, in describing some " bashful Irishmen," (December, 1841), mentioned the name of Remmy Sheehan, and one day a savage letter reached Brussels, almost calling the author out. Sheehan was a most influential scribe, whose

---

* Two dull Papers by Mr. H. Addison, on " Bunyan " and " Tennant " had been sent to the editor, which he finally failed to insert.

† A leading agitator of the day, but favourable to moral force, and styled by O'Connell, the head pacificator of Ireland.

‡ Mr. Sheehan, editor of the *Evening Mail.*

§ The Rev. Samuel O'Sullivan, as colossal as his brother, the Rev. Mortimer O'Sullivan, was diminutive.

curling lip always seemed to say *Nemo me impune lacessit.* The *Mail* continued for some time to attack Lever; but finally the wounds of both were patched up: and some amusing anecdotes of their intercourse in Dublin will be told hereafter.

"Addison's fetters" alludes to the irrepressible advances of a literary gentleman of that name, who was a constant visitor at Lever's house. One day he jokingly invoked the devil—if he had any taste for dull company —to fly away with this writer of 148 successful farces, and more tales, essays, poems, sketches, impressions, and reminiscences than the *Times'* steam press could print off in the next three years—but which happily for the world, but most unhappily for the author of "O'Malley," were only in MS., and read, recited, quoted, and dinned into him, from his egg at breakfast to his colocynth pill at night. He told McGlashan that he could fill any magazine from the Notice to Correspondents at page one to the Obituary at the end. Lever saw no reason why a man should not be treated for an incontinence of ink. He had plagued Lever, muddied the water of his imagination, and left the author of " O'Malley " brimful of the indigestion he had contagiously caught. Lever declared that nothing less could suggest his " infernal fancies," whenever he made the cruel error of supposing that a disturbed imagination was a high wrought power of invention. He might as well compare the internal grumblings of a colic to Heaven's own artillery ! Addison had sent to the magazine a paper which McGlashan hesitated to insert. Lever complained that the irrepressible contributor visited him daily, and ate no end of breakfasts, dinners, and suppers at his house—ostensibly for the purpose of abusing the said McGlashan. He begged "Mac" to insert his article, or poor Lorrequer should be eaten up !*

Addison having at a later period given it to be understood that he and Lever were about to become associated in a literary enterprise, the latter replied, that "he had as much intention of grabbing for barnacles off the keel of the *Royal George* as undertaking any literary concern in conjunction with him." Addison is introduced in "Tom Burke" as Captain Bubbington.

As "O'Malley" progressed in numbers, Lever found to his dismay that, owing to the haste with which he wrote, and to the delays in transit, from the peculiar circumstances of his position, more than one name which ought to have been altered remained intact. On looking at his proof in February, 1841, he was terrified to find that he put Maurice Quill's name in full, and unchanged. He wrote to the printer, beseeching of him to alter it, as Maurice had a score of relations ready to make mincemeat of him, and Lever was tired of trying to calm their feelings by explanations. At last

* A good sketch of Colonel Addison from Lever's pen and Gray's pencil may be found in the "D. U. M." for 1841. Shortly before his death he wrote the "Recollections of an Irish Police Magistrate," in which he describes himself quartered with his dragoon regiment in Ennis during the excitement of the Clare election. He left no representative to feel hurt by Lever's comic remarks.

he told the printer to make it Squill, and no one would notice the change, but the mandate came too late; and probably the very circumstance which annoyed him helped to sell the book. The late Captain Quill, a neighbour of Lever's in Talbot Street, was a brother of Maurice's; and to the day of his comparatively recent death, suffered from wounds received in the campaign so spiritedly sketched in "O'Malley." Dr. Mooney, whose name appears in the account of O'Malley's college days, had once been a veritable Don; and a correspondence in the *Warder* (June, 1840), complains of the introduction of his name. Lever had written with ink tinged with tincture of cantharides, and it had blistered his fingers.

Among the worries which beset the author of "O'Malley," was the destruction, in January, 1841, by fire of Folds' printing-office in Dublin, and of the "copy" meant for the forthcoming number—including a chapter on which he had bestowed much care—called "The Tyrol Story." His first emotion was not for his own loss, but for that of "poor Folds',"—for whom he expressed himself much grieved; though he finally had strong reason to dislike him, owing to some unworthy treatment he received in connection with a newspaper which he printed for Lever. In his extremity he scribbled a comic letter for insertion, instead of the burnt copy; but next day he substituted fresh and better matter, and requested that the letter on the fire might be held over, and burnt at the next fire. A contemporary novelist, Mr. James, who happened to be then in Brussels, expressed great sympathy, and advised Lever to write him a letter announcing the fire, to which he would reply; and thus, with a missive from Monsoon, and a bit of a note from Micky Free, Lever suggested to McGlashan that they might make up what could be called the "O'Malley Letter Bag;" and if Otway or Anster would address the Rev. Dr. O'Sullivan in mistake for the author, regretting the loss that the world would sustain in his excellent work, so calculated to do good, the thing, Lever said, would be capital. He added, as a great idea, that possibly he might be able to get another letter from the plenipotentiary, Sir H. Seymour, who wrote admirably. Part of this plan was carried out: James's letter had some wit in it; but in subsequent editions of "O'Malley" it may be vainly searched for. Of the "copy" finally sent, he told the publisher to take his choice. He had now the paving-stones, and the plodding pavior might drive them home as he fancied. Poor Lever was sadly worried; and he feared that Phiz's plates described not only what was burnt, but incidents the author had himself forgotten. Often he told McGlashan that it was important he should see the previous proofs before he could continue his story, as he had not the slightest recollection where he had left his characters, or how they were engaged. With sound philosophy he sought to make the *contretemps* of the fire subservient to the good of his book. He thought of getting Butt or O'Sullivan to insert, as a good advertisement for the work, a paragraph to the effect that an entire volume of O'Malley MS. had been destroyed, but the puff never appeared. Later on it transpired that Fold was to receive £8,000 "for the blaze," and Lever half jokingly suggested, that if so he ought to make him the amende for the burning of his "Tyrol Story." He is found, on the whole, rather out of spirits after this disaster. He did not feel "up" to the continuance of the same people through so many more numbers—though he knew that, being ready-made to his hand, the thing was easy—but its very facility was its difficulty; besides, it was certain that from the tone of the numbers already out, the same hurried flow of incident was essential to the end, and his material would demand opening out, which he detested. He did not fancy "giving the public Clancy" the Beer of Beamish, as *Fraser* said, but the Whiskey of Wyse. Lever had spoken of Beamish when indicating Cork whiskey; but Maginn, a Cork man, and editor of *Fraser*, explained that he should have said Wyse—Beamish being a brewer.

Reluctantly enough, Lever yielded to McGlashan's desire of extending "O'Malley" to two volumes; and he begged "Mac" to pray very fervently that before it was done he didn't wish himself burned along with the MS. The Scot proved himself a somewhat acute critic, and the success of "O'Malley" was largely due to his pruning knife. One day he condemned some passages in the "Adjutant's story,"—a part of "O'Malley." Lever said that he could not see them in the light his publisher did, but he gave him notwithstanding a carte-blanche, to make it as solemn as one of the Rev. John Lever's sermons; and if it didn't do for "O'Malley," they could dress it up for the *Christian Examiner.**

His frequent difficulty in writing "O'Malley"—which appeared in monthly numbers of thirty-two pages each —was not to fill but to avoid overflowing them. He had seen a great deal of life; most amusing scenes and characters occupied his mind. But, as usual, he had no regular story, and his stock of unconnected incidents reminded him of the materials the Chinese employed for his plum pudding, and who forgot to tie them in the bag which enclosed them.† Just as Dickens found Forster's critical eye of great use, Lever, though he maintained no regular relations with a reviser, embraced any favourable opportunity of securing such friendly aid as casually offered. Sir William, then Dr. Wilde, visited Lever at Brussels, and, after spending a delightful day with him, was handed a bundle of proofs, with a request that he should throw his eye over them and say what he thought. Wilde brought the slips home that night, and getting into a large "four-poster" in which he read them, found, ere long, the ponderous bed

---

* McGlashan wished him to resume in the magazine his "Continental Gossipings," with a further allowance of Lorrequerism, but Lever begged of him, for his great popularity sake, to keep him under the real counterpane and in his sheets. Apropos of the wrapper of "O'Malley," Lever wished that the red should be less frappant.

† This simile is introduced by Lever in a suppressed preface to "O'Malley," dated January, 1857.

shaking in every joint from the hearty laughter produced by O'Malley's freaks. Next day they visited the
field of Waterloo. Lever made numerous notes from
hints supplied by his guide, Sergeant-Major Cotton,
and just as they reached the mound on which the
Belgian lion is reared, a gust of wind carried off
Wilde's hat—whereupon Lever cried out "Hurrah for
Hougoumont!" at the same time flourishing his own.
They returned to Brussels to dinner. A portly Peninsular officer, Commissary-General M—— was announced,
who soon proved to be the Major Monsoon of
"O'Malley"—that comical cross between Falstaff and
Dalgetty. Sir W. Wilde seemed to think that M——'s
daughters were the originals of the wonderful Dalrymple
girls, "who were as well-known in the army as Lord
Fitzroy Somerset, or Picton, from Cape Coast to Chatham,
from Belfast to the Bermudas;" but this impression as
regards their identity is not in accord with that retained
by other friends.

"At an early stage of the proceedings," observes Sir
William Wilde, "he (Monsoon) got tipsy, exhibiting
throughout a marked illustration of '*in vino veritas*,'
and ended the night in paroxysms of maudlin piety."
Just as Thackeray, day after day, invited to his table an
eccentric Celt, still alive, all brogue and blarney, who
furnished material for Captain Costigan, Lever continued daily to feast this retired but not retiring Commissary-General. He well knew the uses to which his
presence was to serve, but Lever's wine was so good,

and his napoleons so bright, that he merely contented himself with pleasantly upbraiding his host now and then for the too free dashes with which his portrait was put in from number to number. The General's son took this liberty in less pleasant part, and having made a special journey to Brussels for the purpose of calling him out, was at once so disarmed by Lever's genial manners that, in the end, he also remained as his guest.

Lever, in some final jottings from Trieste shortly before his death, thus reports one of his conversations with old M——, who, on this particular occasion, was dining with him in company with an English consul:

" 'Let me have the money down on the nail, and I'll give you leave to have me and my whole life, every adventure that ever befel me, aye and, if you like, every moral reflection that my experiences have suggested.'

" 'Done!' cried I, 'I agree!'

" 'Not so fast,' cried the diplomatist, 'we must make a protocol of this, the high contracting parties must know what they give and what they receive. I'll draw out the treaty.'

"He did so at full length on a sheet of that solemn blue tinted paper, so dedicated to dispatch purposes— he duly set forth the concession and the consideration. We each signed the document, he witnessed and sealed it, and Monsoon pocketed my five napoleons, filling a bumper to any success the bargain might bring me, and of which I have never had reason to express deep disappointment.

"That I did not entirely fail in giving my Major some faint resemblance to the great original, I may mention that he was speedily recognised in print by the Marquis of Londonderry, the well-known Sir Charles Stewart of the Peninsular campaign. "I know that fellow well,' said he; 'he once sent me a challenge, and I had to make him a very humble apology.'"

Thus it would appear that Lever acted wisely in having a preliminary arrangement signed, sealed, and delivered with the irascible Commissary, who under other circumstances would not view unmoved the liberties taken with him by a comic novelist.

In closing this notice of M——, we are bound to add, that, when he liked, no man could present a more gentlemanly bearing. A suppressed preface to "O'Malley" says that he had manners sufficiently well-bred for any company, but that when the author introduced Monsoon in the novel he always tried to subdue this impression of him.

Among the veritable figures whose names and characters appear at full length in "O'Malley" may be mentioned Wellington and Picton; while in his sketch of Trinity College we have Jacky Barrett, the eccentric Fellow—a portrait so grotesque that it would be hard to caricature it; and Lever's letters show that he introduced Barrett solely at McGlashan's request. The absurdities performed by Barrett, and to which Dublin became at last quite used, struck McGlashan the more forcibly because he was not himself an Irishman.

The anecdote of tying a string to a halfpenny which, when Barrett stooped to pick up, was rapidly pulled out of his reach, is all quite true. But he does not tell in the novel—though he elsewhere did—how Barrett, having once sent an old woman for a ha'porth of milk, who fell and broke her leg, his first inquiry on hearing of the calamity was for his halfpenny!

The character and name of another veritable personage, appears in the novel unaltered, but no attempt to travesty Wellington was made. Lever had, we believe, at least one interview with him; and he probably felt, on that occasion at all events, that he was sitting, not to a caricaturist but to an artist.

The saying has been attributed to Lever by Dr. Waller, " I never took a portrait without the consent of the sitter." We think there must be some mistake in this, for several instances to the contrary are known to us. He himself says: " The principle of natural selection adapts itself to novels as to nature, and it would have demanded an effort above my strength to have disabused myself at the desk of all the impressions of the dinner-table, and to have forgotten features which interested or amused me." Again. In his preface to " The Daltons " he tells us that a number of the characters therein introduced were drawn from life, and that one or two had been already recognised; but he hoped that the peculiarities touched upon were inoffensive, and that he depicted only such traits as should " point a moral " without wounding the possessor.

It may be well to say, though Lever does not avow it
in his introductions to the novel, that the original of
Godfrey O'Malley, M.P. was Dick Martin of Conne-
mara, a noted duellist, who survived to Lever's time,
and often boasted of the sixty miles of strand which
formed the avenue to his mansion. A veritable incident in Martin's life is engrafted on the character
of Godfrey O'Malley. Martin lived in a stronghold
which no bailiff was ever known to penetrate. When
serving in the Irish Parliament, he found himself one
morning in danger of arrest consequent on a dissolution.
With ready wit he personated his own—got an account
of his death inserted in the papers, and absolutely succeeded in getting himself removed in a hearse until the
safe side of the Shannon was reached. From the top of
the hearse he addressed his constituents, who richly
enjoyed the joke, and he vowed that he would die for
them much more thoroughly in earnest than when, a
few hours previously, he had counterfeited death.
George the Fourth asked Martin who would be the new
members for Galway, and was answered, " Daly, your
Majesty, and the survivor."

Mickey Free, who attained a celebrity second only to
Sam Weller, and who, as he tells us, sang duets with
the Commander-in-Chief in the Peninsula, and wore a
masterpiece of Murillo for a seat to his trousers, was
originally intended as a mere stage servant, for the
removal, so to speak, of tables and chairs ; but Lever
finding him prove a capital vehicle for enunciating the

good things he had picked up, altered his plan, and made him an important figure in the book.* Writing, shortly previous to his death, and subsequent to his last visit to Dublin, he tells us:

"Of Mickey Free I had not one, but one thousand—types. Indeed, I am not quite sure that in my last visit to Dublin I did not chance on a living specimen of the 'Free' family, much readier in repartee, quicker with an apropos, and droller in an illustration than my own Mickey. This fellow was 'boots' at a great hotel; and I owe him more amusement and more heartier laughs than it has been always my fortune to enjoy in a party of wits. His criticisms on my sketches of Irish character were about the shrewdest and the best I ever listened to; and that I am not bribed to this opinion by any flattery, I may remark that they were more often severe than complimentary, and that he hit every blunder of image, every mistake in figure, of my peasant characters with an acuteness and correctness which made me very grateful to know that his daily occupations were limited to blacking boots, and not polishing off authors."

* Mickey Free was recently quoted in Parliament in a debate on the Eastern Question by Major O'Gorman :—

> "For I haven't a janius for work,
>   It was never a gift of the Bradies;
> But I'd make a most illigant Turk,
>   For I'm fond of tobacco and ladies."

The house roared; and even Lord Beaconsfield's impassive face relaxed.

The character of Mickey Free was a mosaic, made up of an immense number of funny traits gathered from many sources, though the first idea of the character was suggested by a servant of Lever's, half groom, half valet. Differently constructed was "Tipperary Joe" in "Jack Hinton," another successful sketch from low life. Lever was the son of an Englishman, and the mellifluous brogue of Ireland with its quaintness of dialect and ringing hits, fell the more freshly on his ear. He remarked that the subtle equivoque in the polished witticism that amuses the gentleman is never lost on the untutored ear of the unlettered peasant, and asked, "Is there any other land of which one could say as much?" Lever's talent in dressing up old stories for his novels was only equalled by the tact with which he made a *réchauffé* in his semi-political papers of sundry points which have long constituted the stock in trade of Conservative journalism. "His fame as a novelist," observes a critic, "is certainly based upon his wonderful power of invention and his audacious fun." The latter part of the criticism is probably more correct than the first.* Mr. Brophy, the late State

---

* Some pleasant evenings were passed in the little dining-room of that old Huguenot House in Dawson Street, filled with historic memorials of Ireland's worthies—when round the hospitable board of Brophy sat Griffin, Bishop of Limerick, Dean Butler, Lord Rossmore, O'Donovan and O'Curry, the great Celtic scholars—Mortimer O'Sullivan and Father Tom Maguire, opponents in controversy, but friends socially ; Frank Thorpe Porter, Edmund Casey, D.L., Dr. Tisdall and, occasionally, the present writer. The *Noctes* spent round Brophy's table, though sometimes stormy, were starry, and, as such, were nights to be remembered.

dentist, a perfect cyclopædia of anecdote, was frequently put under contribution by Lever. The incident in " Lorrequer " of the officer coming on parade without remembering to wash the black off his face which had made him a capital Othello at private theatricals the previous night, really happened to Captain Frizelle, an ancestor of the present writer's family.

" Baby Blake," famous for her light-hearted gaiety, high courage, womanly tenderness, and native fun in " O'Malley," found her original in Miss French of Moneyroe, near Castle Blakeney, who followed the hounds over five-barred gates—not the lady known by this sobriquet in Dublin previous to the publication of " O'Malley." " Frank Webber," whose veracious adventures proved profitable stock-in-trade to Lever, was Robert Boyle, as his own family assure us. But his real name is not disclosed in the professedly explanatory introduction to " O'Malley." One incident, however, of which Webber is made the hero, is due to our late friend Dr. Seward, whose ventriloquial hoax will be remembered. Lever found the adventures of Webber succeed so well that, as he tells McGlashan, he had some thoughts of making him the hero of a distinct book, to be called " Frank Webber."

To McGlashan, he said, during the progress of " O'Malley " that in Brussels he was as on a desolate island, and neither knew nor heard of books. To supply fuel to the flame he sent Lever a few stories which he had picked up. Colonel B——, Grand Master of the Orange

Society, of whom a memoir appeared in the magazine, enjoyed the reputation of a *bon raconteur* ; but Lever, on examining some of his stories, declared that it would need a cleverer fellow than he to convert such "lead into gold."

He preferred a request that McGlashan could not possibly entertain. He asked for a month's vacation after volume one should have been out—and to suspend for a short time the publication of the second, thus gaining time to glean and arrange fresh material for "O'Malley." The Scot knew Lever better than to agree to this proposal; he would as soon think seriously of suspending payment. Lever never did anything well which he took much time to study and mature. His best hits were those which came from him in rapid, electrical strokes. Lever was always apt to weary of his own characters, and often felt tempted to bow the company out at the first convenient opportunity. But more than once he told McGlashan not to let this caprice or unceremoniousness influence *him*, but command if he wished that the characters be longer retained. Again and again, his confidence in the vitality of the characters would be shaken. Were the public content to go on with O'Malley's galloping career for another heat as long as the first, or were they blown? McGlashan knew them better than the author, who was surrounded far more by the persons of his book than the readers of it. Lever was convinced by the force of his own argument, but was ready, like a true Irishman, to "hear rayson."

Again, he feared that eleven numbers of blood and battles was a bold experiment—but then he could close whenever he found the public sleepy.

One day a shell burst which threw all ideal ones into the shade. His banker failed. But Lever learned, when too late, that the number of English in Brussels without anything but debts made banking speculation there something like *Rouge et Noir.* Worst of all, he complained of having been shamefully tricked by persons of the first rank, including a viscount who juggled him out of £160. He wished greatly to visit Ireland, and said he needs must go even though he should consult Jews * about it—of whom, he said with a sigh, he knew much more than his brother, though he preached about them.

To Erin he accordingly steered his course—conferred with Phiz in London, dined with Lord Charleville—and complained that some heartless man awoke him in the Holyhead boat to return thanks for his health which had been drunk by a dozen ill-looking fellows at the table—the said man turning out to be Pierce Egan—and leading to the reflection that letters like poverty puts one to bed with strange company.

McGlashan used to pay him in bills at two, three, and four months. One day he asked him to let him have not what Freney † prayed for, " A long day my lord," but the shortest his convenience could compass—

* The sixteenth chapter of " Roland Cashel" graphically describes an interview with one of the fraternity : the effect of which is enhanced by the sharp pencil of Phiz.

† A noted highwayman—introduced into " the Knight of Gywnne."

for they had not in Brussels that estimable Scotch system
of banking, McGlashan loved to laud—"but a most palpable and d——ble robbery—to which stopping the mail
was only petty larceny in comparison." McGlashan's
final arrangement with Lever was £60 per part, of 32
pp., with a *carte blanche* as to their number. For
"Jack Hinton," still better terms were obtained.

Some of the London publishers made overtures to the
young author, about this time; and he took an opportunity of very quietly letting McGlashan know that
Mr. Bentley was wooing him, while Colburn ogled for a
new book, about something funny—which Colburn knew
not, and added Lever, "I'll be hanged if I do either."

In 1839, Mr. Bentley asked Lever to contribute
papers to his "Miscellany." Lever acquiesced, saying
that the publisher was not obliged to publish them
collectedly, or even to continue them any longer than
he liked, and not amenable to the innkeeper's law—
that having uncorked the bottle he must pay for the
wine. In the following year their correspondence was
renewed. Mr. Bentley offered him £400 for a story in 3
vols. In reply, Lever proposed to write twelve numbers,
of 32 pp. each, for £500—ten numbers like "Nickleby"
being about equal to 3 vols.—so that, at £40 per number,
it was Mr. Bentley's original proposal extended *plus*
£20 for Lever's pains and the discovery. He apologised
for dictating the mode of publication, but asked him to
remember it was pardonable in a parent to discuss the
costume of his own bantling—an example set by Tristram

Shandy's father. Lever was averse to publication in three volumes, and tried to impress upon Mr. Bentley the advantage an author wields in watching what characters and incidents tell best with his readers—in fact, as the French proverb has it, "*Pour saisonner la soupe en mangeant!*"

Lever was of opinion that he could not, without protracting it to undue length, extend the action of the story to Waterloo, as McGlashan wished. He reminded him that four numbers alone had been devoted to the year 1809, which threatened to make the work as long in proportion as "Chevy Chase," and run to 80 numbers, and he made a simile about Lord Nugent following the fox while dogs, huntsmen and whipper-in had gone home to dinner! By rushing over the intervening space, Lever feared that the unity of the whole would be damaged. Would the advantages be commensurate with the probable weariness of his readers? McGlashan argued him out of his doubts—and Lever finally exclaimed, "D—— the unities; ye gods, annihilate both time and space, and make O'Malley twenty!"

Months elapsed—his pen flew—and McGlashan was at last apprised that all kinds of material had been gathered for the "catastrophical number"—and even the Duke would be astonished by his account of Waterloo!

Lever's Irish readers specially liked his battle-scenes; and more than one newspaper was sent to him urging him to go on in the same vein. In reply, he promised them lots of blood and wounds, with three days' fighting

at Talavera, and as the newspapers had taken to cater
for his readers, he expressed himself ready to cook the
prog. His only doubt being, had they not enough
already? But he feared that the public taste in Ireland
for this kind of fare, was like Mick Malone's request at
Lord Louth's dinner, " Corn beef, corn beef!" to the end
of the repast; he knew no other dish, and was resolved
to be safe in his demand. On this point Lever conferred
fully with McGlashan, who quite approved of the suggestion, adding that whatever both might think of the
bad taste, they would not blab, but keep their secret a
few numbers longer, and then laugh at them heartily
some jolly evening over a flask of real Hermitage. The
wisdom of the Irish criticism was proved eventually
in "Tom Burke;" both were glad to recur to the god of
battles; and a fly-leaf withdrawn from later editions
displayed the following lines :—

> " The march, the muster and the night
>   Around the bivouac—
> The columns moving to the fight,
>   The hot and fierce attack.
> The cheering charge, the storming cry,
>   The pealing thunder's roar,
> That rings from red artillery,
>   O'er fields of blood and gore."

On different days during his sojourn in Dublin, Lever
would drop into the hall of the Four Courts, and gather
from the knots of barristers who thronged it material
for his forthcoming number. One day the novelist
joined a group of pleasant talkers with memories much
better stocked than their bags, and in the midst of whom

our informant, Mr. Porter, stood narrating how in passing through Tralee a short time before, he called to see an old friend, Mr. Roche, stipendiary magistrate there, whose servant when very ill said, " Oh masther, I don't think that is a right sort of a docthur who is attending me, for though he gave me two medicines that he called emetics, neither the one nor the other would rest on my stomach." In the following number of " Charles O'Malley," Mr. Porter recognised the anecdote put into the mouth of Mickey Free.*

Lever passed some weeks pleasantly in Dublin, and on the eve of his departure the old members of the Burschen Club gave him a dinner at Kingstown, which he pronounced a great success. He described his journey back to London as the pleasantest he had ever made. Their coach party, he said, consisted of Serjeant, afterwards Chief Justice Lefroy, Mr. Isaac Butt, the Right Honourable Frederick Shaw, member for the University, and subsequently Recorder, and Mr. Henry West, Q.C., Lever's schoolfellow at Wright's Academy. Lever describing the journey said that they laughed from Liverpool to Euston Square.

Mr. Butt has preserved a vivid recollection of this pleasant journey, and tells us that the only man ever

---

* Judge Longfield observed a similar reproduction. He happened to be present with Lever when Dr. Woodroofe from Cork told Mr. Butt of a man who made freemason's signs to a French soldier and escaped, just as he was on the point of being put to the sword like his companions. Dr. Longfield observed Lever listening attentively, and soon after recognised the story with full details in " Tom Burke."

known to make the pious Serjeant Lefroy laugh was Lever. His stories kept them in continued paroxysms of laughter; while previously he had shown himself not less good-natured than efficient in preserving the party from the penalties of sea-sickness.*

On this occasion Lever had a capital opportunity of making a study of Lefroy. This eminent person sat to him for thirty-six hours; and long after we find Lever in "Sir Brook Fosbrook," depicting with more than ordinarily nice attention to detail and finish—the old Chief Justice of the Queen's Bench.

The excitement attendant on the trip to Ireland was followed by reaction; and a violent attack of gout swelled every joint. Perhaps the sharpest sting was the thought that his feet—of which he had the prettiest —would be permanently enlarged. "What is the nicest thing in boots?" somebody once asked, and to which Mrs. Lever answered, "My husband's foot."

Soon after his return to Brussels he described himself as unable to walk or ride, with spirits greatly depressed, but he declared that an encouraging letter of praise he had just received had done him more good than all his colchicum, and as an anti-gout specific he would begin to try flattery among his patients.

---

* "I perfectly remember the journey and the companions of it," writes Mr. West (Sept. 3rd, 1878). "It can only be called a coach journey, in this sense, that as the railway was not finished all the way up to London, we coached from Rugby to some finished portion of the line. Shaw mentioned was the Recorder, who had some very different passages with Butt some years afterwards."

He begged of his publisher to continue to send friendly notices; the horse leeches of praise cried " Give, give," and his " maw " was insatiable; but he had painful misgivings that his appetite would not last, and the supply might fail. He had, as he said, the knottiest knuckles in Belgium, and was driven to try dictation, but he complained that it cost as much fatigue as the personal effort at writing. He described himself at different times as covered with leeches, and once he praised them for behaving like trumps, or O'Malley's career would certainly have closed at Talavera! No wonder, therefore, that in June, 1841, he should have lost two stone of flesh.* A gouty cough tore his frame and destroyed his rest—but, he said, what annoyed him most was that that old villain Monsoon, after fifty years of every excess under heaven, was laughing at him without pain or ache in his old wine-skin.

This man Sir W. Wilde described to us, on the occasion that Lever asked him to meet Monsoon, as " indulging in paroxysms of maudlin piety." We were, therefore, not surprised to find that he called on Lever soon after, to consult upon a work on religious subjects—and Lever

* His good-nature often led him to exert himself when ill able for the effort. Mr. Quinlan, well known in connection with the liberal press of Dublin, when passing through Brussels *en route* to Germany found, on Saturday, that he was too late to obtain the indispensable formula of a passport, and should wait until the following Monday ere it could be procured. This delay would seriously inconvenience him; but he thought of his good-natured countryman and, though personally unknown, wrote to solicit his aid. To his surprise he received by a diplomatic messenger on Sunday, the passport duly perfected.

jokingly wrote to McGlashan to ask him if "Monsoon on the Prophecies" would lie in his way. Lever's plan was to introduce him again in "Our Mess," in connection with the American war—Monsoon having been governor of Annersburgh during the siege—so that, if he found it expedient the major might quote Solomon in another hemisphere, but Lever luckily relinquished the risk of a twice-told tale.

Though scrupulous in small things Monsoon practised kleptomania on a monster scale. "When the British entered a town," said Lever to Hayman, "the Commissary General hastened to the nearest church and appropriated whatever plate or costly reliquaries he could seize. He had once a narrow escape from hanging, after having actually undergone a drum-head court martial; and thenceforth he abandoned his evil courses. When the Allied Armies entered Paris, Wellington was of course the constant figure of attraction. At a grand *fête* he took wine (or went through the form of it) with any officer whose face was remembered by him. The Commissary M—— was a guest at this entertainment, and Wellington's eye rested on him. Up went the hand and glass as a signal, and bows were well nigh exchanged, when thundered out the Duke, 'Oh, I thought I had hanged you at Badajos. Never mind, I'll do it next time. I drink your health!'"

In different petty ways his patience was tried. Sometimes we find his proofs following his Excellency the Ambassador, Sir H. Seymour, through the Highlands and enjoying the sports of the season at the Duke of Athol's. Sometimes he would complain that a " she devil " of a housemaid committed savage murders, and often made an *auto da fé* of such inflammable material as Monsoon's escapades. Anon he got a panic lest the American Minister, who brought to Ireland for him a sheaf of MS., had carelessly executed his trust in pique for an attack on the Yankees which Lever had written.

The new Postage Bill of Rowland Hill in 1841, at last closed the embassy bag to Lever, and while a contemporary rejoiced that,

> From John O'Groats to England's end,
> From Norfolk to Kilkenny,
> A letter now might reach a friend,
> And only costs a penny,

Lever thoroughly anathematised a public boon which had the effect of costing him henceforth £3 a week. He complained that every bore who could handle a pen plagued and regarded him as a kind of general agent for providing governesses, French maids, chaplaincies, and smuggled laces—besides being obliged to answer all questions as to prices of beef, tea, pork, and potatoes, with a summary of the climate, seasons, and habits of the Continent—closing all with an apology for the immorality of its customs to every fusty old maid that ever longed for the chances of a general war.

In 1841 we find him in treaty with Mr. Bentley for a book on Continental life—viewed in its more humorous phases—and Lever made arrangements for a ramble about Germany, to serve as a refresher upon old acquaintance — but characters not cathedrals — cockneys not churches—patlanders and not pictures—constituted his project, which, however, was never carried out. Another contemplated book was the "Campaigns of Hannibal, by his aide-de-camp Terence McHale."

At the last moment new difficulties beset him. He found that the 14th never was at Waterloo—and he told McGlashan he felt strongly disposed to finish with Toulouse and keep the 18th of June for "Our Mess." This idea McGlashan overruled, and "O'Malley" effectively ended with Waterloo and the Duchess of Richmond's Ball. Thackeray liked the effect so well that he adopted the same plan in "Vanity Fair."

McGlashan had a musical ear. Some of the songs Lever used to make him sing as a sort of experimental rehearsal. About this time he begged the worthy publisher to practise himself in the air of Paddy O'Carroll, as he had a song for that tune ready for a coming number.

Bad luck to this marching,
Pipe-claying and starching,
How neat one must be to be killed by the French !
I'm sick of parading
Through wet and cowld wading,
Or standing all night to be shot in a trench !
To the tune of a fife
They dispose of your life,
You surrender your soul to some illigant lilt ;
Now I like Garryowen,
When I hear it at home,
But it's not half so sweet when you're going to be kilt !

Sparkled by song and story " O'Malley " went ahead. Of the songs a critic truly observed " it is almost impossible to read them without singing them, and almost impossible to hear them sung without wishing to fight, drink, or dance." But this sort of thing could not go on for ever. At last he sent McGlashan word to keep open some pages for a grand finale—and then "Hurrah for Jack Hinton ! "

Lever tried to obtain the Duke of Wellington's consent to dedicate " O'Malley " to him—but could only succeed in procuring that of his son Lord Douro. To him, therefore, was inscribed " his attempt to picture forth the most brilliant period of his country's history to the son of him who gave that era its glory, and as a souvenir of many delightful hours long since passed in his society."

It was important that McGlashan and Lever should hold a personal conference in reference to the *dramatis personæ* of the new book; and one day the publisher arrived by the Antwerp steamer, met Monsoon at dinner, and with Lever as guide, visited Bruges.

Among other pleasant threats, he said that if Mr. Orr kept him waiting for his proofs of Jack, as he did of Charley, he would go down to St. Gudules and curse him if he had to turn Papist to do it. Later on he complained that the printers had made a sad mess of " Our Mess."

For ceaseless action and high pressure " O'Malley " had no parallel : few would believe that it was written

with the knottiest knuckles in Belgium, as he assured
McGlashan. The breath of the critic was taken away
in the whirlwind; luckily he had no time to cavil;
and when he got to the end he found little to complain
of unless the soreness of his sides from laughing. A
larger debt of gratitude is due for Lever's labours in
producing hilarity than might, at first sight, appear.
Just as he himself often sat down to write in bad
spirits, from which he gradually rose, in how many
thousand cases has he not relieved, by laughter, the
solitude of the hermit, or the gloom of the hypo-
chondriac? The old novelist, Richardson, speaking of
his levity, says—and the same thought, refined through
the medium of Byron's mind, occurs in Don Juan—"I
struggle and try to buffet down my cruel reflections as
they rise; and when I cannot, I am forced to try to
make myself laugh, that I may not cry; for one or
other I must do: and is it not philosophy carried to
the highest pitch, for a man to conquer such tumults of
soul as I am sometimes agitated by, and, in the very
height of the storm, to be able to quaver out an *horse
laugh?*"

That "O'Malley" made its way without the aid of
reviewers, is shown in the poverty of the "opinions"
which the publisher gathered for his advertisement.
They are cited from a few obscure provincial prints—
one line from the "Standard" being the only metro-
politan utterance. "I would rather," says Dr. Johnson, "be attacked than unnoticed. For the worst thing

you can do to an author is to be silent as to his works. An assault upon a town is a bad thing, but starving it is still worse."

The superfine reviews cut the rollicking Irishman; but it was truly confessed by the greatest critic of our time, Macaulay, that "the place of books in the public estimation is fixed not by what is written about them but by what is written of them."

In America "O'Malley" did not, at first, fare much better than at home. Edgar Allen Poe reviewed it severely, but he began by saying that in point of popularity "it surpassed even the inimitable compositions of Mr. Dickens." He argued that a book may be exceedingly popular without any high literary merit.* Howard, however, has said that "in proportion as a work rises in the scale of intellect it must necessarily become limited in the number of its admirers. For this reason the judicious artist, even in his loftiest

---

* Poe went on to complain that we hear too much of "devilled kidneys" —that some of Lever's best stories were spoiled by "exaggerating anticipation respecting them;" that we have perpetually *eat*, the present, for *ate*, the perfect; and pronounces as a meaningless affectation the word *L'Envoy*, which is made the heading of two prefaces. Poe remarked that "in the story proper are repetitions without end; that the hero saves the life of his mistress twice, and of her father twice"—but had he known the difficulties under which the book was written, greater charity would doubtless have been shown. The enterprise noticed by Poe gave offence in Galway. An election mob is described frightening the horses of Sir George Dashwood, the unpopular candidate, whereby Lucy Dashwood was hurled into the river, and rescued by our light dragoon. Dr. Maginn mutters in "Fraser" *apropos* of this—"I' faith, doctor, I would not like to be in your b——s if ever they should visit Connaught. The air of Galway is too keen, even in fancy for Lever. It has something like an intoxicating effect upon him."

efforts, will endeavour to introduce some of those qualities which are interesting to all, as a passport for those of a more intellectual character."

America regarded " Lorrequer " and " O'Malley " somewhat in the light of " Cocktails " and " Smashers." The piquancy and exhilaration of both books pleased brother Jonathan. Near forty years have since elapsed, and like Waterloo Port, " O'Malley " seems to have richly mellowed to his taste. Fourteen Editions of it lie before us. " What a romance! " exclaims a recent voice from New York. " The high-spirited lad who leads his rival to the jaws of the grave in the hunting field, and follows him in a ride of death against the unbroken front of Cambronne's battalions on the blood-stained field of Waterloo! What a picture of old Peninsular days! What portraits of Napoleon, of the 'Iron Duke,' the gallant Picton, and his great captains! What glimpses of dark-eyed senoritas and haughty hidalgos; of lion-hearted sons of Erin charging to the cry of Faugh-a-ballagh, and leading forlorn hopes with saucy jokes upon their laughing lips."

Lever when starting forth on the mission of life felt within him an inexhaustible spring of fun and buoyancy, and he had, as he tells us, an impression that Englishmen too often " laboured under a sad-coloured temperament, took depressing views of life, and were proportionately grateful to anyone who would rally them, even passingly, out of their despondency, and give them a laugh without much trouble in going to look for it."

Our Doctor was right in his diagnosis. Dyspepsia with its attendant gloom—the penalties usually of repletion in diet—have long been the besetting disease of England; and it is well known to the faculty that laughter aids digestion quite as much as gastric juice. He once said that his buoyant tone was prompted by reasons more intelligible to a physician than to a publisher. Indeed our Doctor would appear to have regarded "Fun" as a great hygienic agent; and in adopting views befitting a man of progress he energetically put his own shoulder to the wheel. His medical studies had made him acquainted with cases of danger and difficulty in which laughter led to complete recovery. They are not without interest; and, but for the objection of digressiveness, might be effectively marshalled here.

Lever reluctantly yielded to McGlashan's wish that a portrait should be appended to his new book; but modestly urged that, if given at all, he should be put in a quiet vignette and mounted on a cob. McGlashan thought otherwise, and sent over Sam Lover to paint him on ivory. When it was completed he declared that the artist had flattered him, but that as he was to be presented to the public it was perhaps only fair to put the best face on the matter.

At the same time that Sam Lover was sent to Brussels to take the likeness of the successful author, Mr. Hablot Knight Browne received an invitation, which he accepted, to accompany him. The object of this visit of "Phiz" was to confer with Lever in reference to the illustrations intended for "Jack Hinton." Lever described his throng of characters as they may be said to have remained in the green-room of his Irish fancy preparatory to "coming on," and "Phiz" made sketches of them under Lever's eye. The latter informed McGlashan that "Phiz" was disposed to take much more pains with them than those in "O'Malley," and both artist and author were quite in heart about them.

Samuel Lover wrote home a wonderful description of their "orgies" at Lever's house. They laughed themselves sick over Monsoon, who dined there daily. They held an installation of the Knights of Alcantara, Lover, Lever, and "Phiz," being made Grand Crosses of the Order, with music, procession, and a grand ballet to conclude: they did nothing all day, or, in some instances, all night, but eat, drink, and laugh.*

Lever finally begged of "Phiz" to go over with him to Dublin, and see "Paddy au naturel," not that wretched

* Monsoon proved a source of irresistible amusement. An attempt at revolt took place at Brussels in 1841, and Monsoon told them that he waited upon the Minister at War to say that, from secret information which had reached him, he was to be one of the first victims of the revolution—his known attachment to King Leopold, and the affection that he and his always maintained towards him and the reigning family marking him for the dagger of the assassin. Outrage to "Madame et les Mademoiselles" were included in the picture, and the old Minister actually reported all he had heard to the King, who, however, was far too deep for that sort of thing, and Monsoon received neither the cross, nor even an invitation to dinner—and expressed his fury freely, the story having got abroad—adding, that there was a decided deal more in the plot than they thought, but that Leopold was but a poor kind of fellow after all, and one would not wonder if they sent him packing !

misrepresentation of him—*au sauce piquante de St. Giles* that London offers. His constant effort was to restrain "Phiz" from caricaturing his countrymen—and he used to say that his reputation for travestie, for which S. C. Hall and others attacked him, was due to "Phiz."

At the Belgian Court Lever made an imposing figure, wearing the borrowed plumage of a commanding officer, and more silver lace, he confesses, than the regulation ever contemplated. The King was on the most friendly terms with him, and would sometimes discourse with him for half an hour, as he tells us, on the exploits of O'Malley or Lorrequer.

Lever was now pretty generally recognised as the Marryat of Land; but, like the Captain, his pen occasionally slipped. For instance, he makes the dashing dragoon a Roman Catholic, forgetting that his uncle, Godfrey O'Malley, M.P. for Galway, of whom we hear so much, could not have sat in the Irish Parliament if a member of the proscribed creed.

The opinions of friends he had been always anxious to elicit. When he came to correct the numbers in proof the matter often struck him as tame, but he declared that so tired of the details was he before they appeared in print, that all judgment on his own part was out of the question.

McGlashan was immensely proud of the success of "O'Malley," and at last wrote with thorough *abandon*, to say so. Lever, in reply, said that if he had a glass of champagne left (they had finished nine dozen in the sixteen days Lover and "Phiz" spent with him) he would drink the health of Jemmy McGlashan. For the first time he felt that "Phiz" and himself had become sworn allies—having arranged on an admirable footing all their future operations.

Liston, when greatly out of spirits, once presented himself before Abernethy. "The physic I prescribe," said the Doctor, "is, go and see Liston to-night, and take my word for it, you must laugh." "Alas!" was the reply, "I am that hapless man myself." All the while that Lever's farcical performances were appearing he also suffered periodically from depression, as numerous confessions from his own pen prove. When he thought himself in vein, he wrote for very many hours without stopping, not knowing when the good day might again come. Like Moore, who sang, "Think not my spirits are always so light," Lever had his hours of reaction too.

When McGlashan did not answer his letters he was racked by suspense and torn by doubts. Once he told him that any longer silence on his part would cost him a pint of colchicum, and a rivulet full of gorged leeches! It is known that the late Lord Derby finally succumbed not to his old enemy the gout, but to the depressing influence of the colchicum which was administered to eject it. There can be no doubt that to the same cause we may ascribe much of that periodic prostration to which Lever often refers in his letters. Colchicum, formerly regarded as a specific for gout,

is now falling fast into disrepute and disuse. His
exhaustion at times made him fly to the brisk and
evanescent stimulus of champagne; but while relieving
gloom, he was sowing fresh gout in his system.

His invaluable treatment for sickness was that of
Sangrado in "Gil Blas." Copious bleeding reduced
the man rather than the local ills which teased him.
That he should have bowed to the barbarous system of
the day amazes us. The faculty, wiser now, regard the
blood as the life. Their statistics show that up to the
year 1839, 1,000,000 leeches were supplied yearly to
the Parisian hospitals, which during the last twelve
years the annual supply has been only 50,000.

To Mr. Hayman, three years later, he described himself
as trying to cool a hot head by phlebotomy; but cerebral
pain seems to have been much increased by that deple-
tion. When Dickens complained of a "hot head," he
rushed off for a walk at dusk, and tried to cool it by
contact with the night wind. Neither treatment proved
very successful. Probably the best way to avoid such
penalties is never to overtask the fragile machinery of
the brain.

Pleasant as he found the composition of "O'Malley,"
and profitable as it proved, its publication was attended
by results still more gratifying. Lever, like Goldsmith,
had a brother in the Church, and to this good clergyman a letter was one day forwarded, the grateful expression of a mother, who said, "I am the widow of a field
officer, and with an only son for whom I obtained a

presentation to Woolwich; but seeing in my boy's nature certain traits of nervousness and timidity, which induced me to hesitate on embarking him in the career of a soldier, I became very unhappy, and uncertain which course to decide on.

"While in this state of uncertainty, I chanced to make him a birthday present of 'Charles O'Malley,' the reading of which seemed to act like a charm on his whole character, inspiring him with a passion for movement and adventure, and spiriting him to an eager desire for a military life. Seeing that this was no passing enthusiasm, but a decided and determined bent, I accepted the cadetship for him; and his career has been not alone distinguished as a student, but one which has marked him out for an almost hare-brained courage, and for a dash and heroism that give high promise for his future. Thank your brother for me," wrote she, "a mother's thanks for the welfare of an only son, and say how I wish that my best wishes for him and his could recompense him for what I owe him."

Old general officers as well as beardless striplings felt the influence of this fascination. Sir. W. Napier is the personage meant by Lever when he wrote: "No small satisfaction has it been to me occasionally to hear that out of the over-abundance of my own buoyancy and lightheartedness—and I had a great deal of both long ago—I have been able to share with my neighbour, and given him part of my sunshine, and only felt the warmer myself. A great writer—one of the most eloquent historians who ever illustrated the military achievements of his country—once told me that, as he lay sick and care-worn after a fever, it was in my reckless stories of soldier life he found the cheeriest moments of his solitude ; and now let me hasten to say that I tell this in no spirit of boastfulness, but with the heartfelt gratitude of one who gained more by hearing that confession, than Harry Lorrequer ever acquired by all his own."

We have seen with what misgivings he introduced so many battles into " O'Malley ; " but when he remembered the passion of the Irish people—of both sexes—for witnessing sham battles and reviews, despite the drawback of that sudden downpour with which the proverbially moist climate rarely fails to saturate fashionable finery—he felt that he erred on the safe side. In his pictures of battle fields Lever seemed a little Livy. Readers are hurried on like the men who follow an inspiring commander, thrilled with expectation. A few mistakes he certainly made, pardonable in one who knew more of the lancet than of the sword. He speaks of " fixed bayonets ! " forgetting that they are always fixed from the moment the tug of war begins. He was also twitted for not having the fear of Æschylus before his eyes, and for constantly using such phrases as " withering volley." *

---

* A critic caustically said that, notwithstanding the display of university and military experience in " O'Malley," the author could not possibly be either a Trinity College man or a soldier. To this he replied in print, that

The Rev. John Lever was much pleased with the termination of "O'Malley." The battle he pronounced magnificent, and he recognised the judiciousness of winding up at once, as anything after this would have been as dull as a family party, after the guests had taken leave.

Lord Combermere declared that his narrative of the Douro was like the statement of an eye witness—as indeed it was, having been written from the oral description of Lord Londonderry. As to the duke he was perhaps more puzzled than pleased.

"One day, at Apsley House," writes the Rev. Samuel Hayman in one of his letters, brimful of recollections, "the Duke was seated in a window recess reading 'O'Malley,' and in another part of the room was his son, the Marquis of Douro, who overheard him, saying: 'Good! but where did the fellow (*i.e.*, the author,) get that story? 'Tis not in the histories, nor in the despatches; nor could anyone know of it unless he was present.' Mayne, or as he is styled in the book,

"he held both a degree and a commission," volunteering no information as to the source of either. A lengthy correspondence passed between the present writer and the Secretary of State for War, who finally referred us to the Chief Secretary's office, Dublin Castle, but neither could furnish the name of the Regiment in which Lever held a commission. From Colonel Sir R. Stewart, he received his appointment to the Derry militia; but we doubt if he were once called out for training. Funnily enough, he said to an inquisitive friend who wished to know how the marvellously military tone of "O'Malley" was derived : "Unde derivatur Miles" ? and which he freely translated, "In the Derry Militia !" The questions for examination were, at that time, put in Latin, and always began "Unde derivatur:" and Lever wished to show that he was conversant with university practices.

Monsoon, was present, and hence the freshness of the incident.

Notwithstanding the inconvenience attending the introduction of real names, he continued this habit to the last.

"Writing rapidly," as he says, "and with details derived from books, and a variety of anecdotic matter communicated by friends, it is not, perhaps, to be wondered at if I was often unable to determine what was historical fact, and what merely traditionary gossip. In the same way I became confused about proper names, and actually hit upon real names where I fervently believed I was inventing."

Just as a real Ichabod Crane once remonstrated with Washington Irving on the liberty he had taken to use his name in fiction, a similar incident befell Lever in writing "Tom Burke." "In my sketch of a French duellist, I had set down some traits by no means flattering or attractive. To this character I gave the name of Amedee Pichot, most conscientiously believing that I had invented that name as well as every other incident about him. What was my surprise on my return home after some weeks' absence, to discover a note addressed to me, along with a card of Amedee Pichot, the note being a courteous assurance that he was not a dangerous swordsman, but a very quietly disposed man of peaceful pursuits, and the editor of the 'Revue Britanique,' at Paris."

Beamish of Cork, who played so amusing a part on

Lever's canvas, is broadly stated by "Fraser" of the day to pourtray the then M.P. for Cork, and whose name was Beamish; but the similitude was quite superficial. Our author in like manner describes Powers, O'Gradys, Dillons, de Veres, Bodkins, Considines, O'Flahertys, Dalys, Frenches, Mahons, Martins,* and Ulick Burkes in Galway, to say nothing of "Burke of Ours," and a family named Bellew, who received the honour of a baronetcy. And when he sang

> "'Tis said the Blakes
> Are no great shakes,"

half Galway vowed he had vast impudence. Then again, the successful aspirant to the hand of Widow Malone is one Lucius O'Brien—

> "From Clare—how quare,
> 'Tis little for blushing they care,
> > Down there !"

And as to O'Shaughnessy, who runs through the entire novel of "O'Malley," his "ancestry were Kings of Ennis in the time of Nero, and he was only waiting for a trifle of money to revive the title." Even the rare cognomen

---

* "No man," saith the proverb, "is a hero to his own valet." It must be taken, however, not always literally, for, as Mr. Hubert Burke writes, "Many of the scenes in 'O'Malley' were furnished in substance by a man named William Murray, who had been valet to Colonel Martin for thirty-three years." A subsequent novel was entitled and specially devoted to "the Martins." Of his fine character of Mary Martin, a Galway lady, Lever found it necessary to state in a final manifesto, that it was fictitious —a declaration the more necessary, "since there was once a young lady," he writes, "of this very name—many traits of whose affection for the people and efforts for their wellbeing might be supposed to have been my original."

borne by "The Lion of the Fold of Judah," as O'Connell called him, proved not sacred.

> " His ancestors were kings before Moses was born ;
> His mother descended from great Grana Uaile ;
> He laughed all the Blakes and the Frenches to scorn,
> They were mushrooms compared to old Larry M'Hale."

A tone of more dignity and repose with a greater breadth of colouring gradually overspread the canvas on which his touches fell.

The real names so freely introduced did no harm in the end ; they helped to make the characters a reality. They possess in truth a robustness, and will live with a vitality not often met with in fiction; there is less sham about them than many men one meets. Lever's characters we regard not as contemporaries only, but as real friends. They seem full of flesh, muscle, and animal spirits ; we feel that we knew them, and experienced the pressure of their warm hands, the exhilaration of their wine, and the charm of their talk. The girls they loved, we love ; we share the excitement of the battles they fought. Somebody said that a reperusal of "Lorrequer" and "O'Malley" was like reading one's old love letters, or hearing a friend recount the frolics of one's own youth.

It has been objected by some of Lever's earlier admirers, including Miss Mitford, that the style and matter of his later novels exhibit a striking change of tone. They are more thoughtful, more dignified, and display less trace of that idiosyncrasy which led

Thackeray to call him "Harry Jolly-cur," and on another occasion "Rollicker." There is less of farce and more of moral force about them. From having been a votary of Anacreon he became a warm appreciator of Horace. Though Lever, until chilled by approaching death, never lost his strong flow of animal spirits, he appears in his later books a sadder and a wiser man. In this thorough change of tone he showed good taste and some will say good sense, while making at the same time atonement for the occasional laxity of early exuberance.

Mr. F. N. Keane describes Lever in 1832 as "nervous and retiring." Lever, addressing his publisher, seven years later, begs of him to keep up his pluck and to stimulate his activity, and we find the same prayer perpetually preferred throughout the progress of "O'Malley" and "Hinton." In November, 1840, he is "so nervous" that McGlashan is asked in case the newspapers abuse him not to mention it.

In 1865 he amusingly referred to the mental torture which his sensitive and unseasoned nature had experienced on overhearing the unknown author of "O'Malley" criticised. "It is twenty-one years since I underwent all this, and the suffering is as fresh as if it was yesterday. I remember the very table where they cut me up. I can recall the chair on which I sat to be lacerated. I can bring to mind the drivelling idiot that had got bits of my unhappy production as he thought by heart, and declaimed them, with interpolated bosh of his own, till my reason actually wandered under the infliction."

CHAPTER X.

THE success of " O'Malley " gave Lever courage, and
when asked if he could supply a new story in the same
vein, he replied, " I could give you not one—but *fifty*."
His first thought was to make in the campaign of Napoleon
an Irishman a soldier of France, who would thus have
on his side certain sympathies, which would not readily
attach to a foreigner.   Lever at once surrounded himself
with all the books and papers he could find bearing
upon the Consulate and the Empire; and he lived
entirely amidst the vast events which began at Marengo
and ended at Waterloo.   The magnitude of the theme,
however, overpowered him, and, beyond detached notes,
he had made no progress when the publisher applied to
him for the title of his story with a view to advertise it.

It was in the pleasant days of " Hood's Own " when
that great humorist, under a print of children daub-
ing themselves at a hurried meal of jam, inscribed

" Infantry at Mess," that Lever became familiar with
the phrase. In order to get out of all noise and interruption, so as to arrange material for " Our Mess,"
Lever retired to the quiet hamlet of Terveuren, " but
villanous cooking and a bottle of bad chambertin drove
me rapidly back to Brussels, were, for some time, I
denied myself to all comers, as though my patients were
all Marchands de Vin." Knowing of how much importance it was to an author to have the public with him in
a first number, he strained every nerve to throw as
much movement into it as possible, and also to introduce his characters to their notice favourably. He told
McGlashan that it was not his intention to hurry himself
as heretofore, but rather to let the story unravel itself
gradually—taking more pains to present *striking tableaux
of society and manners*, than, to detail adventures and
recount events. On reading the first proof he preferred
it to "O'Malley"; but, as Phiz had not written a line to
him he was torn by fears lest the illustrations should
have been neglected—Lever was most anxious to get
forward—for, as he told McGlashan, he only worked
well when warm in the harness, and, like a spavined
hack, he stiffened by standing !

In October, 1841, gout again prostrates him ; and he
boasted that he ordered himself no remedy but champagne
—-traces of which, rather than of gout, he hoped would
be found in " Jack Hinton."

Whether our doctor showed his skill in prescribing
champagne to check his gout—the wine which above all

others the faculty now unanimously caution gouty patients to abjure—few will be disposed to admit; but what he lost in his limbs by the indulgence, he more than gained by the accession of that mental vigour which the earlier chapters of " Jack Hinton " specially show. Their buoyancy received aid from a healthier and better source. Ere the month was out, he told a friend that he had " nine miles to ride for his dinner and scarce an hour to do it in."

For the next two months we find him hard at work on " Jack." He declared that the confounded book would drive him clean mad; that he could think or dream of nothing else, and felt, that until he had it finished he should enjoy no rest. He was wise enough to give himself a holiday on completing the third number. Then it was he found himself knocked up by overwork —for, thinking he was in vein, his pen had never paused a moment for three weeks. He still had his joke, and told McGlashan how much he regretted that he had not made some *proviso* with him that in the event of his going mad before " Hinton " was finished, he'd do something for his widow and orphans. All the while his pen flew his wife and children were, as he said, unceasingly before him. Within three weeks she is announced as suffering much in health and spirits, which unhinged Lever in no common degree—and sleepless nights are painfully described. This penalty may be partly due to his confession, that latterly he had relinquished all exercise. Before the year was out we find him correcting in real earnest that fatal tendency to inertia, which, beginning in cobwebs, ends too often in iron chains.

The coveted holiday he desired to spend in Ireland. It was due to him. " Jack" had showed proofs of hard work so far; and he told McGlashan that all work and no play might make Jack a dull boy.

He wished to cross in January, attend the Viceroy's levees, see everything and everybody within a fortnight, and write four numbers which were simmering in his heated head. He asked McGlashan to find out if he could be lodged at the Bilton, or if not at Gresham's, but not to say so even to his brother, who was constantly inculcating upon him the wisdom of economy. He was also very anxious to obtain the candid criticism of Mortimer O'Sullivan on "Jack Hinton," and asked McGlashan to elicit it for himself, without any reference to the author whose feelings O'Sullivan's friendship would lead him to spare. Lever himself thought "Jack" done in better taste, and with more vigour than either of its predecessors. The original idea which suggested it, is found confessed in the following lines—almost the last penned by him—and proves that, though the son of an Englishman, he was Ipsis Hibernicis Hiberniores.

"Some disparaging remarks," he writes, "on Ireland and Irishmen in the London press, not very unfrequent at the time, nor altogether obsolete even now, had provoked me at the moment, and the sudden thought occurred of a reprisal by showing the many instances in which the Englishman would almost of necessity mistake and misjudge my countrymen, and that out of these blunders and misapprehensions situations might arise that, if welded into a story, might be amusing. I know that there was not a class nor a condition in Ireland, which had not marked differences from the correlative rank in England; and that not only the Irish squire, Irish priest, and the Irish peasant, were unlike anything in the larger island, but that the Dublin professional man, the official, and the shopkeeper, had traits essentially their own. I had frequently heard opinions pronounced on Irish habits, which I could easily trace to that habit of my countrymen, who never can deny themselves the enjoyment of playing on the credulity of the traveller—all the more eagerly when they see his note-book taken out to record their shortcomings and absurdities. These thoughts suggested "Jack Hinton"; and led me to turn from my intention to follow the French arms, or rather to postpone the plan, for it had got too strong hold on me to be utterly abandoned."

Had he desired to caricature English ignorance as to Ireland in the person of his Guardsman nothing would have been easier; but Lever preferred merely exposing him to such errors as might throw into stronger relief the peculiarities of Irishmen, and while offering something to laugh at, give no offence to either. When he had got fairly over the ruts at starting, "Jack Hinton" amused him greatly while rattling along, less, he said, by what he recorded, than what he abstained from inditing. "Indeed, I had not at that time exhausted the cask of a buoyancy of temperament, which carried me along through my daily life in the sort of spirit one rides a fresh horse over a swelling sward."*

"Jack Hinton" introduced the famous Father Tom Loftus, drawn from the Rev Michael Comyns, whom Lever had known in Clare. Different opinions have been expressed, as to the general effect of the priest's portrait as sketched by Lever, and somewhat caricatured by Phiz. Some persons, perhaps without sufficient inquiry, and forgetting other effective attitudes imparted to Father Tom, declared that the character had been overdrawn for dramatic effect, and in deference to that party whose traditional prejudices Lever upheld; but allowance should be made for a man of the avowed Lorrequer type, ardently anxious for adventure, and ready to turn to literary account the result of his experiences.

The character of Father Loftus, if we except some undignified expressions at the card-table, is, on the whole, a tolerably correct picture of the traditional

---

* The moment he perceived that his English readers were beginning to tire of Irish scenes and manners, he shifted his ground. "Arthur O'Leary: his Wanderings and Ponderings in many lands," opened a new field for that "fresh horse," full of grace and speed, with which he scampered over the "swelling sward." He cleared difficulties in story-telling with the same ease wherewith he cleared the mule-cart at Coleraine. The hunting field and cavalry charges once more excited and amazed. The example of his heroes was infectious, and led to the breaking of more bones than all the six-foot walls and double ditches from Kilruddery to Galway.

Soggarth aroon. The cruiskeen, so prominently displayed in pictures of him, seems to have been provided rather for the delectation of his guests than for selfish enjoyment. But certainly the weakness is suggested, if not openly imputed, of a disposition to imbibe like the Father Tom of Boucicault's "Colleen Bawn," which that accomplished re-dresser of old character must have borrowed from Lever. Vainly was it represented to Mr. Comyns, that the character of Father Loftus was interesting and even venerable, that the use of stimulants by the Irish clergy was noticed as a characteristic by Giraldus Cambrensis, the great Welsh bishop—who, however, praised them for chastity. It was all to no use; the pastor of Kilkee folded his arms in anger, and refused to give absolution to the author of the "Confessions," who meanwhile continued his genuflexions, but more in the attitude of coaxing than of penitence.*

It was the caricature of the priest by Phiz, flask in hand, rather than the description of him by Lever, which hurt Father Comyns. A copy of it appeared in

---

* A clergyman who officiated in his parish writes : " He was of a large frame, well proportioned, of a manly type of beauty, had a magnificent presence, as playful as a child but a lion in courage. Though very hospitable, yet perhaps no person ever saw him under the influence of spirituous drink. He appeared to entertain some crotchety notions on the working of the poor laws. His idea was that the more paupers were sent to the workhouse the more speedy would be the downfall of landlords, and rather than pay his share of the rates he allowed his kitchen full of bacon to be auctioned away." The value of a strong panegyric upon him, publicly expressed by the fastidious Father Kenyon, may be estimated when we remember that the same priest shortly before had denounced O'Connell while his body remained unburied. Father Comyns died in November, 1853.

showy colours on the cover of the cheap edition ; but a design less sensational has been substituted. Much erroneous impression in regard to Lever's tone is due to the free and pointed pencil of Hablot Browne.

Thackeray nicknamed Lever "Harry Rollicker," from the love he seemed to evince for rollicking adventures. Lever, in a document before us, says, *apropos* of the said illustrations to "Jack Hinton," "Browne's sketches are as usual caricatures, and make my scenes really too riotous and disorderly. The character of my books for uproarious people and incident I owe mainly to Master Phiz."

Lever, as his stories sped, gradually relinquished his favourite figure of the jolly priest. He at last found that the few he had met in remote dioceses were not to be regarded as true types of the body, a confession made in the last preface to "Jack Hinton."

In "Jack Hinton" old historic names and characters were freely worked up,—boiled down in the same crucible with domestic acquaintances.* Sir Boyle

---

* A Tullamore correspondent, the Rev. G. Craig, Rector of Kilbride, writes :—" Some of Lever's novels were written in this house. People have told me that a servant of his brother's was the model of one of his characters, 'the Haythens, the Turks !'" Our correspondent of course alludes to Corney Delany in "Jack Hinton," who is constantly heard muttering this cruel comment. The Tullamore tradition, however, is not quite accurate. On inquiry from Lever's family it appears that the Rev. John Lever's herd, Peter Gill, formed the prototype of one character only, which was introduced by Lever in his last novel, "Lord Kilgobbin" ; and that it was young Charley's nurse, who, having once tumbled down stairs with the child in her arms, and because Mrs. Lever ran first to the aid of her little son, indignantly exclaimed, "the Haythens, the Turks !"

Roche is introduced as Sir Harry Boyle; while a veritable act of Sir Boyle's, exhibiting pistol-bullets as "capital pills to cure a cough," when an attempt was made to cough him down, is adroitly transferred to Daly in the "Knight of Gwynne;" while Beauchamp Bagenal was the prototype of Bagenal Daly,* and not Bowes Daly as some supposed. Curran is not only introduced by name, but is made to utter several of his own "mots," and to sing his famous song, "The Monks of the Screw." This is, we think, an error of taste, for Lever, like Lysaght, could throw off with ease racy original verse. The introduction of Curran at all proved a greater mistake, for when we remember Byron's remark that he heard more poetry from Curran in one night than he had heard, read, or imagined in a lifetime, the wonder only is that Lever should venture on galvanising into artificial life the long-closed lips of the dead wit.

A prominent character in "Jack Hinton" is "Mr. Paul Rooney, of Stephen's Green, Solicitor," and Lever in his preface says that he had not to draw on his imagination for the portrait. According to the traditions of the Irish Law Club, the original of this character was the late P. M——, though we believe Mr. M—— himself seemed unaware of it. The portrait can be viewed only as a clever pen-and-ink sketch, full of dash and freedom, wanting the truth of a photograph

---

* This is evident by referring to Barrington's "Rise and Fall of the Irish Nation," pp. 164–5, original edition.

and the breadth of oils. Mr. M——, a man of mark and weight, had already attached himself to the Liberal interest, and Lever, in depicting the character of Paul Rooney, made it subservient to the advancement of those principles of Conservatism which had fired his writings to a certain point. Tarring and feathering an attorney has been an old species of practical joke in Ireland. This process was accomplished by the brush which dashed off Paul so cruelly, while at the same time cutting his throat with a feather.*

Who would expect to find in an olla-podrida delectable bits cut with strict attention to artistic accuracy? The fact of making Mr. and Mrs. Paul Rooney frequenters of Dublin Castle during the Richmond Viceroyalty in 1810 is one of those anachronisms which Lever never scrupled to commit. The same licence is shown in introducing the "Monks of the Screw," who ceased to exist as a body in 1789. "Tom Burke," following close on the spurred heels of "Jack Hinton," made another historic slip. A fine glimpse is got in Chapter XI. of a procession of public men hurrying to a division at the time of the Union. The carriages of Bingham, Browne, Corry, Toler, Egan, Castlereagh, and Grattan are alternately cheered or hissed as they pass.

---

* One of the best things, however, said to P. M ——, Lever does not tell, though Mr. Pearce often heard him repeat it. The swell society in which Mr. M—— moved led to jealousy; and many efforts were made to take down the pride supposed to be fostered by such privileges. "I dined at the Duke's yesterday," he once said, "and strange to say there was no fish." "Oh, perhaps, they ate it all in the parlour," was the reply of Pat Costello.

"Ha, Broken Beak, there you go!"—"Ha, old Vulture Flood!" is made to greet one in the *cortége*, while from the College ascends on high "three cheers for Flood." Lever forgot that Flood died ten years previously, namely, on December 2nd, 1791. In "Sir Jasper Carew" we find a more serious anachronism with respect to the Duke of Orleans, though a letter to McGlashan seeks to explain it away. But the same blemish might be urged against Shakespeare himself, who, in "King John" and "Macbeth," speaks of cannon, makes Coriolanus a contemporary of Alexander the Great, Cato, and Galen, and, in the "Comedy of Errors," alludes to a clock striking in ancient Ephesus.

Lever was greatly struck by the talk and tact of the Anglo-Irishman, and some critics may consider that we have more than enough of the first. The last introduction to "Jack Hinton," tells us that "Tipperary Joe was a real personage, and that those who remember the old coaching-days between Dublin and Kilkenny will recall the curious figure, clad in a scarlet hunting coat and black velvet cap, who used, between Carlow and the "Royal Oak," to emerge from some field beside the road, and after a trot of a mile or so beside the horses, crawl up at the back of the coach and over the roof, collecting what he called his rent from the passengers; a very humble tribute generally, but the occasion for a good deal of jesting, not diminished if an English traveller were present who could neither comprehend the relations between Joe and the gentlemen nor the marvellous freedom with which this poor ragged fellow discussed the passengers and their opinions."

Lever goes on to say that Joe, rigged in this odd attire, made his way to Dublin for the purpose of visiting him, and claiming money from him on the ground that he had put him in a book.

Tipperary Joe was not the only prototype who claimed "ready money down" for the material presented in the eccentricities of the very character who personally made this strange demand. Burns expressed a hope that God would give mankind the power of seeing themselves as others saw them; but Major Monsoon at least, it will be remembered, was awake to his own absurdities, and needed not that prayer.

Until the last number of "Jack Hinton," the name of Lever as writer of these pleasant books was not disclosed. But Mr. R. Sheehan, the journalist, had previously pulled his visor off, much to his annoyance. In a paper of Lever's, contributed to "The University" in December, 1839, we trace the reasons which had mainly led to previous reticence:—

"Any taste for the fine arts, any leanings to literature, any knowledge of the more graceful accomplishments which render man's social hours lighter to himself, and more agreeable to his friends, are forbidden to the physician, under the heavy penalty of the world's displeasure."

Lever, when he at last revealed his name, had resigned the encouraging smiles, which, as he says, had been so often dispensed as value for a guinea, in favour of the laborious life of a hard-working scribe.

Several letters are preserved from the Rev. John Lever, strongly urging Charles to content himself with putting merely " Harry Lorrequer " on the title page of " Our Mess." He submitted that though the veil be thin, yet it carried mystery in wearing it ; and that the public love to be in possession of the secret of authorship even when the secret is thread-bare. The prudent parson went further, and urged that " the Author " should alone be affixed to his portrait—leaving the riddle to the sons of Œdipus. And in another letter he is reminded that the concluding words in " O'Malley " intimate a desire of preserving his incognito. John Lever expressed anxiety that the portrait in preparation should be a good one; and specially hoped that the artist, Lover, himself a poet, would not make him too poetical. He urges him to take special care in spelling French words, and adds that it was oversights of this sort which gave the reviewers such an awful handle against Lady Morgan. All this time he was working very hard, and from his brother's letters we gather at the rate of six hours per diem.

Midwinter brought to Lever an invitation from Mr. Bentley to connect himself with his " Miscellany," Harrison Ainsworth, who succeeded Dickens as editor, having quarrelled with him, and retired to set up for himself. This proposal stimulated a plan which Lever had been revolving in his mind, and one more likely to suit him, namely, to assume the editorial reins of the Irish magazine in which his own stories had been for some years appearing, and to live at Tullamore with his brother. He told McGlashan that he was anxious to realise a feeling strong within him that he could make it go in the winner before "Ebony" and "Fraser" ere two years were out, and that he did not know another pair who could carry out this scheme, while the pay might be an increasing scale with the circulation.

In throwing up his medical practice and appointments he seems to have had something more than a literary vista to tempt him. Major D——, his confidant from boyhood, supplies the secret history of the negotiation. "He had in 1841 taken up his pen in the pages of the 'Dublin University Magazine,' in defence of Lord Eliot, afterwards Lord St. Germains, then recently appointed Irish Secretary, against an attack made on him in the leading Tory organ of Dublin, edited by Remy Sheehan. This led through the British Minister at Brussels to some *pourparlers*, the result of which was that Lever went to Dublin to undertake the editorship of 'Maga.'"

Lever, without explaining the circumstances, refers to the movement in his last introduction to "O'Malley":—

"To do this I was not alone to change my abode and country, but to alter the whole destiny of my life. I was at the time a practising physician attached to the British Legation, with the best practice of any Englishman in the place, a most pleasant society, and, what I valued not less than them all, the intimacy of the most agreeable and companionable man I ever knew in my life, whose friendship I have never ceased to treasure with pride and affection."

This alludes to Sir H. Seymour, Minister Plenipotentiary at Brussels, whose regard for Lever, as expressed to the present writer, was equally strong. The temptation to remain was alluring, but the circumstances were peculiar, and at last led Lever to accept the terms offered by McGlashan.

In sending the vindication of Lord Eliot to the Magazine, he confidentially remarked that it afforded him the double opportunity of correcting a mis-statement, and he hoped of doing a service to one able and willing to acknowledge it. Sir H. Seymour was Eliot's oldest and best friend, and offered valuable aid. Lever promised to add, on receiving a proof, the concluding paragraphs with, he hoped, a semi-official statement of the intentions of the Irish Government. He was in high spirits, and scribbled, "Hurrah for the land of Saints—a private Sec—why not play first fiddle yet?" He would go back to Dublin, and carry on with a stretch of canvas of which the small craft never dreamed.

This article he at the time said, was the only thing he had ever done with which, in every respect, he felt satisfied—but he added that McGlashan was just the man to mutter "It's nothing the better for that!"

Lord Eliot wrote to Sir H. Seymour, expressing his thanks for Lever's advocacy, but added a remark which led Lever to recast what he had written, and eliminate all tone of controversy. He finally submitted the MS. to Dr. Mortimer O'Sullivan, in whose judgment, he said, he had the same faith as in his friendship—adding too sanguinely, that if he could get anything diplomatic, he would not refuse it.

A passage in the paper did not hesitate to express almost as much. The ruling powers were urged "to confer the patronage of the Crown, not on the hungry expectants and infuriated leaders of a faction, but upon those whose lives were as conspicuous for excellence, as their abilities were commanding." The title finally determined on for the paper was "Ireland and her Rulers "—the same name bestowed by Mr. D. O. Maddyn on a work published in the following year.

Lord Eliot, the new Irish Secretary, must have been much pleased by Lever's allusions to him :—

"The duties of his office not only place him in intimate relation with the other members of the executive and the law officers of the crown, but they also bring him into contact with a large body of the resident gentry and the magistracy. It is impossible that, for the discharge of such functions, the choice could have fallen upon a more able or competent person than Lord Eliot. Independently of his claims as a man of business and profound political sagacity, he possesses a singularly happy and seductive manner, a warmth amounting even to cordiality, and an unassuming simplicity towards his inferiors in station, highly conducive to the advantage of a station which places its possessor in constant intercourse with persons of all classes. It is not our intention here to enter into the newspaper controversy concerning Lord Eliot's private character; we look indeed upon the attack, if it can be called such, as one of those chance ebullitions of political bitterness, by which newspaper writers occasionally season their columns, while they affect a knowledge of things of which they know little, and persons of whom, perhaps, they know less." *

When, some weeks later, the idea of returning to Ireland became more fixed, he told McGlashan, as he had often done before, that he never wished him to be biassed by any consideration for him to the exclusion of his own individual interests, and that the way to remain good friends was by frank and straightforward dealing. High terms were not his object. In thorough confidence and honesty, he told him that he wished to have a valid reason for returning to Ireland, where he hoped to get something from the Government. He had not a doubt of being able to double the circulation of his magazine, and not leave the other monthlies a leg to stand on; and he soon convinced the publisher that their mutual interest might be served by adopting his suggestion.

He, however, rather dreaded the avalanche of bills which were sure to come upon him when a rumour of his projected departure should get abroad—but feared more the slanderous statement that he had levanted—

* " D. U. M.," vol. xviii., p. 633.

English character at Brussels standing not too high for the supposition.

Again he sought solace in the thought that an Under-secretaryship of State, a commissionership of Lunacy, or, failing both, a Stipendiary Magistracy, or a Surgeoncy in Ordinary to the Household, would recoup him for past loss or worry. The seat of Irish Government—the Castle—rose before him, and castles in the air floated gaily above it. Four years later he thus wrote of a habit which he fostered to the end.

"Notwithstanding all that we hear said against castle-building, how few among the unbought pleasures of life are so amusing; nor are we certain that these shadowy speculations—these 'white lies' that we tell to our own conscience—are not so many incentives to noble deeds and generous actions. These 'imaginary con-versations' lift us out of the jog-trot path of daily intercourse, and call up hopes and aspirations that lie buried under the heavy load of wearisome common-places of which life is made up, and thus permit a man, immersed as he may be in the fatigues of a pro-fession, harassed by law, or worried by the Three per Cents., to be a hero to his own heart at least for a few minutes once a week."

Lever had given no decided answer to the flattering invitation from Mr. Bentley; and Mr. A——n waited upon him one day, to know if he would not accept it. Lever interpreted the eagerness of Mr. A——n to a hope that whenever he should hold the helm of the craft,

Mr. A——n might be sure of employment—but in truth, as he said, he would not accept of him as pig ballast!

McGlashan liked to hold a pruning knife, and Lever feared its exercise. He told him firmly that he would not think of accepting a divided responsibility, and recoiled from the idea of being the mere *farceur* of a journal. It was the conviction, right or wrong, that he was qualified to conduct a magazine, that led him to desert what was an easier path. He took the reins to try whether, with the same cattle, he could not spin along some fifteen miles an hour, *vice* six Irish. He proposed to hold a social meeting of the staff when the new reign would open, and the oath of allegiance be sworn to!

McGlashan did not abuse the confidence reposed in him, and offered Lever handsome terms. He motioned him to the editorial chair of the magazine, and suggested that he should contribute some portion of a story monthly, for which £100 a month or £1,200 a year was offered, with half profits on all he wrote.

Lever was in high glee. Where was he to be housed; was the domicile dry; had it lots of stabling; what was the duty on furniture, old and new, and on an old carriage; what of that delicious thought—an Elizabethan cottage in Wicklow—these were some of the questions he feverishly asked. Meanwhile he wrote to Colley Grattan, Johnson, and others, telling them to hold their pens in readiness to aid.

In a perfect fidget was he. He could not sit down to write, he said, until his home became more cheerful, and his plans fixed. He was all impatience to know how soon he was to don his harness like a spirited steed, and pawed the ground, so to speak, with eagerness to go ahead.

The usually impassive McGlashan was hardly less elated when he thought of his magazine being brought so intimately amongst the ministerialists. Removing the pen from his ear, indulging in a prolonged pinch of Rapée, and giving himself a day's rest from his desk, he started on a tramp to the country, where he, at last, selected a place likely to suit Lever, who, in acknowledgment, said, that when he had a roof over him, he would tell him, more fittingly, how much he felt his zeal and promptitude. He begged of him not to consult about their plans a certain connection of his, who had a diabolical faculty for mismanaging everything on which he put his hand. This weakness would seem to have been a family failing, for just as Lever was about to leave Brussels, he announced to McGlashan that he had made a sad mess of his horses and furniture, having sold all his traps, just to get rid of them, for £600 less than he had not long previously paid. He begs of him not to mention his folly, for he was ashamed to confess it even to himself. Bills he was paying twice over—having lost the receipts, and he feared he should be sent to England like a pauper to his parish!

Pleasant and sparkling thoughts soon chased dull care away. Part of his scheme was to make a French tour through Ireland, accompanied by his wife and a French maid—and not to speak anything but broken

English, and write the result for the magazine. They would go to Killarney—the west—and even the north—and Lever wagered £100, would not be detected. At Tullamore, he would not even tell his own brother—and the thing, he added, would be the most perfect piece of successful humbug ever practised! Another project—the "Weekly Quiz" with sketches by "Phiz"—danced pleasantly through his fancy—not to speak of "The Blarney"—a half sheet, small 8vo, with a droll picture on the cover of all the world blarneying.—The Duke blarneying the Queen; Dan the Paddies; Bulwer the Booksellers; Brodie and the Doctors the Apothecaries; a Lawyer the Attorneys; the Military the Ladies; and "Harry Lorrequer" everybody. He told McGlashan to advertise it for the 1st of April—all Fool's day—and to share the profits with him. Some sheets of a series to be called *Noctes Lorrequeriana* he threw off, but finally burnt. "O'Leary in Belgium, with thoughts on Bones and Balls," shared the same fate.

In January, 1842, Lever had resigned the rod of Æsculapius, and sent word that if any worthy fellow worth taking trouble about cared to come and grasp it, there was at his service £600 per annum, which *his* introduction could secure him. Dr. Parkinson succeeded to Lever's preferment and practice in Brussels.

The Wicklow mountains were covered with snow when their night-capped tops arrested Lever's eye—and the ground, on every side, was hard with hoary frost. The Sugar Loaf never looked more like the monster cone to which it had been compared. He had not been many days in his new house, when illness plagued him. Early in February, he announced himself as half dead with a confounded attack, and unable to hear or speak. He also complained that the house, though professedly a furnished one, far from deserved that character, as Mrs. Lever and he had been furnishing it all day, and should necessarily continue to do till the end of their term.

In March, 1842, we find him fairly in editorial harness; and ordering one of the staff to prepare sugar-plum notices of a new book by Archbishop Whately, and of "Modern Flirtations," by Catharine Sinclair: directions are given to allot to the prelate a good place among the petticoats. Lever had sat up half the night going through the MSS. which had inundated his box, and did not find, he declared, by any accident, a single paper approaching to good. To such of the writers as he knew, he wrote direct; and as regards "the great unknown" literati, he declared that they eminently deserved to be such.

During the following month he is still found doing the drudging duties of a reader, rather than presiding as editorial autocrat. This time he sat up all night. Some of the MSS. were, he said, crude ill-digested trash: a few were good, but the majority "Awfully bad—even unto *Gasparism*." * A budget of papers were duly sifted, and some condemned as execrable, including " Priestcraft

---

* A tedious tale "To be continued," known as "Gaspar the Pirate," had appeared in the Magazine prior to Lever's régime.

versus *Witchcraft.* What was to be done with the great rejected? Coals were dear. Clondalkin Tower might be retained. The Magazine doubtless would need grouting from the wall, and it should not be, more than a pudding, all sugar-plums; but no journal could afford a trimestrial paper such as those he had doomed, without being most deservedly d——d. He thought a capital paper might be made out of the last will of the late editor, beginning: "I, Anthony Poplar,* of sound mind: but grievously suffering from various contributors; do give and bequeath, &c., all my interest, titles, letters, &c. in D. U. Mag.—to my dearly beloved Harry Lorrequer—with all my interest, such as it is, in Gaspar the Pirate. whom I earnestly hope that in proportion as the world neglects and despises, he will use kindly and affectionately," &c. &c. The other contributors also came in for a share.

If Lever discharged the drudging duties of a reader, he also undertook the *rôle* of Chancellor of the Exchequer; and he would press upon the best of the staff, such as Hayman, cheques, not, he said, as an adequate remuneration for their aid, but such as the Proprietors had placed at his disposal.

The Rev. John Lever, though he took care to say that all such criticism is somewhat out of his line, lost

* Anthony Poplar was the *nom de plume* of the Rev. C. S. Stanford, original editor of the D. U. M. He published an edition of Plato, in 1833 ; of Ovid, in 1835 ; and was editor of the " Christian Examiner," from 1843 to 1868. He became rector of St. Michan's, Dublin, in 1844, and died at Surbiton, Surrey, in 1873.

no opportunity of putting Charles " in heart " by words of encouragement, which he well knew, from experience, he at all times needed, if real progress was desired. He thought " Jack Hinton " began promisingly; and that Cross Corney was capable of being made very much of— enough, in fact, to compensate for the death of Mickey Free. The illustrations he liked not much, unless Corney; the points he thought muddy and confused, and he declared that " Phiz" always succeeded best with single figures, or a group of three.

Lever continued to work with a will on "Jack Hinton." A preface to it, issued in 1859, but afterwards withdrawn, naively states that "for the characters of his story, there is not one for which he had not 'a real sitter;" and that for Mrs. P. Rooney, Father Loftus, Mahon, O'Grady, Tipperary Joe, and even Corney himself, " I have scarcely added a touch which Nature has not given them, while, assuredly, I have failed to impart many a fine and delicate tint far above 'the reach of—my —art,' which might have presented them in stronger lights than I have dared to attempt." The final preface, dated Trieste, 1872, declares that he had not to draw on imagination for these characters, but that he never heard one correct guess as to the originals. On the latter point he does not enlighten us, but the late Rev. J. Comyn, P.P. of Kilkee, as he lolled in his easy chair, sat, it is said, for the portrait of Father Tom. His character is believed to have also furnished a large share of the material which enabled Lever in other books to draw his sacerdotal sketches. Our author's early life embraced solely Protestant society, and until he met the Priests of Clare, he knew nothing of their order. It has been asserted that the Priest in Lever's eye was Father Maguire, the famous controversialist; but we are not aware he ever met Maguire, unless casually travelling by canal-boat or coach. He belonged to the diocese of Ardagh, in which Lever at no time lived. The Father Tom whom on a drizzling day he met on board the boat, playing five and ten with a Quaker, paying compliments to Mrs. Carney, drinking punch, and engaged in controversial discussion, does not seem the same Father Tom whom we know and love through the remainder of the story.* The chief part of the scene is quoted in *Fraser* of the day by the dashing reviewer, Dr. Maginn; and we are distinctly told that "this Priest, gentle reader, shadowed out to you, is Tom Maguire, a man of mighty fame in almost every way in which fame can be won by a civilian, and who deserves to be celebrated hereafter as we ourselves can celebrate him." † *Fraser*, though expressing what seems author-

---

* See "Jack Hinton" ch. xix.

† Those who remember Maginn, or his picture in the "Prout Papers," presiding at the head of a genial group of wits, will not be surprised to hear that he longed to know Lever. "We had rather," he writes, "borrow money to drink with the author of 'O'Malley' than get drunk at the costliest expense of any other scribbler." He would indeed have been a welcome accession to a board round which Southey, Coleridge, Hook, Hogg, Ainsworth, Thackeray, Croker, Galt, Mahoney, Murphy and Moir, were wont to cluster. Lever and Maginn, however, never met. The witty critic fell with the leaves in 1842; and some of his final allusions to Lever appeared after his death—an event which put letters in mourning.

ised announcements, is repudiated in Lever's letters of the time, and pronounced to be more injurious than useful to him.

As regards Maguire, whom we personally knew, the sketch which Maginn relished is a broad caricature, though dashed off with the strength of a Hogarth, and the piquancy of a Cham. It may be added that Maguire was a frequent guest of Mr. P. Brophy, well known to Lever, and famous for slang anecdotes, who told us that the moment any joke bearing upon levity was raised, no bust of St. Patrick could present a more impassive gravity. The sketch of the Priest on board the boat cannot, therefore, have been like him. It seems to have been rapidly made, not by a fireside friend, but by a fellow-passenger on a public route, alive to peculiarities of character, and keenly on the watch to caricature them. Maguire was just the man—if formally introduced to Lever—to detect his design, and fold himself in reserve. A less astute Priest presented himself in the person of Father Comyns, with whom, it will be remembered, Lever was well acquainted, and he thereupon rolled the two into one. The Father Tom of the canal-boat altogether alters as the tale proceeds. Lever worked somewhat on the principle adopted by Dickens, whose biographer has let us into the secret of how this sort of thing is done. We learn that "nothing complete is ever taken from life by a genuine writer, but only leading traits, or such as may give greater finish; and that the fine artist will embody in his portraiture of one person his experiences of many."

The good parson's "God speed!" his counsel and his correction, proved of real use to Charles. From St. Catherine's, on the 20th January, 1842, he writes:—

"Jack goes on flourishingly—the dialogue is piquant and racy—and without the bustle of 'O'Malley.' The incidents follow after one another in natural succession. Let me call your attention, however, to the extraordinary hallucination of pp. 83 and 94, in which the same individual is alternately Lord George or Lord Dudley, De Vere, or Herbert, as the printer pleases. The author must choose what name to call his man by, and then let him have no *alias*. As for the picture, the likeness is most spirited and striking; a little too much of *fierté* of air—but altogether excellent. 'Tis Charley himself—especially forehead and eye."

The elder Lever goes on to say that there was good taste and good sense shown by Charles in not bringing his people out—he had already given us some good duels—and need not fight over again. He added a wish that it had not been said that "Sir Roger de Coverley was an emblem of eternity." A flattering notice is enclosed "to put him in good-humour and sharpen his pen."

John Lever knew his brother's nature well.

"Newspapers" writes Charles, "are the spurs which make me spring to exertion when disposed to be idle, which is my natural tendency, alas and alack!"

In sheltering his own name and concocting, as he

believed, imaginary ones like Monsoon, Lever little dreamt that a veritable Jack Hinton would turn up in Wexford.*

The many families whose names he had borrowed for his books, richly enjoyed an amusing retribution—pillorying his own name—which fell upon him at this time. "Charles Lever, the Man of the Nineteenth Century," by the Rev. W. Gresley, M.A. Prebendary of Lichfield; was published in London. The tale set forth the career, from cradle to grave, of a remarkable character described throughout as Charles Lever.† To this circumstance our author, in his "Notice Preliminary of O'Leary," made allusion: "To disclaim any or all of

* Besides making contemporary public characters figure under a half-veiled guise, Lever, in a later book successfully tried the experiment of introducing prolonged allusions to some by name—amongst others to Cardinal Cullen, but never availed himself of the vast power at his command of placing in a ludicrous light men to whom his traditional prejudices had been opposed. He goes farther and puts into the mouth of Kenny Dodd an earnest protest against some strictures on Archbishop Cullen for an opinion alleged to be held by him.

† The annoyance with which our author read such passages as the following may be guessed. "Placed in the atmosphere of a Christian household; all the better feelings of Charles Lever's heart revived and expanded; his conviction of his own errors became daily fixed more deeply; his faith in Christ waxed stronger, and his resolutions of amendment more confirmed" (p. 216).

A letter addressed to us by Mrs. Gresley, dated Boyne Hill Vicarage, March 1st, 1877, states that Canon Gresley, the writer of "Charles Lever, the Man of the Nineteenth century," died in November 1876, and that the coincidence of name was purely accidental. But this was not so provoking as the case of the adventurer Graham, who, under the name of Charles Lever, was charged before Mr. Chance with obtaining money by means of advertisements addressed to "Inexperienced Persons," anxious to appear upon the stage. Numbers replied, and all were promised, on the payment of a commission, a capital opening and salaried engagements.

the intentions attributed to us in Mr. O'Leary's letter, would have been perfectly useless. * * * To little purpose should we adduce that our Alter Ego was the hero of a book by the Prebendary of Lichfield, and Charles Lever given to the world as a socialist."

Lever, who from boyhood possessed almost naturally "the give and take" of good society, was always *au fait* in the salon, especially if a race ball or a hunt ball;* but it is in the open air, clearing a five-barred gate, guiding a runaway Croydon; heading a column; pursuing a flirtation in some romantic dell; or, by vast strength of lungs and muscle, rescuing some dear Galway girl from infuriate Atlantic waves, that he always appears to best advantage. Some of his finest heroines—perhaps more spirited than *spirituel*—are those who well know the secret of planting roses in their cheeks by a keen relish of out-door life.

"Diamond cut diamond" was exemplified in the career of that Bird of Paradise, who could bring down her bird at sixty yards!

> "She'd ride a wall, she'd draw a team,
> Or with a fly she'd whip a stream,
> Or maybe sing you ' Rousseau's Dream,'
> For nothing could escape her ;
> I've seen her, too, upon my word—
> At sixty yards bring down her bird.
> Oh ! she charm'd all the forty-third,
>   Did lovely Mary Draper !"

As a physician Lever knew the importance of the

* See ch. xxvii. of "Jack Hinton," where a Galway ball is inimitably described.

open air in producing the *mens sana in corpore sano*—the real secret of his own success, and the happiness of those who did likewise. His seasonable descriptions, sometimes redolent of the hawthorn but more frequently braced by the scent of the heather, or the aroma of Atlantic sea-weed where waves roll in unbroken from Labrador, equal those of Scott, and surpass Smollett's.*

To the last, he continued his open air system, though sometimes in a novel way. When boating, as he daily did, in the Bay of Spezzia, he would lie often, for an hour at a time, on his back gazing on the bright blue sky, and breathing the bracing air.

The graphic glimpses of Galway belles and balls disclosed by these tales bear so strong an impress of intimate personal acquaintance, that we are not surprised to hear from Major Darcy that Lever's figure at Galway dances is now, after thirty years, clearly before him—his face redolent of enjoyment; his limbs all activity; his coat thrown back, and displaying a large amount of snow-white vest and shirt.†

---

* But, unlike Scott, he cared little for archæological attraction. One catches a good glimpse of his character in a critique he wrote on Otway's " Connaught."

"We are too eager to breathe the mountain air to wait, on any account whatever, at Cong. Away ! we care nothing for your caves—'Our heart's in the highlands.' We are hill-folk—no troglodytes. Don't attempt to stop us with Patrick's tooth ! Your crozier ? would it serve us for a walking-staff ? would it help us up the long hill at Minterown ?"

† Galway was the favourite theatre of his novels. No part of Ireland is so rich in its preservation of comical situations, and startling traditions regarding society there sixty years ago. With these, Joseph Miles McDonnell, of Doo Castle, plied Lever freely.

"The genius of the rest of Ireland," he writes, "uses Connaught as a species of literary store-farm. Ulster, Leinster, and Munster, breed men of genius who, so soon as they have exhausted their own provinces of lay and legend, incontinently cross the Shannon to carry on a predatory warfare against Fin Varra, and Grana Uaile. These they rob and pillage without mercy; driving preys of ghost stories, and taking black mail of songs and tunes as unceremoniously as ever the Finns of old lifted sheep and black cattle. Meanwhile, the Connasians go on coshering, and story telling, and droning on their bagpipes; fighting, joking, ghost-seeing; acting comedies and romances every day of their lives; but never dreaming of taking pen in hand to turn themselves to account;"* and again, "you might as well attempt to eat down a corcass meadow as to exhaust this El Dorado of literary material, by transporting into it any given number of tourists, statists, legend-

---

* D. U. M., August, 1839, p. 124.

Many traits as he gave of Galway oddities, he could have added numerous others hitherto untold. Writs and duns daily dogged the Galway gentry. We are informed by Mr. B—— that bailiffs having one morning obtained access to the hall while his ancestor was dressing, "The masther," thus surprised, with one half of his face shaved, and the other in a lather, jumped from his bed-room window to the yard, and mounting, barebacked a favourite horse, galloped across the country, and presented himself for admission at the house of a popular baronet. The figure he cut, bareheaded. his face in a lather, and minus all clothing but a flannel vest and drawers, exciting consternation among the ladies, and hearty laughter among the men! When we find that incidents such as this were of daily occurrence, it is clear that Lever by no means overdrew the pictures he presented. Some of his most amusing stories were drawn from the life of Mr. Giles Eyre, Master of the Galway hounds.

hunters, whim-catchers, trait-trappers, and historians." This remark was *à propos* to Cæsar Otway, who, in 1839, made a gallant dash into Joyce's country, and came back laden with spoil. Wilde took the hint thus dropped, and produced his book on Connaught scenery.

If Lever provoked laughter, he could also draw forth tears. Less expert in killing than in creating, as much cannot be said of him, as of Dickens, that Paul Dombey's death placed a whole nation in mourning; but, it may be urged that the death of Mary Martin is, in pathetic touch, not inferior to the death of Little Nell. The graphic strength of Lever's sketches, and the depth of his powers of social diagnosis, derived an element of success from the position he occupied as a physician. The picture of a sick chamber in " Luttrell of Arran," and the dying girl, pallid on her pillow, but united in mock marriage by a base clique at her bedside, is full of dramatic strength and skill. In " Luttrell," too, is graphically described that attendance by the bedside of a fair and dying patient, for which the doctor declines to receive any fee but a tress of her golden hair.

In the knowledge drawn from medical practice, Dr. Lever held a decided vantage ground. " The life of a physician," he writes, " has nothing so thoroughly rewarding, nothing so cheering, so full of hearty encouragement as in the occasional friendships to which it opens the way. The doctor attains to a degree of intimacy, and stands on a footing of confidence so entirely exceptional, that, if personal qualities lend aid to the position, his intercourse becomes friendship. Whether, therefore, my old career gave me any assistance in new roads, whether it imparted to me any habits of investigation as applicable to the full, in morals as to matter, it certainly imparted to me the happy accident of standing on good terms with—I was going to say—my patient, and perhaps no better word could be found for him who has heard me so long, trusted me so much, given me so large a share of his favour, and come to look on me with such friendliness."

Some of Lever's curiosities of medical experience were amusing. A stud-groom of the King of Holland had been under his care for ague. He got well, and on his return to the Hague thought proper to visit his former doctor—the King's physician—to show himself cured and extol Lever's merits. The Dutch M.D. was amazed at what he conceived a small miracle, and hearing that the wonderful man who worked it was an author, sent off an express to Bruxelles for Dr. Lever's works. They sent him " Harry Lorrequer," and " Charley O'Malley ! " and the luckless leech nearly lost his senses at the shock, besides being made the laughing stock of Holland, where the whole story was known, from the king downwards. Lever said, as he told the story, that in college he learned that Homer should be read for his anatomy alone; but he had never dreamt of " Lorrequer's practice of physic " * becoming a handbook for the faculty. It will be remembered that " Lorrequer practising Physic," from the pencil of Phiz, richly illustrates a most comical chapter of the " Confessions."

It may be added, that Lever complained that a garbled version of " O'Malley " had been published at Paris under the title of " Deux filles et Maries," the greatest sting being that the writer passed off the lucubration as his own—though on reflection, Lever felt little inclined to contest the parentage. With greater chagrin he read in successive issues of a leading New York journal continued chapters of " Major O'Connor, by the author of ' Charles O'Malley ; ' " but a manifesto from Lever's publishers, in August 1841, repudiates it as " an impudent forgery."

CHAPTER XI.

In April, 1842, Lever publicly entered on his editorial
duties. To select a literary workshop in a neighbourhood not likely to be bored by barrel-organs, or troublesome visitors, would seem, with McGlashan, at least to
have been a primary object; but pending the search we
find Lever at Thornhill, Stillorgan, for a brief *séjour*,
and, later, at Woodpark, Kingstown. Templeogue, a
popular place of resort in the last century, but latterly
like the chalybeate Spas of Lucan and Finglass deserted,
was eventually chosen as the ground whereon to pitch
his camp.

The chief feature of Lever's first number was a
sketch, pen and pencilled, of Tom Moore. Prefixed to
the Magazine we find an address from the new editor,
with a flattering tribute to the redeeming virtues of its
previous career.

"Seeking by every available means, and at every
occasion opportunities of benefiting our native country,
illustrating its antiquities, elevating its literary tastes,

fostering its art and encouraging its industry; and above all seeking to induce on the common ground of literature and science, a bond of union between men of all parties and denominations, while at the same time it never compromised a principle nor flinched from its avowed opinions."

But he saw room for improvement.

" Some time must elapse before I can hope to accomplish the whole or even the greater part of my wishes. I have succeeded to an estate with certain vested rights, and, although the old leases shall not in some instances have renewals, yet while running my life against them, I shall, I trust, treat the tenants in possession with every due courtesy. Lastly, to all anonymous contributors, I would say that, gout excepted, I am by nature of a ' temperament smooth as oil, soft as young down,' yet that I have really no sympathy in common with that large and amiable class who send 100 pages of ill-written MS. and expect a reply by return." His *corps* being ample for all purposes, he begged, therefore, to be spared either the labour of replying to unsought-for applications, or the rudeness of leaving them unanswered.

This address was written before Lever assumed the direction of his team. It cannot be denied that distance lent enchantment to the view. On taking the reins he found his cattle—as he tells the Rev. Edward Johnson in June, 1842—" as groggy a set of screws as ever man held in harness," adding, " God forgive me for my editorial puff of them." By degrees he got rid of the worst of the staff, and enlisted more muscular aid.

His "Nuts and Nut-crackers"—suggested by the *guêpes* in France—were now begun. He wisely felt that the popular topics of the day would afford him abundant matter for ridicule, and sometimes for sharp satire. But he desired anonymity because its personalities like its politics would hit all sides: and more freedom would thereby be allowed to him.*

It will be remembered that he expressed a wish to attend the court of the Viceroy, Lord de Grey. A great Q.C., whose long horse-hair wig made him look an oracle of wisdom, accompanied Lever to the Castle. Both halted at the house of Alexander Spencer *en route*, and partook of some refreshment while giving a finishing arrangement

---

* One of his first Nuts was a pinch for the "Christian Examiner," which brought a note of protest from the Rev. John Lever. Canon Hayman, a contributor to both the D. U. M. and this evangelical organ, tells us that John was not pleased at a remark in those very clever "Nuts," (papers not appreciated as they deserved), about "talking shop," as the phrase is. "Harry Lorrequer, in his 'Nuts,' was constantly combating current notions, in the gayest fashion—indulging in fun and badinage to the utmost. So he averred that multitudes never fell into the error of talking of their professions (giving instances, and among them this)—he had 'dined a dozen times in company with parsons, yet he *never heard a word of piety from them.*' This remark, made in pure frivolity, was taken hold of by some dullard who could not see its innocent quizzing, and poor Lever was hauled up before the public as an insulter of the Protestant clergy. At the very moment that men, like Mortimer O'Sullivan, were thoroughly enjoying the joke, Lever felt the injustice with which he was treated. He wrote to me at the time, as you will see, asking whether I was offended at his levity? I could only reply, that I laughed over and over again at his witticism— adding, however, that I feared his observation was often well founded."

to their dress. A book produced during his stay in Ireland (the "O'Donoghue") contains a chapter headed "St. Patrick's Ball," in which the hero, when attending for the first time those formal scenes, is described as feeling "a bit nervous;" and from the account given of Lever by early friends some personal experience possibly exists in the detail. This feeling of diffidence was cured by whispered counsel in a way specially characteristic of Dublin society.

"With such success did he demolish reputations—so fatally did his sarcasm depreciate those against whom they were directed—that ere long, Mark moved along in utter contempt for that gorgeous throng which at first had impressed him so profoundly. To hear that the proud-looking general, his coat a blaze of orders, was a coward; that the benign and mild faced judge was merciless and unrelenting; that the bishop, whose simple bearing and gentle quietude of manner were most winning, was in reality a crafty place-hunter and a subtle intriguant—such were the lessons Talbot poured into his ear, while amid the ranks of beauty still more deadly calumnies pointed all he said."

Lever held aloof from general society in Dublin, but the ice once broken, he enjoyed a dance at the Castle balls. How often in criticism, printed and oral, has he been represented as "the rollicking and roistering novelist;" but the thorough purity of his heart, when in the height of festive fun, is shown by what he says of Jullien's Irish Quadrilles, then all the rage. In his

"Nuts"—a series of passing hits—he deprecates the introduction of airs heard only at riotous carousals and roistering festivals; whose every bar is associated with words,
which in his maturer years he blushes to have listened
to! He stares about him in wonderment for a moment,
he forgets that the young lady who dances with such
evident enjoyment of the air, is ignorant of its history;
he watches her sparkling eyes and animated gesture
without remembering that she knows nothing of the
associations at which her partner is perhaps smirking;
he sees her *vis-à-vis* exchanging looks with his friend,
that denote their estimation of the music; and, in very
truth, so puzzled is he, he begins to distrust his senses.
The air ceases and is succeeded by another, no less
known, no less steeped in the same class of associations, and so to the conclusion, till the whole is capped
with a melody to which even the restraints of society
are scarcely able to prevent a humming accompani-
ment of concurring voices, and—these are the Irish
Quadrilles!

"If we wished for a set," he adds, "how many good
and suitable airs have we not really at our hands? Is not
our national music proverbially rich, and in the very
character of music that would suit us? Are there not
airs in hundreds whose very names are linked with
pleasing and poetic memories admirably adapted to the
purpose? Why commit the choice, as in this case, to a
foreigner who knew nothing of them, nor of us? And
why permit him to introduce into our drawing-rooms,

through the means of a quadrille band, a class of reminiscences which suggest levity in young men, and shame in old ones." *

It is said that over the gates of Bandon was once inscribed

> Turk, Jew, or Atheist,
> May enter here, but not a Papist—

and that Swift wittily supplemented the lines with

> Whoever wrote this, wrote it well,
> The same is written on the Gates of Hell.

This stronghold Lever felt a passing fancy, if not to represent, at least publicly to aspire to, believing that by this course he would gain favour with the great party then in power. In politics he seems to have been a good-humoured Conservative, and the thought of standing for Bandon occurred to him merely as a stroke of business, not unmixed with the waggery inseparable from his nature.†

---

* Lever's nice delicacy of feeling when in full blooded manhood is here seen. Jullien's reign, marked by flourish of trumpets and din of drum, was a bright one. But at a concert one night in Dublin having been applauded into giving a reluctant encore he lost temper, and called his auditory "a sixpenny mob." The benches were torn up, the orchestra smashed, the chandeliers pulled down, and Jullien himself with dishevelled ringlets fled from a throne which he never afterwards ventured to reascend.

† A parliamentary orator said that, he had himself read this inscription on the gate, but Mr. Bennett in his "History of Bandon," denies that it ever existed, though the authenticity of Swift's lines are not disputed. A dozen additional lines of Swift, hardly known, follow the often-quoted couplet. We are assured by a respectable solicitor, a native of Bandon, that he himself has been shown in the records of its Corporation a bye-law prohibiting any "Papist" to sleep in the town, and that he remembers to have been pointed out the first Catholic to whom that permission was extended.

McGlashan, backed by the Rev. John Lever, continued to urge anonymity; but our author finally disregarded the counsel of both, and the last number of " Jack Hinton " displayed " By Charles Lever, Esq." Indeed further concealment now would have savoured of affectation.

There was nothing amused him more, while living at Kingstown, than the people he met when travelling thither by train. The Dublin and Kingstown Railway had shot into activity within the period which elapsed between his appointment to Derry and return to Ireland. Lever said that if the wise Caliph who studied mankind by sitting on the bridge at Bagdad had lived in Dublin and in our times, he certainly would have become a subscriber to the Kingstown Railway, where for ten pounds per annum he might have indulged his peculiar vein and obtained a greater insight into character, inasmuch as the objects of his investigation would be all sitting shots. Segur's " Quatre Ages de la Vie," he added, " never marked out mankind like the half-hour trains." To the careless observer the company would appear a heterogeneous mass of old and young of both sexes, but Lever read every face with profit. The 8·30 train he found was filled with attorneys. " The ways of Providence are inscrutable: it arrives safely in Dublin." By the 9·0 train comes a fresh jovial-looking set of fellows with bushy whiskers and geraniums in button-holes. They are traders, but have, however, half an acre divided into meadow and tillage near

Kingstown. 9·30, the housekeepers' train, 10·0, the barristers'. "Fierce faces look out at the weather with the stern glance they are accustomed to, and stare at the sun in the face as though to say, 'None of your prevarication with *me*. Answer me, on your oath, is it to rain or not?'" At 10·30 the doctors return, and at 11·0 the men of wit and pleasure—men Lever confessed rather difficult of detection—travel in pairs.

Templeogue House, into which he finally settled down, is described as the former resort of the Knights Templars, and is one of several other mansions in which James the Second has been traditionally said to have slept on the night of his defeat at the Boyne. Its great court-yards with their impregnably high walls and gate piers twenty feet high, the old Dutch waterfall, terraced walks, gigantic grottoes, expansive gardens, and avenues of elms, attest the former importance of Templeogue House. Its sweeping avenue is entered by a massive old iron gate between high piers surmounted by globes of granite. Around it quietude reigned, broken only by the rush of foaming water and the groans of a ponderous wheel, which, with the lofty mill in front, presents a picturesque view, reminding one of the well-known scene in "La Sonnambula," while farther off in front stands Montpelier and its castellated tower, once the resort of the "Hell-fire Club." The sward—part of it suggestive of "Green grow the Rushes, O," the rest of "Shamrock so Green"—was prettily laid out, and quite to Lever's taste. Templeogue latterly had not been much frequented by the votaries of pleasure or fashion ; but some pleasant men whom Lever brought to his house made the reunions there most enjoyable. Men of wit and letters were by degrees recruited, generally summoned by such welcome missives as "Come and dine to meet the Magazine." On those occasions, we are told, he handled his reins so dexterously in driving his team, and used his whip (on the rare occasions that he did so) with such skill and judgment, that you heard but the crack that cheered and stimulated, and not the lash that kept all to the traces.

Writing from Trieste a few months before his death, he says, "I had drawn around me a circle of men of great and varied powers, and when I mention such names as Archie Butler, Petrie, Griffin, the late Bishop of Limerick, Isaac Butt, Mortimer O'Sullivan, &c., I may be believed when I assert that conversation took a range, and was maintained with a brilliancy that left us nothing to regret of the more famous gatherings at Holland or Gore House. Indeed, Thackeray himself assured me he had met no such collective agreeability anywhere."

To one of these spirits we owe the following reminiscence. "These were halcyon days for the corps of the Irish periodical. To that pleasant retreat resorted all the best spirits that could be found—men of letters, men of art, whoever could play a good game of whist, tell a good story or sing a good song,—all found a hearty welcome, and like Jack Falstaff and Justice Shallow, many a time they heard the chimes of midnight. Here the material of the next number was often discussed, many a bright fancy evoked, and many a bright thought born. No one shone with greater lustre than the host himself. No matter who began to talk, somehow ere long we all found ourselves listeners. How this happened one never stopped to consider. A spiritual magnetism, whose operations were unseen, but whose effects were visible enough, drew us all to him; and his cheery laugh—for he laughed with all his heart—was the most infectious thing in the world, and set the table in a roar."

"If," writes Lever himself in 1871, "the men who wrote for the 'University,' were all more or less engrossed in their several careers as churchmen, barristers, and physicians, and there was consequently less of that bond of professional spirit which they who make literature a career possess, there was on the other hand a great breadth from the diversity of daily occupation, vast variety from the divers contrasts of experiences, and a total absence of all the rivalries and jealousies that unhappily attend men when seeking distinction by the same road. I will not say that quizzing, a very Irish defect, was not rife amongst us, and that any lapses into tall talk, or any slips of ' sentimentality' in an article, would not have met very summary punishment as we sat after dinner; but on the whole there was great good humour and great good fellowship, and to the very few who remain—for alas! the ranks are grievously thinned—my heart warms as I write these words of memory."

"Ah," writes a survivor, "the hand which traced these lines has lost its cunning, and the heart which glowed with nationality and friendship's fire has since followed other hearts now stilled for ever."

It often happened that when Lever produced something he considered specially good, McGlashan unhesitatingly condemned it. On the other hand the things he thought his worst proved, not unfrequently, real hits. The Rev. Samuel Hayman, an acute critic, pronounced "O'Leary" a masterpiece, and now, after the lapse of thirty years, regards it as the best of his writings. In January, 1842, Lever besought Hayman—if he loved him—not to mention "O'Leary"—he detested it from his heart; but being obliged to do something for the Magazine, he patched up that stuff, which he said took labour to read, but none to write!

Encouraged by Hayman, the modest author continued month by month "The Wanderings and Ponderings of Arthur O'Leary." Hayman's genial criticism sent him into his oak snuggery with such courage, he said, that he could work, and work hard, when an impertinent paragraph or some malicious sneer would leave him biting his pen and sketching caricatures on his paper for hours after. Later on he described himself as quite in a flutter as to the reception poor "O'Leary" would meet from English critics when presented in complete

outfit ; and though he had perfect faith in the liberality
with which Colburn paid for puffs, not even his own
"New Monthly" could requite him for the acrimony of
the unpaid and uncivil ones.

He eventually had good reason to rejoice, five hundred
copies, as he announced, having been subscribed the
first day in the Row. With the illustrations too he
was greatly gratified.* The Controller at Dublin
Castle told him that "O'Leary" had been read aloud
with great success in the boudoir of the Viceroy,
Lord De Grey. "Who the reader was," writes Lever,
"I forgot to ask : but heaven help poor O'Leary if he
trickled through the conventional lispings of a Cockney
Guardsman. As for me, it is the only success of a book
of mine I ever heard of with pique, for I hold the
powers that be as cheap as I do the Repealers." It
must be confessed that Lever felt sore that the Viceroy
had not taken more notice of him. Whereupon some
of his castles in the air began to melt away like the
saccharine pagodas which graced his Excellency's board,
and tempted his guests.

---

* The late George Cruikshank writes from 263, Hampstead Road :—

I had the honour and the pleasure of being personally acquainted with
the late Charles Lever, and I regret that I was only able to illustrate one of
his works, "Arthur O'Leary," my engagements on "Jack Sheppard," &c. at
that time prevented me from illustrating his other works which he wished
me to have done, but I do not remember ever having any written
correspondence with him, as the MS. or printed matter was placed in my
hands for illustration ; and then I had entirely to deal with the publisher.
Mr. Charles Lever was an author whom I held in high estimation.

GEORGE CRUIKSHANK.

That the success of "O'Leary" became so marked is largely due to Hayman's encouragement. Lever on assuming the editorial reins had recognised in this genial churchman a critic of rare acumen, and assured him that he had not a reader more ready to sympathise with the telling hits he so forcibly dealt out to flimsy literature than himself—adding, with his usual modesty, that this speech was no small piece of liberality from a man who grew nothing but mushrooms, and many of them hard enough to digest.

"Hardly had Lever seated himself in his new home," Canon Hayman writes, "but he must needs have me with him; and my memories of Templeogue are most pleasant. Looking back through the vista of years, I can hardly pronounce which were happiest (inasmuch as each had a charm of its own), those quiet evenings with my friend, Madame and the 'leverets,' as I fondly called them; or seasons, when choicest spirits joined our company; or the menagerie feasts, with the publisher and the general staff of the Magazine. The establishment was costly; the style of living luxurious; yet I never saw excess either with host or guests. All were made happy—innocently happy.

"Riding on horseback was a passion with Lever; and never was he in blither spirits than when far away on the Wicklow hills, with a friend by his side and his children around him on their ponies. He kept a dozen horses, named from his books. 'Pioche' (*vide* Tom Burke) was commonly allotted to me."

Almost the last now left of that once bright group, who gathered round Lever at Templeogue, tells, amid the interruption of bronchial coughs, " We all listened to some new sally as he poured out from the fulness of his memory some pleasant adventure or witty saying, or gave some of his shrewd experiences or humorous portraitures. In truth, he had great conversational powers, and prided himself on the possession of them, and few men knew better their value, or when and how to use them. These pleasant *noctes* are well remembered—the beaming face of our host, every muscle trembling with humour, the light of his merry eye, the smile that expanded his mouth and showed his fine white teeth, the musical, ringing laugh that stirred every heart, the finely modulated voice, uttering some witty *mot*, telling some droll incident or some strange adventure."

In different memoirs of Lever the name of Sir Samuel Ferguson has been mentioned among the men of genius whom he gathered round him on undertaking the editorship of the Magazine; but so annoyed was Dr. Ferguson with him for accepting Thackeray's dedication of the " Irish Sketch Book "—in which the country was to some extent travestied—that he declined to join the Magazine under Lever, and did not care to meet him.*

* This dedication, it must be confessed, was neatly put, and graciously accepted. " Allow me to dedicate my little book to a good Irishman, the hearty charity of whose visionary red coats, some substantial personages in black might imitate to advantage." Bishop Doyle was the only Irishman whom Thackeray enthusiastically praised.

Lever and Thackeray were no doubt intimately associated at this time; but it is a mistake to assume that the "Sketch Book" was in any way inspired by Lever, though he certainly reviewed it favourably afterwards.*

Thirty years later, he writes:—"Poor Thackeray was on a visit with me while I was writing 'Tom Burke.' He at that time was engaged on his 'Irish Sketch Book,' and I believe, though we discussed every other book and book writer, neither of us ever by a chance alluded to what the other was employed on. Nay, I am wrong, Thackeray once referred to his Irish book. It was in the drawing-room after dinner, when I had some twelve or fourteen friends anxious to meet him. 'Can any one of your friends here,' whispered he, 'cram me on the subject of the Irish corporation?' it was the time of O'Connell's mayoralty—'I must give them a page or two.'

"'There's your man,' said I, leading him to Isaac Butt. 'He is an alderman, and in a question of 'cram' equal to anything—from the siege of Troy to Donnybrook Fair.'"

"My friend Butt did not discredit the reputation I gave him. He invited us both to breakfast for the following Monday; and for Thackeray's enlightenment

* He praised it, however, on such healthy grounds as Thackeray's condemnation of that fulsome taste for " Lord-worship " too often met with in Ireland, and of the idle lives the young men of Dublin lead. D. U. M. vol. XXI. pp. 651-4. Lever's lordly guest at Brussels had taught him a lesson.

and amusement, he got up a debate, which incidentally opened the question of the Repeal of the Union, and called up the Liberator himself to speak with an amount of temper and passion, that showed he had detected the spirit of the discussion, and knew it to be merely a "field day," got up to amuse the stranger." *

Lever was a great admirer of Butt, and said that he was one of the very few lawyers he had known whose subtlety did not cramp his intellect.

Thackeray made himself very agreeable during his stay, and was a favourite with the children. A letter to Lever after his departure said, "Remember me to your little people—including Madame."

Major D—— was one of the friends whom Lever had assembled to meet Thackeray at Templeogue. He has supplied us with a very full account of the conversation at dinner, and subsequently—compiled from notes made at the time—and this valuable document will be found in our Portfolio. The Major was deputed by Lever to act as Thackeray's guide. From his careful

---

* The chief change which struck Lever on arriving in Dublin after his long exile, was the substitution of the new corporation headed by O'Connell, as its first Lord Mayor- for the rampantly Orange body which, among other displays of partisanship—loved to paint King William's statue in gaudy party colours. One of his first Magazine Papers (Jan. 1843) declares that " No clue is left to the absentee of a few years, by which to guide his path. He may look in vain even for the old landmarks which he remembered in boyhood ; for somehow he finds them all in masquerade," and after enumerating many changes he expresses amazement when he learns " who are deemed the fashionable entertainers of the day, at whose boards sit lords and baronets."

record of intercourse it is clear that the characteristics
of both these popular writers had little in common.
Thackeray's tomahawk fell upon the heads of women;
and their tongues lashed his name in retort. An expressive estimate of Lever is found in the praise which
ladies lavishly bestow on him. Miss Edgeworth declared that she was enchanted by his books; and the
generous, warm-hearted man in reply, said: "Amid
the thousands you have made better, and wiser, and
happier by your writings, you cannot count one who
feels more proudly the common tie of country with you,
or who more sincerely admires your goodness and your
genius." Miss Mitford, in writing to a friend on July
the 7th, 1843, pronounces "Jack Hinton" as "charming,"
"O'Donoghue" even better; and she adds, "I think
him one of our best living writers of fiction." * Unlike
Thackeray's all Lever's heroines are full of refinement,
good breeding, and elegance, and seem, indeed, incapable of an unworthy thought.

Lever's unruffled good humour is shown in many
ways, including the thorough enjoyment with which he
seemed to view the caricature of his style penned soon
after by the great satirist. In the last edition of "Tom

---

* Lever's friends should be glad of this criticism. Maginn described
Mary Mitford's literary flowers as sweet smelling, and all of the true English
oil—not redolent of turf and whiskey like the strong-scented bog-lilies which
others offered. "Mary's basket," he adds, "is arranged in so neat, so nice,
so trim, so comely—in a word so very English a manner, that it is a perfect
pleasure to see her tripping with it to market." She gracefully took Lever's
ram, and looked up in his face with loving eyes, and sunny smile—a conquest of which to be proud.

Burke " he pronounced as " inimitable " this burlesque; adding how " thoroughly it was relished by the well-quizzed object of it."

Still better was Thackeray's attempt at Lever's style of song—the error of supposing " dis " and " dat " Irishisms notwithstanding.

> " You've all heard of Larry O'Toole,
>   Of the beautiful town of Drumgoole ;
>   He had but one eye,
>   To ogle* ye by—
>   O, murther, but that was a jew'l !
>   A fool
>   He made of de girls, dis O'Toole.
>
> " 'Twas he was the boy didn't fail,
>   That tuck down pataties and mail ;
>   He never would shrink
>   From any sthrong dthrink,
>   Was it whiskey or Drogheda ale ;
>   I'm bail
>   This Larry would swallow a pail.
>
> " O, many a night, at the bowl,
>   With Larry I've sot cheek by jowl ;
>   He's gone to his rest,
>   Where there's dthrink of the best,
>   And so let us give his old sowl
>   A howl,
>   For 'twas he made the noggin to rowl."

Lever, true to the impulses of a gentleman, seemed to enjoy all this, but those who have read his letters

* " Ogle " was a favourite word with Lever.

> " They don't ogle a man
>   O'er the tips of their fan."

And in " O'Malley " " he frowns at his rival, he ogles his fair."

know how hypersensitive he was to any criticism which aimed to turn the laugh against himself. Thackeray's travesty had doubtless due effect in bringing about that thorough change in style which we find soon after inaugurated—much to the since avowed disappointment of Miss Mitford and others.

Lever repeatedly affirmed that praise was the spur which solely nerved him to exertion. Under irony he winced, and it may be said, succumbed. We find no more books of the "O'Malley" and "Tom Burke" family, once Thackeray's travesty appeared. After "Phil Fogarty: a novel by an Eminent Hand," Lever declared he might shut up shop. Stirring scenes and racy jokes fell in brisk succession from the mimic "Lorrequer." A great scene was that when General Picton and Sir Lowry Cole head the storming parties, while nine hundred and ninety-nine guns from the batteries open "withering fire." An army Doctor introduced is made to say, "Who's going to dance? the ball's begun. Ha! there goes poor Jack Delamere's head off! The ball chose a soft one, any how. Come here, Tim, till I mend your leg. Your wife has need only knit half as many stockings next year, Doolan, my boy. Faix! there goes a big one: had well nigh shut me up; bedad! it has snuffed the feather off my cocked hat!" Thus, with eighty-four pounders roaring over us like hail, the un- daunted Doctor pursued his jokes and his duty. That he had a feeling heart, all who served with him knew, and none more so than Philip Fogarty, the humble writer of these confessions. All this was too much for Lever himself, and henceforth such jokes were mostly reserved for fireside friends.

In June, 1840, Lever had described himself to McGlashan as overwhelmed with business, patching up Peel, Philpotts, Brougham, and Lyndhurst, physicking half the continent, advising the Prince de Polignac what to eat, drink, and avoid, and with hardly a moment for literary work. Some remarks, penned shortly before his death, go on to say :—

" Having given up the profession for which I believe I had some aptitude, to follow the precarious life of a writer, I suppose I am only admitting what many others under like circumstances might declare, that I have had my moments, and more than mere moments of doubt and misgiving that I made the wiser choice, and bating the intense pleasure an occasional success has afforded, I have been led to think that the career I had abandoned would have been more rewarding, more safe from reverses, and less exposed to those variations of public taste which are the terrors of all who live in the world's favour."*

---

* "Harry Lorrequer," twenty-first edition, Preface dated Trieste, 1872.
From time immemorial Letters and Physic have formed no unnatural alliance—even Æsculapius is represented in mythology as the son of Apollo. In relinquishing the craft and its gold-headed cane, Lever did not drop the spectacles of the physician. Through those penetrating lenses he continued to the end to view humanity around him. In "O'Dowd" he writes :—" London is a hypertrophied heart ; it has almost outgrown its functions, and has to labour immensely to maintain the circulation ; while in Paris the life-blood bounds freely along, animating, stimulating, and invigorating."

Elsewhere he expressed regret that he should have adopted authorship rather than continue medical practice, in which he thinks he might have risen to wealth and eminence, but it is a question if his choice were not the better one. He is described by his fellow-students at the medical schools of Dublin as failing to indicate any special promise; and, almost instinctively, we perceive that a man of the Lorrequer type would have had need to struggle against the temptation to indulge in that charlatanical finesse to which some of the highest of the faculty, as their brethren know, have not been above resorting. Lever was never so thoroughly happy as when duping the credulous by his practical jokes or plausible " fibs." We shall not soon forget the chapter, or the etching, where Lorrequer is represented " practising physic," utterly duping the patient as well as deceiving the two physicians with whom he had been in consultation, while to crown both the joke and the offence, he pockets his fee with a stiff bow. The disease under which this patient laboured is stated to have been " a stay-at-home-with-us " (steatomatous) tumour !

We have seen that a disposition exists amongst men

Describing a snub to a grand duchess, he says : " This moral turn was a beneficial alterative after our late repulse ;" and the small Italian town in which he lived so long, it appears, had " a condensed public opinion, like those essences a spoonful of which is equal to a pint of the ordinary decoction ; and I defy the most refractory spirit to brave its judgments or make light of its decrees."

His account of a trip to Killarney in wet weather states dryly, " You think of your dropsical integuments, and your atrophied purse." His remarks on parsonitis, or parson's sore throat, are full of humour.

who made medical studies with Lever to decry his claims to professional status. But we have heard them rebuked by senior heads with the remark, that it is experience alone has ever made the doctor eminent, and that no case exists on record of one attaining eminence under the age of forty years. Lever in 1839 was thirty-three only, and who can tell to what distinction he might not have risen in a few years more, had he continued to practise? Certes, Mr. Cusack had good hopes of him, as Lever's brother-in-law, Mr. Lauder, tells.

Far better that he should have occupied himself as he did in delightful story-telling, and died worth four thousand pounds only, than roll in a well splashed carriage as Sir Charles Lever, Bart., realising an enormous fortune as Physician to the British Embassy and practitioner general to the public at large. His gains would have been our losses.

END OF VOL. I.

CHAPMAN AND HALL'S ANNOUNCEMENTS.

December, 1878.

2 vols., demy 8vo, 32s.

The Public Life of the Earl of Beaconsfield.

By FRANCIS HITCHMAN.

Demy 8vo.

Imperial India.

By VAL PRINSEP.

Containing Numerous Illustrations made during a Tour to the Courts of the Principal Rajahs and Princes of India.

2 vols., demy 8vo, with Illustrations and Maps.

Sport in Burmah and Assam.

By LIEUT.-COL. POLLOK.

With Notes of Sport in the Hilly Districts of the Northern Division, Madras Presidency.

1 vol., large crown 8vo.

Pillars of the Empire.

WITH AN INTRODUCTION BY T. H. S. ESCOTT.

With Six Illustrations.   1 vol., demy 8vo, 16s.   Uniform with "On the Frontier."

On Foot in Spain.

By MAJOR CAMPION.

2 vols., large crown 8vo, 21s.

Shooting Adventures, Canine Lore, and Sea-Fishing Trips.

By "WILDFOWLER," "SNAPSHOT."

Demy 8vo.

Memoirs of Sir Joshua Walmsley.

By COLONEL WALMSLEY.

Illustrated. 1 vol., demy 8vo, 6s.

Pretty Arts for the Employment of Leisure Hours.

By ELLIS A. DAVIDSON.

Small crown 8vo.

The Pleasures and Profits of Our Little Poultry Farm.

By MISS G. HILL.

New Volumes of the Library of Contemporary Science.

ESTHETICS. By EUGENE VÉRON.

PHILOSOPHY. Historical and Critical. By ANDRÉ LEFÈVRE.

South Kensington Art Handbooks.

New Vols. Illustrated.

SPANISH ART. By SEÑOR RIAÑO.

GLASS. By ALEXANDER NESBITT.

Large crown 8vo, with Portraits, 18s.

Hibernia Venatica.

By M. O'C. MORRIS, Author of "Triviata."

Large crown 8vo, 8s.

Autobiography of Sir G. Biddlecombe.

With a Portrait.

Foolscap 8vo, 6s.

Bismarck's Letters.

TRANSLATED BY FITZ[H] MAXSE.

THE CHRONICLES OF BARSETSHIRE.

Messrs. CHAPMAN AND HALL

Also beg to announce the republication, in Monthly Volumes and under the above name, of the six following novels by

MR. ANTHONY TROLLOPE:

THE WARDEN & BARCHESTER TOWERS.

2 vols.

DR. THORNE.

1 vol.

FRAMLEY PARSONAGE.

1 vol.

THE LAST CHRONICLES OF BARSET.

2 vols.

Each Volume will contain a Frontispiece, and will be handsomely printed on large crown 8vo paper.

THE SECOND VOLUME IS NOW READY.

Price 6s.

DICKENS'S WORKS.

MESSRS. CHAPMAN & HALL

BEG TO ANNOUNCE

A RE-ISSUE OF THE LIBRARY EDITION,

UNDER THE TITLE OF THE

Popular Library Edition.

This Edition will be printed on good paper, and contain Illustrations that have appeared in the Household Edition, printed on plate paper.

Each Volume will consist of about 460 *pages of Letterpress and*

SIXTEEN ILLUSTRATIONS.

The Second Volume, "CHRISTMAS BOOKS," is now ready.

Large crown 8vo. Price 3s. 6d.

193, *Piccadilly, London, W.*
December, 1878.

Chapman and Hall's

CATALOGUE OF BOOKS.

INCLUDING

DRAWING EXAMPLES, DIAGRAMS, MODELS, INSTRUMENTS, ETC.

ISSUED UNDER THE AUTHORITY OF

THE SCIENCE AND ART DEPARTMENT SOUTH KENSINGTON,

FOR THE USE OF SCHOOLS AND ART AND SCIENCE CLASSES.

NEW NOVELS.

A SECRET MARRIAGE AND ITS CONSEQUENCES.
By THE AUTHOR OF "FASHION AND PASSION," &c.
[3 vols.

ROY'S WIFE.
By G. J. WHYTE-MELVILLE.
New Edition. In One Volume. 6s.

SUNSHINE AND SNOW.
By HAWLEY SMART. [3 vols.

NEAR THE LAGUNAS; OR, SCENES IN THE STATES OF LA PLATA.
By THE AUTHOR OF "PONCE DE LEON." [2 vols.

LAND AHEAD.
By COURTENEY GRANT,
Author of "Little Lady Lorraine," "Our Next Neighbour," &c. [3 vols.

ARTHUR JESSIESON.
By JOSEPH CRAWFORD SCOTT. [2 vols.

CECIL CROFTON'S REPENTANCE.
By VERE GRAY. [2 vols.

JOHN SMITH.
By THE HON. MRS. CRADOCK. [2 vols.

BOOKS

PUBLISHED BY

CHAPMAN AND HALL.

ABBOTT (EDWIN)—Formerly Head-Master of the Philological School—
A CONCORDANCE OF THE ORIGINAL POETICAL
WORKS OF ALEXANDER POPE. With an Introduction on the English of
Pope, by EDWIN A. ABBOTT, D.D., Author of "A Shakespearian Grammar,"
&c. &c. Medium 8vo, price £1 1s.

ABBOTT (SAMUEL)—
ARDENMOHR: AMONG THE HILLS. A Record of
Scenery and Sport in the Highlands of Scotland. With Sketches and Etchings by
the Author. Demy 8vo, 12s. 6d.

ADAMS (FRANCIS)—
THE FREE-SCHOOL SYSTEM OF THE UNITED
STATES. Demy 8vo, 9s.

ADON—
LAYS OF MODERN OXFORD. Illustrated by M. E.
EDWARDS, F. LOCKWOOD, and THE AUTHOR. Fcap. 4to, cloth, 6s.

AUSTIN (ALFRED)—
LESZKO THE BASTARD. A Tale of Polish Grief.
Crown 8vo, 3s. 6d.

BARTLEY (G. C. T.)—
A HANDY BOOK FOR GUARDIANS OF THE POOR:
being a Complete Manual of the Duties of the Office, the Treatment of Typical
Cases, with Practical Examples, &c. Crown 8vo, cloth, 3s.

THE PARISH NET: HOW IT'S DRAGGED AND
WHAT IT CATCHES. Crown 8vo, cloth, 7s. 6d.

THE SEVEN AGES OF A VILLAGE PAUPER. Crown
8vo, cloth, 5s.

*BEESLY (EDWARD SPENCER)—Professor of History in University College,
London—*
CATILINE, CLODIUS, AND TIBERIUS. Large crown
8vo, 6s.

BENNETT (W. C.)—
SEA SONGS. Crown 8vo, 4s.

A 2

BENSON (W.)—

MANUAL OF THE SCIENCE OF COLOUR. Coloured
Frontispiece and Illustrations. 12mo, cloth, 2s. 6d.

PRINCIPLES OF THE SCIENCE OF COLOUR. Small
4to, cloth, 15s.

BIDDLECOMBE (SIR GEORGE) C.B., Captain R.N.—

AUTOBIOGRAPHY OF SIR GEORGE BIDDLE-
COMBE, C.B., Captain R.N. Large crown 8vo, 8s.

BLAKE (EDITH OSBORNE)—

TWELVE MONTHS IN SOUTHERN EUROPE. With
Illustrations. Demy 8vo, 14s.

BLYTH (COLONEL)—

THE WHIST-PLAYER. With Coloured Plates of " Hands."
Third Edition. Imp. 16mo, cloth, 5s.

BRADLEY (THOMAS)—of the Royal Military Academy, Woolwich—

ELEMENTS OF GEOMETRICAL DRAWING. In Two
Parts, with Sixty Plates. Oblong folio, half-bound, each Part 16s.

Selection (from the above) of Twenty Plates for the use of
the Royal Military Academy, Woolwich. Oblong folio, half-bound, 16s.

BUCKLAND (FRANK)—

LOG-BOOK OF A FISHERMAN AND ZOOLOGIST.
Second Edition. With numerous Illustrations. Large crown 8vo, 12s.

BURCHETT (R.)—

DEFINITIONS OF GEOMETRY. New Edition. 24mo,
cloth, 5d.

LINEAR PERSPECTIVE, for the Use of Schools of Art.
Twenty-first Thousand. With Illustrations. Post 8vo, cloth, 7s.

PRACTICAL GEOMETRY : The Course of Construction
of Plane Geometrical Figures. With 137 Diagrams. Eighteenth Edition. Post
8vo, cloth, 5s.

CADDY (MRS.)—

HOUSEHOLD ORGANIZATION. Crown 8vo, 4s.

CAITHNESS (COUNTESS)—

OLD TRUTHS IN A NEW LIGHT : or, an Earnest
Endeavour to Reconcile Material Science with Spiritual Science and Scripture.
Demy 8vo, 15s.

CAMPION (J. S.), late Major, Staff, 1st Br. C.N.G., U.S.A.—

ON THE FRONTIER. Reminiscences of Wild Sport,
Personal Adventures, and Strange Scenes. With Illustrations. Demy 8vo. Second
Edition, 16s.

ON FOOT IN SPAIN. With Illustrations. Demy 8vo.

CARLYLE (DR.)—

DANTE'S DIVINE COMEDY.—Literal Prose Transla-
tion of THE INFERNO, with Text and Notes. Second Edition. Post 8vo, 14s.

CARLYLE (THOMAS)—See pages 17 and 18.

CLINTON (R. H.)—

A COMPENDIUM OF ENGLISH HISTORY, from the
Earliest Times to A.D. 1872. With Copious Quotations on the Leading Events and the Constitutional History, together with Appendices. Post 8vo, 7s. 6d.

CRAIK (GEORGE LILLIE)—

ENGLISH OF SHAKESPEARE. Illustrated in a Philo-
logical Commentary on his Julius Cæsar. Fifth Edition. Post 8vo, cloth, 5s.

OUTLINES OF THE HISTORY OF THE ENGLISH
LANGUAGE. Ninth Edition. Post 8vo, cloth, 2s. 6d.

DASENT (SIR G. W.)—

JEST AND EARNEST. A Collection of Reviews and
Essays. 2 vols. Post 8vo, cloth, £1 1s.

TALES FROM THE FJELD. A Second Series of
Popular Tales from the Norse of P. Ch. Asbjörnsen. Small 8vo, cloth, 10s. 6d.

DAUBOURG (E.)—

INTERIOR ARCHITECTURE. Doors, Vestibules, Stair-
cases, Anterooms, Drawing, Dining, and Bed Rooms, Libraries, Bank and News-paper Offices, Shop Fronts and Interiors. With detailed Plans, Sections, and Elevations. A purely practical work, intended for Architects, Joiners, Cabinet Makers, Marble Workers, Decorators; as well as for the owners of houses who wish to have them ornamented by artisans of their own choice. Half-imperial, cloth, £2 12s. 6d.

DAVIDSON (ELLIS A.)—

PRETTY ARTS FOR THE EMPLOYMENT OF
LEISURE HOURS. A Book for Ladies. With Illustrations. Demy 8vo.

THE AMATEUR HOUSE CARPENTER: a Guide in
Building, Making, and Repairing. With numerous Illustrations, drawn on Wood by the Author. Royal 8vo, 10s. 6d.

DAVISON (THE MISSES)—

TRIQUETI MARBLES IN THE ALBERT MEMORIAL
CHAPEL, WINDSOR. A Series of Photographs. Dedicated by express per-mission to Her Majesty the Queen. The Work consists of 117 Photographs, with descriptive Letterpress, mounted on 49 sheets of cardboard, half-imperial. Price £10 10s.

DE COIN (COLONEL ROBERT L.)—

HISTORY AND CULTIVATION OF COTTON AND
TOBACCO. Post 8vo, cloth, 9s.

DE KONINCK (L. L.) and DIETZ (E.)—

PRACTICAL MANUAL OF CHEMICAL ASSAYING,
as applied to the Manufacture of Iron from its Ores, and to Cast Iron, Wrought Iron, and Steel, as found in Commerce. Edited, with notes, by ROBERT MALLET. Post 8vo, cloth, 6s.

DE LEUVILLE (LE MARQUIS)—

ENTRE-NOUS. With Portrait. Fourth Edition. Demy
8vo, 5s.

A Smaller Edition, with Portrait. Crown 8vo, 3s.

DE POMAR (THE DUKE)—

FASHION AND PASSION; or, Life in Mayfair. New
Edition. Crown 8vo, 6s.

THE HEIR TO THE CROWN. Crown 8vo, 7s. 6d.

DE WORMS (BARON HENRY)—

ENGLAND'S POLICY IN THE EAST. An Account of
the Policy and Interest of England in the Eastern Question, as compared with
those of the other European Powers. Sixth Edition. To this Edition has been
added the Tripartite Treaty of 1856, and the Black Sea Treaty of 1871.
Sixth Edition. Demy 8vo, 5s.

THE AUSTRO-HUNGARIAN EMPIRE: A Poli-
tical Sketch of Men and Events since 1868. Revised and Corrected, with an
Additional Chapter on the Present Crisis in the East. With Maps. Second
Edition. Demy 8vo, cloth, 9s.

DICKENS (CHARLES)—See pages 19—22.

DYCE'S COLLECTION. A Catalogue of Printed Books and
Manuscripts bequeathed by the REV. ALEXANDER DYCE to the South Kensington
Museum. 2 vols. Royal 8vo, half-morocco, 14s.

A Collection of Paintings, Miniatures, Drawings, Engravings,
Rings, and Miscellaneous Objects, bequeathed by the REV. ALEXANDER DYCE
to the South Kensington Museum. Royal 8vo, half-morocco, 7s.

DICKENS (CHARLES)—Conducted by—

ALL THE YEAR ROUND. First Series. 20 vols.
Royal 8vo, cloth, 5s. 6d. each.

New Series. Vols. 1 to 12. Royal 8vo, cloth, 5s. 6d. each.

DIXON (W. HEPWORTH)—

THE HOLY LAND. Fourth Edition. With 2 Steel and
12 Wood Engravings. Post 8vo, 10s. 6d.

DRAYSON (LIEUT.-COL. A. W.)—

THE CAUSE OF THE SUPPOSED PROPER MOTION
OF THE FIXED STARS, with other Geometrical Problems in Astronomy hitherto
unsolved. Demy 8vo, cloth, 10s.

THE CAUSE, DATE, AND DURATION OF THE
LAST GLACIAL EPOCH OF GEOLOGY, with an Investigation of a New
Movement of the Earth. Demy 8vo, cloth, 10s.

PRACTICAL MILITARY SURVEYING AND
SKETCHING. Fifth Edition. Post 8vo, cloth, 4s. 6d.

DYCE (WILLIAM), R.A.—

DRAWING-BOOK OF THE GOVERNMENT SCHOOL
OF DESIGN; OR, ELEMENTARY OUTLINES OF ORNAMENT. Fifty
selected Plates. Folio, sewed, 5s.; mounted, 18s.

Text to Ditto. Sewed, 6d.

ELLIOT (FRANCES)—

OLD COURT LIFE IN FRANCE. Third Edition.
Demy 8vo, cloth, 10s. 6d.

THE DIARY OF AN IDLE WOMAN IN ITALY.
Second Edition. Post 8vo, cloth, 6s.

PICTURES OF OLD ROME. New Edition. Post 8vo,
cloth, 6s.

ELLIOT (ROBERT H.)—

EXPERIENCES OF A PLANTER IN THE JUNGLES
OF MYSORE. With Illustrations and a Map. 2 vols. 8vo, cloth, £1 4s.

CONCERNING JOHN'S INDIAN AFFAIRS. 8vo,
cloth, 9s.

ENGEL (CARL)—

A DESCRIPTIVE AND ILLUSTRATED CATALOGUE
OF THE MUSICAL INSTRUMENTS in the SOUTH KENSINGTON
MUSEUM, preceded by an Essay on the History of Musical Instruments. Second
Edition. Royal 8vo, half-morocco, 12s.

ESCOTT (T. H. S.)—

PILLARS OF THE EMPIRE: Short Biographical
Sketches. Demy 8vo.

EWALD (ALEXANDER CHARLES), F.S.A.—

THE LIFE AND TIMES OF PRINCE CHARLES
STUART, COUNT OF ALBANY, commonly called The Young Pretender.
From the State Papers and other Sources. Author of "The Life and Times of
Algernon Sydney," "The Crown and its Advisers," &c. 2 vols. Demy 8vo, £1 8s.

SIR ROBERT WALPOLE. A Political Biography,
1676—1745. Demy 8vo, 18s.

FALLOUX (COUNT DE), of the French Academy—

AUGUSTIN COCHIN. Translated from the French by
AUGUSTUS CRAVEN. Large crown 8vo, 9s.

FANE (VIOLET)—

DENZIL PLACE: a Story in Verse. Crown 8vo, cloth, 8s.

QUEEN OF THE FAIRIES (A Village Story), and other
Poems. By the Author of "Denzil Place." Crown 8vo, 6s.

ANTHONY BABINGTON: a Drama. By the Author of
"Denzil Place," "The Queen of the Fairies," &c. Crown 8vo, 6s.

FLEMING (GEORGE), F.R.C.S.—

ANIMAL PLAGUES: THEIR HISTORY, NATURE,
AND PREVENTION. 8vo, cloth, 15s.

HORSES AND HORSE-SHOEING: their Origin, History,
Uses, and Abuses. 210 Engravings. 8vo, cloth, £1 1s.

PRACTICAL HORSE-SHOEING: With 37 Illustrations.
Second Edition, enlarged. 8vo, sewed, 2s.

RABIES AND HYDROPHOBIA: THEIR HISTORY,
NATURE, CAUSES, SYMPTOMS, AND PREVENTION. With 8 Illustrations. 8vo, cloth, 15s.

A MANUAL OF VETERINARY SANITARY SCIENCE
AND POLICE. With 33 Illustrations. 2 vols. Demy 8vo, 36s.

FORSTER (JOHN)—

THE LIFE OF CHARLES DICKENS. Uniform with
the "C. D." Edition of his Works. With Numerous Illustrations. 2 vols. 7s.

THE LIFE OF CHARLES DICKENS. With Portraits
and other Illustrations. 15th Thousand. 3 vols. 8vo, cloth, £2 2s.

A New Edition in 2 vols. Demy 8vo, uniform with the
Illustrated Edition of Dickens's Works. £1 8s.

FORSTER (JOHN) Continued—

SIR JOHN ELIOT : a Biography. With Portraits. New
and cheaper Edition. 2 vols. Post 8vo, cloth, 14s.

OLIVER GOLDSMITH : a Biography. Cheap Edition in
one volume. Small 8vo, cloth, 6s.

WALTER SAVAGE LANDOR : a Biography, 1775–1864.
With Portraits and Vignettes. A New and Revised Edition, in 1 vol. Demy 8vo, 14s.

FORTNUM (C. D. E.)—

A DESCRIPTIVE AND ILLUSTRATED CATALOGUE
OF THE BRONZES OF EUROPEAN ORIGIN in the SOUTH KEN-
SINGTON MUSEUM, with an Introductory Notice. Royal 8vo, half-morocco,
£1 10s.

A DESCRIPTIVE AND ILLUSTRATED CATALOGUE
OF MAIOLICA, HISPANO-MORESCO, PERSIAN, DAMASCUS, AND
RHODIAN WARES in the SOUTH KENSINGTON MUSEUM. Royal
8vo, half-morocco, £2.

FRANCATELLI (C. E.)—

ROYAL CONFECTIONER : English and Foreign. A
Practical Treatise. With Coloured Illustrations. 3rd Edition. Post 8vo, cloth, 7s. 6d.

GILLMORE (PARKER)—

PRAIRIE AND FOREST: a Description of the Game of
North America, with personal Adventures in their pursuit. With numerous Illustrations. 8vo, cloth, 12s.

HALL (SIDNEY)—

A TRAVELLING ATLAS OF THE ENGLISH COUN-
TIES. Fifty Maps, coloured. New Edition, including the Railways, corrected
up to the present date. Demy 8vo, in roan tuck, 10s. 6d.

HARDY (CAPT. C.)—

FOREST LIFE IN ACADIE ; and Sketches of Sport and
Natural History in the Lower Provinces of the Canadian Dominion. With Illustrations. 8vo, cloth, 18s.

HITCHMAN (FRANCIS)—

THE PUBLIC LIFE OF THE EARL OF BEACONS-
FIELD. 2 vols. Demy 8vo.

HOLBEIN—

TWELVE HEADS AFTER HOLBEIN. Selected from
Drawings in Her Majesty's Collection at Windsor. Reproduced in Autotype, in
portfolio. 36s.

HOVELACQUE (ABEL)—

THE SCIENCE OF LANGUAGE : LINGUISTICS,
PHILOLOGY, AND ETYMOLOGY. With Maps. Large crown 8vo, cloth, 5s.
Being the first volume of "The Library of Contemporary Science."
(*For list of other Works of the same Series, see page 24.*)

HUMPHRIS (H. D.)—

PRINCIPLES OF PERSPECTIVE. Illustrated in a
Series of Examples. Oblong folio, half-bound, and Text 8vo, cloth, £1 1s.

JACQUEMART (ALBERT)—

THE HISTORY OF FURNITURE. Researches and
Notes on Objects of Art which form Articles of Furniture, or would be interesting
to Collectors. Translated from the French and Edited by Mrs. Bury
Palliser. With 200 Illustrations. Imperial 8vo. 31s. 6d.

JAGOR (F.)—

PHILIPPINE ISLANDS, THE. With numerous Illustrations and a Map. Demy 8vo, 16s.

JARRY (GENERAL)—

NAPIER (MAJ.-GEN. W. C. E.)—OUTPOST DUTY.
Translated, with TREATISES ON MILITARY RECONNAISSANCE AND
ON ROAD-MAKING. Third Edition. Crown 8vo, 5s.

KEBBEL (T. E.)—

THE AGRICULTURAL LABOURER. A Short Survey
of his Position. Crown 8vo, 6s.

KELLEY, M.D. (E. G.)—

THE PHILOSOPHY OF EXISTENCE.—The Reality and
Romance of Histories. Demy 8vo, 16s.

KEMPIS (THOMAS À)—

OF THE IMITATION OF CHRIST. Four Books.
Beautifully Illustrated Edition. Demy 8vo, 16s.

KLACZKO (M. JULIAN)—

TWO CHANCELLORS: PRINCE GORTCHAKOF and
PRINCE BISMARCK. Translated by Mrs. Tait. New and cheaper edition, 6s.

LEFÈVRE (ANDRÉ)—

PHILOSOPHY, Historical and Critical.   *[In the Press.*

LEGGE (ALFRED OWEN)—

PIUS IX. The Story of his Life to the Restoration in
1850, with Glimpses of the National Movement in Italy. Author of "The Growth
of the Temporal Power in Italy." 2 vols. Demy 8vo, £1 12s.

LENNOX (LORD WILLIAM)—

FASHION THEN AND NOW. 2 vols. Demy 8vo, 28s.

LETOURNEAU (DR. CHARLES)—

BIOLOGY. Translated by William MacCall. With Illustrations. Large crown 8vo, 6s.

LUCAS (CAPTAIN)—

CAMP LIFE AND SPORT IN SOUTH AFRICA.
With Episodes in Kaffir Warfare. With Illustrations. Demy 8vo, 12s.

LYNCH (REV. T. T.)—

MEMORIALS OF THEOPHILUS TRINAL,
STUDENT. New Edition, enlarged. Crown 8vo, cloth extra, 6s.

LYTTON (ROBERT, LORD)—

POETICAL WORKS—COLLECTED EDITION. Complete in 5 vols.
FABLES IN SONG. 2 vols. Fcap. 8vo, 12s.
LUCILE. Fcap. 8vo, 6s.
THE WANDERER. Fcap. 8vo, 6s.
POEMS, HISTORICAL AND CHARACTERISTIC. Fcap. 6s.

MALLET (DR. J. W.)—

COTTON: THE CHEMICAL, &c., CONDITIONS OF ITS SUCCESSFUL CULTIVATION. Post 8vo, cloth, 7s. 6d.

MALLET (ROBERT)—

GREAT NEAPOLITAN EARTHQUAKE OF 1857. First Principles of Observational Seismology, as developed in the Report to the Royal Society of London, of the Expedition made into the Interior of the Kingdom of Naples, to investigate the circumstances of the great Earthquake of December, 1857. Maps and numerous Illustrations. 2 vols. Royal 8vo, cloth, £3 3s.

MASKELL (WILLIAM)—

A DESCRIPTION OF THE IVORIES, ANCIENT AND MEDIÆVAL, in the SOUTH KENSINGTON MUSEUM, with a Preface. With numerous Photographs and Woodcuts. Royal 8vo, half-morocco, £1 1s.

MAXSE (FITZH.)—

PRINCE BISMARCK'S LETTERS. Translated from the German. Small crown 8vo, cloth, 6s.

MAZADE (CHARLES DE)—

THE LIFE OF COUNT CAVOUR. Translated from the French. Demy 8vo, 16s.

MELVILLE (G. J. WHYTE-)—

RIDING RECOLLECTIONS. With Illustrations by EDGAR GIBERNE. Large crown 8vo. Fifth Edition. 12s.

ROSINE. With Illustrations. Demy 8vo. Uniform with "Katerfelto," 16s.

SISTER LOUISE; or, The Story of a Woman's Repentance. With Illustrations by MIRIAM KERNS. Demy 8vo, 16s.

KATERFELTO: A Story of Exmoor. With 12 Illustrations by COLONEL H. HOPE CREALOCKE. Fourth Edition. Large crown, 8s.
(For Cheap Editions of other Works, see page 25.)

MEREDITH (GEORGE)—

MODERN LOVE, AND POEMS OF THE ENGLISH ROADSIDE, with Poems and Ballads. Fcap. 8vo, cloth, 6s.

MILLER (JOAQUIN)—

THE SHIP IN THE DESERT. By the Author of "Songs of the Sierras," &c. Fcap. 8vo, 6s.

MOLESWORTH (W. NASSAU)—

HISTORY OF ENGLAND FROM THE YEAR 1830 TO THE RESIGNATION OF THE GLADSTONE MINISTRY.
A Cheap Edition, carefully revised, and carried up to March, 1874. 3 vols. crown 8vo, 18s.
A School Edition. Post 8vo, 7s. 6d.

MONTAGU (THE RIGHT HON. LORD ROBERT, M.P.)—

FOREIGN POLICY: ENGLAND AND THE EASTERN QUESTION. Second Edition. Demy 8vo, 14s.

MORLEY (HENRY)—

ENGLISH WRITERS. Vol. I. Part I. THE CELTS AND ANGLO-SAXONS. With an Introductory Sketch of the Four Periods of English Literature. Part II. FROM THE CONQUEST TO CHAUCER. (Making 2 vols.) 8vo, cloth, £1 2s.

*** Each Part is indexed separately. The Two Parts complete the account of English Literature during the Period of the Formation of the Language, or of THE WRITERS BEFORE CHAUCER.

Vol. II. Part I. FROM CHAUCER TO DUNBAR. 8vo, cloth, 12s.

TABLES OF ENGLISH LITERATURE. Containing 20 Charts. Second Edition, with Index. Royal 4to, cloth, 12s.

In Three Parts. Parts I. and II., containing Three Charts, each 1s. 6d.

Part III., containing 14 Charts, 7s. Part III. also kept in Sections, 1, 2, and 5, 1s. 6d. each; 3 and 4 together, 3s. *** The Charts sold separately.

MORLEY (JOHN)—

DIDEROT AND THE ENCYCLOPÆDISTS. 2 Vols. demy 8vo, 26s.

CRITICAL MISCELLANIES. Second Series. France in the Eighteenth Century—Robespierre—Turgot—Death of Mr. Mill—Mr. Mill on Religion—On Popular Culture—Macaulay. Demy 8vo, cloth, 14s.

CRITICAL MISCELLANIES. First Series. Demy 8vo, 14s.

NEW UNIFORM EDITION.

VOLTAIRE. Large crown 8vo, 6s.

ROUSSEAU. Large crown 8vo, 9s.

CRITICAL MISCELLANIES. First Series. *[In the Press.*

CRITICAL MISCELLANIES. Second Series. *[In the Press.*

ON COMPROMISE. New Edition. Crown 8vo, 3s. 6d.

STRUGGLE FOR NATIONAL EDUCATION. Third Edition. 8vo, cloth, 3s.

MORRIS (M. O'CONNOR)—

HIBERNICA VENATICA. With Portraits of the Marchioness of Waterford, the Marchioness of Ormonde, Lady Randolph Churchill, Hon. Mrs. Malone, Miss Persse (of Moyode Castle', Mrs. Stewart Duckett, and Miss Myra Watson. Large crown 8vo, 18s.

TRIVIATA ; or, Cross Road Chronicles of Passages in Irish Hunting History during the season of 1875-76. With Illustrations. Large crown 8vo, 16s.

NEWTON (E. TULLEY, F.G.S.)—Assistant-Naturalist H.M. Geological Survey—

THE TYPICAL PARTS IN THE SKELETONS OF A CAT, DUCK, AND CODFISH, being a Catalogue with Comparative Descriptions arranged in a Tabular Form. Demy 8vo, cloth, 3s.

O'CONNELL (MRS. MORGAN JOHN)—

CHARLES BIANCONI. A Biography. 1786-1875. By his Daughter. With Illustrations. Demy 8vo, 10s. 6d.

OLIVER (PROFESSOR), F.R.S., &c.—

ILLUSTRATIONS OF THE PRINCIPAL NATURAL ORDERS OF THE VEGETABLE KINGDOM, PREPARED FOR THE SCIENCE AND ART DEPARTMENT, SOUTH KENSINGTON. Oblong 8vo, with 109 Plates. Price, plain, 16s. ; coloured, £1 6s.

OZANE (I. W.)—

THREE YEARS IN ROUMANIA. Large crown 8vo, 7s. 6d.

PARR (HARRIETT)—Author of "Essays in the Silver Age," &c.—

DE GUÉRIN (MAURICE AND EUGÉNIE). A Monograph. Crown 8vo, cloth, 6s.

PIERCE (GILBERT A.)—

THE DICKENS DICTIONARY: a Key to the Characters and Principal Incidents in the Tales of Charles Dickens. With Additions by WILLIAM A. WHEELER. Large crown 8vo, 10s. 6d.

PIM (B.) and SEEMAN (B.)—

DOTTINGS ON THE ROADSIDE IN PANAMA, NICARAGUA, AND MOSQUITO. With Plates and Maps. 8vo, cloth, 18s.

POLLEN (J. H.)—

ANCIENT AND MODERN FURNITURE AND WOODWORK IN THE SOUTH KENSINGTON MUSEUM. With an Introduction, and Illustrated with numerous Coloured Photographs and Woodcuts. Royal 8vo, half-morocco, £1 1s.

PUCKETT (R. CAMPBELL)—Head-Master of the Bath School of Art—

SCIOGRAPHY; or, Radial Projection of Shadows. New Edition. Crown 8vo, cloth, 6s.

RANKEN (W. H. L.)—

THE DOMINION OF AUSTRALIA. An Account of its Foundations. Post 8vo, cloth, 12s.

REDGRAVE (RICHARD)—

MANUAL AND CATECHISM ON COLOUR. 24mo, cloth, 9d.

REDGRAVE (SAMUEL)—

A DESCRIPTIVE CATALOGUE OF THE HISTORICAL COLLECTION OF WATER-COLOUR PAINTINGS IN THE SOUTH KENSINGTON MUSEUM. With an Introductory Notice by SAMUEL REDGRAVE. With numerous Chromo-lithographs and other Illustrations. Published for the Science and Art Department of the Committee of Council on Education. Royal 8vo, £1 1s.

RIDGE (DR. BENJAMIN)—

OURSELVES, OUR FOOD, AND OUR PHYSIC. Twelfth Edition. Fcap. 8vo, cloth, 1s. 6d.

ROBINSON (C. E.)—

THE CRUISE OF THE *WIDGEON*: 700 Miles in a Ten-Ton Yawl, from Swanage to Hamburg, through the Dutch Canals and the Zuyder Zee, German Ocean, and the River Elbe. With 4 Illustrations, drawn on Wood, by the Author. Second Edition. Large crown 8vo, 9s.

ROBINSON (J. C.)—

ITALIAN SCULPTURE OF THE MIDDLE AGES AND PERIOD OF THE REVIVAL OF ART. A descriptive Catalogue of that Section of the South Kensington Museum comprising an Account of the Acquisitions from the Gigli and Campana Collections. With 20 Engravings. Royal 8vo, cloth, 7s. 6d.

ROBSON (GEORGE)—

ELEMENTARY BUILDING CONSTRUCTION. Illustrated by a Design for an Entrance, Lodge, and Gate. 15 Plates. Oblong folio, sewed, 8s.

ROBSON (REV. J. H., M.A., LL.M.)—late Foundation Scholar of Downing College, Cambridge—

AN ELEMENTARY TREATISE ON ALGEBRA.
Post 8vo, 6s.

ROCK (THE VERY REV. CANON, D.D.)—

ON TEXTILE FABRICS. A Descriptive and Illustrated
Catalogue of the Collection of Church Vestments, Dresses, Silk Stuffs, Needlework, and Tapestries in the South Kensington Museum. Royal 8vo, half-morocco, £1 11s. 6d.

SALUSBURY (PHILIP H. B.)—Lieut. 1st Royal Cheshire Light Infantry—

TWO MONTHS WITH TCHERNAIEFF IN SERVIA.
Large crown 8vo, 9s.

SCHMID (HERMAN) and STIELER (KARL)—

BAVARIAN HIGHLANDS (THE) AND THE SALZ-
KAMMERGUT. Profusely illustrated by G. Closs, W. Diez, A. von Ramberg, K. Raupp, J. G. Steffan, F. Voltz, J. Watter, and others. With an Account of the Habits and Manners of the Hunters, Poachers, and Peasantry of these Districts. Super-royal 4to, cloth, £1 5s.

SCOTT (SIR SIBBALD D.)—

TO JAMAICA AND BACK. With Frontispiece. Crown
8vo, 10s. 6d.

SHIRREFF (EMILY)—

A SKETCH OF THE LIFE OF FRIEDRICH
FRÖBEL, together with a Notice of Madame von Marenholtz Bulow's Personal Recollections of F. Fröbel. Crown 8vo, sewn, 1s.

SHUTE (ANNA CLARA)—

POSTHUMOUS POEMS. Crown 8vo, cloth, 8s.

SKERTCHLY (J. A.)—

DAHOMEY AS IT IS: being a Narrative of Eight
Months' Residence in that Country, with a Full Account of the Notorious Annual Customs, and the Social and Religious Institutions of the Ffons. With Illustrations. 8vo, cloth, £1 1s.

SMITHARD (MARIAN)—First-Class Diplomée from National Training School, South Kensington—

COOKERY FOR THE ARTIZAN AND OTHERS:
being a Selection of over Two Hundred Useful Receipts. Sewed, 1s.

SPALDING (CAPTAIN)—

KHIVA AND TURKESTAN, translated from the Russian,
with Map. Large crown 8vo, 9s.

ST. CLAIR (S. G. B., Captain late 21st Fusiliers) and CHARLES A. BROPHY—

TWELVE YEARS' RESIDENCE IN BULGARIA.
Revised Edition. Demy 8vo, 9s.

STORY (W. W.)—

ROBA DI ROMA. Seventh Edition, with Additions and
Portrait. Post 8vo, cloth, 10s. 6d.

THE PROPORTIONS OF THE HUMAN FRAME,
ACCORDING TO A NEW CANON. With Plates. Royal 8vo, cloth, 10s.

CASTLE ST. ANGELO. Uniform with "Roba di Roma."
With Illustrations. Large crown 8vo, 10s. 6d.

STREETER (E. W.)—

PRECIOUS STONES AND GEMS. An exhaustive and
practical Work for the Merchant, Connoisseur, or the Private Buyer. Treats upon all descriptions of Precious Stones, giving their History, Habitat, Value, and Uses for Ornament, together with much Information regarding their Matrices or Rough State. With Coloured Illustrations, Photographs, &c. Demy 8vo, 18s.

GOLD; OR, LEGAL REGULATIONS FOR THIS
METAL IN DIFFERENT COUNTRIES OF THE WORLD. Crown 8vo, cloth, 3s. 6d.

TOPINARD (DR. PAUL)—

ANTHROPOLOGY. With a Preface by Professor PAUL
BROCA, Secretary of the Société d'Anthropologie, and Translated by ROBERT J. H. BARTLETT, M.D. With numerous Illustrations. Large crown 8vo, 7s. 6d.

TROLLOPE (ANTHONY)—

THE CHRONICLES OF BARSETSHIRE. A Uniform
Edition in the Press, consisting of 6 vols., large crown 8vo, handsomely printed.

VOL. I. THE WARDEN.	DR. THORNE.
With Frontispiece.	FRAMLEY PARSONAGE.
[This month.	LAST CHRONICLE OF
BARCHESTER TOWERS.	BARSET. 2 vols.

Large crown 8vo, each vol. containing Frontispiece.

AUSTRALIA AND NEW ZEALAND. A Cheap Edition
in Four Parts, with Maps. Small 8vo, cloth, 3s. each.

  NEW ZEALAND.
  VICTORIA AND TASMANIA.
  NEW SOUTH WALES AND QUEENSLAND.
  SOUTH AUSTRALIA AND WESTERN AUSTRALIA.

HUNTING SKETCHES. Cloth, 3s. 6d.

TRAVELLING SKETCHES. Cloth, 3s. 6d.

CLERGYMEN OF THE CHURCH OF ENGLAND.
3s. 6d.

SOUTH AFRICA. 2 vols. Large crown 8vo, with Maps.
Fourth Edition. £1 10s.

(For Cheap Editions of other Works, see page 25.)

TROLLOPE (T. A.)—

HISTORY OF THE PAPAL CONCLAVES. Demy
8vo, 16s.

VERON (EUGENE)—

ÆSTHETICS. Translated by W. ARMSTRONG. Large
crown 8vo, 7s. 6d.

VON GUNTHER (LA COMTESSE)—

TALES AND LEGENDS OF THE TYROL. Collected
and Arranged. Crown 8vo, cloth, 5s.

WAHL (O. H.)—

THE LAND OF THE CZAR. Demy 8vo, 16s.

WESTWOOD (J. O.), M.A., F.L.S., &c. &c.—

A DESCRIPTIVE AND ILLUSTRATED CATALOGUE
OF THE FICTILE IVORIES IN THE SOUTH KENSINGTON MUSEUM. With an Account of the Continental Collections of Classical and Mediæval Ivories. Royal 8vo, half-morocco, £1 4s.

WHEELER (G. P.)—

VISIT OF THE PRINCE OF WALES. A Chronicle of
H.R.H.'s Journeyings in India, Ceylon, Spain, and Portugal. Large crown 8vo, 12s.

WHITE (WALTER)—

HOLIDAYS IN TYROL: Kufstein, Klobenstein, and
Paneveggio. Large crown 8vo, 14s.

EASTERN ENGLAND. From the Thames to the
Humber. 2 vols. Post 8vo, cloth, 18s.

MONTH IN YORKSHIRE. Fourth Edition. With a
Map. Post 8vo, cloth, 4s.

LONDONER'S WALK TO THE LAND'S END, AND
A TRIP TO THE SCILLY ISLES. With 4 Maps. Second Edition. Post 8vo, 4s.

WORNUM (R. N.)—

HOLBEIN (HANS)—LIFE. With Portrait and Illustrations. Imperial 8vo, cloth, £1 11s. 6d.

THE EPOCHS OF PAINTING. A Biographical and
Critical Essay on Painting and Painters of all Times and many Places. With
numerous Illustrations. Demy 8vo, cloth, £1.

ANALYSIS OF ORNAMENT: THE CHARACTER-
ISTICS OF STYLES. An Introduction to the Study of the History of Ornamental
Art. With many Illustrations. Sixth Edition. Royal 8vo, cloth, 8s.

WYON (F. W.)—

HISTORY OF GREAT BRITAIN DURING THE
REIGN OF QUEEN ANNE. 2 vols. Demy 8vo, £1 12s.

YOUNGE (C. D.)—

PARALLEL LIVES OF ANCIENT AND MODERN
HEROES. New Edition. 12mo, cloth, 4s. 6d.

AUSTRALIAN MEAT: RECIPES FOR COOKING AUS-
TRALIAN MEAT, with Directions for Preparing Sauces suitable for the same.
By a Cook. 12mo, sewed, 9d.

CEYLON: being a General Description of the Island, Historical,
Physical, Statistical. Containing the most Recent Information. With Map. By
an Officer, late of the Ceylon Rifles. 2 vols. Demy 8vo, £1 8s.

COLONIAL EXPERIENCES; or, Incidents and Reminiscences
of Thirty-four Years in New Zealand. By an Old Colonist. With a Map.
Crown 8vo, 8s.

ELEMENTARY DRAWING-BOOK. Directions for Intro-
ducing the First Steps of Elementary Drawing in Schools and among Workmen.
Small 4to, cloth, 4s. 6d.

FORTNIGHTLY REVIEW.—First Series, May, 1865, to Dec.
1866. 6 vols. Cloth, 13s. each.

New Series, 1867 to 1872. In Half-yearly Volumes. Cloth,
13s. each.

From January, 1873, to June, 1878, in Half-yearly Volumes.
Cloth, 16s. each.

GERMAN NATIONAL COOKERY FOR ENGLISH
KITCHENS. With Practical Descriptions of the Art of Cookery as performed in
Germany, including small Pastry and Confectionery, Preserving, Pickling, and
making of Vinegars, Liqueurs, and Beverages, warm and cold, also the Manufacture
of the various German Sausages. Post 8vo, cloth, 7s.

HOME LIFE. A Handbook and Elementary Instruction, containing Practical Suggestions addressed to Managers and Teachers of Schools, intended to show how the underlying principles of Home Duties or Domestic Economy may be the basis of National Primary Instruction. Crown 8vo, 3s.

NATIONAL TRAINING SCHOOL FOR COOKERY. Containing Lessons on Cookery ; forming the Course of Instruction in the School. With List of Utensils Necessary, and Lessons on Cleaning Utensils. Compiled by " R. O. C." Large crown 8vo. Second Edition, 8s.

OUR CREED : Being an Appeal to the Church of England regarding some Doubts about the Truth of Ecclesiastical Christianity. By a BARRISTER. Demy 8vo, 6s.

OUR OWN MISANTHROPE. Reprinted from " Vanity Fair." By ISHMAEL. Crown 8vo, 7s.

PAST DAYS IN INDIA ; or, Sporting Reminiscences of the Valley of the Saone and the Basin of Singrowlee. By a late CUSTOMS OFFICER, N.W. Provinces, India. Post 8vo, 10s. 6d.

PRO NIHILO : THE PRELUDE TO THE ARNIM TRIAL. An English Edition. Demy 8vo, 7s. 6d.

SHOOTING, YACHTING, AND SEA-FISHING TRIPS, at Home and on the Continent. Second Series. By " WILDFOWLER," " SNAP-SHOT." 2 vols., crown 8vo, £1 1s.

SHOOTING AND FISHING TRIPS IN ENGLAND, FRANCE, ALSACE, BELGIUM, HOLLAND, AND BAVARIA. By "WILD-FOWLER," "SNAPSHOT." New Edition, with Illustrations. Large crown 8vo, 8s.

SPORT IN MANY LANDS. By " The Old Shekarry." With 164 Illustrations. 2 vols. Demy 8vo, £1 10s.

UNIVERSAL CATALOGUE OF BOOKS ON ART. Compiled for the use of the National Art Library, and the Schools of Art in the United Kingdom. In 2 vols. Crown 4to, half-morocco, £2 2s.

WOLF HUNTING AND WILD SPORT IN BRITTANY. By the Author of " Dartmoor Days," &c. With Illustrations by COLONEL CREALOCKE, C.B. Large crown 8vo, 12s.

SOUTH KENSINGTON MUSEUM SCIENCE AND ART HANDBOOKS.

Published for the Committee of Council on Education.

TAPESTRY. By ALFRED CHAMPEAUX. With Woodcuts. 2s. 6d.

BRONZES. By C. DRURY E. FORTNUM, F.S.A. With numerous Woodcuts. Large crown 8vo, 2s. 6d.

PLAIN WORDS ABOUT WATER. By A. H. CHURCH, M.A., Oxon., Professor of Chemistry in the Agricultural College, Cirencester. Large crown 8vo, sewed, 6d.

ANIMAL PRODUCTS : their Preparation, Commercial Uses, and Value. By T. L. SIMMONDS, Editor of the *Journal of Applied Science.* Large crown 8vo, 7s. 6d.

FOOD : A Short Account of the Sources, Constituents, and Uses of Food ; intended chiefly as a Guide to the Food Collection in the Bethnal Green Museum. By A. H. CHURCH, M.A., Oxon., Professor of Chemistry in the Agricultural College, Cirencester. Large crown 8vo, 3s.

SCIENCE CONFERENCES. Delivered at the South Kensington Museum. Crown 8vo, 2 vols., 6s. each.
VOL. I.—Physics and Mechanics.
VOL. II.—Chemistry, Biology, Physical Geography, Geology, Mineralogy, and Meteorology.

ECONOMIC ENTOMOLOGY. By ANDREW MURRAY, F.L.S., APTERA. With numerous Illustrations. Large crown 8vo, 7s. 6d.

HANDBOOK TO THE SPECIAL LOAN COLLECTION of Scientific Apparatus. Large crown 8vo, 3s.

THE INDUSTRIAL ARTS: Historical Sketches. With 242 Illustrations. Demy 8vo, 7s. 6d.

TEXTILE FABRICS. By the Very Rev. DANIEL ROCK, D.D. With numerous Woodcuts. Large crown 8vo, 2s. 6d.

IVORIES: ANCIENT AND MEDIÆVAL. By WILLIAM MASKELL. With numerous Woodcuts. Large crown 8vo, 2s. 6d.

ANCIENT & MODERN FURNITURE & WOODWORK. By JOHN HUNGERFORD POLLEN. With numerous Woodcuts. Large crown 8vo, 2s. 6d.

MAIOLICA. By C. DRURY E. FORTNUM, F.S.A. With numerous Woodcuts. Large crown 8vo, 2s. 6d.

MUSICAL INSTRUMENTS. By CARL ENGEL. With numerous Woodcuts. Large crown 8vo, 2s. 6d.

MANUAL OF DESIGN, compiled from the Writings and Addresses of RICHARD REDGRAVE, R.A., Surveyor of Her Majesty's Pictures, late Inspector-General for Art, Science and Art Department. By GILBERT R. REDGRAVE. With Woodcuts. Large crown 8vo, 2s. 6d.

PERSIAN ART. By MAJOR R. MURDOCK SMITH, R.E. With Additional Illustrations. [*In the Press.*

FREE EVENING LECTURES. Delivered in connection with the Special Loan Collection of Scientific Apparatus, 1876. Large crown 8vo, 8s.

CARLYLE'S (THOMAS) WORKS.

LIBRARY EDITION COMPLETE.

Handsomely printed in 34 vols. Demy 8vo, cloth, £15.

SARTOR RESARTUS. The Life and Opinions of Herr Teufelsdröckh. With a Portrait, 7s. 6d.

THE FRENCH REVOLUTION. A History. 3 vols., each 9s.

LIFE OF FREDERICK SCHILLER AND EXAMINATION OF HIS WORKS. With Supplement of 1872. Portrait and Plates, 9s. The Supplement *separately*, 2s.

CRITICAL AND MISCELLANEOUS ESSAYS. With Portrait. 6 vols., each 9s.

ON HEROES, HERO WORSHIP, AND THE HEROIC IN HISTORY. 7s. 6d.

PAST AND PRESENT. 9s.

CARLYLE'S (THOMAS) WORKS—*Continued.*

OLIVER CROMWELL'S LETTERS AND SPEECHES. With Portraits. 5 vols., each 9s.

LATTER-DAY PAMPHLETS. 9s.

LIFE OF JOHN STERLING. With Portrait, 9s.

HISTORY OF FREDERICK THE SECOND. 10 vols., each 9s.

TRANSLATIONS FROM THE GERMAN. 3 vols., each 9s.

GENERAL INDEX TO THE LIBRARY EDITION. 8vo, cloth, 6s.

EARLY KINGS OF NORWAY : also AN ESSAY ON THE PORTRAITS OF JOHN KNOX. Crown 8vo, with Portrait Illustrations, 7s. 6d.

CHEAP AND UNIFORM EDITION.

In 23 vols., Crown 8vo, cloth. £7 5s.

THE FRENCH REVOLUTION : A History. 2 vols., 12s.

OLIVER CROMWELL'S LETTERS AND SPEECHES, with Elucidations, &c. 3 vols., 18s.

LIVES OF SCHILLER AND JOHN STERLING. 1 vol., 6s.

CRITICAL AND MISCELLANEOUS ESSAYS. 4 vols., £1 4s.

SARTOR RESARTUS AND LECTURES ON HEROES. 1 vol., 6s.

LATTER-DAY PAMPHLETS. 1 vol., 6s.

CHARTISM AND PAST AND PRESENT. 1 vol., 6s.

TRANSLATIONS FROM THE GERMAN OF MUSÆUS, TIECK, AND RICHTER. 1 vol., 6s.

WILHELM MEISTER, by Göthe. A Translation. 2 vols., 12s.

HISTORY OF FRIEDRICH THE SECOND, called Frederick the Great. Vols. I. and II., containing Part I.—"Friedrich till his Accession." 14s. Vols. III. and IV., containing Part II.—"The First Two Silesian Wars." 14s. Vols. V., VI., VII., completing the Work, £1 1s.

PEOPLE'S EDITION.

In 37 vols., small Crown 8vo. Price 2s. each vol., bound in cloth ; or in sets of 37 vols. in 18, cloth gilt, for £3 14s.

SARTOR RESARTUS.

FRENCH REVOLUTION. 3 vols.

LIFE OF JOHN STERLING.

OLIVER CROMWELL'S LETTERS AND SPEECHES. 5 vols.

ON HEROES AND HERO WORSHIP.

PAST AND PRESENT.

CRITICAL AND MISCELLANEOUS ESSAYS. 7 vols.

LATTER-DAY PAMPHLETS.

LIFE OF SCHILLER.

FREDERICK THE GREAT. 10 vols.

WILHELM MEISTER. 3 vols.

TRANSLATIONS FROM MUSÆUS, TIECK, AND RICHTER. 2 vols.

THE EARLY KINGS OF NORWAY : also an Essay on the Portraits of John Knox, with Illustrations. Small crown 8vo. Bound up with the Index and uniform with the "People's Edition." Now ready.

DICKENS'S (CHARLES) WORKS.

ORIGINAL EDITIONS.

In Demy 8vo.

THE MYSTERY OF EDWIN DROOD. With Illustrations by S. L. Fildes, and a Portrait engraved by Baker. Cloth, 7s. 6d.

OUR MUTUAL FRIEND. With Forty Illustrations by Marcus Stone. Cloth, £1 1s.

THE PICKWICK PAPERS. With Forty-three Illustrations by Seymour and Phiz. Cloth, £1 1s.

NICHOLAS NICKLEBY. With Forty Illustrations by Phiz. Cloth, £1 1s.

SKETCHES BY "BOZ." With Forty Illustrations by George Cruikshank. Cloth, £1 1s.

MARTIN CHUZZLEWIT. With Forty Illustrations by Phiz. Cloth, £1 1s.

DOMBEY AND SON. With Forty Illustrations by Phiz. Cloth, £1 1s.

DAVID COPPERFIELD. With Forty Illustrations by Phiz. Cloth, £1 1s.

BLEAK HOUSE. With Forty Illustrations by Phiz. Cloth, £1 1s.

LITTLE DORRIT. With Forty Illustrations by Phiz. Cloth, £1 1s.

THE OLD CURIOSITY SHOP. With Seventy-five Illustrations by George Cattermole and H. K. Browne. A New Edition. Uniform with the other volumes, £1 1s.

BARNABY RUDGE: a Tale of the Riots of 'Eighty. With Seventy-eight Illustrations by G. Cattermole and H. K. Browne. Uniform with the other volumes, £1 1s.

CHRISTMAS BOOKS: Containing—The Christmas Carol; The Cricket on the Hearth; The Chimes; The Battle of Life; The Haunted House. With all the original Illustrations. Cloth, 12s.

OLIVER TWIST and TALE OF TWO CITIES. In one volume. Cloth, £1 1s.

OLIVER TWIST. Separately. With Twenty-four Illustrations by George Cruikshank.

A TALE OF TWO CITIES. Separately. With Sixteen Illustrations by Phiz. Cloth, 9s.

₊ *The remainder of Dickens's Works were not originally printed in Demy 8vo.*

DICKENS'S (CHARLES) WORKS—*Continued.*

LIBRARY EDITION.

In Post 8vo. With the Original Illustrations, 30 vols., cloth, £12.

				s.	*d.*
PICKWICK PAPERS	43 Illustrns.,	2 vols.		16	0
NICHOLAS NICKLEBY	39	,, 2 vols.		16	0
MARTIN CHUZZLEWIT	40	,, 2 vols.		16	0
OLD CURIOSITY SHOP and REPRINTED PIECES	36	,, 2 vols.		16	0
BARNABY RUDGE and HARD TIMES	36	,, 2 vols.		16	0
BLEAK HOUSE	40	,, 2 vols.		16	0
LITTLE DORRIT	40	,, 2 vols.		16	0
DOMBEY AND SON	38	,, 2 vols.		16	0
DAVID COPPERFIELD	38	,, 2 vols.		16	0
OUR MUTUAL FRIEND	40	,, 2 vols.		16	0
SKETCHES BY "BOZ"	39	,, 1 vol.		8	0
OLIVER TWIST	24	,, 1 vol.		8	0
CHRISTMAS BOOKS	17	,, 1 vol.		8	0
A TALE OF TWO CITIES	16	,, 1 vol.		8	0
GREAT EXPECTATIONS	8	,, 1 vol.		8	0
PICTURES FROM ITALY and AMERICAN NOTES	8	,, 1 vol.		8	0
UNCOMMERCIAL TRAVELLER	8	,, 1 vol.		8	0
CHILD'S HISTORY OF ENGLAND	8	,, 1 vol.		8	0
EDWIN DROOD and MISCELLANIES	12	,, 1 vol.		8	0
CHRISTMAS STORIES from "Household Words," &c..	14	,, 1 vol.		8	0

THE LIFE OF CHARLES DICKENS. By JOHN FORSTER. A New Edition. With Illustrations. Uniform with the Library Edition, post 8vo, of his Works. In one vol. 10s. 6d.

THE "CHARLES DICKENS" EDITION.

In Crown 8vo. In 21 vols., cloth, with Illustrations, £3 9s. 6d.

			s.	*d.*
PICKWICK PAPERS	8 Illustrations		3	6
MARTIN CHUZZLEWIT	8 ,,		3	6
DOMBEY AND SON	8 ,,		3	6
NICHOLAS NICKLEBY	8 ,,		3	6
DAVID COPPERFIELD	8 ,,		3	6
BLEAK HOUSE	8 ,,		3	6
LITTLE DORRIT	8 ,,		3	6
OUR MUTUAL FRIEND	8 ,,		3	6
BARNABY RUDGE	8 ,,		3	6
OLD CURIOSITY SHOP	8 ,,		3	6
A CHILD'S HISTORY OF ENGLAND	4 ,,		3	6
EDWIN DROOD and OTHER STORIES	8 ,,		3	6
CHRISTMAS STORIES, from "Household Words"	8 ,,		3	0
TALE OF TWO CITIES	8 ,,		3	0
SKETCHES BY "BOZ"	8 ,,		3	0
AMERICAN NOTES and REPRINTED PIECES	8 ,,		3	0
CHRISTMAS BOOKS	8 ,,		3	0
OLIVER TWIST	8 ,,		3	0
GREAT EXPECTATIONS	8 ,,		3	0
HARD TIMES and PICTURES FROM ITALY	8 ,,		3	0
UNCOMMERCIAL TRAVELLER	4 ,,		3	0

THE LIFE OF CHARLES DICKENS. Uniform with this Edition, with Numerous Illustrations. 2 vols. 3s. 6d. each.

DICKENS'S (CHARLES) WORKS—*Continued.*

THE ILLUSTRATED LIBRARY EDITION.

Complete in 30 Volumes.　Demy 8vo, 10s. each; or set, £15.

This Edition is printed on a finer paper and in a larger type than has been employed in any previous edition.　The type has been cast especially for it, and the page is of a size to admit of the introduction of all the original illustrations.

No such attractive issue has been made of the writings of Mr. Dickens, which, various as have been the forms of publication adapted to the demands of an ever widely-increasing popularity, have never yet been worthily presented in a really handsome library form.

The collection comprises all the minor writings it was Mr. Dickens's wish to preserve.

SKETCHES BY " BOZ." With 40 Illustrations by George Cruikshank.

PICKWICK PAPERS. 2 vols. With 42 Illustrations by Phiz.

OLIVER TWIST. With 24 Illustrations by Cruikshank.

NICHOLAS NICKLEBY. 2 vols. With 40 Illustrations by Phiz.

OLD CURIOSITY SHOP and REPRINTED PIECES. 2 vols. With Illustrations by Cattermole, &c.

BARNABY RUDGE and HARD TIMES. 2 vols. With Illustrations by Cattermole, &c.

MARTIN CHUZZLEWIT. 2 vols. With 40 Illustrations by Phiz.

AMERICAN NOTES and PICTURES FROM ITALY. 1 vol. With 8 Illustrations.

DOMBEY AND SON. 2 vols. With 40 Illustrations by Phiz.

DAVID COPPERFIELD. 2 vols. With 40 Illustrations by Phiz.

BLEAK HOUSE. 2 vols. With 40 Illustrations by Phiz.

LITTLE DORRIT. 2 vols. With 40 Illustrations by Phiz.

A TALE OF TWO CITIES. With 16 Illustrations by Phiz.

THE UNCOMMERCIAL TRAVELLER. With 8 Illustrations by Marcus Stone.

GREAT EXPECTATIONS. With 8 Illustrations by Marcus Stone.

OUR MUTUAL FRIEND. 2 vols. With 40 Illustrations by Marcus Stone.

CHRISTMAS BOOKS. With 17 Illustrations by Sir Edwin Landseer, R.A., Maclise, R.A., &c. &c.

HISTORY OF ENGLAND. With 8 Illustrations by Marcus Stone.

CHRISTMAS STORIES. (From " Household Words " and "All the Year Round.") With 14 Illustrations.

EDWIN DROOD AND OTHER STORIES. With 12 Illustrations by S. L. Fildes.

DICKENS'S (CHARLES) WORKS—*Continued*—

HOUSEHOLD EDITION.

In Crown 4to vols. Now Publishing, Sixpenny Monthly Parts.

19 Volumes completed.

OLIVER TWIST, with 28 Illustrations, cloth, 2s. 6d. ; paper, 1s. 9d.

MARTIN CHUZZLEWIT, with 59 Illustrations, cloth, 4s. ; paper, 3s.

DAVID COPPERFIELD, with 60 Illustrations and a Portrait, cloth, 4s. ; paper, 3s.

BLEAK HOUSE, with 61 Illustrations, cloth, 4s. ; paper, 3s.

LITTLE DORRIT, with 58 Illustrations, cloth, 4s. ; paper, 3s.

PICKWICK PAPERS, with 56 Illustrations, cloth, 4s. ; paper, 3s.

BARNABY RUDGE, with 46 Illustrations, cloth, 4s. ; paper, 3s.

A TALE OF TWO CITIES, with 25 Illustrations, cloth, 2s. 6d. ; paper, 1s. 9d.

OUR MUTUAL FRIEND, with 58 Illustrations, cloth, 4s. ; paper, 3s.

NICHOLAS NICKLEBY, with 59 Illustrations, cloth, 4s. ; paper, 3s.

GREAT EXPECTATIONS, with 26 Illustrations, cloth, 2s. 6d. ; paper, 1s. 9d.

OLD CURIOSITY SHOP, with 39 Illustrations, cloth, 4s. ; paper, 3s.

SKETCHES BY " BOZ," with 36 Illustrations, cloth, 2s. 6d. ; paper, 1s. 9d.

HARD TIMES, with 20 Illustrations, cloth, 2s. ; paper, 1s. 6d.

DOMBEY AND SON, with 61 Illustrations, cloth, 4s. ; paper, 3s.

UNCOMMERCIAL TRAVELLER, with 26 Illustrations, cloth, 2s. 6d. ; paper, 1s. 9d.

CHRISTMAS BOOKS, with 28 Illustrations, cloth, 2s. 6d. ; sewed, 1s. 9d.

THE HISTORY OF ENGLAND, with 15 Illustrations, cloth, 2s. 6d. ; paper, 1s. 9d.

AMERICAN NOTES and PICTURES FROM ITALY, with 18 New Illustrations, cloth, 2s. 6d. ; paper, 1s. 9d.

EDWIN DROOD; STORIES; and REPRINTED PIECES, with Illustrations, now ready.

Besides the above will be included—

THE CHRISTMAS STORIES.

THE LIFE OF DICKENS. By JOHN FORSTER.

Messrs. CHAPMAN & HALL trust that by this Edition they will be enabled to place the works of the most popular British Author of the present day in the hands of all English readers.

PEOPLE'S EDITION.

PICKWICK PAPERS. In Boards. Illustrated. 2s.

SKETCHES BY BOZ. In Boards. Illustrated. 2s.

OLIVER TWIST. In Boards. Illustrated. 2s.

NICHOLAS NICKLEBY. In Boards. Illustrated. 2s.

MARTIN CHUZZLEWIT. In Boards. Illustrated. 2s.

MR. DICKENS'S READINGS.

Fcap. 8vo, sewed.

CHRISTMAS CAROL IN PROSE. 1s.   STORY OF LITTLE DOMBEY. 1s.

CRICKET ON THE HEARTH. 1s.   POOR TRAVELLER, BOOTS AT THE HOLLY-TREE INN, and MRS. GAMP. 1s.

CHIMES: A GOBLIN STORY. 1s.

A CHRISTMAS CAROL, with the Original Coloured Plates ;

being a reprint of the Original Edition. Small 8vo, red cloth, gilt edges, 5s.

THE LIBRARY

OF

CONTEMPORARY SCIENCE.

Some degree of truth has been admitted in the charge not unfrequently brought against the English, that they are assiduous rather than solid readers. They give themselves too much to the lighter forms of literature. Technical Science is almost exclusively restricted to its professed votaries, and, but for some of the Quarterlies and Monthlies, very little solid matter would come within the reach of the general public.

But the circulation enjoyed by many of these very periodicals, and the increase of the scientific journals, may be taken for sufficient proof that a taste for more serious subjects of study is now growing. Indeed there is good reason to believe that if strictly scientific subjects are not more universally cultivated, it is mainly because they are not rendered more accessible to the people. Such themes are treated either too elaborately, or in too forbidding a style, or else brought out in too costly a form to be easily available to all classes.

With the view of remedying this manifold and increasing inconvenience, we are glad to be able to take advantage of a comprehensive project recently set on foot in France, emphatically the land of Popular Science. The well-known publishers MM. Reinwald and Co., have made satisfactory arrangements with some of the leading *savants* of that country to supply an exhaustive series of works on each and all of the sciences of the day, treated in a style at once lucid, popular, and strictly methodic.

The names of MM. P. Broca, Secretary of the Société d'Anthropologie ; Ch. Martins, Montpellier University ; C. Vogt, University of Geneva ; G. de Mortillet, Museum of Saint Germain ; A. Guillemin, author of " Ciel " and " Phénomènes de la Physique ;" A. Hovelacque, editor of the " Revue de Linguistique ;" Dr. Dally, Dr. Letourneau, and many others, whose co-operation has already been secured, are a guarantee that their respective subjects will receive thorough treatment, and will in all cases be written up to the very latest discoveries, and kept in every respect fully abreast of the times.

We have, on our part, been fortunate in making such further arrangements with some of the best writers and recognised authorities here, as will enable us to present the series in a thoroughly English dress to the reading public of this country. In so doing we feel convinced that we are taking the best means of supplying a want that has long been deeply felt.

[OVER.

LIBRARY OF CONTEMPORARY SCIENCE—*Continued*—

The volumes in actual course of execution, or contemplated, will embrace such subjects as :

SCIENCE OF LANGUAGE. [*Published*.	PHYSICAL AND COMMERCIAL GEOGRAPHY.
BIOLOGY. ,,	ARCHITECTURE.
ANTHROPOLOGY. ,,	CHEMISTRY.
ÆSTHETICS.	EDUCATION.
PHILOSOPHY. [*In the Press*.	GENERAL ANATOMY.
COMPARATIVE MYTHOLOGY.	ZOOLOGY.
ASTRONOMY.	BOTANY.
PREHISTORIC ARCHÆOLOGY.	METEOROLOGY.
ETHNOGRAPHY.	HISTORY.
GEOLOGY.	FINANCE.
HYGIENE.	MECHANICS.
POLITICAL ECONOMY.	STATISTICS, &c. &c.

All the volumes, while complete and so far independent in themselves, will be of uniform appearance, slightly varying, according to the nature of the subject, in bulk and in price.

When finished they will form a Complete Collection of Standard Works of Reference on all the physical and mental sciences, thus fully justifying the general title chosen for the series—"LIBRARY OF CONTEMPORARY SCIENCE."

LEVER'S (CHARLES) WORKS.

THE ORIGINAL EDITION with THE ILLUSTRATIONS.

In 17 vols.   Demy 8vo.   Cloth, 6s. each.

CHEAP EDITION.

Fancy boards, 2s. 6d.

CHARLES O'MALLEY.	THE DALTONS.
TOM BURKE.	ROLAND CASHEL.
THE KNIGHT OF GWYNNE.	DAVENPORT DUNN.
MARTINS OF CROMARTIN.	DODD FAMILY.

Fancy boards, 2s.

THE O'DONOGHUE.	LORD KILGOBBIN.
FORTUNES OF GLENCORE.	LUTTRELL OF ARRAN.
HARRY LORREQUER.	RENT IN THE CLOUD and ST. PATRICK'S EVE.
ONE OF THEM.	
A DAY'S RIDE.	CON CREGAN.
JACK HINTON.	ARTHUR O'LEARY.
BARRINGTON.	THAT BOY OF NORCOTT'S.
TONY BUTLER.	CORNELIUS O'DOWD.
MAURICE TIERNAY.	SIR JASPER CAREW.
SIR BROOKE FOSBROOKE.	NUTS AND NUT-CRACKERS.
BRAMLEIGHS OF BISHOP'S FOLLY.	

Also in sets, 27 vols., cloth, for £4 4s.

TROLLOPE'S (ANTHONY) WORKS.
CHEAP EDITION.

Boards, 2s. 6d., cloth, 3s. 6d.

2s. 6d. vols.

THE PRIME MINISTER.	PHINEAS REDUX.
PHINEAS FINN.	HE KNEW HE WAS RIGHT.
ORLEY FARM.	EUSTACE DIAMONDS.
CAN YOU FORGIVE HER?	

2s. vols.

VICAR OF BULLHAMPTON.	LADY ANNA.
RALPH THE HEIR.	HARRY HOTSPUR.
THE BERTRAMS.	RACHEL RAY.
KELLYS AND O'KELLYS.	TALES OF ALL COUNTRIES.
McDERMOT OF BALLYCLORAN.	MARY GRESLEY.
CASTLE RICHMOND.	LOTTA SCHMIDT.
BELTON ESTATE.	LA VENDÉE.
MISS MACKENSIE.	DOCTOR THORNE.

WHYTE-MELVILLE'S WORKS.
CHEAP EDITION.

Crown 8vo, fancy boards, 2s. each, or 2s. 6d. in cloth.

UNCLE JOHN. A Novel.

THE WHITE ROSE.

CERISE. A Tale of the Last Century.

BROOKES OF BRIDLEMERE.

"BONES AND I;" or, The Skeleton at Home.

"M., OR N." Similia Similibus Curantur.

CONTRABAND; or, A Losing Hazard.

MARKET HARBOROUGH; or, How Mr. Sawyer went to the Shires.

SARCHEDON. A Legend of the Great Queen.

SONGS AND VERSES.

SATANELLA. A Story of Punchestown.

THE TRUE CROSS. A Legend of the Church.

KATERFELTO. A Story of Exmoor.

SISTER LOUISE; or, A Story of a Woman's Repentance.

ROSINE.

CHAPMAN & HALL'S

List of Books, Drawing Examples, Diagrams, Models, Instruments, &c.

INCLUDING

THOSE ISSUED UNDER THE AUTHORITY OF THE SCIENCE AND ART DEPARTMENT, SOUTH KENSINGTON, FOR THE USE OF SCHOOLS AND ART AND SCIENCE CLASSES.

BARTLEY (G. C. T.)—

CATALOGUE OF MODERN WORKS ON SCIENCE AND TECHNOLOGY. Post 8vo, sewed, 1s.

BENSON (H.)—

PRINCIPLES OF THE SCIENCE OF COLOUR. Small 4to, cloth, 15s.

MANUAL OF THE SCIENCE OF COLOUR. Coloured Frontispiece and Illustrations. 12mo, cloth, 2s. 6d.

BRADLEY (THOMAS)—of the Royal Military Academy, Woolwich—

ELEMENTS OF GEOMETRICAL DRAWING. In Two Parts, with 60 Plates. Oblong folio, half-bound, each part 16s.

> Selections (from the above) of 20 Plates, for the use of the Royal Military Academy, Woolwich. Oblong folio, half-bound, 16s.

BURCHETT—

LINEAR PERSPECTIVE. With Illustrations. Post 8vo, cloth, 7s.

PRACTICAL GEOMETRY. Post 8vo, cloth, 5s.

DEFINITIONS OF GEOMETRY. Third Edition. 24mo, sewed, 5d.

CARROLL (JOHN)—

FREEHAND DRAWING LESSONS FOR THE BLACK BOARD. 6s.

CUBLEY (W. H.)—

A SYSTEM OF ELEMENTARY DRAWING. With Illustrations and Examples. Imperial 4to, sewed, 8s.

DAVISON (ELLIS A.)—

DRAWING FOR ELEMENTARY SCHOOLS. Post 8vo, cloth, 3s.

MODEL DRAWING. 12mo, cloth, 3s.

THE AMATEUR HOUSE CARPENTER: A Guide in Building, Making, and Repairing. With numerous Illustrations, drawn on Wood by the Author. Demy 8vo, 10s. 6d.

DELAMOTTE (P. H.)—

PROGRESSIVE DRAWING-BOOK FOR BEGINNERS. 12mo, 3s. 6d.

DICKSEE (J. R.)—

SCHOOL PERSPECTIVE. 8vo, cloth, 5s.

DYCE—

DRAWING-BOOK OF THE GOVERNMENT SCHOOL
OF DESIGN: ELEMENTARY OUTLINES OF ORNAMENT. 50 Plates.
Small folio, sewed, 5s.; mounted, 18s.

INTRODUCTION TO DITTO. Fcap. 8vo, 6d.

FOSTER (VERE)—

DRAWING-BOOKS:
(*a*) Forty Numbers, at 1d. each.
(*b*) Fifty-two Numbers, at 3d. each. The set *b* includes the subjects in *a*.

HENSLOW (PROFESSOR)—

ILLUSTRATIONS TO BE EMPLOYED IN THE
PRACTICAL LESSONS ON BOTANY. Prepared for South Kensington
Museum. Post 8vo, sewed, 6d.

JACOBSTHAL (E.)—

GRAMMATIK DER ORNAMENTE, in 7 Parts of 20
Plates each. Price, unmounted, £3 13s. 6d.; mounted on cardboard, £11 4s.
The Parts can be had separately.

JEWITT—

HANDBOOK OF PRACTICAL PERSPECTIVE. 18mo,
cloth, 1s. 6d.

KENNEDY (JOHN)—

FIRST GRADE PRACTICAL GEOMETRY. 12mo, 6d.

FREEHAND DRAWING-BOOK. 16mo, cloth, 1s. 6d.

LINDLEY (JOHN)—

SYMMETRY OF VEGETATION: Principles to be
observed in the delineation of Plants. 12mo, sewed, 1s.

MARSHALL—

HUMAN BODY. Text and Plates reduced from the large
Diagrams. 2 vols., cloth, £1 1s.

NEWTON (E. TULLEY, F.G.S.)—

THE TYPICAL PARTS IN THE SKELETONS OF A
CAT, DUCK, AND CODFISH, being a Catalogue with Comparative Descriptions arranged in a Tabular Form. Demy 8vo, 3s.

OLIVER (PROFESSOR)—

ILLUSTRATIONS OF THE VEGETABLE KINGDOM.
109 Plates. Oblong 8vo, cloth. Plain, 16s.; coloured, £1 6s.

PUCKETT (R. CAMPBELL)—

SCIOGRAPHY, OR RADIAL PROJECTION OF
SHADOWS. Crown 8vo, cloth, 6s.

REDGRAVE—

MANUAL AND CATECHISM ON COLOUR. Fifth
Edition. 24mo, sewed, 9d.

ROBSON (GEORGE)—

ELEMENTARY BUILDING CONSTRUCTION. Oblong
folio, sewed, 8s.

WALLIS (GEORGE)—

DRAWING-BOOK. Oblong, sewed, 3s. 6d.; mounted, 8s.

WORNUM (R. N.)—

THE CHARACTERISTICS OF STYLES: An Introduction to the Study of the History of Ornamental Art. Royal 8vo, cloth, 8s.

DIRECTIONS FOR INTRODUCING ELEMENTARY DRAWING IN SCHOOLS AND AMONG WORKMEN. Published at the Request of the Society of Arts. Small 4to, cloth, 4s. 6d.

DRAWING FOR YOUNG CHILDREN. Containing 150 Copies. 16mo, cloth, 3s. 6d.

EDUCATIONAL DIVISION OF SOUTH KENSINGTON MUSEUM: CLASSIFIED CATALOGUE OF. Ninth Edition. 8vo, 7s.

ELEMENTARY DRAWING COPY-BOOKS, for the use of Children from four years old and upwards, in Schools and Families. Compiled by a Student certificated by the Science and Art Department as an Art Teacher. Seven Books in 4to, sewed:

Book I. Letters, 8d.	Book IV. Objects, 8d.
„ II. Ditto, 8d.	„ V. Leaves, 8d.
„ III. Geometrical and Ornamental Forms, 8d.	„ VI. Birds, Animals, &c., 8d.
	„ VII. Leaves, Flowers, and Sprays, 8d.

Or in Sets of Seven Books, 4s. 6d.

ENGINEER AND MACHINIST DRAWING-BOOK, 16 Parts, 71 Plates. Folio, £1 12s.; mounted, £3 4s.

EXAMINATION PAPERS FOR SCIENCE SCHOOLS AND CLASSES. Published Annually, 6d. (Postage, 2d.)

PRINCIPLES OF DECORATIVE ART. Folio, sewed, 1s.

SCIENCE DIRECTORY. 12mo, sewed, 6d. (Postage, 3d.)

ART DIRECTORY. 12mo, sewed, 1s. (Postage, 3d.)

DIAGRAM OF THE COLOURS OF THE SPECTRUM, with Explanatory Letterpress, on roller, 10s. 6d.

COPIES FOR OUTLINE DRAWING:

DYCE'S ELEMENTARY OUTLINES OF ORNAMENT, 50 Selected Plates, mounted back and front, 18s.; unmounted, sewed, 5s.

WEITBRICHT'S OUTLINES OF ORNAMENT, reproduced by Herman, 12 Plates, mounted back and front, 8s. 6d.; unmounted, 2s.

MORGHEN'S OUTLINES OF THE HUMAN FIGURE reproduced by Herman, 20 Plates, mounted back and front, 15s.; unmounted, 3s. 4d.

ONE SET OF FOUR PLATES, Outlines of Tarsia, from Gruner, mounted, 3s. 6d.; unmounted, 7d.

ALBERTOLLI'S FOLIAGE, one set of Four Plates, mounted, 3s. 6d.; unmounted, 5d.

OUTLINE OF TRAJAN FRIEZE, mounted, 1s.

WALLIS'S DRAWING-BOOK, mounted, 8s.; unmounted, 3s. 6d.

OUTLINE DRAWINGS OF FLOWERS, Eight Sheets, mounted, 3s. 6d.; unmounted, 8d.

COPIES FOR SHADED DRAWING:

COURSE OF DESIGN. By Ch. Bargue (French), 20 Selected Sheets, 11 at 2s., and 9 at 3s. each. £2 9s.

RENAISSANCE ROSETTE, mounted, 9d.

SHADED ORNAMENT, mounted, 1s. 2d.

PART OF A PILASTER FROM THE ALTAR OF ST. BIAGIO AT PISA, mounted, 2s.; unmounted, 1s.

COPIES FOR SHADED DRAWING—*Continued—*

GOTHIC PATERA, mounted, 1s.
RENAISSANCE SCROLL, Tomb in S. M. Dei Frari, Venice, mounted, 1s. 4d.
MOULDING OF SCULPTURED FOLIAGE, decorated, mounted, 1s. 4d.
ARCHITECTURAL STUDIES. By J. B. TRIPON. 20 Plates, £2.
MECHANICAL STUDIES. By J. B. TRIPON. 15s. per dozen.
FOLIATED SCROLL FROM THE VATICAN, unmounted, 5d.; mounted, 1s. 3d.
TWELVE HEADS after Holbein, selected from his drawings in Her Majesty's
Collection at Windsor. Reproduced in Autotype. Half-imperial, 36s.
LESSONS IN SEPIA, 9s. per dozen, or 1s. each.
SMALL SEPIA DRAWING COPIES, 9s. per dozen, or 1s. each.

COLOURED EXAMPLES :

A SMALL DIAGRAM OF COLOUR, mounted, 1s. 6d.; unmounted, 9d.
TWO PLATES OF ELEMENTARY DESIGN, unmounted, 1s.; mounted, 3s. 9d.
PETUNIA, mounted, 3s. 9d.; unmounted, 2s. 9d.
PELARGONIUM, mounted, 3s. 9d.; unmounted, 2s. 9d.
CAMELLIA, mounted, 3s. 9d. ; unmounted, 2s. 9d.
NASTURTIUM, mounted, 3s. 9d.; unmounted, 2s. 9d.
OLEANDER, mounted, 3s. 9d.; unmounted, 2s. 9d.
TORRENIA ASIATICA. Mounted, 3s. 9d.; unmounted, 2s. 9d.
PYNE'S LANDSCAPES IN CHROMO-LITHOGRAPHY (6), each, mounted,
7s. 6d. ; or the set, £2 5s.
COTMAN'S PENCIL LANDSCAPES (set of 9), mounted, 15s.
,,   SEPIA DRAWINGS (set of 5), mounted, £1.
ALLONGE'S LANDSCAPES IN CHARCOAL (6), at 4s. each, or the set, £1 4s.
4017. BOUQUET OF FLOWERS, LARGE ROSES, &c., 4s. 6d.

4018.	,,	,,	ROSES AND HEARTSEASE, 3s. 6d.
4020.	,,	,,	POPPIES, &c., 3s. 6d.
4039.	,,	,,	CHRYSANTHEMUMS, 4s. 6d.
4040.	,,	,,	LARGE CAMELLIAS, 4s. 6d.
4077.	,,	,,	LILAC AND GERANIUM, 3s. 6d.
4080.	,,	,,	CAMELLIA AND ROSE, 3s. 6d.
4082.	,,	,,	LARGE DAHLIAS, 4s. 6d.
4083.	,,	,,	ROSES AND LILIES, 4s. 6d.
4090.	,,	,,	ROSES AND SWEET PEAS, 3s. 6d.
4094.	,,	,,	LARGE ROSES AND HEARTSEASE, 4s.
4180.	,,	,,	LARGE BOUQUET OF LILAC, 6s. 6d.
4190.	,,	,,	DAHLIAS AND FUCHSIAS, 6s. 6d.

SOLID MODELS, &c. :

*Box of Models, £1 4s.
A Stand with a universal joint, to show the solid models, &c., £1 18s.
*One wire quadrangle, with a circle and cross within it, and one straight wire. One solid
cube. One skeleton wire cube. One sphere. One cone. One cylinder. One
hexagonal prism. £2 2s.
Skeleton cube in wood, 3s. 6d.
18-inch skeleton cube in wood, 12s.
*Three objects of *form* in Pottery :
Indian Jar, ⎫
Celadon Jar, ⎬ 18s. 6d.
Bottle, ⎭
*Five selected Vases in Majolica Ware, £2 11s.
*Three selected Vases in Earthenware, 18s.
Imperial Deal Frames, glazed, without sunk rings, 10s.
*Davidson's Smaller Solid Models, in Box, £2, containing—

2 Square Slabs.	Octagon Prism.	Triangular Prism.
9 Oblong Blocks (steps).	Cylinder.	Pyramid, Equilateral.
2 Cubes.	Cone.	Pyramid, Isosceles.
4 Square Blocks.	Jointed Cross.	Square Block.

SOLID MODELS, &c.—*Continued*—

*Davidson's Advanced Drawing Models (10 models), £9.—The following is a brief description of the models :—An Obelisk—composed of 2 Octagonal Slabs, 26 and 20 inches across, and each 3 inches high ; 1 Cube, 12 inches edge ; 1 Monolith (forming the body of the obelisk), 3 feet high ; 1 Pyramid, 6 inches base ; the complete object is thus nearly 5 feet high. A Market Cross—composed of 3 Slabs, 24, 18, and 12 inches across, and each 3 inches high ; 1 Upright, 3 feet high ; 2 Cross Arms, united by mortise and tenon joints ; complete height, 3 feet 9 inches. A Step-Ladder, 23 inches high. A Kitchen Table, 14½ inches high. A Chair to correspond. A Four-legged Stool, with projecting top and cross rails, height 14 inches. A Tub, with handles and projecting hoops, and the divisions between the staves plainly marked. A strong Trestle, 18 inches high. A Hollow Cylinder, 9 inches in diameter, and 12 inches long, divided lengthwise. A Hollow Sphere, 9 inches in diameter, divided into semi-spheres, one of which is again divided into quarters ; the semi-sphere, when placed on the cylinder, gives the form and principles of shading a Dome, whilst one of the quarters placed on half the cylinder forms a Niche.

*Davidson's Apparatus for Teaching Practical Geometry (22 models), £5.

*Binn's Models for illustrating the elementary principles of orthographic projection as applied to mechanical drawing, in box, £1 10s.

Miller's Class Drawing Models.—These Models are particularly adapted for teaching large classes ; the stand is very strong, and the universal joint will hold the Models in any position. *Wood Models* : Square Prism, 12 inches side, 18 inches high ; Hexagonal Prism, 14 inches side, 18 inches high ; Cube, 14 inches side ; Cylinder, 13 inches diameter, 16 inches high ; Hexagon Pyramid, 14 inches diameter, 22½ inches side : Square Pyramid, 14 inches side, 22½ inches side ; Cone, 13 inches diameter, 22½ inches side ; Skeleton Cube, 19 inches solid wood 1¾ inch square ; Intersecting Circles, 19 inches solid wood 2¼ by 1½ inches. *Wire Models* : Triangular Prism, 17 inches side, 22 inches high ; Square Prism, 14 inches side, 20 inches high ; Hexagonal Prism, 16 inches diameter, 21 inches high ; Cylinder, 14 inches diameter, 21 inches high ; Hexagon Pyramid, 18 inches diameter, 24 inches high ; Square Pyramid, 17 inches side, 24 inches high ; Cone, 17 inches side, 24 inches high ; Skeleton Cube, 19 inches side ; Intersecting Circles, 19 inches side ; Plain Circle, 19 inches side ; Plain Square, 19 inches side. Table, 27 inches by 21½ inches. Stand. The Set complete, £14 13s.

Vulcanite set square, 5s.

Large compasses with chalk-holder, 5s.

*Slip, two set squares and T square, 5s.

*Parkes's case of instruments, containing 6-inch compasses with pen and pencil leg, 5s.

*Prize instrument case, with 6-inch compasses, pen and pencil leg, 2 small compasses, pen and scale, 18s.

6-inch compasses with shifting pen and point, 4s. 6d.

Small compass in case, 1s.

* Models, &c., entered as sets, cannot be supplied singly.

LARGE DIAGRAMS.

ASTRONOMICAL :

TWELVE SHEETS. Prepared for the Committee of Council on Education by JOHN DREW, Ph. Dr., F.R.S.A. £2 8s.; on rollers and varnished, £4 4s.

BOTANICAL :

NINE SHEETS. Illustrating a Practical Method of Teaching Botany. By Professor HENSLOW, F.L.S. £2 ; on canvas and rollers, and varnished, £3 3s.

CLASS.	DIVISION.	SECTION.	DIAGRAM.
		Thalamifloral	1
	Angiospermous ..	Calycifloral	2 & 3
Dicotyledon		Corollifloral	4
		Incomplete	5
	Gymnospermous ..	.. ..	6
	Petaloid	Superior	7
Monocotyledons ..		Inferior..	8
	Glumaceous.. ..	.. ..	9

ILLUSTRATIONS OF THE PRINCIPAL NATURAL ORDERS OF THE VEGETABLE KINGDOM. By Professor OLIVER, F.R.S., F.L.S. 70 Imperial sheets, containing examples of dried Plants, representing the different Orders. £5 5s. the set.

Catalogue and Index to Oliver's Diagrams, 1s.

BUILDING CONSTRUCTION :

TEN SHEETS. By WILLIAM J. GLENNY, Professor of Drawing, King's College. In sets, £1 1s.

LAXTON'S EXAMPLES OF BUILDING CONSTRUCTION IN TWO DIVISIONS, containing 32 Imperial Plates, 20s.

BUSBRIDGE'S DRAWINGS OF BUILDING CONSTRUCTION. 11 Sheets. Mounted, 5s. 6d.; unmounted. 2s. 9d.

GEOLOGICAL :

DIAGRAM OF BRITISH STRATA. By H. W. BRISTOW, F.R.S., F.G.S. A Sheet, 4s.; mounted on roller and varnished, 7s. 6d.

MECHANICAL :

DIAGRAMS OF THE MECHANICAL POWERS, AND THEIR APPLICATIONS IN MACHINERY AND THE ARTS GENERALLY. By DR. JOHN ANDERSON.

This Series consists of 8 Diagrams, highly coloured on stout paper, 3 feet 6 inches by 2 feet 6 inches, price £1 per set ; mounted on rollers, £2.

DIAGRAMS OF THE STEAM-ENGINE. By Professor GOODEVE and Professor SHELLEY. Stout paper, 40 inches by 27 inches, highly coloured.

The price per set of 41 Diagrams (52½ Sheets), £6 6s.; varnished and mounted on rollers, £11 11s.

EXAMPLES OF MACHINE DETAILS. A Series of 16 Coloured Diagrams. By Professor UNWIN. £2 2s.; mounted on rollers and varnished, £3 14s.

SELECTED EXAMPLES OF MACHINES, OF IRON AND WOOD (French). By STANISLAS PETTIT. 60 Sheets, £3 5s.; 13s. per dozen.

BUSBRIDGE'S DRAWINGS OF MACHINE CONSTRUCTION (50). Mounted, 25s.; unmounted, 11s.

LESSONS IN MECHANICAL DRAWING. By STANISLAS PETTIT. 1s. per dozen ; also larger Sheets, being more advanced copies, 2s. per dozen.

LESSONS IN ARCHITECTURAL DRAWING. By STANISLAS PETTIT. 1s. per dozen ; also larger Sheets, being more advanced copies, 2s. per dozen.

PHYSIOLOGICAL :

ELEVEN SHEETS. Illustrating Human Physiology, Life size and Coloured from Nature. Prepared under the direction of JOHN MARSHALL, F.R.S., F.R.C.S., &c. Each Sheet, 12s. 6d. On canvas and rollers, varnished, £1 1s.

1. THE SKELETON AND LIGAMENTS.
2. THE MUSCLES, JOINTS, AND ANIMAL MECHANICS.
3. THE VISCERA IN POSITION.—THE STRUCTURE OF THE LUNGS.
4. THE ORGANS OF CIRCULATION.
5. THE LYMPHATICS OR ABSORBENTS.
6. THE ORGANS OF DIGESTION.
7. THE BRAIN AND NERVES.—THE ORGANS OF THE VOICE.
8. THE ORGANS OF THE SENSES, Plate 1.
9. THE ORGANS OF THE SENSES, Plate 2.
10. THE MICROSCOPIC STRUCTURE OF THE TEXTURES AND ORGANS, Plate 1.
11. THE MICROSCOPIC STRUCTURE OF THE TEXTURES AND ORGANS, Plate 2.

HUMAN BODY, LIFE SIZE. By JOHN MARSHALL, F.R.S. F.R.C.S.

1. THE SKELETON, Front View.	5. THE SKELETON, Side View.
2. THE MUSCLES, Front View.	6. THE MUSCLES, Side View.
3. THE SKELETON, Back View.	7. THE FEMALE SKELETON,
4. THE MUSCLES, Back View.	Front View.

Each Sheet, 12s. 6d. ; on canvas and rollers, varnished, £1 1s.
Explanatory Key, 1s.

ZOOLOGICAL :

TEN SHEETS. Illustrating the Classification of Animals. By ROBERT PATTERSON, £2 ; on canvas and rollers, varnished, £3 10s.

The same, reduced in size on Royal paper, in 9 Sheets, uncoloured, 12s.

THE FORTNIGHTLY REVIEW.

Edited by JOHN MORLEY.

THE FORTNIGHTLY REVIEW is published on the 1st of every month (the issue on the 15th being suspended), and a Volume is completed every Six Months.

The following are among the Contributors :—

SIR RUTHERFORD ALCOCK.
PROFESSOR BAIN.
PROFESSOR BEESLY.
DR. BRIDGES.
HON. GEORGE C. BRODRICK.
SIR GEORGE CAMPBELL, M.P.
J. CHAMBERLAIN, M.P.
PROFESSOR CLIFFORD, F.R.S.
PROFESSOR SIDNEY COLVIN.
MONTAGUE COOKSON, Q.C.
L. H. COURTNEY, M.P.
G. H. DARWIN.
F. W. FARRAR.
PROFESSOR FAWCETT, M.P.
EDWARD A. FREEMAN.
MRS. GARRET-ANDERSON.
M. E. GRANT DUFF, M.P.
THOMAS HARE.
F. HARRISON.
LORD HOUGHTON.
PROFESSOR HUXLEY.
PROFESSOR JEVONS.
ÉMILE DE LAVELEYE.
T. E. CLIFFE LESLIE.
GEORGE HENRY LEWES.
RIGHT HON. R. LOWE, M.P.

SIR JOHN LUBBOCK, M.P.
LORD LYTTON.
SIR H. S. MAINE.
DR. MAUDSLEY.
PROFESSOR MAX MÜLLER.
PROFESSOR HENRY MORLEY.
G. OSBORNE MORGAN, Q.C., M.P.
WILLIAM MORRIS.
F. W. NEWMAN.
W. G. PALGRAVE.
WALTER H. PATER.
RT. HON. LYON PLAYFAIR, M.P.
DANTE GABRIEL ROSSETTI.
HERBERT SPENCER.
HON. E. L. STANLEY.
SIR J. FITZJAMES STEPHEN, Q.C.
LESLIE STEPHEN.
J. HUTCHISON STIRLING.
A. C. SWINBURNE.
DR. VON SYBEL.
J. A. SYMONDS.
W. T. THORNTON.
HON. LIONEL A. TOLLEMACHE.
ANTHONY TROLLOPE.
PROFESSOR TYNDALL.
THE EDITOR.

&c. &c. &c.

THE FORTNIGHTLY REVIEW *is published at 2s. 6d.*

CHAPMAN & HALL, 193, PICCADILLY.